Here Dreaming Though Wide Awake

Here Dreaming Though Wide Awake by Shawna Woodland

Published by Shawna Woodland

This book is a work of fiction. Any references to historical events, real people, or real places are used fictitiously. Other names, characters, places, and events are products of the author's imagination, and any resemblance to actual events or places or persons, living or dead, is purely coincidental.

Interior Design by Shawna Woodland
Cover by Michaela @jane_bydesign
Chapter Art by Shawna Woodland

Printed in Canada
Edits by Ryan Edits LLC
First Edition
ISBN 978-1-7387461-4-9 (paperback)
ISBN 978-1-7387461-5-6 (e-book)

Here Dreaming Though Wide Awake

Shawna Woodland

Note to the Reader:

This book contains lighter themes, but also heavier ones. I respect and understand that certain readers are affected by certain thematic elements. Therefore, I have compiled a list to help you make an informed decision on whether it is the right time for you to read this story.

Triggers and content include, but are not limited to, the following:

- Grief
- Alcohol consumption
- Mental Health Difficulties such as anxiety attacks, depression, generational trauma, PTSD, etc.
- Abuse or assault (on and off page)

Dearest Reader,

People will try to tell you that fairytales are not real. They'll sound very convincing. You might be tempted to believe them. But one must wonder... If fairytales don't exist, where did the stories come from?

They came from heroes like you. Yes, like you. A hero battling to conquer their monsters, or a hero hiding from them in the dark, as well as every sort of hero in-between. You see, villains are always capable of being defeated, even when found in our mirror reflections.

That's why fairytales are real, we live them every day.

This book is a fairytale. There are no magic spells and the attention to historical accuracies are used in moderation. Still, as with all fairytales, I feel I must warn you that this is a love story, and the journeys to happy endings take different pathways. But within these pages is hope. Hope after discomfort and darkness. Hope like a blanket or a ray of sun. Hope in places and people you never expected to find it.

May you find courage to face your monsters, comfort during the dark, and bravery to keep chasing your sunrise.

Yours,

Shawna Woodland

For the softies who feel lost or shadowed.
Chase your sunrise.

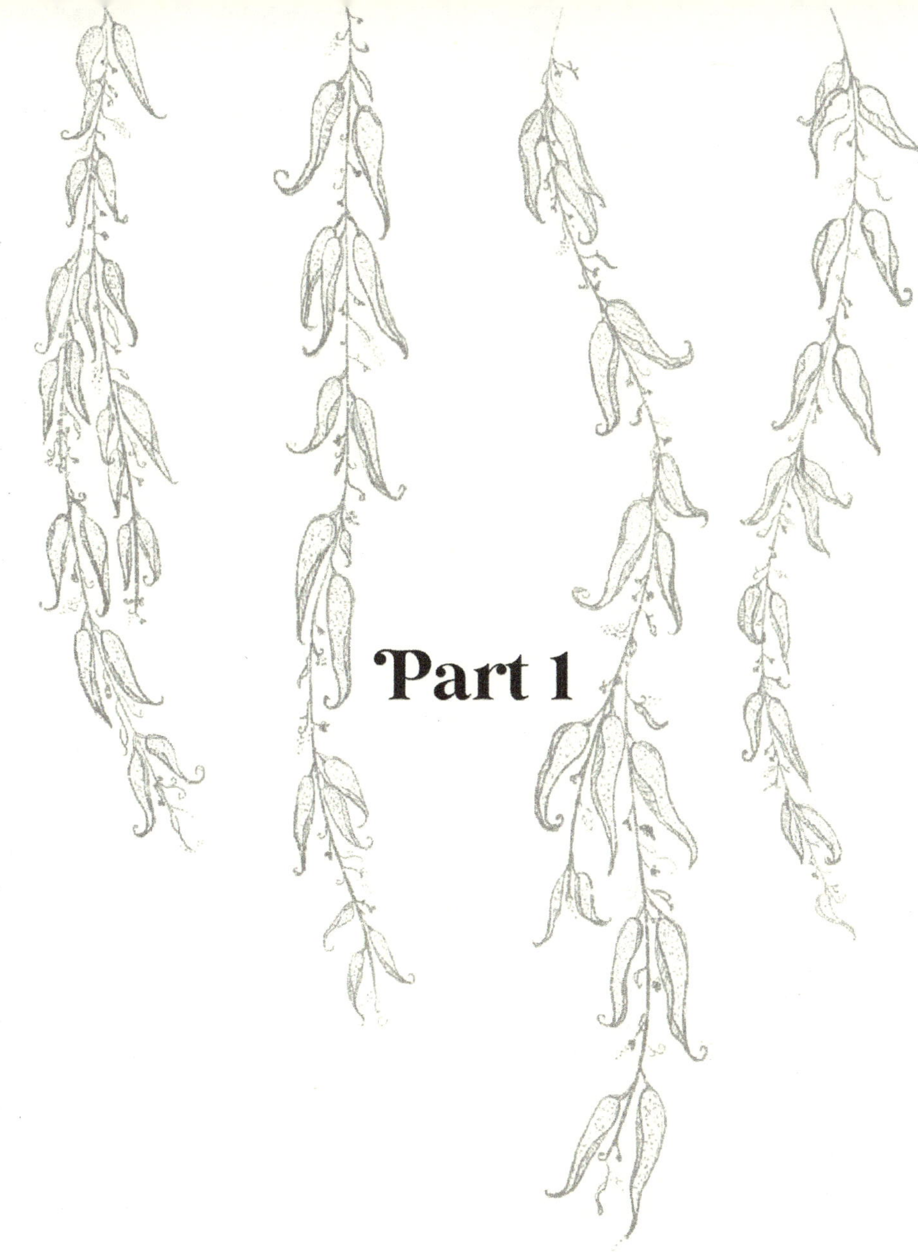

Part 1

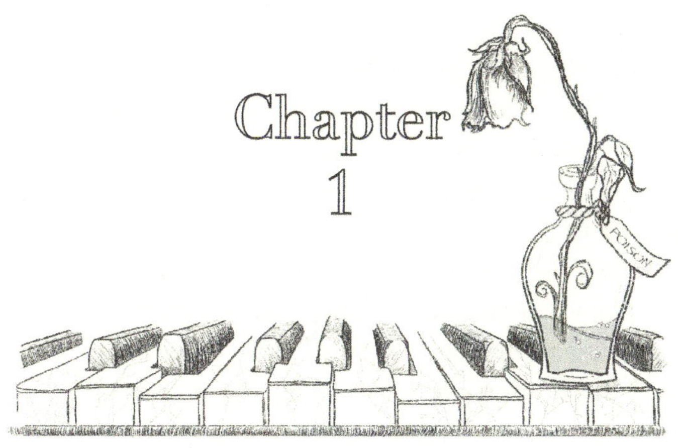

Chapter 1

Late Autumn, 1904

All fairytales come at a price—especially for those performing the role of hero. Which was why heroics and happily ever afters were not investments George Clarington had ever itched to acquire.

Rather, through the power of song, he defined himself as the keeper of monsters. A role he could fulfill in solitude; where bars of music were as bars of iron, and the right ballad could lock away a variety of vile beasts. Creatures crafted by his darkest shadows; his deepest regrets.

He conducted his life through songs, mingling tunes with colours bright enough to ignore the shadows and reprise them as different stories.

The most amusing part of music to George, however, was that it was something to be played—for he never could resist a game.

"You cheated!" Desmond shouted, slamming his cards onto the little wobbling table. He tugged his sleeves up as far as he could, the cream cuffs only making it halfway up his forearms, and combed back his gold curls from his face.

"I have never been any good at cheating." George gathered up the cards, handing them to Thomas who proceeded to shuffle them.

Thomas looked almost like he would laugh, except he never really laughed at anything. He rolled his eyes as the cards flitted around his hands and looked out across the large room of his home to where his family was dancing.

No one outside their group had even noticed Desmond's outburst.

The Towson house was loud, as it always was. Yellow walls met dusty floors where furniture was pressed under the windows, making room for people in the throws of musical madness. The modest and humble home had just enough space for a trio of dancing couples and the four young Towson girls, whose frenzied jumping around might also be called dancing.

Desmond studied George's face. "You've never been good at lying either."

George kept his smile. If Desmond had been a song, he'd have been a rather chaotic one. It wasn't an insult—a life without chaos would be colourless.

Thomas hummed as he dealt out fresh cards. It wasn't a happy song, as Thomas never really indulged in that sort of thing. But the tune struck a sharp chord deep within George's chest, unravelling something that had been locked away, triggering an old memory he refused to acknowledge. He smiled through the pain, not letting on that the rhythm of his pulse had become uncomfortable.

He left his cards face down on the table as he delicately rolled up the sleeves of his sweater. The burgundy knit reminded him of burnt roses and melancholy dreams. He closed his eyes to hide his leftover discomfort and waited for the swirling colours of his memories to fade into grey before opening his eyes again.

He stretched his neck from side to side, lifted his cards, and slipped back into his casual persona as easily as he'd slip on a hat.

Thomas glanced up through dark brown hair that sat in uneven ways. While the Towson family were known for their wide grins and jolly laughs, Thomas was the exception. Thomas was cloaked in the deeper shades of kindness. His penetrating brown eyes never shone very bright, but somehow they saw through and illuminated the things George preferred to keep in the shadows.

Thomas handed George one last card, and then began the game.

Play by play, George won yet again.

"This is ridiculous." Desmond's leg bounced under the table as his smile coiled uneasily. "I don't think I can play anymore if you're going to keep cheating."

"That's offensive. I'm the most trustworthy person at this table."

"Excuse me?" Thomas furrowed his brows.

"Shush, Thomas. Don't interrupt." George sent him a smile before turning back to Desmond. "What're you going to do?"

Desmond shook his head. "I'm trying to decide if I want to stay for another hand or not."

"Typical." George sighed as Thomas began to shuffle. "It comes as no surprise that you're thinking of running away just because things are getting a little troublesome for you."

"What's troublesome is the pleasure you get from your dastardly tricks." Desmond sat back in his chair and stretched his arms behind him.

"Does that mean you're staying?"

"I don't know. I have a rather good reason to leave." Desmond turned to watch the dancing.

George didn't have to follow Desmond's gaze to know exactly who he was looking at. It wasn't Thomas' parents, Jack and Valerie Towson, dancing in elegant strides through the room. Nor was it Jeremy and Victoria who twirled together in perfect unison despite their lack of coordination.

George scooped the black fringes of his hair out of his eyes and gathered the cards that had been dealt. "There's always a good reason if you look hard enough."

"Didn't have to look hard for this one."

"Time to make your choice, Desmond."

"If I leave, are you going to hold it against me?"

"Possibly. But if you stay"—George jutted his chin to where Molly was dancing with Thomas' younger brother—"Linus might steal that girl away from you."

"He wouldn't do that."

"He might," Thomas grumbled. "Linus wants everything worth having."

"It's why we don't let him play cards," George added with a mock tone of seriousness.

Desmond looked between them. "You're forcing me to choose right now?"

"Shouldn't be that hard a choice," Thomas groaned.

George thrummed his fingers on the table, held his grin, and watched Desmond as he fidgeted in his chair.

"You're dastardly!" Desmond turned to smile at Molly, and his bouncing stopped. "I think I'm going to go."

George chuckled. "At least you're predictable."

"Have fun with your cards, boys," Desmond said and pushed himself away from the table. He walked to the edge of the dance floor, seemingly entranced with all the energy. It was an easy thing to get lost in at the Towson home.

"Finally," Thomas muttered. "I thought he was never going to leave."

"I told you it would work," George stated proudly.

"I'm done stacking the deck for you now that he's gone. I want a fair chance to win back my money."

George laughed.

Thomas played with his shuffling, sliding the cards over and under in a way that showcased the skill that had just been so helpful.

"Do you always manipulate circumstances to your advantage?" Thomas asked, dealing out another round.

"I never manipulate for my own benefit," George admitted with a wink. "We did what we needed to do for their happiness. Not mine."

"I'm surprised he was over here at all when he could've been dancing with Molly."

"Desmond was doing your entire family a service by not dancing. The amount of injuries he could have caused is astronomical."

Thomas made a deep solid tone. "Still. You know how my family feels about people who don't dance."

"They've voiced their opinion to me more than once." George switched a card in his hand for one from the pile. "And I happen to be a very trustworthy person."

"Says the man who just manipulated his friend."

"That was a joint effort. And it was for the greater good."

Thomas arched his brows. "And whose good is that?"

George scowled. "Are we playing cards or giving life lessons?"

"A little bit of both."

Using the knuckles of his right hand to soothe away the tension on his forehead, George battled against a storm of thoughts. He didn't crave things like *greater goods*. It was why he'd spent months helping Jeremy and Victoria achieve their happiness without worrying about his own. And how he knew with every heartbeat that he'd be there to do the same for Desmond. It was why, after years of preparing, he was setting out to oversee certain sectors of the factories his grandfather owned. At twenty-one years, he'd be the youngest man to ever hold a position of charge there. But he didn't fear the challenge, or the distraction, it could prove to be. Not when it would give his grandparents some much needed time together—without the business in the way. Which reminded him...

He smoothed his expression into a smirk. "I'll fire you from your job if you treat me that way."

"Again with the manipulation." With a hint of a smile, Thomas placed his cards down. It was a winning hand. "Can you even win when I'm not stacking the cards for you?"

George gathered up the cards to try shuffling himself. "I never win because I never want to."

"You deserve to win sometimes." Thomas sighed, took the cards away, and shuffled on his own. His loose navy sweater gave him the freedom of movement to play guitar. Soon, Thomas would be leaving to share his music. Their time to play cards was slipping away.

With an old and loved piano along the wall, George was always invited to share in the fun. But his fingers ached with an unfinished melody. A serenade of secrets bound around him, leaving no chance for escape.

His music, his songs written in his colours, were not to be shared with anyone. He had already risked an opportunity to play his current song while Molly had sat with Desmond by the fire in her parlour. And while George wasn't necessarily afraid of taking risks, he most certainly knew it was important to choose which ones he took and when. Until it was time, he'd suffer through the relentless ticking between seconds and howling of hours, waiting for the creatures to be put at bay.

"No more life lessons, Thomas."

"One way or another the lessons are going to catch up to you," Thomas warned.

George shook his head as another smile crept up. "Why out of all the Towson children, I decided to be friends with you, I'll never know."

"You didn't have a choice," Thomas droned. "You needed me, the realist, to tell you all of the things you don't want to hear when you need to hear them most."

"Sounds about right." George rocked back in his chair. He cradled his head into his laced fingers and looked out to the dancing crowd.

The music came to a lull. Desmond jumped from his seat and smiled with everything he had. There weren't many times George remembered seeing his best friend look like he was on top of the world. But finally, Desmond seemed as happy as he'd always deserved to be. Seeing that dared George to be happy, too.

Molly rushed over, throwing her arms around Desmond's shoulders as their smiles grew to an impossible size. Her hair spiralled loosely around her shoulders, curls drooping around Desmond before he lightly brushed them aside with his fingertips. He leaned in, whispering in her ear secret words that made her smile blossom further. He took her hand in his and led them away from the dancing.

George turned back to Thomas, who was already staring at him.

"This is one of those times I need to tell you something you need to hear, even though you don't want to hear it," Thomas stated.

"Perfect," George groaned and leaned onto the table with his elbows. "What's that?"

"It's time to end your games with Victoria and Jeremy." Thomas picked up his cards as if he hadn't just said something of importance—something George had already known. Now that Jeremy and Victoria were engaged, it would only be a matter of time before his charade of courting her would come to a close. He would need to find a new way of avoiding the agonizing conversation about his own future marriage, but he'd deal with that later.

"I happen to agree with you."

"And don't start any new ones." Thomas gave a pointed look to where Desmond stood with Molly by the door.

"It's too late for that, Thomas," George drawled as he reorganized his cards, lining them up in his desired way—perfectly tailored in a backwards sort of way. "Desmond needs me."

Thomas made no reply as he placed his cards on the table.

George stared at the misfortune before topping them with his own unbeatable hand.

"You won." Thomas' eyebrows rose about as high as they could go.

"I have no idea how it happened. I was rooting for you."

Thomas laughed in two sturdy sounds and stretched out to deal again.

George turned back to the blushing couple.

The porch door opened, bringing a vibrant yellow glow into the room and encasing Desmond and Molly as they walked outside. The lush green of Desmond's suit accentuated the lilac of Molly's blouse, like leaves that enrich their flowers as they soak in the sun.

Tick-tock, his secrets whispered. Though, he didn't dwell on their whisperings much.

Desmond did need him. Maybe not in that exact moment. But most certainly the following evening, when Desmond's parents had invited them all for dinner. Only time would tell why the invitation had George's barrier walls lurching and groaning in shifts. Why he suddenly felt as though he stood on a flimsy plank of wood over a dark tempestuous sea. Off balance. Shackled by the horrors of his past. Just waiting, dreadful and expecting, for that final drop.

Chapter 2

Everything was magic.

Molly's fingers entwined with Desmond's as they walked through the autumn ridden yard. Leaves danced on a shivering wind, the world was blanketed with warm hues, and the cradle of comfort Desmond carried with him had her settling into the peaceful quiet.

"Are you having a good time?" Desmond asked.

"The best, Dez."

He lifted her hand and gave it a quick kiss. "You're sure you didn't want to keep dancing?"

"I'm sure." She skipped ahead, never releasing his hand as she twirled to face him. "One of these days I'll teach you the dances so that you don't have to worry about hurting anyone."

Desmond chuckled, a deep awkward sound that lifted his shoulders closer to his ears. "That would be good, yes."

She wrapped herself under his arm and pulled in close. Crinkling blades of grass beneath her feet filled the air with riveting songs, reminding her of the last time she had been in the Towsons' yard. Her life had been changed in countless ways since then.

"The last time I was here," she smiled with the memories, "it was snowing."

"This is where you were?"

She twirled out from his arms until she landed right where she had been not even a week earlier. "I'll never forget the exact moment I really started to feel like myself again. I was out here dancing. All of the children were out here dancing, too. Even George was dancing."

"When you said all of the children I assumed George was one of them." Desmond found his place next to her. "I wondered what you were doing to celebrate your beloved first snow of the year."

Molly sighed, as one does when so pleasantly happy the body can't help but let a little bit of it out. "What were you doing when it snowed?"

"I admired it from under a porch for a while. After getting the job offering I told you about, I decided to walk to the inn for the night. I figured if I was in the snow, it was almost like being with you."

She tilted her head up to look at him, loving how he was smiling down at her. The golden flecks in his green eyes were easy to get lost in. Curling tufts of his hair defied the wind that blew around them. Unlike her own hair, which blew over and across her face.

"Your hair is doing wild things today, Molly," Desmond said. "Do you have anything to tie it?"

"I don't," she slid her hair aside, secretly entranced by the chaos ensuing from it.

He combed her hair behind her neck and held it safe, using the movement to bring them closer together. "I guess it's still nowhere near as wild as what it was the first time we met."

"The first time we met?"

"You don't remember, do you?"

Not entirely. "The details are a little fuzzy."

"Then I'll do my best to remind you," he promised with an earth shattering smile.

He lowered onto the leaf-strewn lawn, aiding Molly in crouching down next to him. She curled into his arms as Desmond's words swept her away, pulling her eleven years back in time.

Desmond hadn't expected to find anyone after he ran away to the woods; not anything besides looming trees and satisfying earth. So when a scraggy girl called out to him from across the creek waters, he startled. Then he could only stare.

"Who are you?" she repeated.

"Desmond Prescott," he said, unsure of how she carried herself in such a sure way. The girl looked more than happy with her hair a mess around her shoulders and a handful of perfect flowers in her grasp. "Who are you?"

"Molly Jones." She lowered into an energetic curtsey and bounced back up with a gleaming smile. When he didn't return her smile, she tilted her head to the side and studied him. "How old are you, Desmond Prescott?"

"I'm eight and a half. You?"

"Seven whole years. And loving it." She rested her fistful of flowers on her hip. "Are you okay?"

He dug his toes into the pebbles on the forest floor, mindful not to get his shoes too dirty incase his mother should find them.

"My parents were yelling again," he admitted reluctantly.

"They were yelling at you?" Molly's eyes widened into full circles. "Again?"

He shrugged. "Not as loud as they normally do. It wasn't anything horrible."

Her jaw went slack, and the flowers tumbled from her grip to the ground.

She closed her gaping mouth and bent over to pick up the flowers that had scattered around her feet, mixing with twigs and moss. It was then that he noticed she wasn't wearing any shoes.

"It's a good thing you came out here," she said, clutching the poor beaten flowers in her arms. Some dangled upside down, others knotted around clumps of earth. She glanced his way and locked onto his eyes. "Trees never yell. They're much too kind for that."

"The trees?"

"That's right." She began to spin in circles, hair and skirts drifting in waves, flowers shedding petals in the wind. "But there's more."

He headed closer to the water. "What might that be?"

"If you listen closely enough, they'll sing. Trees sing the most magical songs if you just give them the chance."

"How am I supposed to do that?"

She stopped spinning and wobbled on her bare feet to regain balance. "Don't worry. I'm going teach you."

He laughed and shook his head. "You're something else, Molly Jones."

"You have no idea, Desmond Prescott." She grinned. "Now that we're friends, would you like to join me as I visit the fairies?"

"There are no such things," he protested.

"If we're going to be friends, you have to promise to never say that again." Her voice became oddly stern until she smiled again. "Promise?"

Desmond smiled a bit skeptically. He knew a few boys in town, but there was only one he called a friend.

"I promise, Molly Jones."

"Good! I'm glad we've settled that." She trudged though the water, unfazed by the way it soaked the bottom of her dress, and marched until she was standing right next to him. "Can I call you Dez? You look like a Dez."

That was the exact moment Desmond knew he was never going to be able to disagree with much of what Molly Jones would ever say. Somehow he knew he'd never want to. "You can call me Dez."

"...and so you took me to sacrifice your flowers to the fairies," Desmond concluded, and her own soft laughter fogged into the cool air between them.

"I'm not sure how many times I need to tell you this, but I never sacrificed any flowers."

"Well, it felt a lot like a sacrifice of some sort."

His hand cupped around the tender spot by her ear, sending little tickling sensations across her skin. He twirled the loose waves of hair trailing down her back with his fingertips, tucking them away tenderly as his hand found its way up and around her shoulder.

The first daring touch of his lips filled her thoughts with trails of stardust that left her dizzy when he pulled away. When her eyes fluttered open, he smiled before leaning in and kissing her again. The second kiss was always her favourite.

Hesitant as endings always are, the tip of his nose brushed along hers, staying close as he kissed the apples of her cheeks.

"You two are so adorable it's making me sick," called Linus as he followed his younger sisters into the yard. He had donned one of his brothers' jackets it seemed, since it was much too big for him. His shaggy ash blond hair curled around his ears, and his round cheeks were rosy in the cool air.

"Is all of the dancing done?" Desmond asked, ignoring the slight jest.

"Yes. It's safe for you to go back inside now." Linus laughed.

Desmond turned to Molly. "Would you like to go back inside?"

"I'm happy right where I am, Dez. I like being out here with you."

"I think we're going to stay," Desmond said to the ever smiling Linus.

"Suit yourselves," he said with a shrug. "Don't say I didn't warn you about my sisters though."

As if on cue, the little girls swarmed them, dancing and singing and playing on with all sorts of childish nonsense.

Desmond lost his hold around Molly, shifting in his place whenever a child got too close.

"Maybe we should go inside?" he said in a low voice.

Molly let out a laugh. "Yes. Let's go inside." She nudged him playfully with her elbow, then jumped to her feet.

"Time to wake up," Desmond whispered, lifting Molly gently from his shoulder, releasing her from what had been a wonderful dream.

One moment George had driven them just past the outskirts of London, and now she was being escorted towards the front door of her home. The moonlight played off the stone steps beneath her feet, glittering in waves that seemed to beckon her back to her dreams.

Victoria snuck into their home, and when George realized no one was around who needed the show of his presence, he left, patted Desmond's shoulder and told him to take his time before making a swift exit.

Desmond took a gentle hold of both of Molly's hands and looked into her eyes. "I should get going. There is this paperwork I was supposed to do for my father last night that I never did." His panic rose, colouring his features. "If I don't have it done by tomorrow he's going to be furious."

Molly drew in a sharp breath, knowing a little of what his father's tempers entailed and hating the vision of Desmond on the wrong side of it. "Go home and finish the paperwork. I'll be seeing you tomorrow."

"Tomorrow?" He squinted towards his shoes, concentrating, remembering. "The dinner! I forgot about that."

His grip around her fingers tightened, the worries weighing heavy, slumping him over till he looked like half the man he ought to.

"It's going to be fine," she tried.

"I just can't wait until we're away from here. Away from all this, from my parents!" He looked back at her with all his saddened hopes hanging above them.

There were many things about the future that would need to be sorted out. The prospect of Desmond's new job, the pathway of their relationship, and how the two would somehow work together. But when it came to the way Desmond's parents treated him, she'd spend all of her wishes to get him as far away from them as possible.

"We'll get you out of there soon," she promised. "Let's get this dinner over with first, and then we'll figure out the rest."

"I can't wait." He turned her hand in his so her palm was facing up, placed a soft kiss inside it and curled her fingers around the kiss.

"Me neither." She held her hand closed, revelling in the little tingles that spread across her skin.

Desmond shovelled back his hair and started down the main stairs, one step at a time with careful footing. Molly spun a lock of hair around her fingers as she watched him reach the driveway.

There was a pause after he fell into the car before it began rolling away. Molly could only imagine what sort of words were being exchanged.

"He's complaining already!" George shouted, followed by an "Ow."

And so Molly headed into the house, smiling towards the kiss enclosed in her hand.

Everything was magic, and she dreamt it always would be.

Chapter 3

Desmond crept into his parents' estate. He untied his shoes and put them away. He undid his jacket and hung it up as quietly as possible. With a glance in every direction around the ill decorated foyer, checking twice to make sure the way was clear, he bolted for the stairs.

He barely felt the banister beneath his hands.

Desmond had never been able to go up or down the stairs without taking care. It was something his mother had managed to ingrain in him since he was a young boy. He remembered the conversation well, as it was one of the only times he'd ever felt she truly cared about his well-being.

After making it into his private room with as much stealth as possible, he closed the door behind him and rested against the distressed wood.

There were days he wished he wasn't fearful about spending time with his own parents. But he had given up on feeling like that ever again. They had proven that there was no chance at appeasing them.

He grumbled and headed towards the writing desk where scattered papers were waiting. He flopped down, clicked on the lamp, and waited for the light to brighten. After stacking the papers and preparing his ink, he sat with his head in his hands, combing his hair with his fingers.

Shouting.

His parents' heated argument roared through the estate, rising up from the lower level.

Desmond's fingers grasped tightly in his hair as his legs became restless. Run. His body begged him to run. Get away. Find a place to feel safe.

He squeezed his eyes shut to block it all out. The responding pounding of his heart was a most welcome noise.

He craved a new life. He thought of Molly—how safe she would be, how safe *he* would be, if only he could get away.

"Desmond!" His father slammed a fist against his door.

Desmond took a deep steadying breath, knowing what was about to happen.

The door burst open, and his father, Harold Prescott, prowled into the room with a staggering amount of fury. Desmond's knee bounced against his will and hit his desk.

"Where were you today?" his father shouted.

"I was out with George."

"Neglecting your work?" His father marched closer to the desk and grabbed the stack of papers.

Desmond needed a collected reply to counteract how unsteady he felt inside. "You said you needed it completed by tomorrow."

"Pathetic." The word came out like venom.

Desmond waited silently, watching as his father flipped through the papers at an increasingly aggressive pace.

"This is ridiculous! This is horrible! The worst work you've ever done!" His father threw the papers across the room. "If you weren't a Prescott, I'd have fired you by now. Start over! It needs to be ready first thing in the morning."

The papers hadn't even landed on the ground when his father left, the door slamming behind him.

Desmond's body finally went still. The interaction hadn't been as bad as it could have been.

He crouched down and collected the papers from the floor. Most of them were untouched—whatever his father had called horrible wasn't something he had done. So he carefully tucked those papers into one pile to continue on, and the rest he would start from scratch.

More screaming slithered through the halls. His father's voice battling with his mother's for no good reason.

Oh, to get away.

A lighter knock came at his door. His mother.

"Come in." Letting her come in without protest always helped things.

"Your father is having a bad day," she said as she walked in, spotting him on the floor and not making any note of the mess.

"I had no idea." Desmond braced himself to stand and walked over to his desk, placing the two separate piles of paper down on it.

"Don't be that way Desmond," she hissed. "You know it gets worse if you aggravate things with your sarcasm."

With that comment, Desmond elected to stay silent for the majority of whatever conversation his mother had come in there to have.

"Your father and I have invited the Jones family over for dinner tomorrow." She rolled her shoulders up to stand taller.

He nodded, refusing to show her his true thoughts on the matter.

"We will be talking about certain things pertaining to your future with Audrey and the wedding."

Desmond masked any emotion. Though he did wonder why that information would need to be shared.

"Also," she groomed her dress with her pointed fingernails, "you will refrain from going anywhere near the young Jones girl while she's here. I don't want to see you talking to her or sitting next to her at the dinner table again."

Fine. As long as Molly didn't sit next to either of his parents, he didn't care if she had to sit next to someone other than him. He would do anything to keep her away from them.

"Any questions?" his mother asked, mistaking his silence as waiting for permission to speak.

"No questions," he stated plainly. "George said he was accompanying Victoria, so I already knew about the dinner."

"George is coming?" Alice's eyes flared wide. "Why is he coming?"

Desmond tried not to smile or show that he was enjoying her shock. "Tomorrow night is his usual dinner night with the Jones family, and they're coming here. So now he is as well."

His mother darted her eyes around the room before they eventually landed on Desmond again. "It's just like them to do something as vile as inviting their own guest to *my* dinner."

Numerous replies came to Desmond's mind. He reeled them in tight and didn't let any of them go. He wouldn't give her the satisfaction of knowing who he thought was truly the vile one.

"We will work it to our advantage nonetheless." She let out a huff and turned to take her leave, holding her head as high as it would go. She bid him goodnight, but Desmond said nothing.

When the door clicked shut, Desmond turned back to the desk and started on his work. He reached for the first sheet of paper. His hand shook, though he couldn't feel it and couldn't stop. He reached out to hold it with his other hand, but it too was shaking. He sat his arms on his desk and rested his head on them.

More yelling came through the halls. No doubt, his mother had informed his father about George's planned presence at the dinner. Maybe he shouldn't have said anything. But he supposed it was for the best. If his parents yelled and screamed about it all night, there was less of a chance they would be doing so at the dinner.

The momentum of his bouncing legs had turned into a gallop beneath his desk. His arms kept quivering, and the whole room rattled. He needed to get his work done. He knew how much worse his father would be in the morning if the paperwork went unfinished. But his body refused to comply.

The argument on the other side of the door grew in violence and volume. Desmond's head pounded.

He collected the papers, the writing utensils, and oil lamp before heading into his closet. He closed the door behind him, lining the bottom of it with the first article of clothing he could find.

Finally, the world became quiet.

He switched the lamp on, set the papers down, and stretched out his shoulders. As he lowered to the floor, his body settled.

Leaving. Soon he would be leaving. He had a whole new life out there waiting for him. He couldn't get to it fast enough.

Desmond woke up and swiped a hand down his face, rubbing away the dust from his eyes before he realized where he was. On the floor in his closet. His heart ricocheted against his ribs. He flung open the door and looked towards his windows. The sun hadn't yet risen, though the sky was showing signs that it was about to start glowing.

He ran his fingers through his hair, combing it into place, then collected the papers for his father. He made sure they were organized into the correct order before straightening his suit enough to head downstairs. Maybe he should have taken a moment to get changed into new clothes. But getting in trouble for making his father late would have been worse than getting insulted for how he looked.

"Desmond," his father grumbled upon his arrival downstairs. "You look horrible, and you almost made me late."

"Almost, but not quite," he tried to say enthusiastically, though perhaps he was trying to be subtly sarcastic.

His father snatched the papers from him and flipped through the pages. His grumblings became increasingly worse variations of words beginning with the letter 'm'. "Mediocre. Messy. Miserable," the list went on.

"I triple checked my work," Desmond said loud enough to cut his father's attention away from the papers.

"Done *correctly* and done *properly* are two different things." His father threw the papers into his case and closed it as he walked towards the door. "I expect better from you for being a Prescott. Honestly, I'd never hire a man like you in my life." He left, and the door crashed shut behind him.

According to his father, Desmond was void of any high aspects. Being a Prescott was the only worthy thing about him. Sometimes, he believed it. He allowed the sentiment to stay with him, knowing his name gave him many advantages other men just didn't have. Advantages he could use to his benefit, even ones he could use to help Molly.

Molly...

His mother would be asleep for a while longer, and his father's carriage was pulling down the road already. So the timing was ideal for him to take a little morning walk. The sky was about to glow, soon the sunrise would be raging, and the day would begin. Desmond knew just how he wanted to start it.

Chapter 4

Molly woke up to the sound of rain. She rolled over and plopped the pillow over her head, covering her ears with its fluff. For something she loved as much as rain, it was rather rude of it to wake her from such a very perfect dream.

She flicked up a corner of the pillow to breathe.

Rain didn't make much sense when the glow of the sunrise peeked through her windows. Nor did the rhythm match rain very well.

But there was certainly something.

She threw the blankets off and stepped onto the floor. Her cerulean robe was slung over the arm of the plush chair in the corner by the window. She grabbed it and wrapped it around her night dress as she headed to her balcony.

The morning air was freezing. Clinging to the softness of her robe as she tightened it around her waist, she stepped towards the railing.

Down on the grass she saw a very handsome young man looking up at her. He was dressed in the same green suit he'd had on when she'd seen him last, and his hair was completely disheveled.

"Dez?"

"Good morning," he said with a very sheepish smile. "I was wondering if you wanted to have breakfast with me? I brought you all sorts of pastries."

"You woke me up for pastries?"

"Is that a bad thing?"

"No," she replied with a sleepy curve to her lips. "I'll be right down."

Molly snuck out of her room, happiness coursing over her as the second floor of her home was entirely quiet. Well, with the exception of her father's snoring, which was the best noise possible in that moment.

She tiptoed down the stairs and headed for the cellar door that hid in the corner behind the spiral stairs. The stone floor was ice cold, the air was dry, and somehow also damp. She raced to the exterior door and lifted the hatch.

Desmond still stood beneath her balcony, shuffling his feet along the frosted blades of grass.

"Dez," she called in a whisper.

He smiled and made his way over. "What's this?"

"A secret Victoria shared with me," she said through a mellow yawn.

Desmond brushed a soft kiss against her cheek and stepped past her into the cellar.

She grabbed hold of his free hand and led him into the back corner. A blanket and floor pillows waited for them, along with matches to light a candle.

"Jeremy waits in here sometimes."

Desmond sat down on the blanket, and she fell into place beside him, watching as he struck the match into a flame and the darkness shrunk away. He lifted the top of the basket he had brought along, and the aroma of fresh baked pastries travelled up to her in a most splendid way.

"Mmm," she said involuntarily. "Those smell amazing."

Desmond drew out a napkin and unfolded it, revealing all the treats. He held it out so she could choose whichever one she wanted for herself.

Everything was soaked in butter; baked into a glittering gold. Molly lifted away a swirled muffin and took her first bite. Absolutely divine.

"I also brought this." He reached into the basket and pulled out a large metal flask. "Because I thought you might want some tea."

She caught crumbs in her hands, licking what she could off her chin, and nodded.

"It's going to take a little while to fully steep. The water isn't as hot as when I first left."

She set the breakfast down and pulled his face in close for a kiss. "You prepared a picnic for me."

His rapid breaths against her lips proved she had caught him slightly off guard.

He finally smiled. "I figured if I was going to wake you up, I better make it special."

She stretched out her legs to lay her head onto his lap. "You are special enough all on your own, Dez," she mumbled as her eyelids fell closed.

"The tea will be ready soon," he replied.

"Did you get all of your work done last night?"

"I did. It took half of the night finishing and checking it over."

She forced her eyes open. "And you still came over here so early in the morning?"

Desmond nodded and looked off into the cellar. "I needed to see you before the dinner."

"That's right, the dinner is tonight." She pulled herself up and tried her best to remain in a sitting position.

He looked over at her with a smile that didn't meet his eyes. "My mother is in a frantic way about it. She doesn't want me anywhere near you, and she didn't seem too fond of the idea that George was coming."

"I'm not surprised about you needing to stay away from me. But I thought"—a yawn—"she encouraged your friendship with George."

"I thought so, too." He bent to the side and started pouring her a cup of tea. "She took great offence to him being there. Almost makes me happier that he's coming."

"If George finds out how much he isn't wanted, he'll probably enjoy being there more."

"That is true." He handed her the tea. "I'm sorry, I didn't bring any sugar."

She looked into the cup, felt the steam skim her cheeks in delightful puffs of warmth and savoured each sensation. Molly soaked in the magic and glanced over at Desmond.

He brushed his hands off with his napkin and held it under his mouth as he took a bite of one of the pastries. He caught her watching, and the corner of his lips tugged up.

She returned his smile and took her first sip of tea.

"You know," Desmond began, "I've been worried about him ever since I got back from my trip."

Molly's eyebrows creased. "About George?" She knew he hadn't looked very good the night he found out where his family home had burnt down, the home that had taken his family with it. Even just the brief reminder made her feel sick; it must have been far worse for him.

"He isn't himself." Desmond placed his teacup down and curled one leg under himself as he turned to face her. "Before he went away to school he was different, lighter somehow. I mean he has always had his darkness, but..."

Molly stared at him in a sleepy daze, listening to his words and taking them in, but unable to formulate a response in good time.

"Just the other night, George went on about his father and what a horrible person he was, and that because of it he doesn't want anything to do with love at all. There was something about his mother mixed in there as well, but I don't remember everything. That was a pretty big day for me." A hidden smile appeared on his lips before he went back to his main concern. "But George is different. Something is not right."

She sipped more tea. "So, he needs our help?"

"It's difficult to help George with anything."

"We can still try." Molly laid her head down on Desmond's shoulder and released a tired yawn.

He wrapped his arm around her. "I promise I won't wake you up this early again."

"Don't promise that."

"You're still half asleep."

"It's been a romantic, fresh start to the day."

He smoothed back her hair from her forehead, tucking it behind her ear. "I can't wait for a real fresh start. Away from my parents, and from everything they are. A fresh start on life."

"Do you think they can ever be happy for us?"

"No, I don't." He looked down. "But I don't care. I've spent my whole life trying to make them happy. I've spent sleepless nights worrying I wasn't good enough, or that I would never make them proud. I'm tired of trying. I've given up too much of myself for them. Sometimes I don't even know who I am."

Molly swallowed. "You're a good person, Dez. I hate that they did that to you."

"I don't think I can tell them about us." He faced her again, eyes filled with fear. "They would never let us be together. There's no telling what they would do to either one of us if they found out. I won't let anything bad happen to you, at all. I can't... I can't even think about it."

"So we'll just keep this a secret then?" Her emotions mixed together into new feelings, confusing and untrustworthy. She never could understand how Desmond managed to be so sweet when his parents were so vile.

"I can't think of another way for us to be safe. Not yet."

Molly wanted to be with Desmond more than anything, and making the best of a bad situation was something she was good at. For Desmond, she could give up the little things that wouldn't matter in the long run, and come up with new things to replace them with. As soon as she was more awake, she would try figure it out.

"I understand, Dez." She laid her hand on his.

"Thank you." He combed her hair and held it back as he cupped the nape of her neck. "As soon as we're out of here, they're not going to matter anymore. I'll be free to be whoever

I want. And that includes being a man who so helplessly loves you, that he does crazy things like wake you up for pastries and tea."

A curl broke free from his grasp and dangled alongside her cheek. She swept it away to see him better.

"I can't wait to see who you become," she whispered through a smile.

He leaned in close and pressed his lips softly against hers. "Neither can I."

Molly stole a book from her shelves and curled into the blankets on her bed. One by one, the morning hours ticked away into afternoon ones before a soft knock on her door brought Victoria inside.

She breezed into the room like a personification of day-light—her hair was bright like sunbeams, and her dress was a flirty shade of velvety green.

"I need your help!" she announced, showing off the colourful garments strung over her arm. "I don't know what to wear to the dinner tonight."

Molly pushed up from her comfortable reading position. "Shouldn't I be the one panicking about what to wear?"

Victoria held her nose high. "I'm your sister. If Alice and Harold hate you then I take personal offence to it. Therefore, I need to be looking my absolute finest." She threw the dresses onto the bed next to Molly and started picking them up one by one. "What are you wearing tonight?"

Molly glanced towards her closet and formed a grimace. "I have no idea."

"Not to worry. I couldn't sleep last night, so I went through your entire wardrobe in my mind." Victoria spun to face her with a carefree smile. "Wear the plum dress. The one with all the beading. When you wear that dress, even *I* can't take my eyes off of you."

Molly blushed. "I've only worn it once, to a dinner here at home, and you glared at me the whole night."

"Well of course I did. I mean how could I not when—" Victoria's eyes went wide until she took a deep breath and settled down. "Well you were just so beautiful that night that I may or may not have been a bit jealous. But those days are behind us."

Molly rolled her eyes. "What was that look for?"

"What look?"

"The one you made when you stopped telling me the real reason and ended with a variation of the truth."

"I did no such thing." Victoria threw two dresses to the side and continued to look at the remaining three on the bed. "Now, help me decide between these three dresses. They're my top choices."

Molly slipped off her bed to stand beside her sister.

The gowns were gorgeous. The first was deep blue, embroidered with golden thread that reminded Molly of summer sunlight glistening off crystal waters. There was a cream lace dress that resembled a wedding gown just a little too much but that would suit Victoria perfectly. Lastly there was a red dress, draped in majestic sheer fabric, fit for a queen. And Victoria always looked stunning in red.

"This one." Molly lifted the red gown and held it up to her sister.

"You think?" Victoria grasped the dress by its sleeves and walked over to the mirror where she swayed in delicate motions.

"I know so. Even I won't be able to stop looking at you," she mimicked her sister's previous tone. "Because apparently that's the criteria we are basing our outfits off of today."

Victoria let her laugh ring out as she walked back to the bed. "It's nowhere near as important as it'll be on my wedding day. Jeremy's mother already has so many incredible ideas for our dresses, I'm completely over the moon about them."

Molly felt her smile grow at the mention of Valerie Towson. If anyone could make a dream dress, it was her.

"Think of all the dancing you'll do in such a perfect dress," Victoria nearly sang the words, and Molly didn't blame her.

A chance to dance all night in a perfect dress now that she had Desmond—

Her thoughts halted. If all of the Prescotts were invited to the wedding, Molly was going to have a hard time figuring out how to dance with Desmond at all.

"Where did you go just now?" Victoria asked, crossing her arms.

"What do you mean?"

"A second ago we were laughing about dresses and a wedding, and now you look like you poured sour milk in your tea."

With a deep breath through her nose, Molly walked towards her closet. "Why do I have to explain my face when you don't have to explain yours?"

"Good point."

Molly entered her wardrobe and neared the back corner where all of her favourite dresses waited. She combed through them, admiring each individual gown. She lifted the purple gown down from the rod, ready to walk out with it when its hem caught on a trunk on the floor. She knelt down to lift it away when a small book fell onto her toes, pages open and crayon drawings on display.

Her smile was instantaneous at the sight of this forgotten treasure—her little book of fairytales.

"If you explain your face," came Victoria's voice, "*and* if it's a suitable explanation, I'll explain what I was thinking."

Molly laughed and slid the book back onto the trunk to return to later. She grabbed the purple beaded gown and headed back to Victoria.

"Do you think you'll be inviting the Prescotts to your wedding?"

Victoria beamed. "Of course I'll be inviting them! I expect you and Desmond to dance together all night."

Molly tossed the gown onto her bed and played with her fingers. "I'm not sure that will happen if his parents are there."

"Well they're going to have to get over themselves once Desmond tells them how much you mean to him."

"I don't know when that's going to happen." Molly shrugged to lighten the blow. "You have no idea what they've put him through. They're worse people than you could ever imagine."

"Molly." Victoria looked at her and frowned. "Eventually he's going to have to tell them."

Molly glanced down at her purple gown next to Victoria's red one, loving how they looked together.

"He didn't already tell you he isn't telling them, did he?" Victoria gripped Molly's arms and pulled her closer.

"We talked this morning."

"This morning?"

Molly sent her sister a hard look. "I don't see why you care so much when you not only have a secret relationship yourself, but also a fake one."

"Jeremy and I have a reason to keep secret."

"So does Desmond. I'd argue that his reason is far better than yours."

Victoria stormed away, stomping her foot before whirling around and facing Molly again. "It took us time to decide whether to keep it secret or not. We weighed the good and the bad before we finally knew what was best." She flailed her arms out dramatically and placed her hands on her hips. "As for my fake relationship with George, that is an entirely different subject that we don't have time to get into today."

Molly folded her arms across her chest, unimpressed with her sister's judgments. "Desmond and I have been friends for *years,* Victoria, and we've always had to keep it as much of a secret as possible. We didn't just decide that our romantic relationship needs to be kept a secret. It's *always* been something we needed to do."

"Fine." Victoria huffed, visibly upset but seemingly unable to think of another argument.

Molly let out a heavy breath to brush her own frustrations away. "Now you have to tell me what your face was about."

"No. Your answer wasn't as satisfying as I was hoping," Victoria said with a teasing grin, looking back at the gowns. "I think you need grandmother's clutch tonight. The beading will match perfectly."

Their grandmother's clutch was woven with beads and gems that caught every ray of light, creating reflections that danced around.

"You'd really let me borrow it?"

"Of course!" Victoria shone a more genuine smile. "You need all the help you can get for this dinner."

Molly laughed humourlessly. "Being near Harold and Alice sounds even more exhausting now that I'm with Desmond in this amazing way..." She held out her hands to stop plucking at her fingers. "I hate to be rude to anyone, but they bring out the worst in me. I'm not sure how much longer I can be nice to them."

"Make waves tonight, Molly. They deserve to be told that they're treating you horribly."

"If there's a chance of Desmond telling them about us, I can't risk making waves tonight."

"Oh, boo," Victoria scoffed, walking towards the doorway. "I'm going to go grab the clutch, and then you and I shall start getting ready together. I'll do your hair, and you can do mine. We can tell each other how darling we both look and how the world would crumble at our feet if we were to ever become more beautiful."

"Yes." Molly giggled. "That's exactly what the world will do."

Victoria sent an exaggerated wink before disappearing into the hall. Molly was relieved that she'd have her sister's company while getting ready. Waves were already forming in her stomach, refusing to be tamed. A distraction like Victoria would help with that.

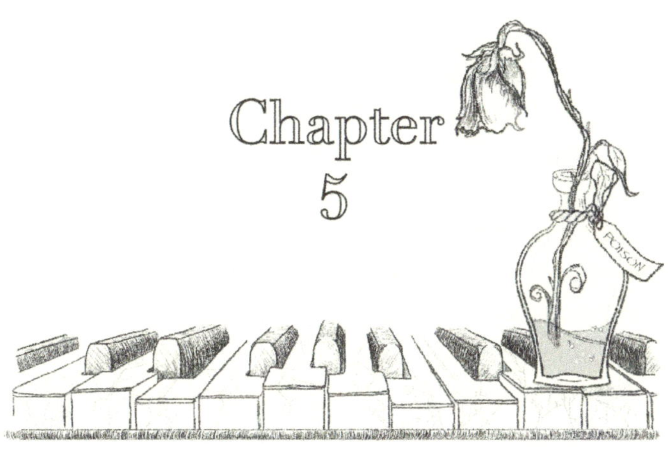

Chapter 5

The orange shroud of a finishing sunset lit the way up the front steps of the Prescott Estate. The ostentatious structure had never seemed like a home, and the shade of light wasn't doing anything to help it appear differently. George looked down at his suit, ignoring the memories of flames as he straightened his tie, pulled at his cufflinks, and fiddled with the chain of his watch. Anything to settle into the person he needed to be tonight. By the time he looked up, he was face to face with one of the hideous gargoyles that had sat atop the steps since he had been a young boy. George had always hated the way they sneered. He dreamed he'd one day get vengeance on the creatures.

"Are we ready?" William Jones looked at each member of his family, acknowledging George before settling his eyes on his wife.

"I'm not sure we'll ever fully be ready, dear," Cathryn Jones answered gently, fixating on the pink hues of her gown.

"There's a reason we only spend time with the Prescotts once a year."

"True," he grumbled.

George rolled back a smile and habitually offered Victoria his arm. While playing his part as a man in love with Victoria had its difficult moments, he had always enjoyed the entertainment value of it.

A quiet woman greeted them at the door, arranging for hats and coats to be discreetly placed away. George turned to look around the foyer, taking in the details of the forbidding home, noting that nothing had changed.

It had been several years since George had last been at the estate, but he remembered feeling just as sickened. Cream coloured walls were accented in deep green trim, maroon curtains matched the maroon carpet woven in a despicable manner. Furniture was sparse, and the walls held no family photographs. Instead, everything was accented with shiny brass trinkets. The Prescotts tried too hard to impress, without doing a very good job of it.

His grandmother, Lady Viola Clarington, changed everything about their home with the seasons. If George remembered correctly—which he always did—Alice Prescott had loved to copy his grandmother's style. What a shame she was no longer able to do so. She hadn't been invited to their home while Desmond had been away at school.

George offered his elbow back to Victoria, whose dress was so red he wondered if she had soaked it in the blood of her enemies. Accepting his arm graciously, she fell into her role as easily as ever. Her trick to the charade was pretending he was someone else entirely. His trick was pretending to be anyone but himself.

In the corner of his vision, George caught sight of Molly. Her familiar dress was a deep plum purple with beads threaded in florals from sleeves to hem. Her uneasy steps along the grotesque carpet swelled into music as the beading swished together. It was a sound he remembered all too well.

George turned back to Victoria, raising a single brow; wearing his questions instead of posing them.

"See something you like?" Victoria asked with a sinister smile. "I may have recommended the dress to her."

"Why?" The word stretched out longer than he had intended, though he was satisfied with the annoyed sharp note of it.

"That dress makes her the most beautiful lady in the room. More than that, it makes her feel like it. In a place as ominous as this, I figured she could use every last bit of help she could get."

"You're evil," he replied, almost impressed by her knack for formulating schemes.

"I know. It's fun." She tucked her chin into her shoulder, playing coy while on his arm.

Victoria looked all around the foyer, forcing George to do so again.

"I feel like I'm going to be sick," Victoria groaned. "This whole place is giving me the creeps."

"Well, if you're going to be ill," he whispered, "make sure to aim for the carpet. It's hideous."

Victoria snorted, earning a stern look from her father.

"Why do I feel like this is a very bad idea?" Molly asked from behind them.

"Probably because this is a bad idea," George said as he and Victoria spun towards her. "But it is going to be okay."

"When people say that, there tends to be a strong possibility of things *not* being okay," was Victoria's addition.

"That was really helpful. Thank you, Victoria." George soaked his words with a heavy dose of sarcasm.

Victoria ignored him. "Where are the Prescotts anyways? This is their house, shouldn't they be here?"

"Victoria." William Jones' voice rumbled through the foyer. He kept a hold of his wife's hand as she stood facing away. "You are all to be on your very best behaviour tonight. The Prescotts demand a certain amount of patience. Be sure to give it to them." He glanced over his shoulder to make sure his wife wasn't listening. "We can make fun of them when we get home."

George hid his laughter behind a smile as Victoria did the same, but Molly's face fell into a vacant mask. George's gaze travelled down to where her fingers plucked at one another through her gloves, then rose to pat her highly restrained hair.

Victoria dragged George to her sister's side, bringing the three of them closer than felt wise.

"It's all of us, versus the two of them," she whispered in Molly's ear. "If they make any comments that I don't like, it'll be taken care of."

Molly showed no signs of answering or even that she'd heard at all. She held her breath, blinking far too rapidly.

"Oh wow! You're all here already."

Everyone's attention shot to the second level of the home.

Desmond held onto the railing as he descended the stairs. He was dressed in colours of the earth—a brown suit and a fern coloured tie. Not one wrinkle could be seen, except the ones near his eyes as he smiled at Molly.

Her breathing returned to normal just at the sight of Desmond, so George relaxed, too. If anyone had the capability of calming her down, it was Desmond.

"Is there a room where we can sit while we wait?" Cathryn Jones asked, gripping tighter onto her husband's arm.

"Of course." Desmond tore his eyes away from Molly as he reached the floor where they were standing. "Right this way." He gestured towards the common sitting room. It was just as boring as the foyer, but at least it gave them all the chance to sit down.

"How have you been, Desmond?" William Jones asked briskly.

George saw the slight flick of Desmond's eyes as they slipped in Molly's direction before turning back to her father.

"Good, sir, I've been good."

William Jones huffed, clearly having seen the stolen glance, then situated himself close to his wife where she sat on an uncomfortable looking sofa.

"When can we go home?" she whispered to no one.

"Now dear, I don't think you should say such things—"

"I'm with mother on this," Victoria hummed, fluffing out her skirt as she reclined in her chair. George stood behind her and propped an arm across the back, leaning into it and pattering his fingers against the scratchy textile of the wings.

"I think even I am," Desmond agreed. "Only not in the same way of course. But I'd like to leave. Not that I have anywhere to go."

"Smooth Desmond," George said with a jesting smile. "I must say, I'm actually fine being here. I'm really curious to know where this is going."

"Really?" Victoria gasped up at him.

George nodded.

"I definitely don't want to be here." Molly twisted her fingers around the beads on her gown, keeping her eyes on the motion.

"So the only person on my side is George?" William Jones asked, looking around the room.

George shrugged. "Seems like it, sir."

William Jones mumbled and shook his head. "I suppose out of the lot of them, you're not the worst person to have on my side."

George slid a hand into his pocket, and grinned. "I won't forget you said that. It gives me great pride."

"Easy boy," William Jones said, hiding a hint of a smile.

Alice and Harold Prescott failed to make timely appearances. William Jones soothed a hand across his wife's shoulders. Desmond's leg levelled up and down at every slightest noise. Molly twirled the beads on her skirt. And Victoria flicked her fingers to shoo George away like a pest.

The sound of the grandfather clock filled his ears, turning the seconds as long as hours, the *tick tick tock* bringing him ever closer to the brink of insanity.

"You're all on time," Alice Prescott cheered as she walked through the doorway, all primed in London's latest fashion, and acting as though she wasn't very late. "Dinner is about to be served. We should all make our way into the dining hall."

William Jones stood first, extending his hand and safety to his wife who looked like she hadn't stopped shaking since Alice Prescott had entered. Desmond followed, stiff as a board, after his mother.

Victoria refused George's assistance as she stood from her chair, pushing him away with a furious elbow.

"Just go in without me, I'm staying with Molly," then under her breath, "which is something *your boy* should have done."

"Things could get so much worse if he did—"

"Doesn't mean he shouldn't." Victoria ignored his protest, and looped her arm through Molly's, guiding her away.

Molly tensed but walked at Victoria's side. She picked her fingers behind her back, and George, following a couple of paces behind, got lost watching the rhythm.

Entering the dining hall felt like entering a theatre. George had forgotten how lavish the Prescotts were in all the worst ways. Even the flowers, in extravagantly horrendous vases, wilted as though trying to escape their porcelain prisons.

The mahogany table was long, but seating was arranged close with everyone huddled tightly at one end. Harold Prescott took his place at the head, but everyone had taken seats to his left, leaving the three odd chairs to his right wide open.

"We'll sit on either side of you," Victoria whispered.

"Stop making a fuss, I'll be fine," said Molly.

"I don't care." With that, Victoria walked around the table, sat next to Harold and had Molly sit next to her. George had no choice but to fall into the chair on the other side of Molly.

Hot soup and fresh salad was followed by a spread of mashed potatoes, gravy-glazed chicken, and fresh bread rolls; all trimmed with seasonal fruits. Everything smelled delicious and was served on luxurious platters—it would have been a great night if the evening could have been judged by the food alone.

"We have some exciting news to share," Alice said with a foul smile, eyeing up Molly as if she were a little mouse.

George filled his fork but hovered it over his plate, waiting for whatever was coming next.

"Is that our definition of exciting or yours?" Victoria airily asked while taking a bite.

George immediately shoved the food into his mouth to fight away a smile.

Harold Prescott glared at Victoria. "Why you—"

"What's this news, Alice?" William Jones interjected, staring Harold Prescott down, daring him to speak to his daughter that way again.

"Our Desmond is getting married," Alice continued, too cheerfully to suit the words.

William Jones kept his eyes on Harold Prescott, who continued his glare at Victoria, but she only sipped at her water as if she didn't have a care in the world.

Desmond grimaced at his plate, and though George waited to catch his eye, he never looked up.

"Well that certainly is...something," Cathryn Jones hummed.

George had a fondness for words. Especially when they were used to keep secrets or to avoid telling unnecessary truths, or how certain phrases became brilliant when the right words were spun together. Cathryn Jones was usually good at that sort of thing, but in that moment, she was anything but her usual self.

Her colourless words roiled around the table, and dread needled its way into George's chest.

"The beautiful Audrey will be here in a couple of weeks from America," Alice Prescott continued, collecting another forkful. "She comes from the most wonderful family, and I know she'll make our Desmond happy."

Victoria let out a vibrant laugh. "I wouldn't have thought you knew how to make anyone happy."

This wasn't unusual behaviour from Victoria, and George had gotten used to it. What was new, however, was that her mother didn't reprimand her; nor did her father.

"Are you going to control that girl's tongue?" Alice Prescott shot to Cathryn and William Jones, who both stared blankly back. Alice Prescott turned her attention to George. "Are you?"

"I have no control over what she says," George answered with a smirk. "Even if I did, I might just have her repeat herself."

"I have *never* been so disrespected in my own home," Alice Prescott shrieked.

"Perhaps you shouldn't have invited us then," Victoria said.

"Enough!" Cathryn Jones cut in. "Now, we all know we were not invited over to your home to talk casually about the marriage plans you have for Desmond. What is this really about?"

George looked at Desmond who was staring right back at him, his green eyes wide, his leg bouncing, and his nerves visibly fraying. There was no way to stop it.

"In view of wedding plans we wanted to discuss the use of the land you have next to your property," Harold Prescott stated coldly.

George lost his grip on his fork, and it clanged against his plate. He stared down at it as the abhorrent sound echoed through his thoughts, trailing away into hues of oranges and greys.

"You mean the land where my entire family died?" he asked, matching the frigid tone that Harold Prescott had used.

"That's—"

"You mean the land where my family died?" he repeated, cutting Alice Prescott's words off and staring her down directly.

She made a proud sound from her throat and sat up taller. "That was a very long time ago."

"Is that supposed to change the morbidity?" George glared into the flames of the candles, and his hands turned into fists.

"We all have our own opinions on that," Alice Prescott said next.

The flames shuddered into flashes of distant screams and smoke. Everything turned to grey ash—nightmares converging on reality.

A light touch on his elbow brought him back to the present. He unclenched his hands, and Molly's hand slipped away. George stretched his fingers out and tapped them along the table's edge.

"Cathryn," Alice Prescott said, taking centre stage, "I was hoping that due to our history you would allow us to use that land for—"

"The land isn't mine." Cathryn Jones slitted her eyes towards Alice. "It belonged to Elizabeth. So now the land belongs to George. You'll have to ask him. Although, I think he already gave you an answer."

George let out a low laugh. "Don't even think—"

"George," Desmond interrupted, and based on his shaking curls, his leg was bouncing beneath the table. He turned to his mother. "Why are you doing this?"

"We want the best future possible for you, Desmond. It would be the perfect piece of land to start you off with. We'll find the two of you a home while a new estate is built—"

"You think I'd want to live that close?" Desmond seemed surprised he'd said the words out loud, as if by admitting that, his parents would know all his secrets.

George adjusted his sleeves, shifting into the person Desmond needed him to be—the friend he was determined to be. He listened closely, so he'd be able to step in quickly if need be.

"It's my life, you can't just plan it all out without so much as mentioning it to me."

"I can do what I want. I'm your mother."

"As if you've ever treated me the way a mother should."

"Don't you dare speak to me that way. Your father and I—"

A laugh.

Cold, penetrating, and bitter.

A terrifying sound to anyone, but especially given it's source—Cathryn Jones.

She calmed and wiped her tears with a handkerchief.

"I'm sorry," she eventually said.

"Mother..." Molly's voice seemed a distant whisper.

"It's okay, Molly darling." Cathryn pushed back her chair and stood up. "I think I just need some fresh air."

"You can't leave until we've settled this." Alice Prescott stood abruptly, knocking the table with her waist.

"I'm done, Alice." Cathryn closed her eyes and placed a hand on her husband's shoulder to steady herself. "I'm leaving."

Alice prowled forward. "We are not done talking about this."

"If you're really so keen to talk, then let's discuss *everything*." Cathryn's eyes bored into Alice. "What were you doing there that night, watching the house burn as everyone was still inside? Let's talk about *why* the Clarington property is empty land."

Time gave up its hold on the world as everything moved in slow motion. Colours lost their lustre, burning into the repulsive shades of George's childhood phobias.

Flames, smoke, ash... All the haunting remnants of his fears came hurtling back.

He forced his eyes open and saw Harold Prescott standing next to William Jones, saying words to the women that George couldn't hear.

Desmond's hands covered his face, his flaxen hair knotted in his fingers, quivering as he tried to hide in plain sight.

Molly's hands hid under the table cloth, surely picking at her nails.

Victoria discreetly rubbed Molly's back and made eye contact with him. "George?"

He nodded, ready to clear the canvas of his mind, eager to formulate an escape plan.

"Tell me!" Harold Prescott boomed, shaking the stemware on the table.

Desmond kept his face hidden behind his hands, though he had stopped shaking. Molly looked across the table at him, but to no avail. The parents all stayed on their feet, grounded in their argument.

"Alice, you tell me right now." Harold Prescott's blaring voice turned his face a despicable red.

Alice Prescott pinched her shoulders back. "There's a chance you're not Desmond's father."

Desmond's head shot up.

The veins in Harold's forehead throbbed. "Who?"

Alice's eyes flicked to George. A whimper escaped her as she turned to her feet. "James."

"Do we know a James?" Victoria asked over her shoulder.

It was a question spoken out of innocent curiosity. Victoria was a lot of things, but never malicious without good reason.

But he only knew of one James.

"My father," he answered to everyone, including himself.

Desmond locked eyes with him, blood leaching from his face, discolouring his skin into shades of terror and shock. He wasn't breathing.

George stretched out his fingers, ready to hold the boy together.

Desmond threw his chair back, sending it crashing to the ground. Without looking at anyone and without a word, he ran from the room.

Chapter 6

Molly sat at the table as the world became a dark and twisted place. Closing her eyes, she cast her face down to her lap, tracing her fingernails with the tips of her thumbs.

She felt movement around her, but the longer she kept her eyes closed, the more it faded away. So she traced, and kept tracing, her nail beds until the rhythm brought her peace.

Even in the black was Desmond, the shock on his face, the pain he was in. And George, how angry and shadowed he had become. Her mother, the sound of her broken laughter and chilling voice.

Molly's fingers stung. She squeezed her eyes tighter and switched to plucking at the beads on her gown.

A small grasp on the back of her arm had her motionless. Silence swam in her ears as she forcibly tried to open her eyes.

The room was excruciatingly bright.

"I came back for you."

Molly turned to the voice, unsure of how to return to the world when her mind was still in a whorl of black clouds.

George sank down beside her chair and looked up to her, his ink black hair tangled back in knots. "You've been sitting at the table alone for ten minutes."

Molly looked around the room. She was alone. Except for George. She couldn't fathom how ten minutes had passed. It didn't make sense. Nothing seemed to make much sense.

"Where is everyone?" she asked.

"I think we both know where Desmond may have gone."

The woods, Desmond had probably ran to the woods.

George continued, "Your parents just left. Victoria had gone outside already."

"They left me."

His blue eyes, usually filled with so many sparks, were dark voids. "We need to get going, too."

George braced her elbows as she stood, maintaining his grasp until she was steady on her feet. Her every footfall was heavy against the ground as it felt further and further away.

Her memories spiralled through her mind in reverse. The shouting, the dinner, the ride over, the laughs she'd shared with Victoria while getting ready...

"My grandmother's purse!" she gasped, clutching her sides in search of it.

"I'll find it," George said softly. "Go get your coat on. I'll be right there."

Molly forced a nod. She found her bearings and left for the foyer, feeling as though the world was made of misty lines when Alice Prescott stormed towards her.

"You!" Alice screamed, and before Molly could react, Alice slapped her across the face.

The stinging pain shot through Molly's fog, waking her up from whatever place she had faded to. She held her fingers to her burning cheek, blinked back tears as the pain traveled to her eyes and watched as the world became solid again. A restlessness in her chest reminded her that she didn't owe Alice one last ounce of kindness.

"You did this! This is all your fault!" Alice raised her hand to strike again.

Molly winced prematurely, readying her arm to block the blow.

Nothing came.

George stood in front of Alice, holding firmly to her wrist. Molly didn't have to see his face to know exactly what sort of expression burned there.

"I think you best be careful as to what you do next." Peeling his hand away one finger at a time, George released his hold on Alice, and she stumbled away.

She glared at Molly, rolling back her shoulders to transform into the poised version of herself. "This was all your fault."

"No, Alice," George corrected, his voice filling the foyer with shadows. "This is all your fault."

Harold Prescott marched over. "You will not speak to her like that in my home, George." He posted himself next to his wife, feigning a sense of loyalty that demanded respect.

George's gaze cast along the floor, turning up when it reached Harold, measuring him from the ground up. The darkness emanating off George froze Molly in place.

"As of now," George began, "the Claringtons' personal connection to the Prescotts, no longer exists, *Harold*. If you wish to address me, you will do so formally."

The authority of the Clarington name laid siege over Harold and Alice Prescott, and neither of them spoke.

George gestured Molly towards her coat. "Let's get out of here."

She rushed over to grab it, slipping into her sleeves and doing up her buttons in frantic clashes. George retrieved his coat, grabbing his hat off its hook so abrasively that the entire rack shook.

Molly looked back at Alice Prescott as she walked towards the door, ignoring George's gentle touch to her arm as he tried to guide her out. There was something she needed to do.

"You never deserved him," Molly said, taking a step towards the Prescotts instead of the door. "You never deserved Desmond, and he always deserved better than you."

Harold Prescott stepped forward. "Watch your tongue, little girl."

An evil smile sliced across Alice's mouth.

So Molly smiled right back. "You really don't get it, do you? You love prestige and attention, when you should have been loving Desmond."

Alice's smile vanished.

"I will do whatever it takes," Molly continued, "to make sure you can never hurt him again."

She spun back to the door and walked out, lighter on her feet and stronger in her heart. Those horrible people had hurt Desmond in ways he'd never admitted—she was determined to make sure they could never do it again.

Gravel crushed under her feet as she walked towards George's car, as the same stones were obliterated under his steps. His open palms slammed onto the hood of his car, barely balancing him.

She looked back to the Prescott Estate and felt sick being that close to the people inside. "What you did back in the house—"

"I'd do it again." He pushed away from the car and raked back his hair, taking one long stride and landing directly before her. "If anyone lays a hand on you, or tries to hurt you, I will embrace every last one of my shadows. And I would never feel a flicker of regret over it. Do you understand?"

She did.

George dipped his chin and guided her into the car, watching as she clumsily lowered into the passenger side. He turned the engine to a start and glanced up to the grey clouds shifting across the otherwise clear sky. Finally, he made his way into his seat, and started to drive. It didn't take long before they were parked in her driveway.

Molly stared at the tree line, searching for something to say, wondering if she could even find the words to match how she was feeling.

"Thank you for not leaving me," she said into the night.

"You'll never have to worry about that." He threw his hat into the backseat of the car and tore out his cufflinks.

Some part of her wanted to reach out to him, to place herself closer, but she lacked the strength. "Do you believe Desmond is your brother?"

"Desmond has always been my brother," he answered in a faraway voice. "What I believe is that he needs you right now."

"What about you?"

He watched the leather stitches between their seats in his car, where their hands almost met. "Are you going inside your home?"

The windows of Quaintrelle Estate were dark, her family most likely in their private rooms, preparing to sleep the night away. "No. I need to go to the woods and find him."

George flexed his hands and curled them into fists. "When you find Desmond, tell him he has a home with me. I'll be going to the clearing and can wait for him there. Tell him not to go back to Harold and Alice."

"I hope he'll take you up on that."

His palms slid up the steering wheel, fingers tapping incessantly as they went. "I'm glad he has you."

Fear crept up between his words, something he wouldn't voice, a secret he seemed to play out with his pattering fingers.

"You should go," George said without looking her way.

So Molly said goodbye and took a gentle leave straight for the woods.

Molly hurried along the water, muttering into the wind. She swung her beaded gown around her legs, holding it high enough to climb up the fallen log.

Straining to see through even the darkest of shadows, she listened and searched for any sign of Desmond. Nothing.

The forest was desolate, the creek shores had not even a whisper of Desmond's presence.

She slid back down to the earth, trying not to panic, not to lose herself in screaming his name.

Tears burned in her throat, unwilling to be shed, swelling into tumultuous waves that crashed in her chest. She could barely breathe.

Every time her eyes closed she saw his face when the announcement had been made—the shock, the rage, the desperation.

She needed to find him.

Wind whipped through the forest, ripping strands of her hair out from the pins she'd used to hold it up. She'd wanted to make a good impression at the dinner, perfected her hair just to do so. How foolish that felt now.

The wind hushed, the rustling leaves coming to a quiet. That's when she heard it. From under the weeping willow, as if the tree had sung her its secret.

Molly nearly tripped over her feet as she raced and brushed past the tendrils of leaves, scooping them to the side to peer underneath.

Sitting at the base of the crackled trunk, his arms wrapped around bent legs, Desmond's face was burrowed between his knees.

"Dez," she cried.

His head shot up, and he rose to his feet, still trembling like he had at the table.

"Molly." His voice was a remnant of who he had been.

She stumbled, breathless already, until she was close enough to throw her arms around his shoulders. She gripped onto his jacket and held as much of him as she could. "I was scared," she whispered into the fabric. "I was so worried, Dez."

He wrapped his arms around her, too, his head dropping down. "I had to leave, Molly."

She brushed his hair away from his eyes and held his face between her trembling hands. "Let's sit down."

It was as if he'd forgotten how to work his own body—but then he remembered to bend his knees and trust the ground as he came to it.

"I had to run," he said in a daze. "I had no choice. I was running before I knew what I was doing."

"It's okay. I found you." She reached out and held onto his hand.

Somehow she knew he needed silence. So she would give that to him. As long as he needed it.

Night sounds filled their silence. The wind through the leaves, the owls, and the streaming waters.

Desmond's eyes hardened as he stared at the forest floor. "You and George are the only family I've ever had. Now he might be my brother. And it was kept from us, our entire lives!"

"Your mother should have told you—"

"That *woman*," he spat, lush with distain, "does not deserve to be called my mother."

Molly flinched.

"I need to go!" He sprang to his feet in an instant, pacing in the open space beneath the willow.

"George said he's waiting in the clearing—"

"No, Molly. I need to go! Away from here, away from London. I need to go!" He flung the branches out of his way and took his pacing to the waters.

Molly forced herself to a stand and followed him to the creek. "What are you talking about?"

Three full strides and he stood right by her feet and grabbed hold of her hands. "You can come with me."

"But Dez—"

"It's all planned out. I have that job, our housing is paid for. We can go! Together."

The ground fell away from beneath her. She squeezed his hands tighter so as not to fall.

Two weeks. That's how long it had taken to figure out if she could live a happy life after running away with him. Two weeks—and so much had transpired since. She couldn't leave now, even as she remembered the days she'd endured crying over it.

"I can't go like this."

He dropped her hands and took a step back. "I decided to stay for you. Can't you decide to leave for me?"

"That was barely two days ago," she pleaded. "I told you to leave. But you said you were staying."

"But now I need to go, can't you see that? I can't stay here with those people!" His words rumbled with brutality as a new version of him came to life.

"I do see that, Dez." She feigned a sense of calm. "That's why I told you to go, because I understand."

"Then why can't you come with me?" He kicked a few stones into the water and stared at the mess of ripples on the surface. His panting breaths seemed to shatter every last piece of him that had remained.

Molly wiped her hands down her gown, spinning the beads as she approached Desmond, careful not to spook him. He wasn't there anymore, not really. She needed to bring him back.

"Alice and Harold treated you horribly." She took his hand in hers, hoping it would keep them together in a way their words had failed to do. "You're allowed to be angry at them. But my family is special to me—I couldn't leave them like this."

"We talked about this already. Where we're going is not that far. You'll see your family all the time!"

"Not if we leave like this, Dez. If I leave with you like this, the rumours people would bring down on my family is not something I want to have happen. It's not something I'll be able to come back from."

"Who cares, Molly?" he yelled, pulling his hands away from hers again. "People will talk no matter what you do! Forget them. Forget them all!"

She caught her breath, feeling tears prickling at her eyes. "I can't forget about what would happen to my family. I think we need to calm down—"

"No. We need to go." His words carved a crevice between them until they stood on opposite sides.

Desmond's palms dug into his eyes, his fingers scratching the tips of his curls. "What if we get married? We can elope so you can come with me without having to worry about your family."

"Your solution is an *elopement?*" She blinked at him.

He shrugged away the heavy suggestion of marriage like it was an everyday conversation. "We already know everything about each other. It would be easy to live the rest of our lives together."

"Live the rest of our lives together..." Her mouth went dry, splicing apart her voice. "Using marriage as a solution to a bigger problem? No, Dez. Marriage is about love. About everyone we love. I want to be surrounded by loved ones on that day. I want my mother to be there—"

"You would choose your mother over me?"

Her jaw tightened. "You didn't just say that."

Desmond stood silent.

She wished for an apology that never came. "I never thought you would ask me to make that choice."

He ran a hand down his face and stole a step closer. "Molly—"

"Stay away, Desmond." She raised a hand between them.

Her hand dropped to her side. The way his full name crossed her lips was a thousand stabbing wounds down her spine. But she couldn't take it back.

Desmond's expression faltered, stretching with pain. It tore away a piece of her—a piece she would never get back.

She plucked at her fingertips, digging down to find a way out of the mess that they had somehow fallen into. Lost, confused, but not without any hope.

"George said you could stay with him. He's waiting at the clearing," she said to her gown, unable and unwilling to face Desmond so soon. "You could stay with him just until we figure things out so that we can leave together."

"I can't do that. I can't risk seeing my parents—" He shook his head. "Alice and Harold."

"Are we not worth the risk of running into them a few times?"

"That's not what I meant."

"It's what you said."

"This can't be happening." He grasped back his hair. "No, not like this, Molly. No."

Molly's heart cracked open in her chest, glass shards ripping her apart and bringing forth her tears. "I cried over you for days because I was ready to let you go," she sobbed, "I knew you needed to leave. I knew we wanted different things. But you—Desmond, you made me believe it when you said you would stay. And then you kissed away my doubts."

"Molly, please." His eyes filled with tears.

Desmond never allowed himself to cry, he always conditioned his emotions to show nothing, even when tears were appropriate. That resolve was wavering now, chipping away at Molly a little bit more.

Wiping away her tears, she stepped back and made her way to the tree stump she had used in all the years of their secret meetings. She collapsed onto it, fighting the instinct to beg him to stay.

But deep down, she knew.

She knew leaving was what was best for him, that if he did, his parents would never hurt him again.

Desmond tossed his hands out, fingers curled into talons. "So you're just going to sit there?"

"Yes," she stated. "I choose staying. I choose working on this together. I will sit here incase you decide you'll be staying, too."

"You're going to make me choose?" It came out in a whine.

"You can tell me that you'll stay with George while we figure this out, together. You can take time to think things through before making your choice."

"I have to leave now, Molly. I have to go!"

"I know you do."

"But I love you," he choked.

"I will always love you, Desmond." Tears streamed down her cheeks, stealing the steady flow of her voice. "If you stay, I will love you more than you could possibly imagine. I will love you until you have forgotten you were never loved enough before. And if you leave, I will love you from afar, in ways that transcend the distance between us. I will love you until you find someone to love you up close."

Desmond's tears fell as he crouched down and held onto her knees for balance. "I don't want to say goodbye. I don't want to lose you."

She raised her hand up to his face, placing her palm on his cheek, brushing away his tears with her thumb. "You will never lose me."

He shook his head and watched her face with feral need. "I can't just walk away from you."

"It's not that I want you to," she managed to whisper. "But you're determined to run away. And we both know that it's exactly what you need to do."

"What if we try letters again?"

Molly dropped her forehead onto his, lacing one hand behind his neck, slipping the other into his hand. "If you walk away tonight Desmond, it means you've left me without trying to figure things out together. That can't be fixed through letters."

"I need to leave, Molly." His hand gripped tighter to hers.

"I know." She felt how quickly he was breaking down inside, and she was broken herself.

Their breaths rolled in sync, tears falling in unison. Their hands tore apart. All that remained were two crushed hearts and a collection of broken dreams, all in the forest that had once brought them together.

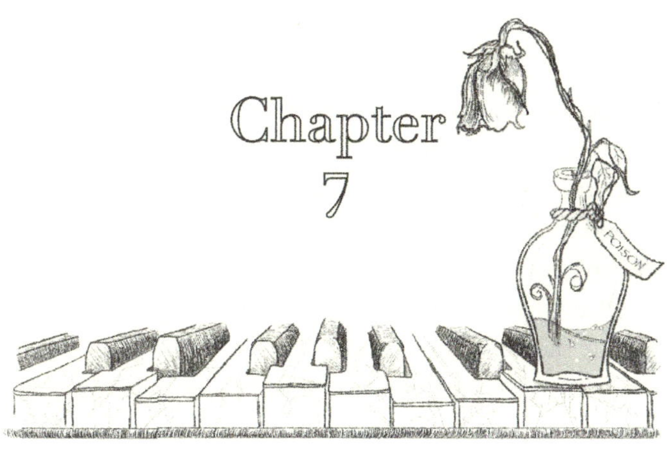

George sat in the long grass as the melody of the breeze spun his shadows together. He didn't know how to feel about anything he'd learned tonight—he couldn't sort his furious thoughts into songs, or lock them in their appropriate boxes.

Plucking a blade of grass, he twisted it around his fingers. If he couldn't play the piano, he'd make do by incapacitating his fingers. Every time he closed his eyes, flames and ash clashed through his internal barriers. He couldn't take it anymore.

He pushed to his feet and walked across the clearing.

The moonlight played tricks with his vision as he trudged through the grass—his family's graves. Step after painful step, he made his way to the car.

When he arrived, Desmond sat on the passenger side.

George released a breath of relief. Then he held his next breath back at the sight of Desmond's suit jacket thrown roughly into the backseat, at his sleeves ripped open, and the disarray of his hair. He looked the way George was sure they both felt.

"I didn't hear you arrive," George said, falling into his seat. There was a part of him that wanted to make light of the evening, to joke, jest the stresses away. But everything he scrambled to come up with, fell flat.

"Thank-you for offering me a place to stay," Desmond muttered as he watched his leg bounce in slow-motion.

"It was the least I could do."

They drove in silence for several excruciating minutes. George turned back to Desmond, desperate to talk about something, anything, before the silence ate away at what was left of his senses.

"You will have the guest room," he tried, getting no response from Desmond. "I see you don't have a bag packed, so you can borrow some of my clothes until we can get yours."

"I'm never going back into that house," Desmond snapped.

George let the attitude slide. "I don't mind getting them for you."

"I don't want *anything* that is connected to those people."

"Desmond, you need clothes."

"This isn't about clothes." Desmond's bouncing rhythm gained momentum, and his voice grew with toxicity and wrath. "This is about how my life, *my entire life,* has been a lie."

George gripped onto the steering wheel, desperate to hold up the walls he felt slipping away. "James might not be your father."

"It doesn't matter," Desmond said as he turned to face the landscape. "To him I will never be his son. And that was the only thing he ever managed to like about me."

"Harold?"

Desmond grunted.

"If it makes you feel any better, I almost hit him."

"You what?" Desmond's face was stone cold, matching the pitch of his voice.

"Yes," George admitted reluctantly. "There was also a moment with your mother that I'm not proud of."

"My mother?"

George wrung the steering wheel in his hands. "She hit Molly, and I reacted—"

"She hit Molly!"

"Molly didn't tell you?"

Desmond grabbed hold of his hair and folded over, head dropping to his knees. "Stop the car, George."

George pulled over immediately.

The rumbling engine echoed through the night, but the headlamps on the car did nothing to shrink away the lurking monsters in the dark. George could hear his regrets growling, waiting, climbing up the crumbled mess of his decimated walls.

"You need to take me back there," Desmond mumbled chaotically. "I need to go see her. I need to go see Molly. We need to fix it—fix everything. I need to go back and see her right now, George."

George's hand had hovered over the wheel, ready to coast the car back onto the road, but now it instinctively dropped into his lap.

"What do you need to fix?" He turned hesitantly, hoping not to hear the words he was expecting.

Desmond shook his head.

"What do you need to fix?" George spoke as slowly as he could so that Desmond, even in his panic, could understand him. "Desmond?"

"I made a mistake, George. I made such a huge mistake."

"I'm going to need you to explain it to me."

Desmond closed his eyes, holding his composure though he was vibrating. "I can't go back. Not to that house. Ever. My life can't be here anymore. I have to leave. I have to. But Molly..."

George dragged a hand down his face. He already knew what Molly would have said to that. "What was your mistake?"

"I left Molly," Desmond said quietly.

George gazed across the road at the lingering haze of London, where murky yellow lamps cast a cloud above the city like the glowing eyes of a most foul beast.

He tried not to picture it, picture her. Being left. Alone. He saw it all too easily, like the vision had been calling out to him from the depths between his monsters...

He slammed his eyes shut. "And now you want me to take you back."

"Yes."

George couldn't move.

"Why aren't you driving? We need to go back. You need to take me back!"

"I will take you back right now." The wind blew strands of his hair before his eyes that he couldn't even start to be bothered by. He stared through them and looked at Desmond, knowing his face bore no sort of comfort. "I will take you back to her. I will help you climb up to her window if I have to. And I will help you fix this—under one condition."

"What is it?"

"You don't leave. You stop running. Forever."

Desmond stared back. "I just need to see her."

"There was a time where I thought there was nothing I wouldn't do for you, nothing I wouldn't sacrifice—" He shut his eyes, fire and ash coated his throat. "But the day has come. I will not be a part of this."

"George, I *need* to go see her."

"Then promise you aren't leaving."

"You don't understand."

"I do, actually."

"How could you possibly understand?" Desmond poisoned his words, and it was more than what George could shove aside into one of his little boxes.

His pitiful laugh scared even him. "Let's see, shall we? First, tonight you found out that your father might not be your father, your father could be *my* father. Tonight I found out that while I've lived my whole life thinking my entire family was dead, it turns out I might have a brother. So on a familial level, I understand just a little."

Words he hadn't wanted to speak kept fighting their way out. "My mother just wanted to be loved by a man who kept hurting her. And he probably hurt her the most by having a child outside of their marriage. Somehow that child is now my best friend. So I understand on whatever level *that* is. And the matter of you leaving and running away from Molly after only two days? Let's not forget I know what that is like as well. I had one night at a party with a girl who constantly haunts my dreams. So yes, Desmond, I understand. Maybe not exactly, but close enough."

"You're angry," Desmond said, sounding apologetic, but he added no apology.

"It appears so." George willed away his shadows and gripped the steering wheel with his shaking hands. "I'm taking you home with me. You will change out of those clothes, and you can burn them in the fireplace for all I care. You will let me play the piano, and then you and I will talk. In the morning you'll tell me where I'm driving you. I will take you to Quaintrelle Estate, or to the trains."

Desmond made no protest to any of the conditions.

George turned the car back to the road and continued their drive to London.

Amongst all the swirling shadows of his past were the broken pieces of all his good intentions—a lifetime spent forming schemes to get his friend anything he needed. Days spanning more than a decade encouraging that friend to keep meeting a girl in the woods. Sleepless nights, hoping it would all work out...

Chasing after any happy endings, even when not for himself, had been all for nought.

That was a mistake he would be sure to never make again.

Chapter 8

The smell of blistering bacon and toasted sourdough lured Desmond to open his eyes. The ceiling that stared back at him was not the one he had expected. The walls were covered in art, the bed was too comfortable, and the blankets too soft. He propped himself up on an elbow and rubbed his eyes with his free fingers. After blinking several times, he remembered everything.

No wonder his head was spinning. Last night had been one of the longest of his life. What had happened. What he had done. Who he had hurt.

He flopped over and dropped his arm over his eyes. He waited to see if he would wake up again, if it was all a dream... But he had never been good at dreams.

Desmond rubbed at his head, thankful to not hear yelling, or to feel afraid of what he'd run into once he opened his door. He was safe in the Clarington home. Even after every horrible thing of the previous night, leaving his old house had brought the relief he had always craved. He couldn't take that for granted.

A voice in the back of his mind refused to believe that Harold wasn't his father, but it didn't matter. Desmond would make it very clear that he didn't want anything from the Claringtons. He didn't want anything from the Prescott inheritance, and he refused to scar the Clarington name based on stories that couldn't be proven true. George had said he was done keeping secrets from his grandparents, but Desmond hoped the news wouldn't go farther than them.

Crawling out of bed, he grabbed the clothes he had borrowed from George. He pulled on the trousers and scooped his arms through the sleeves. The aroma of food was motivation enough to run down the stairs before he even had all the buttons done up on his shirt. He was hungry, as he hadn't truly eaten anything since the breakfast with Molly.

His feet stopped moving just moments before he was at the bottom of the stairs.

Molly.

Desmond's insides turned to rubble.

Running was something he had always done, and it had always served him well. The first time he'd ran away from home it had brought him to Molly. It had brought him peace. This time, it had seemed to shatter him completely.

He forced himself down the last steps and passed the long wall of family portraits. He hesitated there, searching the smiles and finding them genuine. It made sense now why his mother had never hung up any family portraits. They were hardly a family at all.

Desmond pushed down the festering anger in his gut and left for the long table where George was already sitting.

Platters of food sat on top of the deep emerald runner on the table. There seemed to be enough food for a large family, though George's grandparents were still out of town. On the table beside George sat a small leather pouch, but George paid no attention to it as he spun a piece of toast around his plate. "Are you going to sit, Desmond?"

Desmond took a seat across from him. He fumbled with the top buttons of his shirt, before realizing he had missed one at some point, and he had to start over. "This is a lot of food."

George set down his silverware and dabbed the corner of his lips with a napkin. "You remember Edwin and Cecilia? They've help run the Clarington homes for decades, but they're extra family members these days. I think they overheard us last night and wanted to do something nice."

Desmond nodded and served himself.

George scratched at a mark on the table, then tapped his fingers underneath it. His hair was practically matted from sleep, and nothing about his suit really matched. He looked as though he'd scavenged for whatever was the easiest to reach in his closet and thrown it together.

Desmond could relate. All nineteen years of his life that's all he had been doing. Scavenging bits and pieces from any scrap of love he could find. From Molly. From George. Still, he was nothing but a large mess just thrown together.

"Here." George pushed the small leather pouch across the table.

"What is it?"

"A list of addresses to families who would take you in if you got desperate. There is also a fair bit of money to buy some clothes and help get you by for a little while."

Desmond stared across to George, even though he never met his eyes. "You knew I was going to choose to leave?"

"I was hoping you would prove me wrong." George's eyes were a painful blue, rimmed with dark circles and lines of focus. It wasn't a version of George that Desmond was used to.

"I'm sorry."

"No you're not." George poured himself some tea and held the cup between his hands. "If this is the choice you're going to make, then you can't be sorry about it."

"How could I not be sorry about it?"

George shrugged carelessly. "You can be sorry for what you did to Molly, but you shouldn't be sorry about leaving."

Hearing her name penetrated Desmond's chest. He pushed that aside, too. "Will you visit? Once I'm settled."

Tightening his jaw, George nodded. "Send word to me as soon as you're ready, and I'll be there."

Desmond swallowed a bite of food, holding back a grimace as it turned flavourless with his guilt. He needed a sort of validation only George could supply. "And you think it's good for me to leave?"

George leaned back in his chair and latched onto Desmond's gaze. "I think it's good that for the first time in your life, you're doing what's best for you. I'm proud of that. I'm proud of you. No matter how much it hurts."

Desmond poured himself a glass of water. He watched it whorl up the sides and crash over the rim as he set it down. Thoughts of Molly grew into an infection, into puncturing thorns that ravened his lungs.

"Do you think she will be ok?" He couldn't bring himself to say her name.

A dark expression crossed George's face. "I think there's a chance that girl is stronger than the both of us put together."

"So you think she'll be fine?"

George thrummed his fingers against the table, but gave no response.

"I just..." His leg began to tremble. "I just want her to be okay."

"She'll be fine." George lifted his cup and distracted himself with its contents.

"Can you make sure she's okay?"

George spat out his tea, and then tried to play it off as though nothing had happened. "Absolutely not, Desmond."

"Why not?"

"Between helping you tell her how you feel, and all sorts of things with Victoria, I have meddled in her life enough. I'm done. I'm not doing it anymore."

"I just want to make sure she's okay."

"I don't think she would want you to."

"But if something were to happen to her?"

George massaged the tension between his eyes. "Fine. If something life altering happens, and I hear word of it somehow, I'll be sure to let you know. But I'm not getting personally involved."

The dismissal was final.

George pushed away from the table and stood from his chair. "The train will be leaving in half an hour," he said as he left the room. "If you're ready to go, I can be ready to take you."

Alone at the table, Desmond fell deeper into his chair. So that was it—he was running. Nothing was holding him back.

His train was parked and waiting. Crowds circled around, embracing in goodbyes, shedding tears, or sharing excited smiles. They all knew where they were headed and what was waiting.

Desmond had no idea.

He couldn't escape the hurt in the forbidding lines of George's expression, or the way his shoulders remained rigid.

"You're going to be fine," said George, watching Desmond from the corner of his eye.

"How did you get over it?" Desmond asked him. "Running away from the girl at the party?"

"It's a secret." A faint reflection of George's usual confidence held to his words.

"Are you going to share this secret?"

George's lips tipped up with a tinge of sympathy. "I'm not over it, Desmond."

"Wasn't it years ago?"

"So let us hope you fare better than I did."

"But it's Molly."

"I know." George nodded, looking past Desmond towards the train. "This isn't about Molly. This isn't about me. It's about you. Get out there, grow roots, and branch out. Uncover the person you can be."

Desmond picked up his bag and strapped it over his shoulder as different attendants yelled last calls for their passengers.

George brushed off his sleeves and adjusted the knot of his scarf, straightening it into perfection. "You'll find a way to mend your broken heart. You'll find a family, a home. And I'll be here when you do."

Desmond grabbed George's shoulder. "I'll try, if you promise to do the same."

"Do what?"

He walked backward towards the train, eyes remaining on George as he faded into the distance. "Change how scared you are of love."

George couldn't have looked more put off by the idea.

Desmond grinned as wide as he could, its false nature sickening him right to his core. "It's what your mother would have wanted. For you to have what she was never able to get."

"You claim to know an awful lot about mothers for someone who despises their own."

Desmond tugged the step railing and swung himself onto the train. He looked out at George for the final time. "You claim to despise love an awful lot for someone who carries so much of it."

George shone a sarcastic smile and saluted a goodbye.

The train was loud and boisterous. It was hot and reeked of soiled clothing and cigar smoke. Desmond made his way to his seat, watching his shoes scrape against the floor.

He had a long journey ahead, with an unknown destination. Even inwardly, he was lost. He'd grown into someone he didn't know, someone he couldn't recognize. But somewhere out there, was a version of himself he had yet to discover, just waiting to be found.

Part 2

Chapter 9

Desmond stared out at the ocean, the cool mist biting his cheeks, and the salt air opening his chest. He had ventured as far across the country as he could, imagining he'd find something, anything, beyond the profound helplessness of being lost.

No matter how many times he filtered through his past, there was no alternate course of action. Leaving had been his only choice. Leaving Molly behind had to be done.

His early days of sadness had eroded away, replaced by an oily rage that he couldn't rid himself of. One that had been buried beneath his surface like an inheritance from the people who'd raised him. It slithered up into the light of day, strangling out everything he thought he knew of who he was. It became a new facet of his personality.

Desmond turned his back to the water. The wind roared and flapped open his secondhand brown jacket. He tied it shut and reached into its pocket, pulling out the paper that contained the address he was looking for.

He walked towards town, following the directions to John Thompson's residence. The sound of horse hooves on the roads reminded him of London, placing a pit in his stomach for more reasons than one. But Desmond needed to move on. Move on from Molly. Move on from his past. Move on—no matter how gruelling it would be.

He was venturing untravelled pathways, with unkempt baggage. He refused to burrow and give up.

Desmond was welcomed into the house and led to John Thompson's home office. He approached the leather chair that sat before the large desk in the centre of the room.

"It's nice to see you again, Mr Thompson," Desmond said as he reached across to shake Mr Thompson's hand. The impressive moustache the older gentleman bore made him smile in a way that felt more real than anything had in weeks.

"You too, my boy. Please, sit!" Mr Thompson motioned to the chair and sat back in his own. "I was delighted to get your letter. I have things set up for you in all the ways I can, temporary lodging, an office, and some enthusiastic clients."

"Oh." Desmond had known he was throwing himself into a new life, he just hadn't expected that life to catch him so fast. "Thank-you, sir."

"Yes, but call me John."

John went on to explain certain duties Desmond would be required to attend to on a daily, weekly, and monthly basis. It was all lined out on paper so there would be no confusion. The extensive list of duties looked more daunting than it would feel, John assured him more than once. His position in the company suddenly felt all too important.

Hopefully he wouldn't mess up his professional life the way he had so easily done to his personal one.

Remembering the night before he'd left cramped his hands into fists and kick-started his leg into bouncing. His teeth ground together, his pulse pounded in his ears, and his chest contracted.

"Speaking of which," John's bright voice cut through Desmond's emotional fog. "Did your girl come with you?"

Desmond masked his instant contempt at the question by staring at the wall behind John. He noted the wooden picture frame around a large family portrait and counted the scrolled carvings until his lungs loosened, and he was able to look back at John.

"It's just me," Desmond said with a shaking breath, shifting his feet uncomfortably beneath him.

"I see..." John finally answered after what Desmond felt was an eternity. "Will she be joining you eventually?"

Desmond's leg bounced even though he needed it to stay still. "No. She won't be coming."

"I'm sorry to hear that." John's eyes took on a hazy stare. "Do you want to talk about it?"

Talking about Molly sounded...unpleasant.

He shook himself. This pity party wasn't doing him any favours.

"I see." John picked up the papers that sat between them and walked around his desk. He put a reassuring hand on Desmond's shoulder and gestured for them to leave his office.

The halls were lit with chandeliers that dashed their light refractions in bursts of glamour that Desmond had never had in the halls he'd grown up with. Long embroidered carpets were slightly faded in the centre where most traffic would have been—but they looked loved and taken care of in a way he couldn't relate to.

No, that wasn't true. Molly had made him feel that way once. As had George.

He scuffed the heel of his shoe on the carpet, making a promise to never be such a burden to anyone again.

"Desmond Prescott returns!" came a female voice.

Desmond's hackles rose. The voice belonged to a girl with vibrant red hair. He looked up from his feet, seeing John greet her with a fatherly peck on her cheek.

"You remember my daughter, Beatrix." John gestured and returned to walking down the hall, turning the corner and exiting Desmond's sights.

"Where is your lovely girl?" Beatrix trilled. "I've been excited to meet her."

He tried to escape, but she grabbed his wrist and held him regrettably in place. Her orange blouse was draped in long black beads that camouflaged into the pleats of her skirt, shadowing into stripes. Her outfit highlighted the determination in her expression, and she looked like a predator eager on a hunt.

"Where's this girl you are head over heels about?" she challenged again.

Desmond hauled his hand out from her grasp. "Home, I imagine."

"How come?"

Desmond's feet tensed, wanting to get him out of there, wanting to help him accomplish everything he needed to. Step one: evade Beatrix. Step two: prepare for meeting his second employer and co-worker. Step three: stop thinking about Molly. But his feet refused to budge, and he couldn't do a thing about it.

"Why do you need to know?"

His anger made her laugh. "I was looking forward to having a new friend."

"She won't be coming." Desmond tried to maneuver himself around the annoying woman, but to no avail. He pressed himself against the wallpaper, desperate to distance himself as much as possible.

"Why not?" Beatrix's voice gave away that she had assumptions already.

Desmond made one last desperate attempt to squeeze past her, and failed. He huffed and crossed his arms over his chest. "Why won't you let me pass?"

"Why isn't she coming?" Beatrix's ability to interfere in business she didn't belong in was aggravating.

"I ran away," he confessed, willing to do anything to get away at this point.

Beatrix gawked long enough that he had time to escape. He pushed away from the wall and brushed off his jacket. Not that it was anything worth taking care of, just a diluted murky brown garment that had been worn by who knew how many people before him. But he'd needed to look as presentable as possible.

"You actually ran away from her?"

Desmond rolled his eyes at the sound of her following him. "Yes."

"What do you mean?"

He straightened his frayed tie to hide its condition. "She stayed in one place while I ran to another."

"Not right in front of her."

Desmond didn't respond and kept walking.

She gasped. "You actually did this right in front of her?"

He couldn't reply. Not when he was picturing it again in his mind. Not when he could almost feel Molly's tears as they hit his hands as he held onto her for the last time…

"You're a monster!" Beatrix shouted.

It was enough of an accusation for him to whip around and face her.

He placed an expression of mock surprise on his face. "And here I was thinking we would never agree on anything."

He stomped away, finally making it to the sitting room where John was waiting in a high-backed chair.

Beatrix prowled between them. "She watched you leave?"

John motioned for Desmond to sit and let out a low sigh that skittered the ends of his moustache. "Beatrix, let it go."

"Oh father, you know I couldn't stop even if I wanted to." She turned back to Desmond as he fell into his seat. "Do you know what it's like to watch someone leave you behind? Do you have any idea what that does to a person?"

"Beatrix Lorraine," her father warned.

Beatrix's face creased into a cruel smile. She scanned Desmond with the hollow depths of her eyes. "Remember how I said you'd have to call me Beatrix until I decide if we can be friends or not?"

He glared his response.

"We can never be friends. So you shall call me Beatrix Lorraine, or you will not address me at all."

The latter half of the threat did seem rather perfect. He didn't need friends. Certainly not one the likes of her.

What he needed was a purpose, a calling. A distraction to bury away the parts of himself he couldn't stand.

Chapter 10

Winter 1904

Swallowing the final dregs of coffee from his mug and shovelling his paperwork into a tidy pile, Desmond finalized his day at the office. The liquid gold gave him the innate ability to function, something he had barely managed before in his life.

Work had been a good way to keep the thoughts about his heritage deep, deep down inside. Hidden so well that he could sometimes pretend to forget he knew they were there. Still, on this day, he was thrilled to be leaving work early.

Until Beatrix Lorraine's irritating voice sounded through the hall.

He grimaced and snapped his briefcase shut before sneaking into the hall. He crept down the stairs, deliberately avoiding her. Whatever her problem was with him, it was big enough that she still hadn't let it go.

He jumped over the last few steps, rushing to exit into winter's chilly air. Fresh snow littered every surface thanks to the previous night's storm. Even pedestrians walked extra carefully on the sidewalks, boots scuffing along the cobblestones at a slowed pace.

The world was bright and in stark contrast to the solitary man who leaned against his car, rhythmically swatting his hat against his legs.

George studied the wrinkles in his suit through the dark hair falling over his face. His charcoal coloured long coat shrouded him in shadows in a way Desmond still hadn't got used to seeing. All that being the case, when George finally saw him and smiled, the cold atmosphere around them dissipated into a very familiar warmth.

"Desmond!" he called in a voice that broke halfway through.

Desmond tried to ignore it. "I worried you weren't coming due to all the snow."

"Right. The snow." George looked around as if he was seeing it for the first time.

"Is everything alright? You only seem half put together."

George's eyebrows swept up beneath his bangs. "I'd be very offended by that if it wasn't so true." He brushed off his coat and propped his hat onto his head. "I am only half put together, I've been wearing the same thing for almost two days."

"Two days!"

"It's not a big deal."

"That's a *very* big deal. I don't think I've ever seen you wear the same suit twice, let alone two days in a row."

"Again, I find myself almost insulted."

Before Desmond could say anything else, a shrill laugh scampered out from the office building. George whipped his head to see the source, and Desmond reluctantly did the same. He knew before seeing her, that it had come from Beatrix Lorraine.

The obnoxious redhead skipped down the steps with some pretty little friend on her arm.

Desmond turned back to ask George if they could leave, startling himself into taking a step back when George was nowhere to be seen.

He twisted in circles, searching in every direction. George had no business slipping away the way he had.

"Get in," George said in a low voice. "Don't ask any questions."

Desmond bent over and found George ducked inside his car. "How did you—"

"That sounds like a question already."

Stepping through a large snowbank, Desmond stumbled backwards, turning his gaze in Beatrix's direction.

If looks could kill, Desmond was sure he'd be dead. He clutched his briefcase to his chest, ignoring the ever consistent glare from the maddening woman, and lunged into George's car.

"What was that all about?" he asked George through heavy breaths.

George slouched in his seat, barley able to see over the steering wheel. He looked out the windows as best as he could, then pushed himself up. "Is your entire vocabulary dictated in questions?"

"You completely disappeared, George." Desmond fussed, rearranging himself to be more comfortable. "As soon as Beatrix came out you... Were you hiding from her?"

"Hmm?" George flared out a new smile.

"You know Beatrix, don't you?"

He shrugged.

"Why were you hiding from her?"

"We shouldn't ask questions we don't want the answers to." George lifted his hat and scooped back his hair. "Now, be a good friend, and tell me where I'm driving."

Desmond was more than willing to follow the conversation switch. The last thing he wanted to talk about was the trouble that came with Beatrix Lorraine.

He gave the directions to his apartment as George drove, glad to arrive somewhere he felt safe.

Desmond stomped off the snow from his shoes on the doormat and welcomed George inside.

His place was nothing but a small kitchen with crooked cabinets, a sitting area with pre-loved furniture and single bedchamber that waited down what could almost be described as a hallway if it had been the slightest bit wider.

George tugged off his jacket, revealing an even more dishevelled shirt and a lack of tie. His top buttons remained undone, and there were wrinkles...just about everywhere.

"It's a great place," George said as he took it all in.

"Thank-you." Desmond hung up their coats, then joined George at the large window by the small sofa.

The view was of a main street filled with people and carriages. The rush and bustle of the small town filled Desmond with a sense of urgency and belonging that he'd waited his whole life to feel.

"How are you, really?" Desmond asked, watching George plummet down on the sofa.

"My mind is in shambles right now, Desmond. I'm surprised I was able to walk to your door at all," he answered with a dark chuckle. He removed his hat and placed it on the couch beside him.

"Did you...want to talk about it?"

George tilted sideways and crossed an ankle over his leg. "I'm going to be taking over the family business soon. Both factories and the offices. By January, I hope my grandfather can retire so he and Gran can move out of the townhouse and into the Northern Estate—live life the way they were supposed to before I entered the picture."

Desmond forced himself to smile. But the mention of the Northern Estate brought thoughts of Molly.

George eyed him up, seemingly sensing the shift.

Silence hung over them. Who knew if the subject should be breached at all. But Desmond was powerless against the question blurting itself out.

"How is Molly?"

"I thought we agreed not to talk about her?"

But it was too late. Her name had crossed his lips, unleashing something he had been holding back for weeks.

"I know you wanted to stay out of it. But if you know anything, George, I just want to know if she's doing okay."

"Then she's doing okay," he answered shortly.

"Just okay?" Desmond's mind was invaded with worst case scenarios, weaving into knots and tangles of all the horrible things that could have happened. His leg reverted back to its nervous shake.

George pushed on Desmond's knee with two fingers. "Molly is fine, I promise. Things are just a little complicated at the moment."

That addition didn't bring him any relief. "Complicated?"

George pulled back and scratched the side of his neck. "I don't see her much anymore. I ended my charade with Victoria two weeks after you left."

Somehow, Desmond felt like the sentence was targeted at him. He tried to reroute the conversation to stave off his growing frustration.

"But what's complicated about Molly?"

George dropped his fingers to the couch cushions, tapping out a quick, silent melody. "Do you ever feel like you're made up of all sorts of little pieces that, sewn together, make up who you are?"

"Yes," Desmond half lied, not fully understanding what George was asking.

"Suppose I am made up of one thousand little pieces. That would mean, Molly hates all one thousand pieces."

"Molly hates you?"

"Well..." George's head craned sideways. "What I really said, Desmond, was that Molly hates every last thing about me. Which is a bit more dramatic."

It didn't clarify things. "Molly doesn't hate people."

George went back to playing with his hat, avoiding Desmond's gaze.

"It's because of me, isn't it? She hates you because of what I did?" Desmond's knee bounced again.

"I'm your best friend, Desmond," George said gently. "I helped you get together with her in the first place. And then I also helped you run away."

The weight of that sunk in. Molly hated George, which could only be a part of what she felt towards him. It swelled the agony in his stomach.

"There are other reasons. Some don't include you whatsoever. Like certain things about other things. Victoria and whatnot." George watched his hands as his fingers stretched out one by one. "That girl has a lot of reasons to hate me. She isn't even aware of all of them yet."

Desmond shut his eyes and shook the hair back from his face. "And you're certain she hates you?"

"Ooooh yes. I've only seen her three times since you left. The first time she spent her energy insulting me, yelling at me, and throwing things at me."

It was painful to imagine Molly doing those things.

"The second time she didn't talk to me or look at me at all," George continued. "That was almost as bad."

Desmond stared at the floor. "What about the third time?"

"I'm still trying to process the third time." George clicked his tongue. "And if she ever finds out exactly what happened, she will hate me even more. So I have that to look forward to."

Molly was never one to get angry and lash out, never one to hold a grudge. It wasn't her. He knew that. But he also knew he was unworthy of knowing her at all.

George hummed. "All that to say, she's forgiven you for leaving."

Desmond's whole body stilled. "You said she hates you—"

"Yes, she hates *me*. Not you."

Desmond glared into the air between them, the echo of unspoken details and unclear answers.

"One more thing," George began, yanking Desmond from the confusion of his thoughts. "There will never be a chance of Victoria forgiving you for what you did to Molly. If you ever come back to London, you better pray Victoria doesn't hear of it. I fear what she might do."

"I won't be coming back to London."

"That wasn't the point." George fell back into the cushions, his face falling in disappointment.

"I can't do this." Desmond rose from his chair and paced across the small space, his raging pulse quickening his steps. "You're not making any sense. There's no way Molly hates you, I'm the one who left. I'm the one who hurt Molly. And I've let you down. Too many times to count. You're the only two people who ever cared for me! All I do is mess things up! Just as I start feeling that perhaps I am somewhere where I can do *something*, I'm reminded of just how horrible a person I really am!"

Ragged breaths heaved his chest as the sound of his own voice rattled through the room.

George's eyes bore into him. "How long has that been happening?"

"What?"

"This. This isn't you."

"This is me! I got it from *them*." Desmond couldn't bring himself to call them parents. "I have felt this way my whole life, only now I'm able to scream about it!"

"This isn't who you are." George slowly rose to his feet and tucked his hands into his pockets. His voice sounded too brotherly.

Desmond shook his head, disagreeing with all ideas about who George thought he was.

George took a step forward and brushed a speck of dust off Desmond's shoulder. "It sounds like you got away from Harold and Alice without actually leaving them behind."

"Don't—" Desmond's voice gave way. He couldn't bear to hear those names.

He gulped past the lump in his throat. Desperate for air, for relief of the built-up pressure.

"You've removed yourself from a bad situation, and you are left with a blank space," George said like a promise. "Now you get to decide what to fill it with."

"How?"

George's smile warmed up the room. "One decision, every day."

Desmond's foot tapped against the ground. It sounded too simple. "Is that what you do?"

George made a noise that was far from admitting anything and stepped away. "We're not talking about me. We're talking about you."

Desmond placed a fist on his hip. "Where are you going?"

"I thought I was invited here for dinner," he answered with an evil tick to his smile as he meticulously folded up his sleeves. "Right?"

Desmond followed the six steps it took to get to the kitchen. "I did say that. But I'm not all that great with making food."

"Uh huh." George bit back a mischievous grin and rubbed his hands together. "Well that's fine, we'll come up with something."

They collected ingredients and started chopping any vegetable they could find, forming piles of little cubes.

Desmond followed George's direction as he shaved the skin from a potato. "So, you're really taking over the Clarington factories?"

George took a deep breath. "Currently, I'm working on the factory floor."

"On the floor? Your grandfather put you on the floor? Isn't that a bit dangerous?"

"It can be dangerous, sure." George's knife was precariously close to his fingers, but he never flinched as the blade sliced down. "My grandfather actually hates that I'm on the floor."

"Then why aren't you in the offices?"

George shrugged his shoulder nonchalantly. "If I'm going to be running the business one day, I want to know what it's like on the base level. I want to know what they go through everyday so that I can help them in years to come."

Yet there Desmond was, walking into a business he knew nothing about at the second to highest tier. Versus George, gaining his way up from the bottom. Piece that together with what had been done to Molly, and there was an undeniable fact staring at him.

"You're a better man than me, George."

But George just shook his head. "In a lot of ways, you're better than me."

Those were words he'd never agree with. "I've missed you."

"I've missed you too, dear friend."

"So, you and I are good?"

"Absolutely," George agreed enthusiastically. He dropped more prepared vegetables into a boiling pot to thicken and marry into something resembling a soup.

The rest of George's visit was just like old times. They ate, they laughed, they played cards. Desmond won every time.

George pretended to be upset about it. Saying goodbye wasn't even as difficult as Desmond had suspected it would be —not with the promise of George coming back to visit on a monthly basis.

Desmond watched George leave, sending one last wave from the window before closing the curtain.

He spun around and surveyed the apartment.

He was still hungry. He reached for a proper placemat to prepare a decent table setting and paused.

One small decision. To break free.

He dragged a table across the room so that it was within eating distance of his couch—he could enjoy a bowl of soup while watching out the window. He placed his bowl onto a dishtowel and dropped his spoon directly inside. His apartment would not be a place for proper etiquettes.

It could be a home.

A home where he could grow roots, where he could soften the areas around his heart he had forcibly turned to stone.

Scooping his dinner and shovelling it into his mouth less than politely, he finished off every last crumb and dropped his bowl into the waiting sink before hurrying to the door.

A good walk was exactly what he needed. A stroll to muse over the confessions of a little boy who wished he could fly away. Perhaps he'd find a path towards understanding his past —since it was the only one he would ever have.

Maybe one day, a lost boy like him could discover who he could really be.

Chapter 11

If Desmond should have ever guessed anything about himself, that he'd enjoy math wasn't something he'd ever have put money on. But he did enjoy it. Numbers were predictable. There was never something too unexpected or too difficult to figure out. He found it comfortable and even a little fun.

He had learned the ins and outs of the banking industry and got his job done. At night, he went to bed feeling accomplished and unafraid of what the morning would bring. Somehow his life had managed to get itself onto a track—not that he knew where that track was heading exactly.

But he buried himself in his work, feeling a true sense of accomplishment, and only slightly concerned that he didn't deserve it at all.

Huddled over his desk in his office, with the light from his oil lamp bright enough to illuminate the paperwork in an optimistic yellow, Desmond flipped page after page into a pile of completed orders. One hand curled a lock of hair, his other scribbled out tasks he had completed that day. His foot tapped as he finished a couple more calculations, but it wasn't of the sort he didn't have control over.

Loud curses rang out from the office across the hall. Albert had been in there since the previous day, tediously sorting out a client's papers, and still not able to figure things out the way he had hoped. He and Desmond had been set to work together on a particular project, but each of them had agreed to work on it separately.

When Albert threw his office door open, Desmond braced himself.

"We need to work faster." It was a regular greeting from Albert.

Desmond never looked up from his papers. He didn't have to, because he knew exactly what Albert would look like.

Albert Brockton stood at a staggering height, as intimidating as a steep cliff face. His shady blonde hair was always slicked back, and his blue eyes stood out most when they widened into angry craters. He looked like a younger version of Harold.

"I'm working as fast as I can."

Albert grunted. "It's not good enough."

He sounded like Harold, too.

Desmond leaned back in his chair.

Everything about Albert was a horrid reminder of what Desmond had tried to leave behind. His snarling face and taut shoulders. His overall attitude towards others, and the way he demanded respect.

"If we don't have this done by tomorrow," Albert seethed, stomping further into the room, "my father is going to be furious. Not that you would understand."

He could still hear Harold's voice blaring in the background, his insults, the threats he'd throw. He felt those same words on his tongue, ready to be fired on command.

He turned to Albert, feeling the comments writhe around his consciousness.

So Desmond did understand. Not only the fear of harm, but the battle not to become the very thing that hurt you to begin with.

Desmond got to his feet. One decision. A blank space to fill.

He swiped a stack of papers into his hands, and tapped it into order.

"Your father isn't going to be furious," he began, "because we're going to have our work finished."

Albert spun to face him, the red in his face draining away.

Desmond continued, "We'll collect and bring everything to my apartment. It's quiet, has no distractions, and we can get this done fast."

Albert scanned Desmond from head to toe through narrowed eyes. "Why should I trust you?"

It was a question Desmond had wondered about for a very long time. "I'll let you know when I figure that out."

Another moment of hesitation.

"I also know a thing or two about father figures," Desmond added reluctantly.

A knowing look passed over Albert's face. He stepped forward and extended his hand. "Then let's get to work."

Desmond grabbed hold of Albert's hand and shook it.

Work. Numbers. Predictability.

He looked forward to a distraction as comfortable as those.

Chapter 12

Winter 1905

It was another snowy morning as Desmond walked into the office building. He kept his worn brown coat closed with a gripped fist and his face down to shield himself from the burning ice blasting through the chilly wind. He made a mental note to remember to bring home more firewood.

But in addition to the chill, the snow came with bittersweet thoughts of Molly. His feelings had shrivelled and changed since he'd left, leaving a sticky feeling that crept over his skin and through his chest even on the best of days. There was always energy diverted to thinking of her.

He still couldn't picture her angry with anyone, let alone George. No one was insane enough to throw things at or to scream at George. A battle like that was lost before it began.

Desmond had to shake off the visual the same way he shook the snow from his boots.

He paused in the entryway, soaking in the warmth of the offices. But the comfort only lasted a moment.

A fast gush of wind from behind blew loose snow towards him as someone walked in through the doors. Desmond turned around to see Albert mumbling and ranting.

"Morning, Albert," Desmond said as he brushed the new snow off his legs.

"What?" Albert turned to him with a scowl, but then his face relaxed. "Oh. Yeah. Morning."

Desmond chuckled and headed for the stairs. He and Albert had almost been getting along ever since they'd worked together. Which made it all the more fun for Desmond to push the boundaries—just a little.

"What has you in such a chipper mood this morning?" he asked while they trekked up the stairs.

"I have special plans with my girl tonight. Haven't been able to see her in too long." He coughed the words out between grumbles. Albert climbed the stairs at a faster pace than Desmond, catching up and pushing past him to make it to his office first.

John Thompson came towards them in a hurry just then. His large moustache bounced with every step, and his head gleamed in the light—the bald spot the same colour as the walls.

"Boys!" he bellowed.

Desmond heard Albert mutter something under his breath before taking a step out into the hallway again.

"I hope I can borrow one of you tonight. I need your help." John looked between them both, waiting for objections. He took a moment to comb his moustache with his fingers before continuing. "We have an important client in need of several changes to their account, and we need them done by tomorrow."

Albert looked towards his office, shoulders hunched.

Desmond felt the shattering of Albert's already unhappy spirit. "I can do it," he offered, before Albert gave in and cancelled his plans.

"Perfect!" John wrapped his arm around Desmond's shoulder and gave it a pat of approval. "You collect any papers you have on the Thornsberrys' and bring them to my house. We'll work there. It'll be a long night, and I promised Beatrix I would be home for dinner."

John walked away before he noticed the grimace on Desmond's face at the mention of Beatrix Lorraine.

"You didn't need to do that," said Albert.

"If I had known it was going to subject me to Beatrix Lorraine, I might not have," his voice squeezed out of him and everything turned sour as he headed into his office.

"I owe you." Albert stood in the doorway, watching as Desmond fell into his chair.

"Yes." He turned away from Albert and collected the papers John had asked for. "You certainly do."

Desmond skipped dinner and kept working through the hour, feeling on the cusp of solving it all. It was a delightful choice, since it also meant avoiding Beatrix Lorraine.

John's home office had become a familiar and safe place. The desk was more than large enough to host two chairs and dozens of papers. Desmond moved a lamp closer to the page he'd been staring at, feeling much closer to finding the lost numerals.

He shed his suit jacket and tossed it over the chair—not missing how the heavy green twill had kept him too warm. Folding his sleeves up, Desmond pulled apart his tie and set to work more earnestly.

Working for John had made that easy. Desmond wasn't beyond admitting when he was wrong, though John always said there was no such things as failures, just giving up or trying again. Desmond always elected to try again.

He pushed past what he'd previously known as his limits, feeling the excitement building as he solved the problem. A rush coursed through him.

"Yes!" he shouted to the empty room, throwing his arms up in celebration.

He ran around the desk, double checking to make sure he had it all sorted out. And when he'd double and triple checked with the same answers, he knew his smile would be a permanent feature for the rest of the night.

Desmond let himself celebrate.

He picked the papers up, slid himself across the floor on the way back to the original copies, and cheered one final time with a jump and a fist in the air.

"Genius!" he called himself. "Desmond, you did it!"

"Can a person who refers to themselves in the third person still be a genius?"

Desmond's good mood vanished as he turned around. "I'm not surprised you're such a kill-joy, Beatrix Lorraine."

"I'm happy I have that power over you." She leaned against the doorway. Her bold copper gown matched her bold copper hair and defied the glow of the lamps. She twirled a corner of her shawl, making the scrupulous woven beads jitter together in a very annoying sound.

"What do you want?" He spun back to the desk and collected the papers to show John they could be done with work for the evening—more anxious than ever to go home.

"Father sent me to ask you if you wanted a plate of food. I told him I'd rather have you starve, but he sent me anyways."

Desmond shuffled the papers into a neat pile and clipped them together. "How inconvenient for you."

"I heard you sacrificed your full day for him. And for Albert's plans."

"It was pointless of anyone to share that information with you." Desmond placed his case on the desk and rummaged through the desk until everything that could be brought back to the office was safely tucked aside.

He carefully reached for his jacket, avoiding Beatrix Lorraine as much as possible. He hadn't noticed that she had walked up next to him.

She let out a long, sarcastic sigh. "Is this how you always are? Is this why you don't have any friends?"

Desmond could only count one friend, George, but he wasn't about to admit that to her.

"Tell your father I don't need a plate as I'll be heading home as soon as he's finished," he said instead.

"Okay, Desmond," she muttered and turned around to leave.

"Okay, *Beatrix Lorraine*."

She paused in the doorway and peered at him over her shoulder. "Beatrix. Anyone who gives up their time for my father can't be entirely horrible."

Desmond didn't relax until she disappeared.

Once John returned to the office, inspected the work, and patted Desmond's back, his sense of ease returned.

John's type of praise was something he had been waiting for all his life.

He stood taller as he made his way out the door and into the snowy streets.

The frosty air was a reminder about his need for firewood. He spun back around, heading for the corner of town where homes left logs for sale by the street.

He searched through several piles and chose the best bundle he could find. He dropped his coins into the tin, enjoying the musical jingle that reminded him of how George would've planned to write a song about it.

He found a brick of ice and kicked it along his way home. It skidded down the sidewalks, soaking in the moonlight until he accidentally hit it into a snow bank. Then he sank his hands into his pockets and looked up to the winter sky. A form of little clouds whisked by the moon.

Yammering barks drew his attention to the sidewalk behind him, where a scraggly and dirty dog looked up at him expectantly.

"Who are you?" Desmond asked.

The dog tilted its head sideways and rushed up to Desmond's feet, sniffing at his shoes.

The streets were empty. No people, no movement, just the dog.

"It's really cold out," he said, crouching forward to allow the animal to examine his hand before scratching behind its ears. "You should head home."

The dog yipped; a small sound for such a large animal. It ran at Desmond's heels as he tried to leave.

"Go home now."

The animal showed no signs of obeying.

He sighed and carried on his way, jostling logs from one hand to the other as the dog thought it was some sort of game to jump up against them.

Desmond grumbled and looked around. No one was calling out looking for a dumb dog. It was quiet, he could almost hear fresh ice forming on the crisp lamp posts.

He looked down with a groan. "Fine. You can stay with me tonight, but only because it's freezing."

Desmond and the lost pup made it to the steps of his apartment. He wasn't alone as he climbed up his steps, turned the lock on his door, and stepped inside his cold, dark home. The dog scurried around the little room, tumbling clumsily around the furniture and down towards the bedroom.

Desmond smiled and hung his coat, dropping the bag of firewood to the floor.

During his entire walk home, which had been longer than normal, the snow hadn't made him think of Molly.

He slid down the door until he sat on the floor with his legs folded against his chest. He sank his forehead onto his knees as the persisting guilt took over.

The dog returned and licked at his fingers—disgusting. As soon as he thought to shoo the creature away, Desmond turned to face it, and the dog curled into a large heap next to him on the floor.

Its fur was matted, clumped with mud, and it smelled terrible. The poor dog might be just as alone as Desmond was.

He combed his fingers as best he could through the dog's coat and decided that maybe neither of them would have to be alone again.

Chapter 13

Two cups of steaming hot coffee waited on the kitchen counter. One for Desmond. One for Albert.

It was another blustering cold winter day, the sort of day best worked in the warmth and safety of an apartment. Snow, while beautiful, had been something he'd discovered he preferred to look at—not spend time in.

He and Albert had fallen into a pattern of diligent scribbling and tallying numerals that helped the day move along quickly. This was especially the case since Gwen had joined them.

Gwen and Albert had been together for months. They said *I love you* so much that Desmond wondered if he had ever known the meaning of the word prior to knowing them. They said it in place of other phrases, like *thank you* or *you're welcome*. Albert used *love* as a nickname even though it was the same amount of syllables as Gwen's name. And they said it out of the blue, during lengthy silences or in the middle of thick conversation.

Entertaining was what he called it, though neither of them seemed to appreciate it when he did.

Desmond quickly grabbed the mugs and brought them to the couch where Acorn, the lazy dog, was curled up, taking up half the space.

After a good bath, or three, her fur had turned a caramel colour, splotched with white around her soft floppy ears. And now her carefree tail wagged at the sight of any earnest smile.

Acorn wasn't a name Desmond had chosen, but instead it seemed the dog had chosen it all on her own. She had found a stray acorn in the apartment one day and scuttled it along the floors with her nose. The tumbling noise was the sound he had woken up to every morning for the entire month he had searched for her proper owners. When no owner had been found, and Desmond muttered *"Acorn"* every morning while he scrubbed his hands down his face in bed, that was the name that had become hers.

Desmond silently handed the extra coffee to Albert and placed his own on the table, sliding it away from his work so as to not spill droplets on the papers.

Albert dragged his cup closer and chugged the liquid, not even flinching at the temperature. He sat in the chair facing the kitchen, facing Gwen.

Gwen always seemed to be baking, supplying Desmond with enough breakfast goods and late night snacks to satisfy him for a week each time she was there.

As always, her hair was meticulously curled and pinned back in an elegant fashion with ribbons that matched her skirt. Albert always remarked on how impressive it was and how easy she made it all seem. And while words were less important to him while he was in the middle of work, Albert was never at a shortage of them for her.

Acorn ran to the kitchen as Gwen finished preparing her a light snack. The dog wove around her legs as she entered the small living area, and sat pretty to receive the treat.

Gwen laughed and scratched behind Acorn's ears. "I think we'll need a dog, Albert."

"Is that so?" He stretched back in his chair and smiled over at her. "How're you feeling, love?"

"Perfect." Gwen smiled and glanced down at Acorn as she stroked the glossy patch of white fur between the dog's eyes. "How about you?

"Just about the same." Albert leaned forward onto the table and turned to Desmond. "We have been invited to go out tonight. Did you want to come?"

"Me?" Desmond looked between them.

"Yes, you." Gwen laughed. "It'll be fun!"

Desmond looked to Albert for a more honest answer. "Will it really?"

"Depends," Albert replied with a shrug. "How much are you into dancing?"

"Not very."

Albert shrugged again. "Girls?"

Desmond didn't trust himself to feel any way about anybody anytime soon.

Albert furrowed his brow. "Drinking and complaining?"

Desmond smiled. "You almost have me there."

"Well then it's a plan," Albert said with a clap of his hands. "Hear that Gwen? Desmond is coming to drink and complain with me while you go dancing."

"You'll be dancing too," she stated firmly, Acorn letting out a low bark in agreement.

"I'll be dancing too," Albert admitted quietly before turning back to Gwen. "How many times?"

"At least a few."

Albert nodded. "Will you be able to manage without me for a few songs?"

"I'm sure I can," Desmond answered.

"Good." Albert stood and extended a hand to Gwen.

She lit up in a new smile as she swung her hand to meet his. When their hands clasped, she was swooped into the air and they proceeded with a short dance routine right into Desmond's kitchen.

"Please don't break anything," he called out, although part of it was directed towards the dog who ran around them as if she was a much smaller animal than she was.

Gwen laughed as Albert dipped her. She peered up at Desmond from her upside down position. "You need to loosen up, Desmond."

Patting Acorn's back, Desmond hummed in a quiet agreement. There was no denying it. He wasn't excited about leaving the house, and he hadn't spent the night out of his apartment since he moved in. Apparently that was going to change.

Desmond followed Albert and Gwen past the large oak door that led into the dancing club.

Mossy green booths lined the wooden walls, filled with patrons who conversed over jars of lit candles and drinks in various sorts of glassware. Scavenged logs dangled from burlap ribbons across the ceiling and between chandeliers. Walking across the pub floor was like walking inside a hollowed tree.

As stunning as everything was, it didn't take long for Desmond to regret being there. The group they had joined included someone he really didn't want to see.

"You managed to get the rodent out of his burrow?" Beatrix drawled with all her class.

Gwen laughed and looped her arm with Beatrix's, leading her away towards someone they called Emma.

"No one told him she was going to be here?" a young man asked as he walked up to them.

"He wouldn't have came if we did," Albert said quickly, then he left to follow Gwen.

"He's right about that isn't he?" the man asked with a grin.

"Inescapably," Desmond grumbled.

"The name's Jasper." He grasped and shook Desmond's hand. Jasper's dark brown curls bounced with the frenzied movement.

"I don't know what happened between you and Trixie," Jasper said with a laugh. "But so far it's very entertaining for the rest of us."

And with that comment, Desmond understood why Albert and Gwen never liked it when he referred to their relationship as *entertaining*.

Jasper led Desmond to a round table at the back of the club, where a group of people were already waiting. The table sat beneath a circular chandelier held up by random ropes and strings.

Beatrix's hair was so red in the candlelight that she looked as if she was ablaze. Albert hung his expensive silver jacket on an old dirty chair for Gwen to sit on, and adjusted his suspenders to a more comfortable fit. Gwen flared out her colourful skirt and kissed him on the cheek as she sat down.

Desmond lowered onto a chair and looked around the table as drinks were ordered and conversation ensued.

"We're quite the group of misfits, aren't we Desmond?" Emma asked from her seat across him, smiling a sort of smile that was free of worries. It was...very intimidating.

He wasn't about to admit to anything.

"Jasper's my brother," she said with a laugh as she sipped her drink. The relation made sense to Desmond; the two shared the same energetic hazel eyes and the same brown skin.

"Emma and Trixie became friends right after Trixie moved to this area from London," Jasper continued. "Then, a little while ago, Trixie fancied Albert for a while. So when he went out with them I did too, so he wouldn't be alone with boring girl talk."

"It's not boring," Emma argued, flicking her curls off her shoulder and hanging her arm on Beatrix's shoulder.

"And before you ask," Albert began, wrapping his arm around Gwen and pointing an accusing finger at Beatrix. "It was the worst three weeks of my life being with that woman."

"Oh, stop it Albert!" Beatrix shot back.

"Mind your kindness," Gwen cooed, laying her head back against his chest.

"I stand by what I said." Albert turned his attention to Gwen.

"Both he and Trixie were too stubborn to find new friends so we all just stuck it out," Jasper continued through a chuckle. "Then one day the lovely Miss Gwen shows up in our lives. And now there's you."

"Me?" Desmond looked around the table, seeing everyone's eyes back on him.

"If Albert can stand you, then we know the rest of us can," Jasper joked, slapping Albert with the back of his hand. "Besides, we've heard enough about you from Trixie that we know you'll fit."

Desmond turned to Beatrix skeptically. "You talked about me?"

"It wasn't anything good, I assure you," she said with a dismissive flick of her wrist and turned to face Emma.

Soon, Gwen swept Albert onto the dance floor, and Jasper excused himself to find a girl to dance with on his own. Emma left too, and Desmond was stuck with Beatrix at the table.

"We don't have to talk or pretend to be nice to each other." He looked away into the crowd.

"Oh please," she sang. "Whose idea do you think it was to invite you out tonight, hmm? Albert's? That man has no real ideas."

Desmond frowned. "Why would you have wanted me to come out tonight?"

"Because I'm tired of you being boring all of the time."

"I'm not boring," he retorted.

"Are you planning on dancing tonight?"

"No."

"That makes you boring." She leaned forward, shining a very feline smile. "This place is filled with pretty girls, Desmond. Ask one of them to dance. Prove to me you're not as boring as I think you are."

"I'm not going to be bullied into asking a girl to dance." He picked up his drink in hopes of ending the conversation—a trick he had seen work for George more than once. But it didn't work on her.

"If you don't ask a girl to dance, I'll go find a girl to ask you," she said more predatorily.

"Don't," he warned. "Do not do that."

Her wicked grin grew. "The more you protest, the more I want to go do it."

Desmond felt a low growl in his throat as he turned to scoping the crowd.

Gwen and Albert swung around the floor like it belonged to them, with more grace coming from Albert than what seemed possible. Across from them, Jasper danced with a brunette who smiled up at him nearly as much as he did down at her. And Emma twirled her way across the floor on her own, her pink skirt catching the legs of the dancers around her. But none of it made Desmond feel any better.

"There's no winning for me. If I refuse, you'll ruin the entire night. But if I give in, you'll never let me live down the fact that you forced me into it."

Beatrix's smile sharpened. "Life isn't about winning. But if you are that worried, I'll make you a deal. Ask a girl to dance, and I'll forget it was my idea in the first place."

"Promise?"

She crossed her arms, all poise and no mercy. "Are we twelve years old? Yes, Desmond, I promise."

He grumbled and tried not to make it look as though he was scoping for a dance partner, though he didn't really know how to pull that off. He scanned across the room until he saw two girls sitting at a table alone. They were looking back at him, giggling.

"How lucky," Beatrix said, seeing where his eyes had landed. "It's almost as if they're waiting for you."

Desmond didn't bother with a reply and headed to where he had spotted the girls. He didn't even reach them before one stood and dragged him onto the floor to dance.

The music pulsed through the room and into his bones. It slithered over his shoulders as his dance lessons came back to memory. *Stand tall. Shoulders back. Follow the rhythm. Lead her around the floor.*

He stumbled over his partners feet.

"Everything alright?" she asked with glittering eyes.

"Yes, yes." He tipped his head and hoped his smile looked easy.

Desmond tried once more. His mother's voice returned. *Tall. Shoulders. Rhythm. Lead.*

He stumbled again.

"You're sure everything is fine? My toes are taking quite the beating." The girl laughed, though it wasn't condescending.

"I'm a bit rusty." He shook out his cramped foot and apologized to the couple next to them for bumping into their sides. "I'm trying to remember my dance lessons."

She took his hands once more and guided them back to the dance. "Maybe try forgetting those, and remember how to have fun."

Fun.

That was the difference. Everyone was having fun. Most of the men on the floor weren't standing tall with their shoulders back. Some couples didn't follow the rhythm at all, while some ladies even took the lead, throwing their men across the floors with exuberant laughs from both parties.

Fun. It sounded like quite the adventure.

"Let me see what I can do," he said.

He twirled her under his arm, she flung him around in her own way. Together they spun around the floor, graceless and fumbling. Somewhere along the way, that became the best part.

And so Desmond let go. He let go of the rules, of what he assumed people expected. He had fun.

The last bit of worry snaked out of his shoulders as he was dragged to the dance floor by his previous partner's friend. And someone new after that. As the rest of the night went on, he was on the dance floor more often than he was off until the club closed, and the herds of dancers ushered outside.

The misty moonlight shone grey beneath the lampposts. Desmond followed the group of misfits into the night, watching their attached shadows almost still dancing.

Frost crunched beneath his feet. His worn boots were in need of replacement; their laces were frayed at the ends and knotted together where they had once snapped.

Jasper fell in stride beside him, huddled into a deep brown jacket that was too big. He flipped the collar up to cover his ears. "Did you enjoy your night?"

"I think I did," Desmond responded.

"Good," Jasper said, breathing into his hands and rubbing them together for warmth. "Welcome to the family, then."

Desmond tripped at the word. *Family.*

His building stood waiting on the corner. His home. Half opened curtains and foggy glass marked his living room window. No doubt Acorn was scouring the streets, anxious for his return.

"This is goodnight, then," Albert said, arm slung around Gwen's shoulders.

She grinned. "We're glad you came."

Jasper wrapped himself closer to his sister, bumping her with his elbow to pull her out of her conversation with Beatrix.

Emma knocked him back. "We'll see you next time, won't we Desmond?"

He wouldn't refuse an offer to go out again.

They all gave him knowing smiles.

Beatrix only gave him a nod.

Family. Maybe it wasn't a word to stumble over.

Acorn's nails scratched at his door before he'd even reached for the handle. He laughed and stepped into his apartment, kicking off his boots, and dropping his jacket into a chair before falling onto the couch.

Acorn shuffled closer to him, tail swaying in large circles. She sniffed at his cuffs and shoes, then hopped onto the sofa and curled up so her head laid on his lap.

Desmond brushed a hand over Acorn's fur and decided it was time to forget the version of himself he had been that morning. He had stayed cooped up in his apartment for far too long. Allowed the scum of his past to coat his skin—thicken his blood. Now the sediment of filth was finally settling beneath him.

He had found something greater.

A home. A dog. Friends, and possibly family. Somewhere to stay a while.

Chapter 14

Desmond fell into the chair behind his desk, propping his feet on the handles of one of the drawers, and dropping his head back into his laced hands. The sunlight poured in through the window, illuminating the space, so he relaxed just a moment before heading down to fix a mug of coffee.

It was a new year filled with new possibilities. Nights were spent with friends. Days were in the office. Every moment in between was devoted to Acorn—and she was devoted to him. She took him on winter strolls to the park, and he tossed her toys into the snow where she'd dig and burrow under the fluff.

But this day, was an especially good day. He had come into the office early per John's request. Their meeting handed Desmond the best news of his life. New York!

Adventure was out there, calling to him. He could hear his name in the wind travelling across the sea.

He'd be gone a little over a month. Already he was planning how to pack and who could be trusted to watch after

Acorn. He also needed new shoes, and to declutter his brief-case. There was much to do, but New York would be worth it.

"Knock-knock," a familiar voice announced from his open office door.

He looked up. "George!"

George smiled, though it was weaker than it ought to have been. His right hand was placed securely away in his coat pocket, and his hat was slightly skewed to the side. "I know I'm earlier than you expected."

"A lot earlier. I thought you weren't coming until dinner."

George took a step further into the office, his sideways grin curling in its usual sly manner. "Did you know there is a wild beast inside your apartment?"

Desmond laughed. "That's Acorn. And you're not allowed to make fun. She takes better care of me than my parents ever did."

George lifted his left hand in surrender. "I would never make fun of something like that."

Ignoring the strange posture of his friend, Desmond rose from his desk and walked over to greet him. "Would you like a cup of coffee? I was just about to head out and grab one."

"Oh." George's smile transformed into something very strange. "I'm not allowed to have coffee."

"Why not?"

"Apparently it accentuates aspects of my personality that don't necessarily need to be accentuated."

Desmond recorded that information away so that he could bring it out whenever it would be most useful. "If not coffee, what would you like to do? I'll have to start working soon."

George removed his hat and placed it in the crook of his arm beneath the black winter coat that glistened with melting snow. He glanced up at Desmond, an emptiness in his silver-blue eyes. He swallowed hard and looked down. "I'm not myself, and I just wanted to let you know that I can't be here right now. Um..." He looked around the room, shifting his shoulder back while his hand remained in his pocket. "Things aren't great, and I'm not good company."

Desmond blinked. "Is it Molly?"

"Is it Molly?" George's voice rose beyond its normal limits. "I tell you I'm unwell, and your first reaction is to ask about Molly?"

"I didn't mean—"

"No, no, it's fine I get it." George stepped back.

Desmond tapped his foot against the floor, unable to meet George's eyes, and all the thoughts he had locked away came tumbling out. "I have been thinking a lot about it. Well, not a lot. Not as much as I used to. But I have been thinking..."

George's eyes narrowed.

"You said Molly hates you. Hates everything about you. But that doesn't make much sense." Desmond walked the length of his office, exchanging glances between his feet and George as he spoke. "Molly doesn't hate anything. She never has. It's not something she does. So I was thinking, you know. You could apologize."

"Tell me you're not serious." George levelled Desmond with a look that pierced his feet to the ground.

"I am serious," he managed to say.

"Then let me ask you something." George closed the space between them, face sharpened in all its angles. "Have *you* apologized to Molly?"

"What?"

"Have you apologized to her? In the woods, in a letter, in any way at all?"

"I—" Desmond lost his words. "No."

"No," George repeated, stepping back again with a sadistic smile.

"I didn't mean—"

"Did you seriously think your problems would just disappear if you ran away from them?" George raked his fingers through his hair roughly and shoved his hat back on. "Because they didn't. They changed, they morphed and became problems to all of us left behind. You don't know my story, and you don't care what you did to Molly. And I—I'm going to go. I shouldn't have even come."

George was out the door before Desmond could say a word. He stood in the middle of his office, startled into stone, unable to move.

The world went cold.

He scrubbed a hand down his face and approached the window, hopeful to catch a glimpse of George as he drove away—desperate for just a sliver of warmth from the sun.

He had been under the assumption that his problems were his own, that if he left they'd follow him. No one was supposed to get hurt; they were supposed to be safe.

He'd been wrong.

His office door creaked open.

George rushed over and wrapped Desmond in a robust embrace.

He slowly raised his arms and folded them around George's shoulders.

"I'm sorry," George mumbled into the folds of his sleeves as his grip tightened. "Everything is building up, and I can't—" He stepped back, quickly tucking his right hand into his pocket with a flash of white.

"What was that?" Desmond pointed.

"Don't worry about it." George patted his free hand on Desmond's shoulder and squeezed. "You are my dearest friend. You know that, right?"

"Yes." He also knew that when being called a dear friend, George was actually saying—

"I love you, Desmond."

Desmond took pause at the statement he'd only heard from one person before. And that person had certainly not been George. "I love you, too, George."

After a stiff nod, George gestured to the exit with his bent arm. "I have to go, or I'll miss my ride back to London."

"Your ride?"

"Yes." George looked out to the hallway. "Are we meeting up next month?"

"I'll be in New York." The words felt less exciting, almost halfhearted.

"New York?" George replied, pride tinging his voice, reigniting what Desmond had almost lost. "That's fantastic, Desmond."

"Yeah." He nodded. "It is."

"We will plan for the month after then?"

"Absolutely."

George tipped his hat, gave one last crescent smile, and left.

🍁

Desmond got home from work late that night. He took Acorn for her stroll, showed her some of her desired affections, and got himself ready for bed. He slumped into his sleeping attire and relaxed across his mattress.

He adjusted the lit candle beside his bed, pulling it closer on the side table, and opened an ink pot to prepare his pen. He pulled a large sturdy book close, and dragged empty pages onto the cover. It was time to write two letters.

One was filled with words he should have told Molly ages ago. She deserved an apology, and perhaps the slightest update on his life. Nothing too detailed, but a letter worthy of her.

The second was a letter he dreaded having to write almost as much as he dreaded the outcome.

He addressed it to Alice.

There were questions only she could answer; ones about the night a fire tore George away from his family. Because for once, Desmond was going to sacrifice for George. George needed answers, or could at least use them to move beyond the shadows he always carried. So Desmond wrote the letter to Alice, for George. He would meet with Alice, for George. And he would deal with anything else, for George.

Chapter 15

Desmond's legs wobbled as they had at sea. He was ready to drop his bags on the kitchen floor and fall onto his familiar couch. Travelling to New York had been everything he had hoped, but having a place to feel at home—that was different than anything he could have ever imagined.

He unlocked his front door, jiggled the handle until it opened all the way, Acorn announcing his arrival before he even stepped a foot inside. He smiled lazily while taking in the familiar view. Her wagging tale, her butterscotch fur rolling back and forth with the force of her excitement.

"You're back," Jasper called as he strode through the hall.

"I am," Desmond said after a yawn, leaning down to greet Acorn with all the energy he had left.

"I promise I took good care of your apartment and your dog took good care of me."

"I believe it." Desmond fell onto the sofa, propping his elbows on the table, and using his hands to hold his head up, and to stay awake.

Jasper laughed. "I'll go make some coffee."

Desmond hoped he had made some sort of signal that he was thankful but was too asleep to know if he truly had.

In the centre of the table, directly beneath where he had planned to lay his head, was a pile of mail. He grabbed it gruffly, flipping through to make sure nothing required immediate attention. Two envelopes stood out.

The first was from Molly.

> *Dear Desmond,*
>
> *I appreciate your kind apology and accept it full-heartedly. I'm glad to hear you are doing well and have found new friends and a place to call home. You will always be someone special to me, and I will always wish you the best.*
> *My days have been filled with wedding preparations for Victoria and Jeremy. Everything is working well so far.*
> *And I have been doing well, thank you for inquiring.*
>
> *With deepest kindness,*
> *Molly*

Desmond rubbed at his eyes. He had reached out to Molly, and nothing bad had happened. She had even said she was doing well. He was too tired to think about it further than that.

He lifted the next letter. Every muscle in his face tensed as he tore it open.

It was from his mother.

He had offered to meet her in the next town over at a cafe. She had agreed to meet him in two days. His gut held more rocks.

"Everything okay?" Jasper brought over two cups of coffee and sat down on the couch.

"It's my mother. She's coming to visit." Desmond barely looked up from the paper as he spoke. The lines blurred together under his stare.

Jasper muttered under his breath, aware of the few details Desmond had shared with him and Albert, though there were still many topics left to cover.

"Albert and I will be here that night," Jasper said, without leaving room for debate.

Acorn waddled over to Desmond's feet and curled up on top of them as he rubbed behind her ears. He was grateful to be home.

No. He was grateful to *have* a home.

"How was your trip?" Jasper asked.

"Good," he replied, lingering his sip of coffee over his lips, savouring the welcoming warmth.

"Was it everything you ever wanted?"

"No, it wasn't." Desmond smiled. "What I had hoped to find in New York, ended up being something I found right here."

He looked down into his mug, at the swirling steam and dark coffee.

Traversing from one adventure to the next, from dancing in pubs to crossing the ocean, things were clicking into place.

His job and apartment; the safe places just for him. Albert and Gwen, Emma, Jasper, maybe even Beatrix, definitely Acorn, and obviously George. Desmond had family. He had a sense of belonging. He had a home.

"Are you getting all sentimental on me?" Jasper asked warily.

Desmond released an exhausted chuckle. "I used to think that getting away was what I wanted. But if I keep running, escaping my life, then I'm not really living it."

He leaned back and swallowed the rest of his coffee. "I'll go to New York again. I'll go wherever John asks me to, and explore the world one place at a time. But I have a home here. I've never felt like I had a home before. I can't give it up when I've just found it."

"We're stuck with you for a little while then?"

"At least." Desmond grimaced jokingly. "Until Beatrix scares me off for good."

"You'll get used to her." Jasper stood and brought their empty mugs to the sink. "She makes for a good friend eventually."

"Did Albert and her actually have a relationship?" Even thinking about it, Desmond couldn't believe it.

"Sure did. It was short though. Trixie falls in love fast, and out just as quickly." Jasper made his way to sit on the couch again and fully reclined onto it. "She has this one story about falling in love before even knowing the poor guy's name. I swear, every relationship that ends she blames on that story, as if it was the one time she was destined for true love but lost it."

"Sounds chaotic."

Jasper laughed. "But she has lots of stories about lots of things. It's why I love her."

Desmond gaped. He was either too tired to hear correctly, or he was losing his mind. "You love Trixie?"

Jasper sprawled back onto the sofa, his arms lengthening across the back and his feet dragging against the floor. "You can love someone with out being *in* love with them. I love Trixie in the sense that I'd be fine if she's in my life for the rest of it. So long as it's not every day." He shivered dramatically and grinned. "But to be in love with someone, you want to be with them every moment of every day for the rest of your days. You can't even imagine just one without them. Which is *not* what I feel for Trixie."

Desmond stared at the worn floorboards, dusted with Acorn's hair and scratched from the furniture that was always being moved around. He got lost in the patterns as he thought of Molly, and how he was the one who had suggested meeting every other night when they continuously snuck out to be together. He had been the one who couldn't be that attached, the one who couldn't summon enough energy to manage being with Molly every day. She was incredible in every way, but he had never been able to muster the strength to match her enthusiasm.

Jasper sat straight up and gestured to the door. "Let's get out of here. Everyone will be grabbing dinner soon at the pub. The sooner you get there, the sooner you can head back here and sleep."

Desmond nodded. He needed sleep, but he missed his friends.

He grabbed his coat and shoved his arms through the sleeves, thinking once more of Molly. Of how incredible she was, how she deserved to have the world and her dreams.

Then his smile came. Because if anyone could manage anything on their own, it was Molly. She'd get her dreams, she'd get the world she'd want. Nothing could stand in her way.

Chapter 16

Desmond should have assumed his mother would arrive to the cafe in all her pompous glory. Her outfit was primed without fault, her skirt had barely collected dust from the streets, and her hat was as ostentatious as ever.

He had been hoping for a civilized conversation, one most people could have on any given day. But he recognized his mother's stance as battle ready. Her nose was facing north two degrees further than usual, her lips were pressed and angled south, and her eyes were pointed and direct.

Her heels scraped against the stone floor towards his table, clawing in a maniacal way. He could almost hear her prowling thoughts, viewing him as nothing more than a mouse she could easily squash. But that had been his intention, hadn't it?

He'd purposefully chose his most simple suit and the trousers he'd accidentally purchased just a bit too short. His tie was one Acorn had gotten a hold of, and she never really treated things with care. He was an actor playing the part of a mouse. George had always been good at games of pretend, especially for Desmond's benefit. It was time to return that favour.

"Desmond," she said, lowering herself into the chair across from him.

The cafe was nothing spectacular; small, hidden and family owned. But it was beautiful in its own way. Plus, they served the best coffee.

"Mother," Desmond said into his cup with a sly half smile he hoped she'd see. Cats never expected the mouse to be unafraid. "I'm appreciative that you were able to meet with me."

That was another trick he had learned from George, to choose your words wisely to not get caught in a lie, to present the truth in a way where your opponent had to come up with their own version of the full story.

"I was grateful to receive your letter of invitation." Alice whisked forth a handkerchief and laid it across her lap. "I knew you'd reach out eventually. Though I was surprised it took you so long."

Desmond drained the last of his drink and nodded as the waitress offered to refill it. He'd need all the help he could get. "I'm not here to converse with you, to catch up, or mend our burnt bridges. I'm here for George."

"George?" Her eyes widened sharply.

"Yes." Desmond leaned forward. He had expected her to be taken off guard by that. "I asked you here to piece together the story he's been needing to hear his entire life. The story we have all needed to hear our entire lives." He was referring to Molly, George, and himself. But he wouldn't dare speak Molly's name in his mother's presence. Even though he was able to think of Molly without severe pains now, he wouldn't dare grace his mother with a chance to bring her down. Broken hearts would mend, he supposed, so he was grateful that his was on its way.

Alice accepted her cup of tea without so much as acknowledging the woman who'd prepared it for her. She remained silent for too long.

"What you did was horrendous," Desmond began, pulling his mother into looking at him once more. "What you did to Harold, what you did to your friend Elizabeth, what you did to *me.*" He paused to draw in a breath. "Thanks to you, my origin is riddled with your heinous act. But I will not allow it to be my legacy."

Alice squared her shoulders and pursed her lips. "What would you like to know?" she asked in a dismissive purr.

Desmond tried not to laugh at how infuriating she was. "Spare me the details of my ancestry. I do not need to know, or care to know, why you might think James is my father. I'll come to terms with that in my own way. What I need to know right now, is what happened the night of the fire."

Shock passed over her face and settled into the creases by her eyes. "You would make me relive one of the worst moments of my life?"

"You want to mend the ties between us, mother?" Desmond lowered his voice. "This is where it starts."

Alice fixated on her hair, patting it down and grooming rebel strands away. "It was Cathryn's idea." She coated her voice in an irritated tone. "She said I needed to come clean to Elizabeth. She told me William had heard James bragging about the whole escapade at the club one night. So she knew the truth; she knew there was a chance that you weren't

Harold's son. But she knew what type of man Harold could be, so, all she asked was that I came clean to Elizabeth, because that's what friends do."

Here she scoffed and laughed, a sound so cruel it thickened Desmond's blood and turned it rancid.

"So I did." Alice was nearly smiling. "I went to her home once all the children were asleep, and I told her. She wasn't even surprised, although perhaps she was a little hurt. But the woman actually apologized—to me. She apologized for her husband, as if she couldn't believe he would do that to me. The woman was weak." Alice examined her fingernails. "She never should have been a friend of mine."

Desmond forced himself to swallow, his mouth dry. He needed the conversation to be over. But not as much as he needed answers.

"You're right," he fringed his words with ice, "the two of you didn't deserve each other."

His mother angled every perfect feature of her face into a serene smile. "That was the point where George came down from his room. He was just a pathetic little boy back then—too much like his mother. Though, I suppose that hasn't changed much." She sipped at her tea. "Elizabeth asked him to wait in his room, I don't even remember why, but he disappeared after that. By the time Elizabeth went upstairs to check on him, James had returned home."

Alice's facade shuddered, and her pain shone through her eyes—pain or anger, it was hard to tell the difference.

"James was blubbering drunk and could barely stand on his feet. Which was typical." She smacked her lips pompously, as if she had a claim to James' behaviour. "We had reached the second floor of the estate, when James went to hold the lantern Elizabeth was carrying, to help her with George. Well, she didn't want his help. He hit her and she fell back, her head slamming against the corner of the banister as the lamp in her hands shattered and leaked its oil onto her skirt. I screamed, but she wouldn't move. Not even as the flames started to spread across the hall."

Alice's fingers started to shake. "I went for her when James turned on me. He pushed me backward, and I fell down the stairs. I had grasped onto his jacket and he came tumbling down with me."

Her tea cup clapped and jittered against the saucer as she tried to place it down. "The next thing I know, I'm waking up at the foot of the stairs, everything is on fire, and I can still see James on the floor next to me. Elizabeth..."

Alice closed her eyes and took a shallow breath, steadying herself. Desmond took the chance to do the same.

"I managed to drag myself outside. I could barely breathe. It's a miracle I made it out."

Desmond had other words he would have used.

"By the time I regained the strength to stand, the house was already smothered in flames—there was no way I could make it inside. That's when Cathryn showed up with George in tow. I have no idea how the two of them connected. But after several minutes of screaming at the fire, Cathryn went into labour with Molly. And she left." Alice shrugged away the thought, the story no longer important to her. Desmond scowled at the sound of Molly's name passing his mother's lips.

"So that's it then?" Desmond squeezed his hands into fists beneath the table as his leg started one of its ridiculous bounces.

"That's it," she confirmed. "Once I knew George had survived I made sure to keep the two of you together. As some sort of atonement, I suppose."

Desmond froze. "My friendship with George was the only thing you ever did right by me."

Alice's features returned to their usual stone cold arrogance. "So have I answered your question well enough? Was the story as satisfying as you were hoping?"

"The only time you showed just the slightest bit of emotion was when you were talking about yourself, making yourself out to be the victim. But you were not the victim here, mother. Not the only one. There were children in that home, and staff, and your friend! And here you sit," he propped himself towards her on the edge of the table, "barely affected and hardly remorseful for your own actions."

Her face altered into surprise. "You said telling you this story would mend our relationship."

"To what point?" Desmond challenged.

"I want you to come home."

Desmond felt his smile grow just as cruel as hers. "I am home."

Alice pushed her cup away and went to stand up. "I will get you to come home, Desmond. I always get what I want."

"There is nothing you could do to me to make me come back to that place."

Alice grinned, maliciously and unmotherly. "I didn't say I would do something to *you.*" She stood and left the cafe, not once bothering to look over her shoulder at him, or offering to pay for her own drink.

Desmond sucked in his bottom lip and tapped his feet under the table. He shuffled his hair back from his forehead and dropped the weight of his head into his palm. Maybe he should have worried about his mother's threat, tried to decipher it in some way. But he was too concerned with how he would tell George everything he had learned, and how to handle the outcome.

Chapter 17

Spring 1905

T hat's the whole story?" George looked off into the distant corners of Desmond's apartment, eyes taking in visions of the retelling of events. Fires, shadows, monsters.

Desmond had done his best to soften the blow, leaving no room for misinterpretation of his mother's words, while also leaving out the more sinister details he knew he could.

Handing over a cup of steaming coffee, he stood next to George and landed a comforting hand on his shoulder. "I'm sorry."

George nodded and sipped his coffee, his facial expression muted. "I'll figure it out."

"You're taking this a lot better than I imagined."

"I'm surprising myself a little." George looked off towards the window; at the darkness of the night, the flickering candles on Desmond's table, and the lamps on the walls. "I'm sure it'll all catch up with me when I get home."

George stepped towards the sofa, and then got locked in place. His gaze sharpened before his eyes drifted closed. He tipped his head down, shifting it slightly to the side, angling his ears as if he was listening to something that couldn't be heard. He had shed his coat and suit jacket during the long and difficult conversation. It left his white shirt exposed and mostly untucked around his navy suspenders. His hair was an utter mess, which Desmond knew was nothing compared to how George might be faring on the inside.

He bumped George lightly with his elbow. "You should stay here for the night. I'll take the couch."

"Nonsense." George arrived back in the real world and tried more coffee. "I'll have the couch."

Desmond dropped his shoulders. "I thought I'd get more of a battle from you about staying the night."

Lifting his cup again, with the grey billowing steam curling before his crystalline eyes, George broke into a glowing grin. "Give me two more seconds with this cup of coffee, and I'll be a lot more fun."

Acorn scurried around George's legs as he walked, somehow managing to not be tripped on. Neglecting the sofa to sit on the floor, George fell onto the creaking boards, and Acorn took it as an invitation to then sit on him.

"She is not a lap dog," George said from behind the mass of fur. "She is over half my size."

"Good luck trying to get her off of you."

George raised an accusing brow at Desmond and then shook his head as he stroked Acorn's fur.

Three rapping knocks on the door stole George's attention. "Are you expecting more company?"

"No." He went to answer it, not surprised at who was on the other side.

"Gwen made me bring these over." Albert held up a box that was wrapped in floral printed paper.

"And Emma sent me," Jasper added.

"That sounds unlikely, Jasper," Desmond said, taking the box.

"Fine." Jasper rolled his eyes. "But as soon as Gwen sent Albert out, I wasn't about to stay behind with the girls by myself."

Desmond smiled. "What's in the box?"

"Something that smelled really good but that I wasn't allowed to taste," Albert grumbled, looking down the street with a snarl.

"How are things going in there?" Jasper asked hastily, knowing George was hiding in the room.

"Better than I hoped," Desmond replied with a shrug.

"Don't talk about me like I'm not here," George drawled in the background. "And it's bad form to leave guests on the doorstep. Invite them in."

With a tight-lipped smile, Desmond beckoned them inside, and Jasper was all too eager to follow directions.

"You must be George," he said, excitedly reaching out his hand.

George placed his mug onto the floor beside him and leaned over as far as he could to shake Jasper's hand. Acorn refused to budge even to greet new company. The dog had a way of sensing where she was needed—not leaving her post until her job was complete.

"I'm sorry," George looked at Desmond quick, then back at the two new men he had never heard of. "I must have forgotten your names."

"I'm Jasper." He slapped the back of his hand against Albert's arm. "The grump is Albert. Call him whatever you like."

"Call me Albert," Albert corrected grimly.

George smiled with his usual charm, shifting out of one mood into the next the same way he always did. "Did I hear you say that you brought over something that smelled delicious?"

Albert gave a curt nod. "Gwen said it was for you, and I couldn't touch it."

"Me?" George looked at the box as Desmond handed it to him. Acorn rolled aside slightly to let him tear it open. He lifted a square from the box and took a bite, allowing his head to fall back onto the sofa, and relaxed his eyes.

"Well, we did what we needed," Albert said to Jasper. "I'm heading back now."

"Figures," Jasper mumbled. "I wish I could stay, but I have to go walk Emma home."

"Who is Emma?" George sat up straight again, gleaming all his wolfish teeth in Jasper's direction.

"My sister," Jasper admitted, his eyes narrowing, but the glint in his smile was more of a playful challenge than a true one. "You're not allowed anywhere near Emma."

George placed the fingertips of his left hand over where his heart ought to be. "I'm genuinely offended," he mocked. "I have no interest in being near your sister. My heart belongs to another."

"Poor lady." Jasper laughed.

"You have no idea."

"Wait, what?" But Desmond's question went ignored.

"We'll see you later, Desmond." Albert went to push Jasper out the door, offering controlled waves to the boys left behind.

"Say hello to Emma for us," George called with his wide grin.

Jasper's laugh was heard even beyond the closed door. Desmond didn't dwell on the teasing between his friends, or how well they got along. His mind was on one thing: the effects that coffee was rumoured to have on his best friend.

He waited until the coffee mugs were empty. It wasn't long before the thrumming drink crawled it's way through George's veins, ticking movements coming to his fingers as if playing songs on a piano, but in reality were single-handed taps on the floorboards.

Acorn barked and leapt off George's legs, running down the hall towards Desmond's private room. George's grin loosened, his eyes leaving the dog and turning to the floor while his hair bounced with the rhythm of his movements.

"Can I ask you a question?" Desmond leaned forward with what he hoped was an encouraging smile.

"Mhmm." George nodded but didn't look up as he continued in his world of floor-board music.

"Did you just say you were taken?"

George turned to him with raised brows, confusion clouding the blue of his eyes. "Oh, yeah," he laughed in a breath and bit his smile. "I forgot I said that."

"It was two seconds ago."

"Time has never been my friend."

"So is it true?"

George stopped his music and bent his knees, balancing his elbows across them. "No, though it was fun to say."

Desmond studied George a bit further. "One of them is a lie. Either you lied to Jasper or you are lying to me. Either way, I don't like that you've gotten better at this."

George's smile turned a darker shade of evil. "Or maybe neither of them are lies."

"That makes no sense."

"It wasn't supposed to."

"You're infuriating."

"I've been called that before. And I kind of like it." George winked and dropped his chin into his open left palm. "If someone resides in my heart, she'd be taking up space in the worst possible way. Then again..." His lips curved into a cool smirk. "I suppose all of the best ones do."

"So there is a girl."

"Is there?"

Desmond had to remember to give George coffee as often as he could. "Just tell me who it is!"

George's smile faded, and he sat up with better posture. He looked down to the floorboards, dark hair falling in front of his eyes. "She's only a dream. And a nightmare."

"What does that mean?"

George combed back the hair from his eyes, sweeping his hand all the way back until he gripped onto the back of his neck and stretched. "It means I have things to sort out before I have enough space for anyone."

Then his eyes shot up to Desmond, excited again. "Hey!" he exclaimed too loudly. "Here you are asking me about girls when there is one very specific girl you haven't brought up today even though you've brought her up every other time!"

Desmond sighed. "I didn't need to ask about Molly. I wrote her a letter. She responded."

"Right-right-right." George nodded, eyes still wild. "I saw them."

"Them?"

"She was with Christopher at the post office. They were mailing your letter."

"Christopher?"

"You're not allowed to be jealous." George seared him with a warning look.

"I'm not jealous." The feeling he had was something else entirely. "Molly is...special. I don't want her to get hurt again."

"That's not up to you." Something fringed the edges of George's voice, sharp and assuming. He blew out a puff of air that tossed his hair to the side and relaxed. "Christopher strikes me as decent man. You know, helps little old ladies with their groceries—a true gentleman. I mean, he's completely boring, but he is good."

Desmond waited to see if George would divulge any more information. He didn't. He just leaned back until he was laying completely on the floorboards and staring up at the ceiling. "That's nice you wrote her a letter, though. I can't even begin to explain how happy I am not to be in the middle of *that* anymore."

Desmond laughed, imagining how awkward he had made things for George. "In her letter she said she was doing good."

"Huh."

"What is it?"

"It's nothing."

Desmond wasn't satisfied with that. "Is she not doing good?"

"Did she use those words exactly?" George propped himself up on his elbows to look at Desmond better, no longer smiling.

"Close enough. Why?"

George's face exploded into a very vexatious grin. "*You're* doing good, Desmond. Your apartment, your job, your friends. A dog. I'd call that really good. But Molly," he paused to look up into the corner of the ceiling, holding a finger to his lips. "She was being modest. She could have at least used words like *excellent* or *superb* or something of that sort."

Desmond smiled, relieved. "She's really doing that good?"

"Better even." George kept his smile as he laid back down. "The Molly you left behind is different than the Molly you would see today." His hand flicked above him as he gestured along with his words. "It's a good thing you're over her. Otherwise, I would guess, you'd *really* regret leaving."

Chapter 18

Surrounded by clouding smoke, thick liquor aromas, and dangling tree bark, Desmond enjoyed a moment of relaxation after a few spins on the dance floor. He relished the aspect of meeting strangers and interacting with their lives in a way that would only last the night. Dancing until his legs were giving out was only half the fun, the best part was the company, the family he had lucked out on falling into.

Jasper let out a low grunt as he dropped into a chair, his brown curls floating up and then landing down against the collar of his taupe shirt. He laced his fingers and sat his hands on the table, looking out into the crowd. "If that man doesn't get away from my sister soon, we're going to have to go over there."

Desmond followed Jasper's gaze and saw Emma trying her best to evade a gangly man who kept spilling his drink on the people around him.

Jasper reached for his glass of water, never letting his eyes drift away from the man following Emma. "I just wish she would punch him in the nose already."

Desmond laughed. Emma had a reputation for defending her own honour quite well with similar behaviours in the past.

"Who is punching someone in the nose?" Beatrix asked as she flopped into the chair across from him. Her face was as red and glowing as her gown from her quick dance with a man who still wasn't able to look away from her.

"Emma," Desmond replied, shaking his head, noting the poor man Beatrix had danced with was still watching. "I think you broke that man's heart, Beatrix."

"Trixie," she corrected firmly. "And he'll get over me. They always do." She sent the man a wave with just her fingertips.

"Look-look-look!" Jasper lurched forward and pointed to where Emma shouted at the gangly man. He shrank with every phrase she spat out at him.

"Oh, come on!" Jasper groaned. "All she did was talk to him! Where's the action?"

Trixie rolled her eyes and leaned across the table. "Which one of you owns the best suit?"

"Definitely Desmond," Jasper said without looking at her.

"Not true," Desmond pressed back. "I have never bought a fancy suit. Why do you need a suit?"

Trixie pointed between them. "I want one of you to wear it and stand beside me."

"She wants one of us to be her accessory for a night," Jasper clarified as he puffed out a breath of hot air.

"I really don't care who it is." She flicked out her hand, seemingly exhausted of them already. "I have an event I'm going to, and I hope to see a special certain someone. You will be free to do whatever you want once we get there."

"Is this that certain special someone that you've talked about in the past?" Jasper asked, pumping his brows.

Trixie flashed a flirtatious grin. "Very possibly. But if he doesn't turn up alone, then I don't want to either. I don't wish to look the part of a fool."

"I don't think we could help with that." Jasper winked.

"Oh, bug off," she said with a laugh. "Come on boys. Free food! Free drinks! A party unlike any other!"

"Tell you what, Trix," Jasper pulled a deck of cards out from his pocket and slid it across the table. "Desmond and I will play for it. First King wins. Loser takes Trixie to the ball."

"Loser takes me?" She shot a wicked glare between them both. "Shouldn't I be the prize?"

Desmond smiled towards the cards he was shuffling. "The prize is staying home."

He laid out the cards, face up one at a time before him and Jasper.

"This is unbelievable," Trixie said, massaging her temples. "I can't believe the two of you."

"Then why did you ask us?" Jasper smiled as the cards revealed nothing but faceless numbers.

"You're all I have!" She raised both arms dramatically before dropping them. "I need better friends."

"You won't find any." Jasper's smile spread as the king of spades was flipped over in his pile. "First king. Looks like Desmond is your date."

Desmond scratched the back of his neck and dropped his hand into his lap. "Great."

"Oh, it can't possibly be that horrible of a proposition can it?" Trixie asked with eyes full of insults.

"I had to do it last year." Jasper picked up the cards as he spoke. "It's not all dreadful all the time."

"Thanks," she scoffed. "So, Desmond, do you have a nice suit?"

"How nice?"

"Nice enough to make you look worthy of me."

With a long breath, Desmond leaned back in his chair. "I'm going to have to assume that means no. But I have a friend who would lend me one."

"Do you think your friend will lend you his finest suit?"

Desmond laughed before he could stop it. "He would. But I'd never ask for his *finest* suit. And I don't think you'd want me showing up in it either. I'll ask for one of his less finer suits, and it'll still be better than anything I own. I'm sure it'd meet your standards."

"There's nothing wrong with having high standards." Trixie crossed her arms. "Do you think you can get one from him soon? We're leaving for London this weekend."

"London?" Desmond repeated. "No. No, I can't go to London this weekend." George had made sure he wouldn't forget to stay as far away from Victoria as possible.

Trixie studied him. "You already agreed to come."

"I don't think I should go."

"Why not?" Jasper tapped him with the back of his hand, creases forming on his forehead.

Desmond was thankfully interrupted by the arrival of Albert and Gwen, both dressed in matching shades of early spring blossoms.

"What's going on?" Albert asked, his arms roped around Gwen's waist.

"Desmond is going with Trixie to a party this weekend." Jasper was holding back a smile. "For some odd reason, the idea of going to London seems to be more frightening than the idea of being with Trixie."

"There happens to be someone in London who doesn't like me very much," he conceded.

Trixie blew red curls away from her eyes and clicked her nails along the table as she gave him the same glare she had the night he'd first arrived in town.

"The girl you ran away from?" she quipped, still holding a grudge against his actions.

"No. Her sister."

"Makes sense," Jasper drew his words out slowly, fully smiling and drooping his head back into his open hands. "Sisters are crazy."

Emma had returned to the table unbeknownst to Jasper. Her lips turned up as she smacked him on the back of his head, brown curls flying with the motion, his knees bumping the table.

Drinks spilled, flowing together in a mixed coloured puddle that dripped onto the floor. Jasper shot back before it spilled all over him, and Emma bent forward to grip his shoulders.

"Brothers are worse," she said with a huge grin.

And so, Desmond had found a strange little family to be a part of. Maybe it wasn't conventional or anything remotely resembling traditional. But they were his, and he was theirs. Whatever trials waited in London, Desmond would survive.

It'd be an adventure if nothing else. And if all really did fail, at least he had a home to run back to.

A home.

A family.

A place where he belonged.

Nothing else mattered as much as those.

Part 3

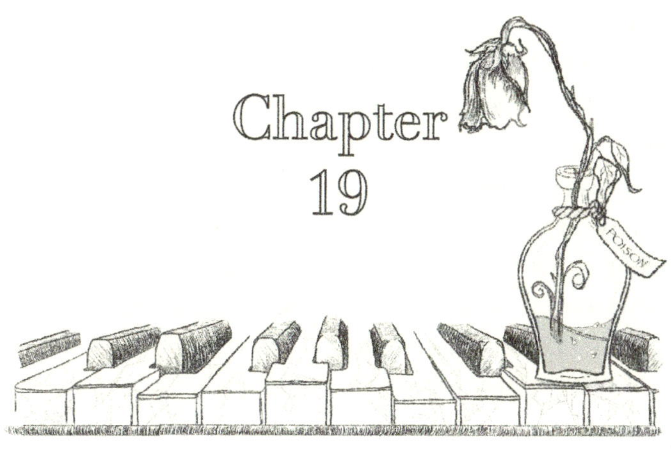

Chapter 19

Autumn 1904

It was George's belief that the piano could transport him to any world imaginable. Worlds that matched the darkness of his shadows and worlds vibrant enough to chase them away. There were worlds of dreams and worlds of nightmares— George took time to visit them all. So while it may have appeared that he was sitting in his solace on the onyx piano bench, there was really no way of truly knowing exactly where he was.

Within the first few intimate caresses of the keys, George sailed away to the stars and swirls of the sky, exchanging his shadows for colours in the only way he knew how.

The song came easily, being one he knew from long ago, secretly eating away at his subconscious in a fashion he couldn't fight away. It had hid in the corners of his mind, sneaking out during a legato of regrets.

"George." Jeremy's voice pulled him out of the music.

George swivelled in his seat, bewildered more by the fact that showing up unannounced was not something Jeremy ever did. The lingering whisper of his song rang through his mind, and George tapped the notes out on the bench in silence.

"I'm sorry to bother you," Jeremy started again, dusting off his yellowed sleeves and taking a seat on the couch that sat adjacent to the piano. "It's just, I've only seen Victoria once since your dear ol' friend left town." He grumbled in aversion to speaking Desmond's name.

Fine. Everyone took Molly's side in the split. George had accepted that.

"What brings you here, then?" He tried to sound more interested than he felt. If there was a chance he had to defend Desmond, he wasn't in the mood.

"Victoria said that she'd get word to me when she's coming to town. I haven't heard from her in over a week, and then I get this." Jeremy pulled out a folded piece of paper and handed it over.

Dearest Jeremy,

I'm sorry, but I don't know when I'll be able to see you next.

With all my heart,

Victoria

"So you see why I'm worried," Jeremy said, voice remaining calm, but the stare in his eyes proved there was more going on beneath the surface. "Right after our engagement she doesn't know when she'll be able to see me next."

"I'm sure she isn't calling off the wedding." George refolded the paper and handed it back. "She still sends her love to you."

"This is not like my Victoria. I can't explain it, but I know something is very wrong."

George cast his face down, allowing his hair to fall out of place. "Jeremy, why did you come here?"

"I need to see her. If something bigger is going on, it would be safest if I show up still under the veil of your relationship."

In the midst of his growling shadows, George had done what he could to grip on to the refuge of melodies. He could hear the notes he should be playing to keep the monsters at bay—but they could wait a little longer.

He pushed himself away from the piano and focused on his arms, folding his sleeves over the tension of his muscles.

"I'll take you right now," he said, slipping his cufflinks through his cuffs as he walked to the foyer.

"Really?" Jeremy asked, running after him.

"Unless this is a bad time?" George lifted his coat off its hook, slipping his hands through in one motion.

"Right now is perfect! You're sure it's okay for you?"

"Why wouldn't it be?" George lifted his scarf and threw it around his neck.

Jeremy's gaze pierced through George's skin as if he scanned for internal issues.

"I'm fine," George stated firmly, believable, even to him.

"Okay."

"Okay. I'll meet you outside."

Once Jeremy had left, George flicked his hat off its hook, catching it during its tumbling spiral. He tried to smile at it, but nothing came out the way he had hoped. With a heavy breath, he headed out the door, prepared to make the long drive to reunite two lovers after their failed attempts without his assistance.

George knocked on the front door of Quaintrelle Estate. Birds flew above him in the cloudless sky, chirping their songs and creating cheerful music that didn't match the day.

Flipping down his collar and straightening his tie, George tried to ignore the itch in his fingers, his craving to play his own song. Instead of making music, he was knocking again, a miserable hollow sound against the old sturdy door. It looked as though Cathryn and William were gone for the day. Perhaps the house was empty.

The door was opened to a silent home by a muted attendant. George removed his hat and stepped inside. At least in the foyer he didn't have to be jealous of little creatures serenading the world when he couldn't so much as see a piano.

"George?" Victoria asked, breezing through the room in a gown so yellow she was nearly blinding. "What on earth are you doing here?"

"I missed you, too," he said, donning what he knew was a very convincing grin.

"Seriously, why are you here?"

"Your sweet Jeremy is all in a tizzy about the note you wrote to him." George inspected his hat, feigning boredom. "He seems to believe you are calling off the engagement, and now he's waiting outside for you."

"He is?" Victoria twisted around, glancing out the window in hopes of catching a glimpse of the tall blonde fellow who was waiting for her.

"Yes. He is. Why would I lie about something like that?"

"I didn't think you were lying, I just..." Victoria approached the window and held her fingers to the glass. "I can't see him."

"You could if you went outside." George slid his hands into his pockets and waited.

"I can't leave."

"He came here so that you don't have to leave. See how that works?"

"My parents left for the countryside and won't be back until tomorrow. I'm not leaving until my mother is back."

"Not even to take a few steps to the car?"

Victoria said nothing. Her nails bit into the glass as they scraped down the pane.

Horrid, horrid sound.

"What's going on, Victoria?" he asked as gently as he could.

"Nothing," she answered, her voice tilting too high, too fast for him to not recognize the lie.

"At least give me the courtesy of the truth."

Victoria placed a hand to her face, still peering out the window. "Jeremy really convinced you to come out of your hiding spot just so he could see me?"

"Yes. Which is why it's really annoying that you don't want to go out and see him."

She swung around fiercely, her eyes glossed over. "I love that he came all the way here to see me. I have longed for him as well. But I can't leave. I'm not leaving Molly."

"Even for two minutes?" George took a moment to listen. Not a sound ticked through the halls, not a clink of china or a rustling of fabrics—no signs that anyone was close by. "She probably won't even know you're gone."

"You're right!" Victoria's forceful words brought forth tears. "But if there is any chance she will come out of her room in the next two minutes, I need to be here. If she comes out, and I'm not here, when I've waited... No. I'm not doing that."

"I don't understand." George followed Victoria as she marched away into their sitting room. "It's two minutes."

"You want to understand, George?" Victoria's tears filled with rage before they trickled down her cheeks. "Then allow me to explain it to you. Your little brother *destroyed* my sister, alright? She hasn't left her room since he left. So I'm not leaving her. Not unless you tell me your idiot little friend is outside so I can kill him!"

George collected himself, his last nerve struck against flint, igniting things he'd tried so hard to hide away. "What did you just say?"

"Don't defend him!"

"Not about *him*. Call *him* whatever you want." He gripped his hands into fists, the antagonizing siren song ever louder and more persistent in his mind. "What did you say about Molly?"

"She is in a really bad way."

"Meaning?"

Victoria flicked the loose hair around her face and cast her eyes down. "I don't know, exactly. She never leaves her room.

She rarely ever eats. I try to make her tea every morning, but it just sits there and goes cold." Victoria wiped away fallen tears with her fingertips. "She packs things away into boxes in the middle of the night. I doubt she sleeps, because I've barely been able to."

Festering colours left reality a blur as a plan came into focus. George spun on his heels, only half aware of what he was doing, of what could be done. "I'll be right back."

"What are you going to do?" Victoria's quick steps followed him into the hallway.

"What I do best." He made it into the foyer and started to climb up the stairs.

"And what's that?"

"Fix things."

Chapter 20

Molly dangled her fingertips over the flickering flame of a candle, thinking of the fireplace in the parlour; the welcoming glow, how her family gathered there. She missed them, but they were better off without her. She'd only be infectious with her frost-covered heart flowing with poison.

Trees no longer sang. Books provided no escape. The sun rose and set without adding a single sparkle to the sky. Even thoughts of Desmond brought no feelings, as if she could only picture the letters of his name and nothing else.

You're worth it, Molly. The memory haunted her.

So, she tore it out and fed it to the angry beasts that waited in the depths beneath her waves, asking them to devour all the pieces of herself she no longer wished to have.

Old. One finger circled the fire.

Alone. A second one.

Unloved—

A knock at her door disrupted her momentum and the flame singed the tip of her thumb. The tiny sensation was a sharp reminder of being alive. It would go away soon. As would whoever knocked at the door. They always did.

She returned to dangling her fingers one by one above the candle, waiting for the fire to reignite anything in her life.

"Are you going to open the door for me, Miss Jones?"

Molly stared at the rose petals carved on the back of her door. Surely, she was hallucinating.

Another knock.

She hesitantly walked towards the sound, feet unsteady as she stepped up to the doorway and opened the door.

Her mind had not been playing tricks.

George leaned against the frame with a single elbow, pressing his fingertips onto the bridge of his nose. His suit was a dismal grey, his dark hair fell over his fingers, and not even a bit of colour was scattered over his waistcoat or tie. All he wore were shades of the ashes she had been seeing everywhere.

"You should know," he said, massaging the space between his closed eyes, "this goes against my better judgment."

She didn't have the energy for this. "Then why are you here?"

George smiled in his irritating way, his eyes too blue compared to the colourless contrasts of the world. "Because my better judgment doesn't know how to have fun."

He walked past her and into the room, looking around the walls, taking note of her bed and floor. She felt like she was taking in the sight of the mess for the first time, too.

Boxes littered every surface, filled with things she used to love. She didn't really love anything anymore.

"What do you want, George?"

"Why are all your books in boxes?" He looked back intently, waiting for an honest reply that wasn't coming.

"Spring cleaning," she said, trying to stand as tall as he was.

"It's the end of Autumn."

"I'm getting an early start."

"Or a late one." He rifled through the piles of books she had packed away. "Either way, I don't believe you."

"Believe what you want."

"I always do." He picked a book out of one of her boxes. "This one is mine. I'm taking it back."

"Oh." She stared at the purple binding and then back up at George himself. "Fine."

"Why is there a purple dress in this one?" He motioned to the box on her bed. She knew where she had placed that memorabilia. She didn't need him to point to it.

"I already told you."

"You mean you lied to me." He held his arms out in a large gesture to the room. "What is going on here?"

Molly didn't know why the question made her eyes well up, but she pushed that away. She hadn't cried since the night with Desmond in the woods. She wasn't about to start again.

"You have your book. You can leave now." She spun away from him and headed towards her dresser. Her hands gripped onto the edge as her head fell forward, her tangled hair blocking out the proof that she wasn't alone.

"Why are you here?" she asked, dabbing the backs of her fingers against the threat of tears.

"I made you a promise."

A laugh jumped out of her as bitter as she felt. "What promise is that?"

"To put you in your place."

She whipped around to face him, remembering that day in front of the fire, with Desmond. A promise to fix things when necessary; to take care of each other and put each other in their place. "That was a three-way promise. And it's been broken."

"Desmond may break his promises, but I do not break mine." The inferno of his voice rolled through the space between them, intimidatingly calm.

"I'm in my place, in my room, in my home. You can leave."

"This is not your place, and I will not be leaving." He took steps towards her, pulling her eyes to match his in a way she couldn't avoid. "This dark, gloomy place filled with shadows and broken hopes? That's not your place. It's mine. I'd appreciate it if you leave."

"I'm not going anywhere."

"Yes, you are." He grinned, sinister beneath his burning gaze. "You have fifteen minutes before I expect you downstairs. So wash up, get dressed, and come down."

The startling command slowed her response until he was just a couple of steps away from leaving her room.

"I'm not coming," she called through clenched teeth, weaker than she wished to be.

"You're coming whether you want to or not." He travelled a few steps back, abandoning his route to the door. "Even if I have to come back up here, throw you over my shoulder and carry you down the stairs myself."

"I'll lock the door."

His devious smirk unsettled her in a whole new way. "Then I will take your door off its hinges, Miss Jones. Much in the same way you unhinge me."

"You wouldn't."

"Don't believe me?" He resumed walking away. "Fifteen minutes."

"That is hardly long enough."

"Lies." He tilted his head back into her room, fingertips tapping against the door frame. "I've been a part of this house for a little over six months now. So I know that when I give you fifteen minutes, it's five extra minutes compared to what you need. But if you want twenty minutes so that you can sit and contemplate whether I'll actually remove your door or not, that's fine. I'll give you twenty minutes. But I expect you down-stairs soon."

He left, and she fell back on her bed. No doubt he would come back and do exactly what he had promised. The exas-perating, arrogant man.

She stared towards her closet with much internal protest. Her skirt was one she'd never liked, and the blouse had never been comfortable. They suited her just fine. For twenty min-utes she'd sit and wonder how necessary having a door truly was.

Life had dwindled away as the cooler months approached. No glitter was left in the world; not even a taste of magic. To think there ever was had been the immature dream of a child. Molly stared at the ordinary realism of the earth, and pitied her old silly notions.

Jeremy helped Victoria from the car and together they made their way up to his home, oblivious to the distinct change of the Towson's house. The bushes by the stairs were brown and shrivelled, flowers were nothing but blackened stems, and little critters ran around the trees and away to the street.

Molly's stomach rolled with nausea. The last time she'd been there, Desmond had been, too.

"Are you going in?" George remained sitting behind the wheel in his car as he faced her.

She crossed her arms over her jacket and braced herself in her seat. "Do I have a choice?"

"Always." He removed his hat and spun it around in his hands. "I don't feel like being surrounded by the cheeriest people I know today, so I won't be submitting myself to that torture."

She studied him, trying to decipher what he was insinuating. "Where are you going?"

A cold, slight smile sliced across his lips. "It's a secret."

"I'm not in the mood for secrets."

"Then stay here."

Laughter erupted from inside the house. Molly cringed. "Are you driving off to your happy place?"

"There will be no happiness whatsoever where I'm heading," he said in a cavalier tone. "And if you come along, I'm assuming there will be even less."

"Less happiness than none at all?"

"That *is* the power you seem to be wielding today."

She thought of throwing some sort of insult at him, a retort, or even just a noise. But it wasn't within her abilities. She plucked at the tips of her gloves, making it plainly obvious that she was too bored to move.

"Too bad you don't have any books." He spun the wheel in his hands and drove the car onto the road. "It's a long drive."

The fact of the matter was, Molly didn't need books to tell her stories anymore. She had pieced several together all on her own.

When she was born, the night of the atrocious Clarington fire, Molly had lost the mother she was supposed to have had —the brave, adventurous woman that Cathryn had supposedly been. After years of playing together and getting along, Victoria had suddenly vanished from her life, too. Friends over the years had moved away. Desmond had gone to school and then ultimately left entirely. Through it all, only one thing had ever stayed true: Everyone who ever left Molly was better for it.

Her mother had to retreat in on herself to survive the torment of losing her dearest friend. Victoria's distance from Molly had led her to Jeremy. And Desmond... Well, she had faith that he would make something of himself, too.

No matter how much good Molly tried to add to people's lives, the best always came when she was out of them.

She kept facing the dull fabric of her skirt, picking at loose threads and folding them over her nails, barely noticing the car had come to a stop.

Her feet stretched out to the ground, leaving the car behind as she slowly looked up to see where she was.

A small stone palace sat in the dip of rolling hills, extravagant in every way. Crisp vines climbed up the bricks—brown leaves and twisted stems proving the vine had spent years carrying life but had fallen asleep for the oncoming season.

"Welcome to the Lake House." George headed to a worn path in the tall grass that led down to the water. He motioned towards his car. "You can carry your own blanket and follow me, if you so choose."

It wasn't what she would call a polite invitation, or any kind of invitation for that matter. She grabbed a knitted blanket from the back seat and followed a few paces behind as he walked all the way down to the pebbled shore.

George unfolded his blanket onto the grey stones and sat on top of it. He glanced at her briefly from under the hair falling over his forehead before turning his back to her.

Water had used to be able to carry so many sparkles. Today it only carried a colourless reflection of a blank sky. The shore was grey with its rocks and stones, and the tree she stood beneath was covered in dull bark; all of its leaves fallen away and forgotten about. She thought about the possibility of falling away and being forgotten about. It was tempting to disappear forever...

"What's really going on, Miss Jones?" George asked, collecting different stones into his hands and crossing his legs on the ground in front of him.

"Nothing," she said, gritting her teeth, not wanting to think about it. She threw open her blanket, not caring that it was rumpled, before crawling on top of it and hugging her knees.

"Don't try to tell me that nothing is wrong when it's evident something is."

She glared at him until he sighed and looked away.

"You forget I've watched someone travel down this same road." He tossed a stone into the water, its splash echoing into the silence. Molly remembered the story of George's cousin.

How she had lost her love of the world, of life. Tears rose in Molly's eyes and in her throat. She swallowed them down.

"I've seen where this path leads," George continued. "And I'm not capable of standing idly by while you receive the same fate." He faced her again, his eyes mirroring the sky. "So talk to me. Because that's what we do. That's what we've always been able to do."

Molly's words were ones she had vowed to never say to anyone. They rolled against the inside of her chest in burning waves, threatening to release themselves even if she didn't find the courage to do so voluntarily.

"I'm in no hurry." George spun his next stone between his palms. "I'll sit here as long as it takes."

She picked up a rock of her own and pinched it between her fingers, her eyes closing against the prickling tears.

"No." She squeezed her eyes tighter, tears escaping her lids and streaming down her cheeks. Emotions she had been trying to hold back boiled to the surface. She rose with them, finding her feet to pace along the shore.

George stood and walked after her.

"I'm fine." Molly wiped away her tears, keeping her hands over her eyes so she couldn't see the world beyond.

"You're not fine. Even Victoria is worried."

A cold laugh jumped out of her throat, twisted with all sorts of villainy. "Victoria doesn't even remember how I take my tea! Why would you trust her feelings towards me at all?"

"Now we're getting somewhere," he stated. "You want to scream about tea? Let's scream about tea."

Molly glared at him and clenched her hands into fists. He tracked the movement and pulled her hands into his.

"I'm serious," he whispered.

His kindness was too much. She ripped her hands out of his grasp and stumbled back.

Molly watched him, skeptical of the ways he'd been able to read her in the past. "People go through heartbreak everyday. I'll be fine the way they are fine."

"Perhaps," his tone changed to a low disagreement. "But this isn't just about losing Desmond."

Molly shrugged and turned her back to him.

"I see it in your eyes," he said, perhaps to himself. "I have never seen them like this, empty, bleak—"

"Only children look at the world with a sparkle in their eye," her voice pitched with sarcasm. "They see magic and love *everywhere.*"

"So do you."

"Did," she corrected, peering over her shoulder at him as she spun around. "You know how all the best fairytales have that one magical kiss? The one that brings you back to life, cancels curses, and marks true love?"

He raked a hand through his hair. "I'm familiar."

She goaded him with a smile as cruel as un-happily-ever-afters. "My first kiss brought me lies and broken promises, my worth stolen away with just footsteps. I was shoved back into the real world, and I hate it here."

George's eyes hardened. "I can't let you hate the world."

"You can't stop me."

He searched the lake waves, each one ebbing and flowing onto the rocks along the shoreline; docile, complacent. They flowed between the stones and disappeared, as if they'd never existed in the first place.

"My turn to confess," George's voice burned into the cool air.

She surveyed him cautiously, battle ready with the restlessness she had built up inside.

"Desmond needed to leave. It's why I drove him to the railway myself." His face was expressionless. "I gave him money to get him as far as he could go, and I gave him as much help as I could offer."

"I'm glad he had you."

George looked across the shore and tapped his fingers on his leg. "I helped him with everything I could. Like you, for example."

"Me?"

"Surely he told you." George straightened his suit; fixing his sleeves and tugging his waistcoat. "He never felt ready to tell you how much he cared for you, I basically had to walk him through it until the very end."

Molly shook her head, not wanting to believe it. "He didn't want to tell me?"

"He didn't think he should. Funny," he clicked his tongue, "maybe he was right about that."

"I'm glad he told me how he felt," she lied.

"Oh, good," George drawled. "Then you're probably also fine with all the scheming I did at the Northern Estate."

"What do you mean?"

"I planned it out, down to every last detail." He took long, arrogant strides towards her. "I never planned on letting Desmond on a horse, and I never intended for you to go riding without him. The goal was to get the two of you alone for the day. You managed to figure that one out, though, yes? You heard the horse story. I would've been a horrible person to let Desmond near my animals."

Her jaw locked. "You might be a horrible person anyways."

He smiled thinly and took another confident step. "You weren't the slightest bit suspicious when Victoria started begging you to come with us? She only did that because I asked her to."

"Stop."

"It was a bit backwards of me, I'll admit that." He tilted his head, one side of his grin deepening. "After all, I'm the one who wanted you to be no part of our fake relationship in the first place."

"Stop. Talking."

"Victoria asked if she could tell you about the false relationship all those months ago. She wanted you to know the truth from the very beginning. But *I* told her no. *I'm* the one who didn't want you near any of it."

Molly took the stone she had been holding on to and threw it at him.

He didn't flinch as it struck him in the chest.

"It was all because of you? Everything?"

He remained still.

"Why?"

He shrugged and slid his hands into his pockets. "Why not?"

She screamed at the world, at nothing and everything all at once.

George had kept Victoria away from her and had pushed Desmond too close. He was the reason she was all alone. He'd had a hand in it all. And he didn't seem the least bit sorry over it.

She grabbed handfuls of her hair, yanked on the pins, only tightening the knots in the strands. More tears escaped.

Stones shifted beneath her feet, rolling towards the water from beneath the tree. She raised her arms, trying to release a pin from her hair, when her sleeve caught on the cursed grey branches. She snapped the branch off and screamed as she threw it away.

Her heart stopped.

Tears stole possession of her breath.

Yelling at trees crumbled her into the smallest, most vile pieces.

She fell apart. *Old. Alone. Unloved.* She was dust.

Her shoulders heaved, opening a crevasse where everything she had shut out crashed in.

Her knees wobbled and gave way entirely. There was a quick second where George grasped her elbows, aiding her fall to the ground. Then he was gone.

Molly curled into a heap on the blanket, and it all came pouring out.

The torturous feelings swirled around her, drowning her, consuming her until there was nothing left. Just darkness; a comfortable place for her to feel all the sadness of its shadows. And a silence where nothing else mattered.

She pulled her knees up to her chest and held herself close, wishing for the world to disappear and for a dream to come take her away.

The sting of sunlight burnt Molly's eyes before they were even open. She had fallen asleep, she had dreamed, she had forgotten...

A splash in the water reminded her of everything.

She pushed onto her elbows, and stretched out until she was sitting.

George sat facing the water, tossing a new stone into the lake as soon as the ripples vanished. He acted as though she wasn't even there.

"How long was I sleeping?" she asked, shielding her eyes beneath her hands.

He tossed another rock into the lake. "Three, possibly four hours."

"Why didn't you wake me?"

He looked over his shoulder and matched her contempt. "I didn't want to."

Molly got off the blanket and snatched it into a ball. "Take me home."

She threw the blanket at him, not waiting to see if he had more to say before taking the path back to his car. As far as she was concerned, she'd never talk to him again.

Chapter 21

Night brought its welcomed darkness as George drove Victoria and Molly home. The girls huddled in the backseat of his car, sometimes whispering, sometimes silent. George paid no attention to their conversation, not caring what they may have been talking about. He'd stopped caring by the time he had gotten Molly back to the Towson house and had watched as she ate a decent amount of food for dinner. By the time he'd pulled his car up to the main doors of her home, George had decided it was the last time he would ever do so.

Molly got out and ran up to her house. Victoria had barely one foot on the ground by the time Molly had disappeared inside. She stood still for a shocked moment before her lips formed an ugly line.

George stepped out of the car and relaxed into the side of it. "I'm assuming you and I need to exchange words."

"What on earth did you do?" Victoria most certainly had a way of getting directly to the point.

"That's an unwise conversation to get into." He swiftly hid his hands in his pockets. "What's more important is that this charade of you and me is done."

Victoria's eyes widened, and she looked off into her yard; at the dying grass, the lifeless greens, as if the answers could have been there. "That's not fair, I need a week."

Bargaining. George was good at bargaining. "I'm not giving you a week, Victoria."

"I need more time."

"You'll have three days."

She jutted out her hip, moonlight catching the ample flash of her gown, and planted a hand on it. "Why are you ending things now?"

"Your parents would find it believable that I ended things with you after finding out about Desmond and my father. So will my grandmother, when I tell her."

"I don't buy it. The timing is suspicious in my opinion."

"Good thing I've never put a value on your opinion."

She stared daggers at him. "Where did you take Molly today?"

George rolled his eyes on his way to staring at his shoes. "My family's summer property."

"You took Molly to the Lake House?" she nearly shrieked. "Why?"

"It's the only thing I could think of."

"And how did that go?"

"Quite well actually." He pushed himself off his car and went to get back inside.

But Victoria filled the space. "Liar."

"I'm not lying. Everything I set out to accomplish, has been done."

"What exactly was it that you set out to accomplish?"

He stretched his back in an arch and looked passively up into the night's sky. "Why do you ask questions you already know the answers to? It's one of your most annoying qualities."

She coughed out a laugh and pulled him by his collar until her nose was a breath away from his. "Molly hates you. Why?"

"Because she needs to." He pushed her hand off him and stood up straight again.

"She has no reason to hate you." Victoria wore her shock well, so well he almost believed her.

"She has many reasons. I only gave her a few." He snarled out a sharp smile.

"What could you even tell her that made her hate you so much?"

"The truth."

"About what?"

"How I helped Desmond leave, and how I maneuvered things for them to be able to get together in the first place."

Victoria let out a saddened breath. "I told you you shouldn't have done that."

"And you were right. Mind you, it has now officially come back to haunt me, so I'm sure you can feel good about that."

Victoria's lips spun to the side, an obvious tell that her thoughts were circling. "So, that was it?"

"I may have also hinted towards how you wanted her to know the truth about our relationship—"

"You told her about that!"

"I hinted." He focused on playing with his hat. "All she knows is that you wanted her to know the truth, and I didn't."

"So you told her half-truths just to get her to hate you."

"I told her just enough truths until she decided to hate me on her own. I would've told her more if I'd needed to."

"You've lost your mind!"

"Aww," he said with a crooked grin. "That's the nicest thing anyone has said to me all day."

"Why did you want her to hate you?"

"Because..." George wanted to be witty, sarcastic, evasive. He stared into the wind. Those parts of him had evaporated. "If she's busy hating me, then she'll be too busy to hate the world."

"You can't do that, George."

"I happen to have an entire repertoire of ways to make her completely despise me," he corrected, with a wink.

"She would have stopped hating the world eventually."

"It is not worth the risk." He tossed his hat into the car and motioned her to step away. "By hating me she gets to see the world in colour again. By hating me, I become black and white and shades of grey."

"You would sacrifice yourself for her world?"

"It's not a sacrifice," he amended. "I was no one to her, but now I can be something to hate. And I can be good at it."

Victoria pouted. "I don't want her to hate you."

George stole the chance to slip into his seat, using the momentum to ignore the honesty of Victoria's statement, the pain in her words, the strain in her voice.

She walked up beside his seat, staring him down. It didn't make him feel any smaller than he had already made himself.

"Why, George?" she whispered.

"You know why." He looked up at Victoria one last time. "Molly slept, she ate, and she's talking to you again. My guess is that tomorrow will be the same, and the day after might be even better. And one more thing."

Victoria nodded. "What is it?"

"Stop putting sugar in her tea, and she might drink it." George pulled out of the driveway without waiting to find out what Victoria would say to that.

He was ready to sit at the piano for as many hours as it took for the shadows he had summoned to go far, far away.

Chapter 22

Winter 1904

Snow raged down from the sky. Chilling winds blew the white dust with George and Thomas as they entered the Towson home. A fire roared in the hearth, billowing smoke up the chimney and sending the scent of embers and ashes coasting through the room. The curtains were closed, keeping whatever warmth they could inside. And the sofas were spun in odd ways, as they always tended to be, making room for whatever madness the Towson girls could create.

It had been a very long day, not only for Thomas who'd worked on the factory floor, but also for George who had only been able to escape to the floor for the morning and had been cooped up in his office the entire afternoon.

Thomas kicked off his shoes and ran down the hall, no doubt racing to scrub off the dirt and grime and whatever other filth always covered him after his shift.

"George!" Linus stepped into the living area. "Are you staying for dinner? I'm cooking!"

The mention of Linus cooking took away his last bit of appetite. "That's a kind offer but—"

"So you're staying!" Linus cheered, continuously stirring the contents in the large bowl he desperately clung to.

"I—"

"Linus, get back in here!" Valerie shouted from the kitchen.

George didn't want to stay for dinner. If he could have only gotten the sentence out, he would have said as much. He only needed a second more of Thomas' time to let him know he wouldn't be able to pick him up in the morning or drive him home.

"George is here!" Mary ran into the living room, giggling as her dark curls bounced with her steps. Her older sisters followed behind with Jeremy, walking at a normal rhythm.

Powerless to little Mary's smiles, George removed his shoes and stepped deeper into the home. He curled into an uncomfortable lump on a worn round carpet, the original colour of which was unknown.

Mary fell into his lap, utilizing the end of his tie to transform her doll into a mermaid and pretending she was swimming through the air. Her sisters' stories about their day were riddled with chaos that really only allowed George to share wavering smiles as he struggled to maintain details.

"Are you staying for dinner?" Mary asked through the imaginary voice of the mermaid.

"I'm sorry, but I don't think I can tonight," he replied, loosening the tie a bit more so he didn't get strangled.

Mary dramatically groaned and rolled off his lap to the floor, bumping into her sisters and causing an uproar of laughs. George smiled and pushed himself back to his feet.

"You only just got here!" Tessa, the second youngest sister, complained.

He ruffled his hand through the top of her hair and turned to leave. "Another time, Tessa, promise."

"Stay." Jeremy's voice caught George's attention. He sat on the sofa, watching discreetly, most likely thankful that George was taking the brunt of his sisters' attention for a while. "If you do, there will be less food for us to suffer through."

"I can hear you!" Linus called from his place in the kitchen.

"Please stay," Jeremy pleaded with a smile, rising to his feet.

The offer was tempting.

Violet, the oldest sister, jumped in between them. "Molly and Victoria are coming for dinner, too!"

The temptation vanished.

"Doesn't that sound like fun." George masked the distain in his voice and turned an unimpressed glare at Jeremy. "You weren't going to mention that yourself?"

Jeremy shrugged. "I knew you'd never agree to stay if I did."

"You were correct."

"Molly can't be mad at you forever."

"She definitely can be." George stepped over the strewn remnants of the girls' toys, anxious to exit the house before any more company showed up. "I've only seen her twice since Desmond left. She threw things at me the first time and pretended I didn't exist the next."

"That was over a month ago," Jeremy called desperately, unable to follow George due to his sisters clinging to his limbs. "Things have changed!"

Thomas had filled George in on what had been an eventful month, from Victoria revealing her relationship with Jeremy to her parents, to the way Molly had done a complete turnaround. He knew William and Cathryn Jones had known the false nature of his relationship with Victoria all along, which was embarrassing. He knew that Victoria took the blame for all their lies, which was strange. And he knew that Molly was laughing again, because it happened often enough for Thomas to complain about it.

Fresh snow gusted through the room with a freezing wind as the front door opened. Girlish laughter sent prickles up George's spine. The time to run had passed.

Of course it had. Time was a menacing foe.

George slouched in annoyance and glared at Jeremy.

Jeremy grinned. The same scheming grin George often wore.

So it hadn't been a coincidence that Jeremy had first appeared behind the group of his sisters, the same little girls who had convinced George to sit—and stay a little too long. It had all just been part of a game that had probably originated with Victoria herself.

"Well played," George grumbled with a smirk.

Jeremy tipped his head in thanks.

George swiped at the wrinkles on his black sleeves, adjusting his monochrome attire and dulled watch-chain, shifting from a disgruntled man into the persona that knew how to pull himself together. As a matter of self-preservation, it was also key to avoid looking at Molly.

His eyes flicked up to the piano that stood alone against the far wall, unable to help him. Then he glanced through his bangs to the entryway where Annabelle, the Jones' housekeeper and volunteer chaperone, had come into the home alongside her husband, Roger. George nodded a greeting as they went to the kitchen, claiming to want to see Valerie.

Victoria slid her coat off her arms and hung it on the nearby coat rack. She tinkered with the belt on her emerald dress so that it hit her favourite curves in her favourite way, and walked around the first sofa to make it to Jeremy's side. She curled under his arm as he slung it around her shoulders.

"Try not to look too glum, George," she teased. "You weren't the only one tricked into coming tonight."

George tucked his hands into his pockets and rocked back on his heels. "You're playing a very dangerous game."

"We thought you liked games," Jeremy said, irritatingly sly.

"What's *he* doing here?" Molly sniped.

George refused to look at her. "Leaving," he said, attempting to make it around Victoria.

Jeremy grabbed his arm. "We already set a place for you."

"It's not impossible to put dishes away," Molly mumbled in a pleased tone.

George pulled out of Jeremy's grasp and flatted his jacket lapels. "It's time for me to go. Especially since Miss Jones finds the prospect of me leaving to be the best news she's heard all day."

"Or all my life."

"Or all her life," George conceded.

Victoria darted her eyes between them. "It's not even like the two of you need to talk. Just sit in the same room as each other."

"Ew."

Victoria's eyes widened at her sister's remark, and Jeremy followed in unison. But George grinned. Molly's voice, even when making a disgusted sound at his expense, was vibrant. He lost the ability to avoid looking her way.

Molly looked regal in a pale-blue gown with detailed scrollwork around every hem. Her stare could tear down empires, let alone rip the hearts out of men. Rose-tinted hues had found their way back to her cheeks, and while perhaps she wasn't smiling at him directly, George could tell that she had finally been smiling again. Not to mention the way she now allowed her hair to flow freely around her shoulders. Her wild determination was back; the waves Victoria loved to brag that Molly made had returned. Although, who was George kidding—he also enjoyed those waves.

Molly shifted, just slightly, and the ruffles of her skirts swayed in a crinoline serenade.

"Did you say *ew?*" he asked, attempting an irritated tone instead of his natural amusement.

She looked beyond him and into a distant corner of the room, curling a lock of her hair around her slender fingers as she contemplated a proper reply.

"I may have," she finally answered, eyes finding his.

George's smile loosened completely. "All right." He turned to face Jeremy. "I'll stay. Although it *may* not be for the reasons you had hoped."

"It's because I said ew, isn't it?" Molly glowered in defiance.

"That's the only thing that could have convinced me." He winked.

Molly huffed and crossed her arms, looking back into the corner she'd previously stared at.

"You're right, this is fun," George said towards the scheming couple. "I'm going to go check in with Thomas real quick."

He stretched his steps over Victoria's feet, ready for escape. But as he reached Molly's side, he hesitated.

Her brown eyes held something achingly soft. It was best to not decipher what she may have been thinking.

"Are you sure my presence won't woo you into forgetting all of the reasons you hate me?" he asked with his darkest note of humour.

Her gaze sharpened. "You think too highly of yourself to assume your presence has any affect on me at all."

He kept walking, allowing himself to smile once he was out of view.

George disappeared into the hallway, grateful as the voices faded into the background. People were tedious. Especially Molly. Thankfully, Thomas was his own little species.

George knocked on the bedroom door and waited for Thomas to grunt out an invitation before he opened it and walked inside. Partially laying down in his bed, the bottom bunk, Thomas cradled his guitar in his lap, strumming it quietly.

His eyes smiled but nothing else. He motioned for George to sit down. "I take it Victoria and Molly arrived."

George dropped onto the chair. "Thanks for the warning. I didn't think you would stab me in the back like that."

"I'm not sorry." Thomas laid the guitar down beside him and turned his focus solely on George, wearing a gentle expression. "You should just apologize."

"We've already talked about this."

"Yet, here we are."

"Hating me has done her a lot of good." George combed his hair out of his eyes to the top of his head, sighing when it fell back in the way.

"Maybe it's done enough good, and you can both move on. She's the only person who would listen to you when you talk about Desmond."

"You listen to me."

"Because you're my boss, and I have to."

George smiled at that. Thomas had turned out to be a good friend whether he admitted it or not. "Speaking of that friend of mine, I can't drive you to work tomorrow. I'm heading out of town to visit him."

"You're actually going to visit him?" Thomas' eyebrows couldn't possibly rise any further.

"It's very much contingent on if I survive the night." George tapped his fingers across the tops of his legs. "I'm not sure what worries me more; the fact that Linus is cooking, or having to face Molly."

"Seriously?"

"You're right. They're both equally horrible prospects."

Thomas stared at him, through George's walls and to his molten core.

"We're going to be late for dinner." George pretended to laugh as he stood. "Are you coming?"

Thomas grumbled and crawled off his bunk to follow George to the door. "Someone has to make sure you don't do anything stupid."

That was probably wise.

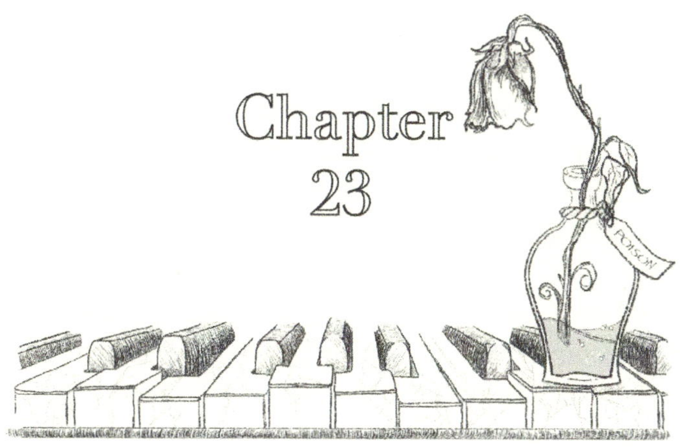

Chapter 23

George couldn't relax. His time had been spent pretending Molly wasn't laughing at things that were not funny, or ignoring how her attention was given to the young Towson girls as they begged her for an impossible amount of things. She'd left to put them all to bed, following through on a promise to tell them bedtime stories. That particular talent would serve her well in her dreams of her own family one day, though he detested how he remembered in detail what her dreams were.

It was exhausting. Especially the impossibility of ignoring any of it—any of *her*—and the uncomfortable feeling of not knowing when he'd have to ignore all of it again.

Roger and Annabelle began to prepare themselves for the journey home, signalling that it was time to say goodbye. Jeremy and Victoria stole a moment for a lengthy farewell, one which everyone in the room gave them privacy for. Linus made jokes under his breath about the whole thing while their father seemed less content to hear them. George turned his back to laugh about it, especially seeing how enormously unimpressed Thomas was.

Roger flung the front door open on his way to finalize preparations of the carriage and the horses. But as everyone noticed rather quickly, Roger never headed outside.

"What is it, Roger?" Annabelle asked from over his shoulder.

"I'm not sure we're heading anywhere tonight." Roger turned around to face the group, awkwardly pulling his hat off and looking down at the floor.

George had a sense of foreboding about what was going to be said next.

"The snow hasn't let up," Roger said. "The carriage can't make it all the way back in this."

"Really?" Victoria weaved past everyone to head to the window. She threw open the curtains, revealing the snow and swirling winds.

Valerie exchanged a glance with her husband, Jack, who gave a curt nod. "You're all welcome to spend the night here. We'll make arrangements."

Jack gave Linus a look. "Get the rollaway bed," he grunted.

Linus darted away as whispers filled the room regarding the horses and who would help get them to shelter.

George discreetly walked to the door, reaching for his coat while no one was looking.

"Don't even think about it," Valerie warned, grabbing a hold of his arm before it had even reached the coatrack.

"If you don't want me driving, I could walk—"

"And catch frostbite on your toes and lose your foot?" She shook a finger at him. "Not on my watch." The mess of curls on Valerie's head mirrored all her movements as she did a quick head count of the room.

"Roger and Annabelle should get the master room," said Jack.

Valerie nodded. "You and George can sleep in the boys' room. Victoria and I will bunk together with the girls."

"What's happening?" Molly tiptoed into the room from the hallway, leaving behind a quiet room of slumbering young girls.

"I knew the count was wrong," Valerie grumbled and tapped everyone's shoulders as she did a final check. "We're going to need to utilize the couches."

"We got snowed in," Victoria whispered to Molly whose eyes widened as she looked towards the windows, smiling at the sight of all the cascading glitter.

"The couches are horrible." Jack's comment was followed by a bickering session with his wife over who should sleep where. The only thing agreed on was that one parent would stay with Victoria and the other with Jeremy. To make sure things stay on the *up-and-up,* Valerie called it.

"I don't mind the couch," Molly interjected, her voice a gentle contrast to the angry whispers.

"The couches are horrible," Valerie argued with a laugh. "I don't wish those on you."

Molly lifted her shoulders. "I can fall asleep anywhere. And it's the simplest solution."

George rolled his eyes. "Or you can take the rollaway bed into the girls' room, and I can take the couch."

Molly glared at him, but before she could protest, Valerie spoke in her place. "Can't put the rollaway bed in the girls' room, there isn't enough space."

"The couch will be fine, I can sleep anywhere." Molly assured.

"It's true," Victoria said, clinging onto Jeremy and clearly thrilled at the evening's new arrangements. "She fell asleep on the cellar floor. We all had to go looking for her."

Molly blushed and twirled a lock of her hair. "So if your couch is more comfortable than a stone floor, I'll be just fine."

Valerie glanced back at Molly. "I'm sure that was ages ago. You're much too grown up for that now."

"It was last week," Victoria clarified.

Everyone faced Molly, including George who'd had every intention of remaining silent up until that point. "Your cellar is a dungeon."

"Your point being?" Molly snapped, all kindness vanishing.

It didn't bother him. Nor did it stunt his curiosity. "What were you doing that had you falling asleep in a dungeon?"

"Oh, the usual things," she replied with a voice so sugary he was only drawn in more. "Reading, writing, daydreaming and...ah, yes,"—one corner of her lips tugged up—"plotting my revenge on you, of course."

The urge to smile was fierce. George held a hand over his mouth to hide how much he actually enjoyed the response before turning away from her completely.

"Enough of this." Valerie stepped between them. "Everyone go to your spaces, and let's all get ready for bed."

Her voice was heavy with command, so everyone did as instructed, disappearing to their designated rooms. The only exception was Jeremy and Victoria, who stood in the middle of the hallway exchanging goodnights and preventing George and Thomas from making it anywhere.

"How long do you think this is going to take?" George muttered to Thomas.

"No idea," he groaned and dropped against the wall.

George thrummed his fingers in a secret rhythm and turned to the room behind him.

Molly sat on the couch beneath the window watching the snowflakes fall as she wrapped herself in a blanket. The locks of her curls falling down around her shoulders flickered in the flaming light.

Blazing reminders of things he desperately wished to forget shattered his vision. He pressed his fingers over his eyes to erase the sight. The roar of fire and smoke filtered through his mind, filling the silence, destroying his songs. If there had been any hope that he could sleep, it was gone.

George watched the shadows dance on the ceiling, each one transforming into malicious memories more sinister than the last. Not even Jack's snoring could drown out the agonizing screams of the past scorching through George's veins.

The room was boiling. He unfastened every button on his shirt, for air, for escape. It didn't do much to help.

Noisy springs squealed beneath his weight as he struggled to swing his feet to the ground and sit. He gripped his hair off his forehead and roughly pushed his sleeves up past his elbows, anything to relieve the pressure of his persistent nightmares.

Time to fix it.

No one was the wiser as George snuck out of the room and into the hall. The faint orange glow was a beacon to the fire, each crackle a secret, each *pop* a memory. His balance wavered with the flames, flickering faster and snapping entirely. He dropped against the yellowed wallpaper, sliding out his feet to anchor himself.

He ran a shaking hand through his hair, tuning out the world as much as he could, ready to wander through the orange until he could watch the fire die.

Someone tripped over his feet, toppling forward. He caught the perpetrator in his arms before they fell, holding them up against him as he utilized the wall for stability.

Molly glared up at him in colourful fury, her frozen fingers burning his skin.

"Your hands are like icicles," he hissed, though the shock of her touch had nothing to do with the temperature.

He couldn't fathom why the most vexing person he knew was roaming the halls past midnight or why she smelled of perfume. His gaze traveled through the tresses of her hair to the layers of her clothes. It would've been more than easy for her to hide flowers somewhere. Surely it wasn't her natural fragrance.

He shook his head to dismiss the distraction of it all, unwilling to entertain any thoughts on the complexities of women. Certainly not the one in front of him.

"Why don't you have a shirt on?" she sneered, eyes narrowing onto his. "It's disgusting."

There was something remarkable about the power of her will, the strength in her loathing. Truly irresistible. So it was easy to slide into one of his grins, knowing the situation called for a persona he could only wrangle with the aid of knowing he was hated.

"If that's what you think, why do you seem so comfortable in my arms?"

She scoffed and pushed away, brushing her hands off on her gown. "I've never met anyone as vile as you. It's disconcerting to women everywhere."

"What a compliment." He laced his hands behind his neck, adjusting his position against the wall. "I didn't realize I had any effect on women everywhere."

Her chin angled up as she made a sound that tilted high and mighty into the room. She gave him a pointed look down her nose and rushed past him to the couch.

The cushions let out a sigh as she fell into them and curled up under the blanket. She played with the ends of her hair, twirling them between her fingers before she turned away. Her hand fluttered out, gesturing carelessly towards the couch under the window. "You can sit over there."

He took hesitant steps into the room, and dropped against a new wall, trying to pretend that he didn't want to take her up on the offer. "Wouldn't you prefer it if I walk away?"

"I'd definitely prefer that," she said with no hesitation, "but I'm not coldhearted. I'm sure you'll leave me once the fire is out. And, with any luck, I'll have forgotten I was ever nice to you by morning."

Well, at least there could be the hope of forgetting. Usually the things you wanted to forget the most were the moments you remembered forever.

George fell onto the opposite couch, not caring that it was less than graceful as he fastened his shirt back together. The cold air blasted down over his neck from the window above, and while the chill was refreshing, it was also annoying.

Molly didn't look at him, and he pretended to only watch the fire. The flames were mesmerizing, dancing together in different shades of golds. He hated it as much as it continued to draw him in. The final log screamed as it gave way to the burning. He pulled his hair in front of his eyes in order to squeeze them shut privately.

"It's snowing again!"

The motion happened fast. Molly rushed the couch until she was sharing the same piece of furniture as him.

She stared out the window, eager to find every falling ice crystal. "I'd say sorry for encroaching on your space, except this is my space and you're in it."

"Is that you asking me to leave?" He crossed one leg over the other.

"No."

"Then at least we still have a survivable distance between us."

"Barely."

He caught her looking at him through the edges of her lashes. "This is why we never could've been friends and why Desmond kept us apart all that time."

"Desmond probably never realized he could have gotten us all together." Her breath fogged the window as she spoke, puffing out of her in a soft, rhythmic lullaby. "I think we could have been good friends had we met all those years ago. You know, before your soul-crushing ego came into play."

"Here I was thinking you were about to say something nice."

"Do you think you could handle it if I said something nice?" she challenged.

"Probably not," he decided out loud.

Molly twirled into the sofa, ignoring the snow as she watched him. Half of her features glowed silver and blue from the snow-hazed moonlight that poured through the window. The other half was flickering gold and yellow from the flames. But her warm brown eyes were as sorrowful as they were curious.

She laid her arms on the back of the couch, lacing her fingers together before resting her chin on her hands. "You wish he was still here, don't you?"

"You say that like you don't wish it yourself," he grumbled, turning away from the flames as they crackled incessantly.

"I wish for a lot of things, but I don't wish he was here. Victoria hates him."

George felt an involuntary tug on his lips at the comment. "She hasn't kept that a secret from anyone."

"Wherever Desmond is, I hope he likes it. He can never come back to London. If Victoria ever hears of him being in town—"

"She'll kill him." George laughed, stopping when he heard Molly did too. Her smile faded, and she went back to watching the snow, eyes dancing all over.

George uncrossed his legs and returned to watching the fire. Only one log remained. Soon it would be down to embers, and once those barely glowed, he would make his way back to his room.

His eyes drooped closed, long enough for him to enjoy the swirling colours beneath his eyelids. The firelight billowed the colours into reds and blues and violets. They flitted about in sporadic melodies. He could easily spend forever there, inventing new songs, creating new worlds...

The hues twisted together, creating forms and transforming into something treacherous. George predicted their next move just in time and opened his eyes.

Motivation was a tricky thing, and never came exactly when or how he wanted it to. He had hoped to stand on his own, but it wasn't until a soft weight landed on his shoulder that he realized he should have moved—only a moment too late.

Molly lay on his arm, off in a dream. She sighed, a mellifluous sound that settled deep into George's fortress of locked away secrets. For a moment, his world wasn't in shreds. For a moment, the lurking shadows weren't tearing him apart.

Unacceptable. He needed to slip away unnoticed, pretend like it had never happened—and she simply would never know.

George slid his arm away, a little too slowly, catching her beneath her neck to place her down lightly on the sofa.

It took him too long to realize he was free. With that, he sunk to the floor.

The fire had finished, not even an ember was glowing, leaving no reason to stay on the floor any longer—except for the fact that his limbs refused to budge.

He swept the hair away from his eyes and stared into the smokey hearth. In a few hours he was supposed to visit Desmond. There was no way of knowing how he was going to handle that anymore.

George rose to a crouching position, daring to look at Molly one final time. She looked peaceful, just as when she had fallen asleep the day he had taken her to the lake, where he had spent too much time watching over her. Everything about that day had left him in pieces. But it hadn't been the first time, nor would it be the last.

"You have no idea how much you break me every time I see you," he whispered to her slumbering silhouette. That was the thing about late night hours; once reality blurred into dreams or nightmares, secrets revealed themselves, whether you wanted them to or not.

Molly made a faint noise that stopped his heart before it was sent beating at a prestissimo. He jolted backwards and stole only one glance to make sure she was still asleep before disappearing down the hall.

At least the house was still. Not a sound was heard. So no one would ever know. And George was free to forget the whole night had even taken place.

Except, a pesky voice reminded him, *you never can forget the things you wish to.*

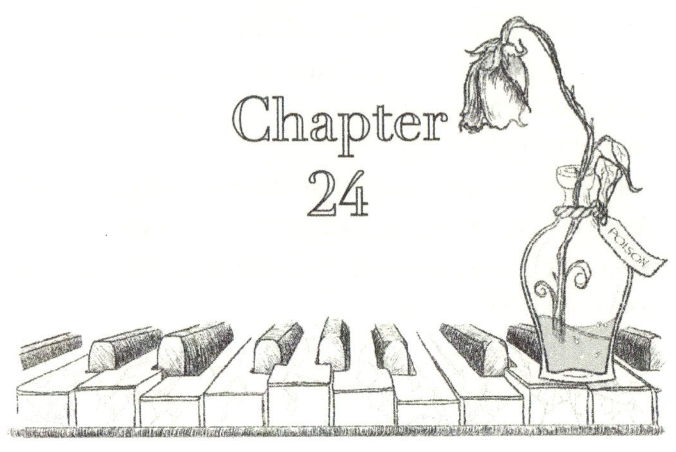

Chapter 24

The whispered yellow of sunbeams through mist.
The secret greens of grass hidden in the shadows.
The murky blues of lake waves stirred up by thrown rocks.

These were the colours chosen as George spun them into a song. His fingers tapped along the keys, each momentum of the melody pulling on him and transporting him somewhere far away.

Somewhere he'd stayed awhile.

George stretched his fingers away from the piano and reached for his glass of water. He widened his eyes and blinked back the fog before he noticed he wasn't alone in the room.

"I waited until your song was finished," Gran said, smiling as she lowered onto the sofa. Her attire was still in mourning blacks, silver hair pinned up and drawing attention to her piercing blue eyes. She was looking right through him as she always did. "How was your visit with Desmond?"

"It was good." He left the piano and sat down next to her.

Gran turned to the fireplace. "Just good?" The lilt of her voice proved she had assumptions.

He knew how he would've played about it; the chords and rhythm that would explain everything. In music there was always a way. Each tune carried a colour, and with enough colours he could create new worlds. Ones where the locks around his reserves vanished, and the prison inside him was nothing but empty cells.

The fire released a burst of sparks, shooting them up the chimney. He winced.

Gran reached out with a reassuring hand to hold his pieces together.

"Do you know what I think?" Her slight smile played off the wrinkles around her eyes. "I think you have poured your heart into helping others. And now you have been forced to confront the fact that you've been neglecting yourself."

George's eyes flicked to the piano, back to the fire, then towards Gran. "I'm not sure I like that interpretation of my feelings."

She squeezed his hand. "Many years ago, when I was already an old lady, I was enjoying a quiet house and relaxing evenings with my husband. Then along comes this boy—the most stubborn young child London has ever seen. Suddenly, the years that should have been filled with leisure were spent raising this child who wanted nothing to do with growing up."

George grinned. "I still want nothing to do with growing up."

"Well, of course not. You're also still very stubborn." She laughed before vanishing her smile. "I didn't spend all of my energy pouring out my love to you only for you to do nothing with it. But you seem so determined to only live half a life, George."

"I'm not sure I'd call it half a life."

She perked her brows. "Then whatever happened to living your life authentically?"

It was a conversation they'd had several times in the past. Though the words had never rang so loud.

"I may have forgotten to do that," he admitted.

"Well don't forget again." Her words fell heavily. "You can't be happy if you don't let others see who you are. Including yourself."

"I've been acting a part my whole life Gran, this is who I am."

She released his hand to count on her fingers. "You're always planning who to be, what to say, what you're going to do. You become the person necessary to fit the situation surrounding you. When was the last time you were truly yourself?"

"Just a few minutes ago, with the piano."

"And around other people?"

He glared at the embers, the hissing smoke and crackling timbers. "Not by choice."

Gran sighed. "I worry that if you don't do this by choice, it will be forced upon you. I only want you to be happy. *You*. Not the person you pretend to be."

"And if the person I turn out to be is repulsive, what happens then?"

"Plan B." Gran winked. "Your grandfather is working on something special."

"Our definition of special tends to be different."

"He's invited a girl to attend the theatre with us next week."

His heart raged. "Who?"

"Someone you don't know." Her smile spread across every feature as she noticed his panic. "How sad I am now that I didn't suggest—"

He let out a growl.

"Could you imagine?" She laughed.

"No. And I don't want to." He gripped his fingers into his hair and leaned fully into the couch.

"It would have been so much fun."

"Gran!" He wanted her to stop, needed her to stop. "She's irritating and gets under my skin in the worst possible way."

She hummed a happy melody while tipping her head side to side. "All the best ones do, George."

He ignored the comment, knowing it would play out in his mind during the days and weeks to come. "Who is the girl Gramps has invited to the theatre with us?"

"Her name is Claire. Most likely she'll be clinging onto me for the night, and you would be free to do as you choose."

"You're already offering me the opportunity to leave you behind?"

She made an unconcerned noise. "It's time for you to stop worrying what others think. Within reason of course, I did raise you to be a gentleman."

He straightened in his seat. "So, if I remain gentlemanly, I'm free to leave you alone with this Claire and go off and do whatever I choose? Gramps would be okay with that?"

"I know you think your grandfather wants you to run the business, get married, and have a family. But all we want is for you to be happy. If you don't want to get married and have a family, then I'll make sure your grandfather stops introducing you to girls."

George rubbed at his forehead, making sure he wasn't hallucinating due to lack of sleep. "You'd be happy without an heir? One to carry on the business, the family name and fortune?"

"If you can promise you'd be happiest alone instead of married, then we would rather you be alone. You would figure out the other things when you had to."

"Really?" This opened up an entirely new future for him; a new world. One where he wouldn't have to bring ruin upon anyone but himself, where he wouldn't have to worry about fires and ashes.

"Really, George." She patted his knee twice, emphasizing her point before pushing up from her seat. "Just promise you'll think about it."

Gran disappeared, filling the room with a perturbing silence between the sparks and flames.

George made his way to the piano, ready to escape to a different place. One where maybe he could be himself, if only he remembered how to do so.

Blazing torches led the way down a long corridor that reeked of mildew and simmering oils. Archways constructed of stone bricks collected water that dripped down to George's feet.

Drip-drip-drop.

George heard the clang of a clock emitting out of the darkness and the low gurgle of something far more frightful.

"George." His mother stood before him.

Her gown was made of wrinkled pages covered with scribbles of ink and smears of red. She held a bouquet of smouldering roses, smoke rising from their petals and mixing into her hair. Each blackened strand fell in twisted ribbons off her shoulders, the tips glowing like embers.

"We don't have much time," she warned.

Her fingers stretched into talons, clawing into his skin as she pulled him forward. Blood oozed from the wounds and puddled to the wooden slats on the ground, meeting up with the darkened water that kept leaking through the walls.

The soles of his shoes clapped off the floor as they become one with the shadows.

A whimpering noise burst out, resounding off the bricks.

His mother held a torchlight closer to the wall, revealing iron bars.

The noise became a wail.

George tore free from his mother's claws, ignoring the pain to grasp at the bars. A small child in tattered clothing sat in the corner, clutching a small stuffed bear.

"Why is he in there?" George shook the bars, aching to pull them apart.

The child cried louder.

His mother stood emotionless by the cell. "Too many fires, not enough time."

The young boy's hand shot through the bars, seizing the torch from his mother's grasp and piercing it into her side.

George cried out.

The flames took over, igniting the papers of his mother's gown, consuming her.

She vanished into ash.

George bolted upright in bed. Breaths were a forgotten pastime.

He sensed the clock on his nightstand and took it in his shaking hands.

He threw his covers away and marched for the window, shoving it open and hurling the clock outside.

George slammed the window closed and wobbled back to the chair beside his bed. He grabbed his robe and draped it on, tying it around his torso as he left the room and headed for the stairs.

It was time for a song. One powerful enough to lock his beastly shadows back in their cages.

Chapter 25

Molly flipped through her closet, passing through frilly things as she searched for the most perfect gown. The theatre was sure to be an experience like no other. A place where stories came to life before her eyes.

"Hurry up!" Victoria called from her waiting spot on Molly's bed. "It's rather boring waiting for you to choose something."

Molly grabbed her outfit of choice and walked out. "How's this?"

"Looks positively darling." Victoria smiled.

Molly stared at the periwinkle gown with its glittering stones and bobbling ribbons.

That's when it hit. The familiarity of the moment—Victoria on her bed, dresses strewn across the covers—brought on waves of memories from the night of the Prescott's dinner. Everything twisted upside down, tumbling over her.

"Here." Victoria held out a cup of tea, taking the gown into her grasp, and placing the porcelain cup into Molly's waiting fingers.

"I'm sorry," Molly whispered. She held the cup close, savouring the comfort as the steam billowed up to kiss her cheeks. Just from the aroma, she knew Victoria had made it perfectly; unsweetened and brewed to a rich flavour.

"What're you sorry for? Never apologize for what happened after Desmond left," Victoria said briskly. She placed a strong arm around Molly and stared into her eyes. "And don't you dare let a boy make you feel like less than what you're worth."

She stood from the bed and walked over to Molly's dresser to play with the bits of jewellery on display. "That boy was never good enough for you."

Molly hid a thankful smile behind her cup. "I don't think it's fair of you to hate Desmond so much."

Victoria examined a gold chain. "I don't hate him. I just have plans if he ever shows his face around here again."

Dribbles of tea burnt her lips as she giggled. "It would only be fair if he knew these plans so he could avoid them."

"Well, George knows them. I'm assuming he'll let Desmond know for me if he gets the chance."

Molly's face soured at the name she had no desire to hear. "Can we not talk about him?"

"We can talk about Desmond who treated you like rubbish, but you don't want to talk about George?"

"Correct."

"You're twisted."

"So are you." Molly joined Victoria by her jewellery. She slid her cup onto the dresser and lifted the pearl drops that would match her gown best. But also the crimson stones which would be an accent in daring contrast.

"Definitely the red," Victoria said.

Molly grinned. "Do you think?"

"I know." Victoria held Molly's shoulders as they gazed upon their own reflections in the mirror. She swept back Molly's hair and held an earring up to its proper place. "The same way I know that Desmond never treated you good enough."

With a dream-like sigh, Victoria retreated back to the bed, lying in a heap of gowns that smothered all her curves.

Molly turned back to her reflection, mulling over more than just earrings.

"Alright, girls." Their mother swung her coat off her shoulders and handed it to the reception desk, revealing her gorgeous plum velvet gown with embroidered scrolls along the torso and sleeves.

"Cathryn..." Their father prowled behind them, tipping his hat and fixing off his gloves. "This is nonsense. I'm sure Johnathon Clarington has retired his archaic tricks."

Molly turned a glance at Victoria who shrugged, also unsure of what their parents were getting at. Victoria was dressed in emerald silk that hugged her in all the right places—or all the wrong ones, according to their father. She looked absolutely divine.

The flowing beads on Molly's dress shone like falling stars, sparkling like wishes waiting to come true. Every time she moved they clashed together in little rivers of twinkling bells.

It was the perfect periwinkle gown, filled with shimmering fairy dust and glittering music.

She stood with her family in an empty hall of the theatre, removed from the distraction of the gorgeous dresses and perfectly tailored tuxedos of all those in attendance.

The fancy theatre had many different wonderful things hiding all around. Lush scarlet curtains hung by the entrances, their golden tassels matching the chandeliers that hung from towering ceilings. Murals of clouded skies were painted between crown moldings and sculptured beams that glistened white in the crystal light.

"This is important," her mother continued in a hushed voice. "For a very short time, I was romantically involved with James Clarington."

"You what?" Victoria shrieked, "George's father?"

"I should have told you this before," her mother mused, eyebrows creasing at the unpleasant memory.

"Or not brought it up at all," her father countered.

Her mother smacked his arm with the back of her clutch and leaned in closer. "My family was very close with the Claringtons. Once I ended things with James, our families wanted to reconcile and make sure there were no underlying strains on the family bonds." She paused to look around. "The night we went to dinner at their house, Johnathon had arranged for James to have a new woman, just for my benefit."

"What?" Victoria said too loudly again, gaining a glare from both parents.

Molly chewed back her smile as she guessed where the story was leading.

Her mother pressed on, "I am positive that Johnathon will be playing the same game tonight for George, arranging to have a girl at his side. And she'll probably be very lovely."

A snort escaped Molly before she held up a hand to cover her mouth. "I'm sorry," she said. Her eyes danced from her mother's startled expression to Victoria's unamused one. "It's funny to me. It sounds like something George would really hate to be a part of."

Neither her mother nor Victoria shared in her humour.

Molly scowled and faced away. It was joyously fascinating that George would spend his evening as uncomfortably as he deserved. And when she caught her father's eyes, he reined in a smirk and nodded in agreement before his wife caught him.

"George and I were hardly involved." Victoria's face contorted as if it did bother her that George wasn't there alone. "Why would he have to be here with someone else?"

"Not everyone knows the truth of your *arrangement* with George," their father grumbled, not holding back his distaste for those months where Victoria thought she was hiding the truth.

"Why are you so bothered by this Victoria?" said Molly.

"Doesn't it bother you?" she asked in reply.

"If George was forced to bring a girl here tonight, that makes me very happy. For many reasons."

As if the whispers of their names drew them into the room, George's grandparents, Johnathon and Viola, floated through the hall, George trailing behind with someone fairly pretty on his arm.

"Isn't that Claire?" Victoria whispered. "The girl you met, when you were trying to buy the same book?"

"Claire..." Molly studied the girl's face, trying to make it look as though she wasn't staring. Claire was beautiful, with kind eyes rimmed with dark lashes, and a quaint little pout. Molly couldn't recognize her, but the story rang true. "If it is, then I like Claire. She's a very sweet girl."

Victoria scoffed. "I do not like this *Claire*."

"You have no reason to not like her." Molly jutted her elbow into Victoria's ribs. "She's very sweet. It's too bad she's stuck with George."

"No one is ever *stuck* with George." Victoria elbowed her back. "I didn't get along with him, but whenever we were out, I ended up having a great time. He knows how to make the best of situations."

Molly left the conversation there. The Claringtons had drawn close, and it wasn't worth continuing anyways.

Johnathon Clarington had on a dazzling black tuxedo complete with shiny shoes. His beard had been trimmed and his grey waves sat atop his head nicely curled to the side. His jolly smile was all too intoxicating.

Viola Clarington was draped in a black gown with sheer sleeves and a prettied neckline that sparkled from the tear drop chandeliers above. Her silver hair was drawn away from her face, revealing the most stunning diamonds. But the way her arm entwined with her husband's proved that her most favourite accessory wasn't any of the sparkling jewels. The smile on her face as she looked up at him, deepened the creases around her eyes and lips; true signs that while her life had been filled with grief, he had given her every possible opportunity to smile.

"How wonderful to see you!" Johnathon Clarington's voice filled the hall as he called out to the Jones family. He mixed the casual greeting with common courtesy and spoke to her parents more directly.

"How are you, dear?" Viola Clarington wrapped Molly into a hug—one she returned with full force.

"I'm wonderful, how are you?"

"Just about the same." She stood back and held onto Molly's hands. "I am so sorry I missed our performance at the Charity Ball."

"Don't worry about that." Molly had almost forgotten about the performance. But with the reminder came the plethora of memories; how she'd ended up singing beside George, how it had led to so many events afterwards...

Viola must have read it all over Molly's face. She stepped in close, and her smile shifted into something sweeter than honey. "I'm sorry about other things, too," she murmured with a tilt of her head towards George, hinting she knew the full story of events that had taken place in her absence.

Swallowing a dryness in her throat, Molly nodded. "I've recovered just fine. There's no way I let boys dictate my worth."

Viola beamed before her laugh clanged off the walls. "Oh, I do love your spirit, girl! Johnathon?" She looked over her shoulder to her husband.

"Yes?" he said, holding on tightly to his jacket lapels.

"I'd like to have Molly over for tea."

"Whatever you desire, dearest."

"That is, of course, if you'd like to join me?" Viola opened the invitation with enough gentle space for Molly to decline without a fear of disappointing her.

She missed their teas, sitting by the piano, windows open to let in the early autumn breeze. Viola always shared the best stories, and Molly had always been eager to listen.

"I'll make sure George is out of our way," Viola added, eyes glimmering in promise.

"Thanks, Gran," George muttered from the background.

Molly paid him no attention. "I'd love to join you for tea."

"Marvellous!" Viola slipped her hands away and backed towards her husband. "I'll be in touch."

The room emptied out as guests made their way to their seats before the show began. Molly's excitement bubbled all through from her head to her toes. It was time to dive into a story; one of a boy who wouldn't grow up.

Chapter 26

A re you coming?" Victoria called from the aisle.

Molly smiled, her eyes still on the stage. "Go on without me, I'll find you."

Fairies. Pirates. Flying.

The audience filtered out to the hall, but Molly never left Neverland.

She made her way to the stage, captivated by the fantasy. Red curtains shimmered as she grazed her fingers against the fringes. The golden tassels glittered and shone bright, illuminating the possibility that perhaps it wasn't a stage at all. Perhaps it was a portal to Neverland itself.

Lights closed all through the auditorium.

"Oh great," Molly mumbled, holding on to the rim of the stage floor as each shuttering sound brought another blast of darkness.

She was alone in a shroud of black.

She blew out a puff of air, long and drawn out. It wasn't as if she was afraid of the dark, or what hid in the shadows. Rather, she found herself quite curious.

"Please don't scream."

The sudden sound made her do exactly that.

A groan, then, "I even said *please*."

Molly's heart thundered in her chest.

"Are you good now, Miss Jones?"

George.

She would have slapped him, if she knew where he was standing. "What do you think you're doing?"

"What do *you* think I'm doing?" His words curled with what she assumed to be a grin.

She really wanted to hit him. "You could have been anybody. A kidnapper. A murderer."

He let out a dark chuckle. The sleeve of his jacket brushed against her arm as he walked past. "Follow me."

"Why?"

"If you want to find out, then you'll need to come along," he called from a good distance away.

She stuck out her tongue and crossed her arms.

Boys were annoying. But he seemed to know where he was going, when she had no clue where the exits were. She stomped her foot and followed him. He mustn't have noticed and stopped in the middle of nowhere. She tripped over him.

His immediate grip on her arm held her up.

"Please stop making me catch you," he complained.

She tore her arm away and brushed off his touch. "As soon as you stop tripping me."

A grumble. "Hold this."

Something structured touched her hands. "What is it?"

"My hat."

"Why do you want me to hold your hat?"

"Would you rather hold my hand?"

She latched on to the hat.

"Good," he said, tugging her along. "Now you won't fall all over me."

They wove through a row of seats, heading towards a dim light that crept through the cracks of a closed door. Anything could be on the other side. Something marvellous, something terrifying, something in-between.

"Where are we?" she asked, releasing the hat as they stopped.

"Patience, Miss Jones."

He opened the door and blinding light flowed towards her as she stepped into the empty hall. She blinked until her vision returned. The little hall was lit with lanterns. Red velvet curtains hid the walls towards a small staircase that led up to a second door.

"You kidnapped me to bring me backstage?"

"I didn't kidnap you." He looked down to brush off his hat. "You came on your own."

"I thought you were leading me somewhere more exciting than this."

His eyes flicked up, igniting mischievous flares. "It's nice to know you haven't lost *all* faith in me."

"That's not what I—"

"Here you are, sir."

Molly's rebuttal was cut off by a man in a long tail coat and a grim smile. He held out a tray of champagne.

"I didn't ask for this," George quickly told the man. But when the tray wasn't removed George sighed and retrieved a glass. "The lady can get her own."

Molly stared at him, then at the bubbling glass of celebratory drink. She took it quickly, knowing beyond any doubts it would help her survive George's company.

The gentleman walked away with the empty tray, leaving them alone. Molly took her first sip, enjoyed the tingle, and turned to George.

"You kidnapped me to bring me backstage for a glass of champagne?"

Confusion etched his features, mixed with something that stole his mischief. His head lolled to the side and he rolled his eyes. "I didn't kidnap you. And there was never champagne involved."

She held up her glass and dramatically examined each bubble as it popped at the surface. "I don't suppose you could tell me what this is, then?"

"I have so many regrets right now," George droned, downing his drink and setting the empty glass on the ground. "I tried to ask you back here nicely, until you started to scream, so that didn't happen. But I didn't bring you here for a glass of champagne."

He took the steps up to the door and raked his fingers through his falling shadow dark hair. "You are owed an apology. What better place to do that"—he turned the doorknob—"than Neverland."

Molly nearly lost the grip on her glass. "What?"

George swung the door open and flipped the switch to a series of lights on the stage. She walked towards it, not believing a word he was saying until she saw it with her own eyes.

Painted trees and fountains of water. Twinkling lights and glittering backdrops. She tip-toed into the world all laid out before her.

She swung around to face him. "Are you bartering for my forgiveness?"

"I am not worthy of your forgiveness." His tone left no room for misinterpretation. "You however, are deserving of an apology."

Molly's breaths rolled in turbulent waves.

George tapped his fingers across his thumb as he found his voice. "Please know that I am very sorry, for everything I have done and did not do. If I could go back and change it, I would." He looked beyond her to the props that littered their surroundings. "I saw how you were pulled away into Neverland tonight, and I had the means to make this happen. I wasn't about to let you miss out on this because of me as well."

Molly followed his gaze to the cutouts of trees and the waves of the sea. She stared into Neverland until the sound of his footsteps brought her back.

"You're leaving?" she asked after him.

George slid his hands into his pockets while taking a step down the stairs. "Enjoy, Miss Jones."

In the final moment before he disappeared, she almost didn't want him to.

Almost.

Molly slipped her shoes off and walked across the stage. The illusion of enchanting things had her falling into the world of dreams. She set her glass of champagne with the trees in the forest and twirled towards the waves.

Her decision about his apology would come later.

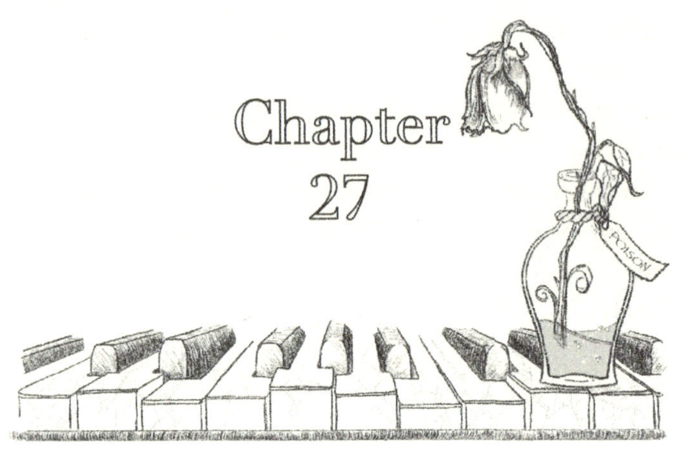

Chapter 27

Winter 1905

The Clarington Townhouse was where George had been raised, his father had grown up, and his grandparents had started their lives together. Now that it solely belonged to him, it was time to make it his own. How was that going to happen? Dragon's blood furniture.

George had always been drawn to that particular shade. It incited an inexorable sum of trouble and afforded him the opportunity to say *dragon* every once in a while. And if he stared at the colour long enough, he could remember every reason he had to lock his authentic self away.

It was an important act of the night. Soon he'd be welcoming company for an evening of listening to wedding plans.

As the grandfather clock struck on the hour, George stood away from the piano and made his way over to the sofa. It had been a long day of sewing his colours into songs; lazy yellows, blazing reds, twinkling pinks all on the backdrop of the darkest sky. Colours reminiscent of the sunrises over the Lake House. Colours that were a reprise to his earliest songs.

He stretched out onto the sofa cushions to lounge a little more comfortably. He felt more like himself in the luxuriant fabrics and trimmed lines of his suit than he had all week in his work attire. Factory clothes did nothing but scratch against his skin. Despite that and all the lectures his grandfather gave him on how to properly run a business, George worked on the factory floor more often than not. It was something he planned to do for a while.

A knock on the front door brought Edwin though the room. George closed his eyes and listened as the dear old man greeted his company. There were the voices he was expecting...and then an extra one.

He bolted straight up and strained to hear.

The door to the room burst open as Thomas rushed inside. His black hair was a mess and dripping wet.

"What did you do," George began, "jump off a boat and swim here?"

"My ship just made port actually," Thomas deadpanned. He went for the couch, ultimately unable to make it past as George grasped the sleeves of his old striped sweater.

"Am I hearing who I think I'm hearing?" George questioned.

Thomas' mouth pulled into a sideways grimace. "Yes."

He released his hold on Thomas and climbed onto the arm of the sofa, placing an ankle over the opposite knee. "She came. Why?"

Thomas sighed as his brows knit together. "Just, do us all a favour, alright? Try to be nice."

Thrumming his fingers over the tops of his legs, George contemplated announcing that he was offended by the silent accusation. "Are *you* asking me to be nice?"

"*Me?* I'm just a lowly sailor making suggestions to the captain." Thomas flung his guitar strap over his shoulder and examined the strings.

Captain. George rather liked the sound of that.

He ran the back of his fingers along the edge of his jaw. "You do realize that girl tends to have an adverse reaction to my kindness."

"I adamantly advise against whatever you're thinking."

"But why?" George pushed up to a stand and slid his hands into his pockets.

Thomas levelled him with a look as the door crashed open a second time.

Jeremy's arm was thrown around Victoria as he towered at a height that made him duck through the doorway. He smiled at his beloved who strode beside him as if she was the owner of the home.

Lingering in the doorway was Molly. A book was tucked beneath her arm, hidden in her billowing aqua sleeves. She twirled a spiral of her loose hair slowly as if savouring the sensation of it as her eyes cast to the floor.

It was unwise to tune in to such little movements or decipher what they may mean.

His hand flexed at his side.

Victoria's laughter rang through the room like tiny little warning bells.

"So," said Victoria. "The grand Clarington Gala is next weekend?"

"If you want to call it that." George fell down onto the piano bench and looked across the room to where she was sitting on one of the blood coloured chairs, curled up next to Jeremy. It was not a piece of furniture designed for two, yet somehow they both fit fine.

"Why do you always speak in riddles?" she scoffed.

"Why do you insist on conversing with me if you don't like how I speak?"

A muffled giggle turned everyone's attention towards Molly. Her eyes went wide at the attention, and she rolled her lips in. She held her fingers along her collar bone and her arm directly over her book as she played with the chain of her necklace.

"Am I not allowed to find something funny?" Molly asked with the sharpness of poison.

"What you found funny was something *George* said." Victoria cast a glare at him.

"I'm hilarious," he answered with an exaggerated grin.

"Actually," Molly roughly corrected, "it was because this is the first room I've been in since planning your wedding, where at least one person isn't afraid to upset you. It's refreshing. Despite the fact it came from him."

"Seriously?" shrieked Victoria. "You're supposed to be on my side. You're my maid-of-honour!"

Molly crossed her arms. "You've spent most of your energy these last few weeks trying to force me into getting along with him, so why are you so upset?"

"Really?" Victoria spat back. "Out of all the moments you could have chosen to get back on the same page as George, it had to be at my expense?"

"We're not on the same page," Molly replied, looking over at him.

He recognized the uncertainty in her eyes, the silent scream. His reflection often bared the same secret.

"But maybe we're in the same book," he said, only half sure of what it meant.

A smallest furling of her lips illuminated the tempestuous spirit she kept beneath the surface.

Dangerous girl.

"I can't believe this," Victoria stated pompously. "This is exactly why—"

"I hope you don't mind me interrupting," George said, half groaning. He couldn't do it. He couldn't sit still and not wonder what it was that was holding Molly back, while simultaneously listening to her sister inflict new wounds.

He rubbed at his temple. "Can we get back to the original question? The Grand Northern Ball is next weekend. Yes, my name is on the invitation as host. But before you ask anymore, I know nothing about it. My grandparents are the ones putting it together."

"Why are they putting it on in your name?" asked Jeremy, who looped his arm protectively around Victoria's shoulders.

"Something to do with initiating my official role as a Clarington in Society—whatever it is I am supposed to do." He waved off the words he didn't feel like saying. "Now, why is this relevant?"

"We want to know a few of the details. Things we should try food wise, or keep an eye out for through the night. Decorations, and music, and whatnot," Victoria sang.

"You're using *my* party to plan *your* wedding?"

Victoria lifted a shoulder and smiled in her condescending way.

George didn't find it to be worth his attention any more. Especially when he noticed Molly slip around the corner.

He combed back his hair, even though it hadn't fully fallen into his eyes, and sat back against the closed piano. Victoria and Jeremy were already in their own conversation.

"Mr Thomas," he drawled in his most lazy, authoritative voice, "would you play us a song?"

Thomas' invisible grin ticked his eyebrows just notch to the north. "Aye, *Captain*."

Chapter 28

Molly snuck into the kitchen somewhere between Victoria's attacks and the first echoing chords of Thomas' guitar playing. She dropped onto an old stool at the kitchen island and enjoyed how it swivelled from side to side. Curling up as much as she could, craving the comfort of being held close, she relaxed and opened her book.

She lifted her gold pendant away from under her blouse and dragged it across the chain. It was a gift she had bought herself, just because she wanted to, and it had quickly become one of her favourites. The little rectangular pendant reminded her of books, not only in shape but in how it opened and closed. Oftentimes she would play with the locket, allowing the rhythm to soothe her into the pages of her favourite storybook moments.

No matter how hard she tried that evening, her thoughts kept retreating to the past—somewhere lonely and overflowing with fickle dreams. Every time she tried to turn back to her most loved chapters it was hard not to wish for her own story, one where she felt the largest and most free. Not that she wouldn't be alone there as well.

"Good book?"

Molly found George walking across the kitchen towards the corner cabinets. It was quite possible he had said something.

"I'm sorry?" she asked lightly.

"The book you snuck into my house." He pointed. "Is it any good?"

"Yes," she replied, knowing it was a good book because she had read it before, not because she was currently enjoying it.

He made a noise of agreement and started rummaging through the cupboard.

His suit jacket folded around his reach in loose creases, opening just enough to show the lining, revealing blues and reds that danced their way behind the deepest black fabric, intricately woven by glistening golden thread.

"How many times have you read this novel before?" George called out next, closing the wooden door, revealing his arrogant grin.

"How did you—" Molly cut her question short, knowing the answer. "Still reading my thoughts?"

"Only a little. I can't figure out why you decided to come here tonight."

"Victoria demanded it."

His smile sliced open. "We both know Victoria couldn't force you to do anything."

"She would have been really annoying for the next few days. By coming here, I chose the lesser of evils."

"I see." He made his way to the island where she was sitting and leaned towards her with his forearms on the edge. "And I'm the lesser evil?"

Molly laid her hands over her book. Entering a standoff with him was easier than entering the story. "It's not too late for that to change."

"I don't mind being a villain, Miss Jones." He chuckled and crouched behind the counter, only his hand visible as he reached up to slide a wooden tray across the island. "I was warned to be nice this evening. But I've always been disinclined to that approach."

"Would that be why you kidnapped me, right before you apologized for being the problem?"

"Most likely."

She clicked her pendant open and closed, using the momentum to lull her reserves. "Well, it worked. I forgave you."

He stood in a flash. "Why?"

"I—" Her face pinched in confusion. "How could I not forgive you? I forgave Desmond and he didn't even apologize."

George's eyes darkened, and his lips pulled into a taunt line. "He should have."

A kettle came to a scream, stealing his attention as his face gradually softened. He poured the steaming water into a teapot that he had also prepared without her noticing, and closed the lid to let it steep.

She turned back to her book, failing to understand the sentence she had read too many times to count.

"How is Mr Darcy doing?" Mischief returned to his voice and hooked around his words.

"Excuse me?" She glared at him from beneath her lashes.

He gestured in the direction of her book before pulling out a ceramic jar. "Is he all broody in ways that make your heart flutter out of control?"

"Are you—"

"He's a bit overrated if you ask me."

"Really?" She raised her hands, flustered. "I literally *just* forgave you."

His laugh was deep and luscious, but mostly infuriating. She immersed herself back into the pages, regardless of whether or not she was getting anything from them.

The clatter of dishes rang in her ears as he collected a few, but she refused to look up. "You're unbelievable."

"How kind," was his haughty reply. "I thought you believed in everything, yet here I stand, unique in my unbelievability."

"It wasn't a compliment."

"I'm taking it as one anyways."

She wasn't going to look at him, she swore she wasn't. But as a new aroma floated her way—rich and buttery with sweet sugars and spiced cinnamon—she was drawn away from her book yet again.

At least George wasn't looking at her as he reached into the opened jar and pulled out three delicious looking biscuits. He dropped two onto a plate that had already been placed on the wooden tray and slipped the last in his mouth. He held it there as he closed the jar, not taking a bite. Then his eyes flicked up and met hers, and his smile curled around the dessert.

He slipped the biscuit between two fingers and turned towards the tea.

It was only while he grabbed the pot that he looked away, then his eyes were back on hers. He lifted the pot far higher than he needed to, pouring the deep saffron coloured tea into a cup and saucer on the tray. Never once losing Molly's eyes. Never once spilling a drop. His gaze glittered with all sorts of trouble and shone impossibly blue. The steam billowed around them, heating the air like a storm, threatening thunder and trickery.

He took a bite of the dessert at last, licking a few stray crumbs from his lips. The corners of his mouth ticked into that smirk he always seemed to wear. She hated realizing she had let her gaze drop before tracing it back up to meet his eyes.

"Is this the part where you finally leave me alone?" she asked a bit breathlessly.

"No," he responded elegantly. "This is the part where you put your ribbon back in your book."

"Why would I do that?"

"Because you're going to follow me."

Molly sat as tall as she could. "I'm fine here."

"You are my guest, Miss Jones." He lifted the tray away from the counter and walked until he stood beside her. "As long as you're in this house, you will not be allowed to settle for mere basics."

Molly glanced down at her book and then back at George. "I don't want to go out there with them right now."

"That's why I'm leading you somewhere else." He left too fast for her to argue further.

He led her down a narrow hallway to a slim excuse of a corridor. They passed several closed doors with dusty knobs and picture frames that held no photographs. Molly was too curious not to wonder about it all when George came to a stop and spun around.

"Do you mind?" he asked, holding the tray out to her.

She placed her open book beside the teapot and took the tray into her hands as he swung open an old and tired door.

On the other side was a dark room. George stepped in, fully vanishing into the shadows until a click sounded, bringing forth a faint yellow glow.

Molly walked inside and stopped in her steps.

George sighed. "I forgot how big a mess it was."

Papers, flat and crumpled, were scattered across every surface—not that there were many of those. The room resembled something more akin to a closet. A wingback chair waited in the corner, worn and obviously loved. An upright piano was clustered against the wall with a tray covered in more papers and a pair of round spectacles.

"Give me a minute, and I'll have it cleaned right up for you." George slipped off his jacket and draped it delicately across the red upholstered chair.

He collected crumpled papers and tossed them into a bin that waited beside the piano, never missing a shot.

"What is this place?" Molly shifted sideways to make room as George headed towards the piano with his loose papers.

"Um..." George tapped the papers against the roof of the piano. "I suppose it's an office of sorts."

Molly hid a smile as George lifted the round spectacles off the tray and put them on. His hair shuffled down his forehead as he examined the papers more thoroughly. He looked—no. She wouldn't allow herself to think he was adorably boyish.

"An office?"

"It's where I've been composing songs." He placed the stack of papers on the piano before collecting more to examine.

"I didn't realize you wrote them down."

"I don't." He switched between two papers in his hands and quickly pulled the glasses off his nose. He looked towards where more papers had slid beneath the chair and rushed over to pick them up.

"If you don't write down your songs, then what are all the papers?" she wondered aloud as he crouched to the floor to scavenge under the chair.

He grinned and flicked his hair back as he sat back on his calves. "An anniversary gift for my grandparents. It'll be fifty years. I'm writing this song down so Gran can play it whenever, or if-ever, she so chooses."

He stood once he was satisfied he had collected every last sheet and went back to the piano.

"I'm not sure I follow."

"It's simple, really." He swung the spectacles back on and held out the new sheet music before his eyes, pulling it closer to his face and then extending it as far as he could. "They told me not to get them any gifts. And there's nothing I could buy them that they wouldn't already have. My grandfather asked me to get a wife instead." George smiled and looked at her over the brim of his glasses. "I'm hoping a song will suffice."

Molly suppressed a giggle. "And the spectacles—are those new?"

He pushed them back up and focused on the written music. "They're my grandfather's. Something about wearing them helps me decipher which way the song needs to go." He pulled the paper as close to his eyes as possible. "But I never remember if they make things bigger or smaller."

He placed two sheets of paper on the piano's front and raked his hair off his face before sitting on the bench. "Feel free to sit down," he called without looking her way. "I need to see which one of these sheets is the one I want to keep."

Molly sat on the red plush chair, balancing the tray on her lap as George settled his fingers over the keys and entered into his song. Piano notes tingled off the walls, gradually spinning together into a brilliant melody.

Lazuli blues, tepid greys, entrancing blacks.

The colours flitted in an elegant dance, flourishing into bolder hues.

Shadows unfolded into scarlet reds and mesmerizing pinks, both glimmering against the backdrop of mellow citrines.

There was peace and joy and hope. Each building upon the other in a crescendo of possibilities.

The first rays of sun, yellow as bright as fresh aspirations.

Luscious red, slashing through the sky, as daring as dawn.

A speckle of flirtatious pink, sparkling as soft as the first gaze from a lover.

All the finest things to wake up to...

The room drifted into silence.

"I think that's the one." George nodded and slipped one page aside, leaving the other where it was before turning around to face her. "Thank you for your patience."

Molly was too stunned to speak. George waited for a response that wasn't coming.

"Miss Jones?"

"I'm sorry." She shook her head and faced the tray of treats in her lap, using her hair as a curtain. She lifted her tea and held the delightful cup in her hands. The warmth was revitalizing, reminding her how to function.

George scrubbed a hand over his mouth. "If there's something wrong with the song, I'm going to need you to tell me what it is."

"There was nothing wrong; I think your grandparents will love it," she confirmed, sipping her first taste of tea. "It felt like waking up in the morning."

She tried the biscuits next. They were buttery and sweet, drizzled with chocolate. Molly felt like a little girl as the crumbs fell down her chin.

She caught George watching her. "What is it?"

He put the glasses on top of the piano and rubbed his eyes with his fingers. He looked back up, steeling her with a look that could have been frightful if it hadn't been so dashing. "That was exactly what the song was about. Surely, it's just a coincidence."

"Surely," she squeaked, opting to take an extra sip of tea.

He leaned away and spun back to the piano, shaking a trembling hand through his hair before hovering it over the keys.

Molly focused on her tea.

A few notes played before he turned to her again. "We should confirm though, yes?"

"I suppose..." Though really she didn't, because she didn't fully comprehend where the coincidence was.

He nodded without looking at her and dropped his fingers.

Sparkling silvers. Dazzling blues. Crystal whites, iridescently glittering over a blank canvas of transcendent clear gems.

Building and then dropping off, climbing and dropping away. They spun in glorious swirls, racing with no finish line before they were building and dropping once more.

Enchanting floating dust, falling all around. Coating each musical embrace with twinkling wonders...

George eagerly spun to face her, watching closely as he crossed his arms over his lap.

Molly shook her head. That song, as beautiful as it was, felt unlike anything she knew.

Each line of his muscles relaxed. "Oh good. It was just a coincidence." He puffed out a breath of air. "You have no idea how much better I feel."

"I'm happy to help." She smiled into her cup of tea. "What was that song about?"

"Ice skating."

Molly marvelled. "Really?"

"Yes."

"You made it sound magical."

George tipped his chin in a thankful motion. "Has it been a while since you've skated?"

"I've never actually been." Molly placed her empty tea cup down and spun the last biscuit around its plate.

"When you were younger?"

"Nope." She loved the idea of it, however. "Not even once, in my entire life."

George eased into a smile, one soft around the edges, sharp in-between, and all kinds of wonderful. It disappeared as quickly as it came.

He cleared his throat. "Well, that means we haven't proved much of anything then, have we?"

"I must admit, I have no idea what you're going on about."

"Allow me to explain." George skid across the piano bench until one half of it was free. "Come. Sit."

"Beside you?"

"We can't leave any space for misinterpretation," he confirmed, turning towards the ivory keys.

It certainly was a curious request. She placed the tray onto the chair as she left it behind.

Her skirt fluttered around her ankles during the descent beside him, the sensation reminiscent to floating, as though gravity had become a fragment of the imagination.

"The piano..." George pattered his fingers against the keys to make tender sounds. "It's like a vessel. One that can take you anywhere you want to go."

"Go?" It felt like a glittering promise. "It could take us anywhere in the world?"

"Not just this world." His eyes met hers, searching and vulnerable all at once. "Any world you could dream of."

Molly reached for her pendant, flipping it open as sweet melodic notes filled the room. The song twirled with twinkling energy, spinning into itself, holding her close. Shimmering lights crossed behind her closed eyelids until they dispersed into something calming and kindly predictable, in a perfectly whimsical way. It was somewhere she imagined she could have stayed for a long time.

The music came to an immediate halt.

"I should go," George announced, jumping away from his place and rushing to retrieve his jacket from the chair.

He swung it through the air, looping it around his arms so they swiftly fell into the appropriate places. He flipped his collar, laying it perfectly around his shoulders and down the front. Patting up and down and checking all his pockets, his hands froze, and he looked towards her with the most quizzical expression.

"Did you forget something?" she asked, reading him as best she could.

George pulled out his pocket-watch and spun the chain around his hands before tucking it away.

"I think I may have," he finally said.

One foot graced over his other as George hurried to the door. He grasped for the handle, his gaze flicking over to her one last time. Then he disappeared into the hall and closed the door.

Molly sat on the bench for a while, working through what had happened. Nothing made much sense.

She stood and took three nimble steps back to the waiting chair. The centre of the cushions had faded to a soft pink where the edges were still a vibrant red, signalling the chair had been around for a while. Molly grazed her fingers across the seams before moving the tray and sitting down.

With a content breath, she laid her head against the wing. For a while she'd get to escape from planning a wedding she was expected to help with, but was never allowed to. She could dive into her book or simply sit in silence and dream. The best part was, she didn't even feel like she had to choose. Her hair rolled into loose swirls off her shoulder as she drew her legs up to curl them beneath her.

Molly stared at the crinkled balls of paper that George had tossed into the bin. They resembled frilly bubbles in the aftermath of a large wave. Perfectly marvellous.

Chapter 29

The whistle blew, and everyone got to work. Blasted whistle, making stupid sounds, pushing them to start the day whether they were ready or not. Perhaps that was something George could change when he took charge of the factories.

"You seem a bit distracted," Thomas yelled over the noise of the busy factory floor. "Tough night?"

George could tell it was a joke, one made at his expense. He closed his eyes and went to carrying things to the conveyer belts. "No life lessons, Thomas. Not today."

"So it *was* rough?" This time, Thomas yelled in concern.

"I don't know what it was," George stated over his shoulder, loud enough to be heard over the roar of the machinery. He tripped over a pipe that had fallen on the floor, and kicked it away.

"Might it have something to do with how you disappeared for a while?" Thomas handed him a stack of metals and turned to watch as George placed it across the slicing path of the conveyer.

George knew he needed to own up to the thing that unsettled him the most. "I played the piano."

Thomas didn't necessarily look shocked, but there was a new tenseness across his shoulders, so he was at least surprised. "With Molly there?"

George scrunched his face. "I believe—and I could be wrong about this—I played it *for* her. On purpose."

It made even less sense when he said it out loud. He turned back to his task, whatever that was.

Thomas blinked. "Are you being serious? Or are you doing that thing where you are only appearing serious but there's an underlying joke I'm not catching?"

"There is no joke." He wished there was.

Thomas faded into silence. George hated silences. He tried to focus on carrying their piles to the blades.

"I think you know why you shared it with Molly," Thomas eventually said.

George dropped his pile onto the belt and straightened it as best as he could, making sure it was perfected.

He was hoping for a better explanation, an epiphany, a strike of lightning, or other such things. Instead, it was something that battled for release, something locked away in one of his boxes, one he'd lost the key to.

"George!!" Thomas screamed, but not within enough time.

White, blinding spots smothered his vision. Seeping sinister red poured over him with the most excruciating pain. He knew he hadn't moved away from his pile before his hand had met the slashing machine.

The entire world went black.

Somewhere in the dark...

Tick...

George curled in on himself for days without respite.
He was left with the visceral roars of the beast. The relent-
lessness of passing time.
Torment laid siege to every wall, every refuge he'd ever
known.

Tick...

No more music. No more colours.
Not even his old friends the shadows.

Tock.

Chapter 30

The luring magic of the frost drew Molly away from her family. Every tower of the Northern Estate glistened in the light of a thousand stars shining through the thin spaces between the heavy grey clouds that promised snow. Molly tiptoed to where the ice-brimmed bricks on the round towers met the glass panes of the Clarington's conservatory. Something marvellous cuddled in the corner.

Hidden by a collection of crystallized droplets, leaning against the warmth from the greenhouse, a rosebush continued to blossom. One bloom held tight to its bright petals, staying vibrant against all odds. Little buds even tried to poke through; kissed by a series of happy accidents.

"Molly!" Victoria called from around the corner. "Come on!"

Molly cupped her hands around the roses in a soft embrace, wishing bravery to the winter blossoms.

She lifted her glittering skirt, hurrying to catch up with her family who had begun to climb the stairs at the grand entrance.

Everything was grand; the sculpted railings, the carpet that had been laid out, the flickering lampposts and lanterns along the way. It all glowed like a fairytale.

"What were you doing?" Victoria sounded less than amused, holding her gown up to ascend the steps. "Do you know how long I've been itching to come to one of the Clarington's Balls? Now that mother is venturing out of the house, we have a chance to be here. Please, don't mess it up."

Molly summoned all her grace to climb the stairs behind her sister. "It's far more magical tonight than I remember from last time."

Victoria gave her a quick, sympathetic glance. "That's because Desmond isn't here."

She should have expected that to be the detail Victoria latched onto.

"Maybe there is someone here who will *actually* kiss you tonight." Victoria suggestively wiggled her brows.

Molly tried not to grimace. "If anyone here so much as thinks about kissing me, I'm going to hit them."

"It's a party. You sneak around for some secret kisses. What's wrong with that?"

Their father theatrically cleared his throat, sending Victoria a glare over his shoulder as their mother snickered.

Johnathon and Viola Clarington stood at the top of the procession line, greeting their guests. They were adorned in matching tones of the most luxuriant berries, their smiles shining beams of light as everyone approached.

"It's so lovely you all came," Viola said kindly.

Johnathon nodded to the whole family. "I do apologize on behalf of my grandson, who was unable to greet you tonight."

Molly's parents made quick comments on how there was no need to apologize, and after being wished a happy time, they made their way fully into the home.

"See," Victoria whispered as they checked their coats. "Even George knows the importance of sneaking away at parties."

"You think he's getting some secret kisses?" Molly tried not to laugh or catch the attention of their father who had seemed increasingly unimpressed with the conversation.

Victoria shrugged. "I don't see why not. It's his party. It would've been foolish for him not to lean the guest list in his favour."

Molly fluttered out her gown to add life into the ice blue layers. She felt like she had walked out of a fantasy. Hooped gossamer sleeves slid down her arms and twirled around her torso into shimmering layers. Delicate blossoms in shades of aqua danced along the sweetheart neckline and into her sleeves. Her skirt reminded her of ocean waves with teardrop shapes edged in silver glitter.

"How do you not have anything to say about this?" Victoria snapped.

Molly dropped her skirt and crossed her arms. She hadn't even been aware they were still discussing anything. "You care about kissing George too much. Almost as though you've kissed him yourself."

Victoria looked horrified. "I have never! Nor will I ever."

Oh, but Molly could see all of the proof. It was in the ever-deepening blush that spread across her sister's nose, the way she spoke too fast with a voice too high, and her quick steps to distance herself.

"I'm off to find Jeremy." Victoria raised her chin and spun around. "Your notion of me kissing George is completely ridiculous. It's making me feel ill."

Molly inwardly promised herself to bring the conversation back up at just the right time.

She travelled further into the home—unaccompanied by anyone who could steal the magic away. The Northern Estate was decorated with such spectacular detail that every hall to every room sang out with the power of granted wishes. However, it was the ballroom that brought the enchantment out in full force.

Clusters of winter flowers hung across the ceiling, embracing the ribbons of tulle strung in waves along the walls. Couples twirled on the dance floor to the most spectacular orchestra. New gentlemen asked new ladies to dance, filling their futures with the possibility of happily-ever-afters. Molly weaved through the crowd, sharing smiles with strangers and making up her own little stories of who they possibly were.

She made it to the tables that sat by the far wall. Each one was filled with towers of edible delicacies. Fancy trays carried tiny sandwiches, petite cakes, and freshly trimmed fruits.

She picked out a plate with a frilly pastry that looked absolutely divine, but proved to be less than satisfactory. She spit out the remnants into her napkin and finished off a cake instead.

Reaching across for a shimmering glass of champagne, Molly went to place her empty plate down, tipping it accidentally onto a gentleman next to her—although, when she got a better look at him, he was no gentleman at all.

"Sorry." Molly reigned in a heavy apology and stared at his sleeve where the secret habitants of her napkin had leaked.

"You're *sorry?*" He angrily brushed away at his sleeve, face turning red in the process. "Out of all the girls I could have run into at this table, it had to be you?"

Molly was less than happy about it herself.

His close companion patted a hand on his shoulder. "I'll catch up with you soon, Boris."

"Right," Boris grumbled, downing an entire glass of champagne. His sharp jawline and artistically carved features were just a bit too perfect to be truly attractive, even if he was one of the most handsome men in the room.

Molly sipped from her glass, twirling its stem between her fingers, hoping he'd disappear soon enough.

"Where's your friend?" Boris grumbled, acknowledging her again. "Shouldn't he be here, protecting you like always?"

Molly had to surmise he was talking about George. "I don't need anyone to protect me, in case you forgot." She hid her smile behind her champagne glass. "Also, George isn't in this room."

"Of course he isn't. He's just the host, why should he be here at all?"

"So angry, Boris. Maybe you should find something that will make you feel better."

"They all seem to be busy at the moment." He stared out to at least three different girls.

"I'm sure you'll figure out a way to sneak them to hidden places to get your secret kisses soon enough." Molly finished off her drink and set it on a passing tray.

"Don't worry, you won't be one of them."

She released a bitter laugh. "I'd rather spend the rest of my life alone, then spend even a dance of it with you."

"Good. That's most likely how you'll end up."

Her jaw dropped. "Pardon me?"

"It seems you heard just fine." Boris finished wiping his sleeve, dropping the soiled napkin to the floor as he walked towards a circle of unsuspecting maidens.

Molly wanted to follow him, ruin his chances with any of them. But as Boris joined their group, their stares turned towards her—just as scornful as Boris' had been.

His words struck deeper in her chest.

He could be right. After all, she'd once felt safe and worthy of love...

Her eyes squeezed shut to remove the visions. The girl she had been around Desmond couldn't have sparkled as ferociously as her current self. And she would never auction off bits of herself just to be loved again.

She forced open her eyes and allowed her gaze to linger high over the twirling couples to the dark night beyond the windows. A soft flutter of white passed down, catching the light. Then another, and another.

Molly took off, running along the wall to the nearest doorway. She journeyed through the halls, not completely sure where she was going until she caught sight of a very large fireplace through a lofty doorway.

Far away from the party, the room waited quietly, only filled with the sound of her footsteps and heartbeat. She passed the hearth and the logs piled up neatly beside it, remembering Desmond... And Boris' accusation.

Molly kept walking, craving an escape.

The library greeted her like a realm of fresh dreams. Dimly lit by the lanterns flickering from outside, everything was faintly illuminated. Towering windows stretched along the wall, complete with sills deep enough to jump into.

She lifted her skirts and took the giant step up. She pressed her hands onto the glass and peered out into the breathtaking snowstorm. Her head fell gently against the stone archway, watching the snowflakes as they cascaded down without a care in the world.

"I should have assumed you'd find your way here once it started snowing," came a voice from the shadows.

Chapter 31

Molly gripped the stones and peeked out into the room, her dress trailing to the floor as she leaned backwards.

George looked out from his seat in the windowsill next to her. "Are you enjoying your evening?"

"I'm having a wonderful time," she lied through a wavering smile. Though, she had been having a wonderful time, until Boris.

She turned back to the snow, watching flakes float past on the light breeze as the world became covered in twinkling dust. Molly pressed her fingertips against the window as her breath fogged the glass. She drew a rose and watched as it faded away. Half of her reflection stared back at her, it too fading with the flickering light from the outdoor lampposts.

She didn't feel like watching things fade anymore and peered over to look at George.

He sat with his legs bent to his chest, a hand in his pocket and the other dangling towards the floor. Locks of dark hair fell like flowing ink, looping at the tips near his eyes and around his ears. He didn't bother to brush it back into place. His suit was made of midnight fabric, featuring grey embellishments on the waistcoat. He was a treasure trove of nightmares.

"I'm sorry I'm not better company," he said, slowly looking her way.

There was something sinister lurking in the undertones of his voice, carving out raw patches where it fell flat. It matched the darkness in his eyes and the slump of his shoulders.

Her feet lowered to the floor as she sat against the window's frame. The teardrop layers of her gown fluttered up, casting off bits of glitter into the air. "You're actually the best company I've had all night."

"I hope that's not true."

She laid her head against the bricks and combed the curtain of tangled hair behind her ear. "Why would you assume you're not good company?"

"I just returned from visiting Desmond."

Oh.

"I may have yelled at him," he admitted. "And then I may have told him I loved him. Quite frankly, I'm not sure what's worse."

She laughed, a fluttering sound that pinned his attention to her.

His eyes brightened.

Molly read past their shine. "Will you tell me what your actual reason is?"

George swung his feet on the ground and peered down at his left hand. He observed it thoroughly, watching the lines in his palm as if he were savouring their very existence. He stretched his fingers out and back in again before dropping it away.

His right hand remained in his pocket.

As his stare turned out to the dark library, gripping onto the individual aisles, he let out a laboured breath. His shoulders fell with his expression. He didn't look her way as he revealed what should have been his second hand.

She gasped.

White bandages peeked out from beneath his sleeve, covering from his wrist to the tips of his fingers, too thick for him to move his hand at all.

"George..."

"I don't want to talk about it."

Molly sprung out from her seat and made her way over to him. "You don't get to not talk about it."

He made a low sound. "It's nothing."

"What a blatant lie," she reprimanded. For some unknown reason, she was angry. Angry that it had happened in the first place. Angry she hadn't noticed sooner.

She lifted his hand in her own, tracing where only the tops of his fingers were seen. Swollen, bruised, and a stark contrast to the white wrappings. "What happened?"

"An accident at work." He slipped out of her fingers and hid the evidence behind him.

"What about the piano?"

"There isn't much of that anymore."

She twisted a glittered tear of her gown between her fingers, feeling the crisp sparkles coat her fingers. "But it's the piano."

George stood from the window seat silently, shrugging as if it didn't matter.

"It's the piano, George." She thought back to the evening at his house, when he'd played for her in his little secret office. His melodies nourished him, held him steady, and kept him whole. Without them...

"The doctors are hopeful," he answered before she could ask. "But there is no absolute."

All it would take was one more step. One step and there would be no distance between them. He wouldn't have to suffer it alone; she'd be there with him, for him.

Piercing echoes of laughter came from the adjacent room.

"My grandparents must be giving a tour." George's eyes widened as he looked over her shoulder. "We can't be caught like this."

Molly nodded absentmindedly. She took in the books on the shelves and the oak cases that held them. She looked at the worn floors and the fringes of the carpets.

"Miss Jones?"

"I'm fine." She faced him again.

Voices trailed through the hallway, past the forbidding fireplace, and into the library.

George shot a quick glance in their direction, turning back to Molly with a worried brow as he took a hesitant step back. "Will you be staying here?"

She looked out the towering windows and watched the snow fall towards the earth, swirling around in the winter winds. There was no reassurance to be found. She turned back to him and was transported back in time.

It was a night she frequented in her dreams, standing and watching as someone walked away. The visions always came back in crashing waves. Some were easy to ride over, others filled her lungs and didn't permit a single breath until it rolled past.

The unknowing guests grew louder.

Molly egged George away, gesturing loosely with her hands so he knew he was fine to go. He spun around to leave and the wisp of his flaring jacket caught a faint light and spun the room into shifting memories.

Bookshelves became imposing pillars, larger than trees. The long carpet flowed like creek waters across the wooden floor, rippling the room into twisted fairytales.

It was no longer George who was walking away.

It was happening again.

Molly gripped the front of her gown, wishing to quiet her heart, holding herself steady and demanding the room to return as it was.

She squeezed her eyes shut and was tossed into the midst of the current, tumbling towards the depths.

An arm roped around her shoulders and pulled her out.

George.

He'd come back.

Molly scurried at his side as they ducked beyond the first two aisles of bookshelves. Her pattering footsteps felt too loud, her entire self felt too hot, and her breaths barely managed to keep up with their race into the shadows.

The distant voices were no longer so distant.

Molly peeked over her shoulder, stealing a glance at the silhouettes on the floor. There had to be at least a dozen people in the library behind them.

George released her and reached towards the end of the bookcase in front of him. There was a click as he pulled the wall out. "Hurry."

She walked inside the shelves, consumed immediately by blackness and the scent of hidden bricks and brittle wood. George entered behind her and slid the plank back into place, shutting them away.

"Where are we?" she wondered into the dark.

"An old tunnel. It used to lead to the North Tower, but it's closed off now."

The idea of being inside a secret passageway should have sent Molly's imagination to the stars, thrilling her with the mystery. But reality crashed down, cramping her hands into fists. If they were caught, there would be no fighting the inevitable away. A ruined reputation would land her a life she didn't want. Forever. *Old... Alone... Unloved...*

A draughty apartment that leaked during inclement weather, where stray cats would creep through the window to chew at her books. Or being banished from her home, forced to reside in a governess's room with her cousin's family, raising his children and never being afforded the opportunity to have her own. She could be forced to get married.

George's hand clasped over her mouth. "They may not be able to see us, but they could hear us."

Molly had no idea how much she had said aloud.

George brought his face beside hers. "I won't ask you to calm down, but to avoid the consequences you just laid out, it's imperative to keep any noise to a faint whispering." His hand lifted away. "Do you think that's something you can do?"

She slowly nodded.

He leaned against the wall beside her and rolled to the side. His jacket brushed against the stones, bringing the hush of falling dust clouding the air.

"Why did you come back?" she whispered.

"I saw you. I couldn't leave."

The visions remained. The apartment, the cats, living in someone else's home. She'd be a part of a family, but it would never be her own. And then her shoulders shuddered as she imagined being married off to an old man that she didn't know; one desperate to marry. Bile rose and burned the back of her throat.

Multiple sets of footsteps headed in their direction, echoing voices drifting down the alley of bookshelves.

"It was around here somewhere, wasn't it Johnathon?" came Viola's chipper voice.

"I believe so, my dearest," Johnathon replied.

"Over here," Viola added, approaching even closer. "There was an old tunnel, hidden inside one of the shelves. It'd be quite lovely if we could find it."

Molly had to collect herself. She set her shoulders back, forcing herself to believe in her own determination.

Knocks blasted against the wooden shelves beside them. She barely held back a frightened squeak and leapt backwards, bumping into George.

Pounding blasted in front of them, and they both startled.

Molly's thoughts thundered.

Old... Alone... Unloved...

She closed her eyes as George's fingers brushed her arm.

"I'm sorry," he murmured, "I know our predicament is far worse now than if I had just left."

The crowd beyond the books pressed closer, filling the little hidden space with the scrubbing sounds of books being slid recklessly around or dropped to the floor.

She drew in a calming breath. "It doesn't matter."

"Of course it matters."

"It never has."

Loud knocking battered in front of them, sending her pulse jumping.

George's arm wrapped around her, and she sunk back into his embrace, willing herself to dream that there was still hope.

"It'll be fine," she assured herself, just loud enough for him to benefit. "I'll find a way to change my dreams. Even if the worst happens right now, I'll figure it out. There's no sense in worrying over being alone, or waiting for someone to love me, when no one cares to know who I am anyways."

"That's not fair."

It wasn't. She didn't want to believe it was true either.

Books clattered to the floor, and she jolted back against him. The intruders kept searching, hammering on shelves nearby. It was only a matter of time before they were found.

George tilted his head over her shoulder. "I know you."

She closed her eyes as his hold around her tightened.

"I know how you take your tea in the morning and your favourite books."

"Those are trivial things."

His thumb brushed against the tips of her sleeves, the rough fabric from the bandages gently scraping against her gown as he pulled her in further. "Whenever you have tea, you hold it for a while, enamoured by the prelude as much as you are for that first taste." The smooth and luscious lustre of his voice sent glittering sparks along Molly's skin. "On days when you're not feeling quite right, you reread your favourite novels, skimming through the pages until you get to your favourite scenes, where you sit and dream for as long as it takes to feel better."

A sliver of light flowed through the slits of wood, bright enough to illuminate his eyes. They locked onto her.

"I can tell how you're feeling just from the sound of your voice or the rhythm of your breaths. So I knew from the moment you smiled by the library windows that you were not having a wonderful time, even though you said otherwise. Because when you truly smile, your eyes resemble a sunrise; bright and colourful, and unafraid of darkness."

Silence enveloped them, held them together with half shared secrets and forbidden stories. It was more than enough, more than addicting, bringing her thoughts to a lull as she nestled into his arms.

"I *was* having a wonderful time," she clarified softly. "Until Boris—"

"Boris?!"

"Did you hear that?" A scratchy voice crept closer to the wall George and Molly hid behind.

"Hear what?" said a second outside voice.

"I thought I heard a noise coming from over here."

Padded footfalls and the clicking of fancy footwear approached their secret corner.

"What sort of noise?"

"Just a regular noise."

"Are you certain?"

"Well..."

Exasperated sighs filled the corridor, and Molly hoped it meant they would stop searching.

She spun around in George's loosened grasp, seeing he had dropped his head against the brick wall and closed his eyes.

"If the worst should happen," he muttered, "can we blame Boris?"

"Yes."

His lips hooked into a grin, something soft and hazy, like lingering remnants of the sweetest dreams. She smiled and laid her head down on his jacket. She could hear the beat of his heart, the constant drum, the fortress harbouring his deepest secrets.

It was easier to blame Boris, than it was to admit that *the worst* no longer seemed like a possibility. Somehow, they'd stumbled into a little world; alone yet together. A world of escape from sobering seasons. A world of winter gardens, where a bit of warmth was all it took to help flowers bloom. A world of serendipitous roses.

"It sounds quiet out there." George dropped his arms away and slinked along the wall towards the exit. He pressed an ear to the wood. "I think my grandparents escorted everyone out."

"We're safe?"

He pushed open the secret door and stepped into the faint light of the library. "We're free."

She stepped up to the main floor, watching as he slid the plank of wood back into place.

They walked back to the large windows in silence; Molly captured by the snowy scene once again. The snow added a touch of magic, a bit of wonder, and all the glamour that it always did.

"Forgive me," George said. "I need to get going in order to switch into a new suit. I'm covered in an incriminating amount of glitter."

He certainly was. Even the distant lights caught every sparkle against the fabric. He lit up like the night's sky.

"Sorry," she replied, knowing she looked nowhere near sorry.

"Don't be. If I hadn't promised my grandparents I'd at least *try* to mingle tonight, I wouldn't be bothering."

"So you're no longer avoiding your lovely guests?"

His smile stretched wide. "I'm not sure I escaped my lovely guests at all."

A breath whooshed out of her, despite her need for it. A man like him needed to come with a map; one with clearly marked plot twists and possible dangers. "Your casual flirtations will get you nowhere with me."

"Now I'm curious." He dropped into a lean against the wall between the windows. "Where do you think I want them to take me?"

Her cheeks heated. "The sorts of places all gentlemen at parties wish their flirtations to take them."

"And that is..?"

"Abandoned rooms and secret kisses."

"Dare I state the obvious?" He spun a finger through the air, gesturing to the empty library as his grin shifted into something more villainous.

She swallowed, and her eyes tracked how his gaze followed the sound.

His eyes shot back to hers, and he stood away from the wall.

"Well," he said, flaring his hands through the air. "I really must be off."

She nodded.

He backed towards the door, not turning away from her.

"Thank you," she called before she could think better of it.

The smile in his eyes flickered back to life. "For..."

"Keeping our tradition." She grasped her hands together and lifted her shoulders. "It's become a habit for you to sneak me away places."

His wispy laugh made their little world feel even smaller. It sent her heart rate into tiny frantic bubbles.

"Tell me, Miss Jones," he said, voice smokey and drawn out. "Do you enjoy being one of my secrets?"

Molly watched as he swiftly exited the room. She couldn't feel anything beneath her feet as she climbed back into the window.

Shimmering flakes fell gently onto the glass. The snow, it seemed, was determined to lure her into trouble all winter long.

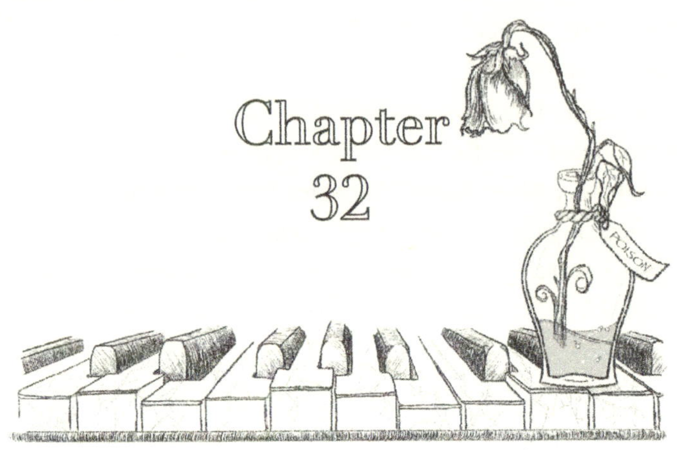

Chapter 32

George flicked a pencil between his fingers, forcing it to hit against his desk in a solid beat. He tossed the pencil away, hearing it tumble to the floor and roll into a dusty corner. He'd been working on rhythm for weeks, pushing his fingers to their limits with little to show for it.

He inspected his right hand where the bandage met his skin. He could still feel the brush of Molly's fingers as she chastised him. He could hear her voice, see the frustration crease her brows and a colour spread across the apples of her cheeks.

It shouldn't have made him smile, but it did. He shouldn't be thinking about Molly. But he was.

More often—*too* often—they had found themselves in each others company. During evenings of wedding planning where Victoria and Jeremy were the only ones allowed to participate. In crowded rooms with too many people doing too many things. Beside starlit carriages while waiting for certain family members to say adieu. George and Molly discovered a place that was only theirs. Or perhaps, they had never escaped the dusty space behind the overpacked bookshelves. The unrelenting chord strung between them drew stolen glances and secret smiles; communication in its simplest and most dangerous form.

George picked up the next pencil and decided to try the rhythm again, this time slower, more concrete, steady.

The pencil snapped in his fingers.

Thomas knocked on the door. "How many pencils have been injured this time?"

George relaxed back and cradled his head into laced fingers. He swivelled in his chair to take in the unsightly scene of discarded pencils on the floor. "A few."

Thomas grunted. "Don't you have a meeting in twenty minutes?"

"Yes!" George clapped and stood up, thriving on the sting that flared across his palm at the sudden contact. "It is time for me to annoy the old men who run the business behind my pretty face." He picked up the pair of cufflinks he'd recently purchased, slipping them into place. They were the only ones he could wear, the only ones his fingers allowed him to use.

"Then how come you haven't mailed those letters yet?" Thomas motioned to the stack of unmarked envelopes.

George looked to the clock. "I have more than enough time to run to the post office and make it back for the meeting."

Thomas posed his questions in heavy brows.

George chuckled and grabbed his jacket off the nearby hook, swinging it around his shoulders. "Five minutes there, five minutes back, ten minutes to sit down and contemplate all my poorly made life choices, followed by an excruciatingly long hour or so at a table with a bunch of men who would much rather have me out of sight—let alone out of the business entirely."

Thomas rolled his eyes. "Your ideas have propelled this company forward. The safety measures you've implemented on the factory floor have increased productivity. You should tell them about the results we've seen so they stop tearing you apart."

George shrugged and scooped the letters up. "If I pretend to not have feelings, then I won't actually *have* any. They don't need to know the truth."

Thomas looked less convinced. "That's not how that works. At all."

George winked and left the room.

He took the stairs two or three at a time, envisioning each plane of wood as if they were piano keys, each thud of his steps a base note to a song he couldn't play. He jumped into the main lobby, flinging his scarf around his neck as he spun his back to press the door open and flip on his hat.

The streets were crusted with refrozen slush, greyed by the passing life. Smoke stacks billowed out their clouds, filling the air with a thickened smog. George blended into the crowd with his polished shoes and charcoal wool jacket. He didn't mind coasting through the smoke; the ambience made him feel mysterious and that was always fun.

He made it to the post office in exactly five minutes. He scrubbed the soles of his shoes onto the welcome carpet and brushed off his coat as best he could with the limits of his bandage, then looked around the building.

Patrons completed various tasks. Women were adorned in blacks and greys and browns, in hats tall or short or round, next to men in the shapes of them all. But in amongst the sea of people, there was one who stood out brighter than the rest. She was impossible to miss, even sheltered behind a broad gentleman in a tan coat and matching hat. George knew him, barely, but enough to know he was in fact a gentleman. What proved it was true, was that Molly was with him.

Her hair was tied into a loose braid with a soft blue ribbon. A few curls fell loose and framed her face, sheltering the depths of her eyes so he couldn't truly decipher her expression. She gripped an envelope in one hand, her other busy tugging at the buttons on her coat.

George made his way past them, disregarding how she wore his favourite colour in a way that made it look entirely new. Not dragon's blood, but the fathomless vibrance of rosebuds right before they bloomed.

He stepped up to the counter, ready to keep it all behind him.

"You're George Clarington aren't you?" the attendant behind the desk asked a little too happily.

"I am," he grumbled.

The man ticked the inside of his cheek. "Shame what happened to your father. Good man."

George fought against the words raging inside. *Them.* What happened to *them.* James Clarington happened to be the least good of all.

"You'll have to fill these out at the designated table." The attendant pointed to where Molly was standing next to… George allowed the list of names he had compiled to fall through his memory. Christopher. Molly and Christopher.

He turned back to the man who was trying to help him. "Is Henry here? He's been helping me fill these out."

"He'll be back soon if you don't mind waiting."

"How long might he be?"

"A few minutes, possibly sooner."

Possibly wasn't good enough; there wasn't time to waste. He spun around and adjusted his hold on the envelopes before discarding them onto the table at the opposite end of where Christopher and Molly stood. The papers slid across the wooden top and would need to be resorted. He went to adjusting them to his best abilities, all the while taking good advantage of a perfect eavesdropping opportunity.

"I can ask Victoria about getting a formal invitation sent to you," said Molly.

"You think she would do that?"

"I think she owes it to me."

"Why, you haven't changed at all, have you?" Christopher asked.

George peeked up just in time to catch Molly's grin, a bit too pointed to be kind, and with all sorts of mischief in the corners.

"That's not exactly true," she replied, earning a less than satisfactory chuckle from Christopher.

George folded in his bottom lip to keep from making any noise of agreement and stared down at his penmanship. It was not up to par with what his best efforts usually provided. His left hand wasn't quite dignified yet, despite the weeks of practice. He glanced at the time. He could still make it back for the council meeting, as long as he kept working.

"It was nice to see you again, Molly." Christopher backed away from the counter and tipped his hat.

"I'll be in touch," she said, watching as he left the building.

George really tried to hold back. Or maybe he didn't. It was getting harder to decipher in her presence. Nevertheless, he found himself speaking. "Found yourself a date to your sister's wedding, did you?"

Molly looked at him through the corner of her eyes. "It's rude to listen to conversations you weren't invited into."

George filled out his final envelope, keeping most of his focus on her. "It was very entertaining."

She dropped her head into her waiting palm, her cheek pushed up with her fingers, increasing the pink of her winter blush. "It's just, Christopher is so..." Her lips swirled to the side. "Well, he happens to be very..."

"Gentlemanly," George offered, lifting his envelopes and ready to leave as soon as she finished her thought. But she remained silent. "Handsome? Romantic? Well-read?"

"Completely and utterly *boring*." Molly's face scrunched up. "He spent the last few minutes explaining how the post works. As if I don't already know!" She gestured around the room. "Do I look like a girl who doesn't know how to mail a letter?"

George noted the small cream envelope that she twirled around in her grasp. "A little."

Her shock was wiped away by her melodic laugh. "Why would you say that?"

His smile was instantaneous. "You've done nothing with the letter in your hands. Surely someone who knows how to mail it would've already done so."

"This is different."

George examined her handwriting and recognized part of the address. "A letter to Desmond?"

She nodded. "I'm not sure I'm going to send it."

George curled his fingers up and stretched them against the strain of his bandage. "Are the two of you trying to work things out?"

She unspooled a curl from behind her ear and it fell in front of her eyes. "I'm sure you have more important things to do instead of listening to why I don't want to send this letter."

"No." The response came quick.

"It's the middle of the work day, is it not?"

He could have joked about it; that's what every instinct screamed to do. Tell her *yes*, he was happy to avoid work. Tell her *sure*, but he never passed up on an excuse to get out of responsibilities. But he couldn't. His occupation had nothing to do with the reasons he had to stay.

"Tell you what," his voice pulled her back in, hope rimming the shades of her cinnamon irises. "You finish this secret, and I'll give you one of mine."

Molly kept playing with her hair, swooping it around her finger and thumb in a hypnotizing rhythm. "It's not exactly a nice thing for me to say."

He leaned towards her and relaxed against the counter. "Since when have you been concerned about only telling me nice things?"

A single corner of her mouth tugged up. "Desmond apologized."

"Did he now?" George's heart rate tripled at the memory of his last visit with Desmond, glad that at least it had resulted in Molly getting the apology she deserved. Maybe the two of them could find their way back to each other somehow.

"He told me about his life and asked about mine. So I wrote him this." She placed the envelope on the table and spun it in circles. "It says I accept his apology and that I'm doing well. But it feels like a lie."

"What's the truth?" George watched the spinning envelope. He hadn't planned on getting involved with any of Molly's romantic interests ever again, and so far, he had already stumbled upon two. Though, he supposed, the first one was more of a misunderstanding.

Her sigh released in dulcet tones. "The truth, George, is that after all that he said, and all he has done, I want to tell him thank you."

"You want to *thank* Desmond?"

"It's a bit more involved than that." She tapped the letters of Desmond's name. "I'd start by telling him how when he left, it destroyed me. How it turned me into a wretched beast. All that was left of me were my least favourite parts. Because of him, because of what he did, I had fallen as low I could. And *then* I would tell him thank you."

She steadied both hands on the table and gave George her smile—her real smile. Not the fake one she had given Christopher, or the polite one she gave to strangers on the street. It was a little wild, a tad extravagant, sprinkled with all sorts of trouble. It was probably George's favourite.

"When I was at my lowest I was presented with the opportunity to build myself back up," she explained, her eyes twinkling in glorious waves. "I recreated myself out of gold and gems and anything that glittered. I am a version of myself that I never could have dreamed! So in some strange, twisted and complicated way, him leaving was the best thing that ever happened to me." Her cheeks flushed as she finished with a heavy breath.

George reminded himself to breathe as well.

"Well," he said through an exhale, proud of how nothing in his voice quavered the way his bones did. "While I do appreciate you sharing that with me, I think I'm just going to take this." He reached forward and slipped the enveloped from her grasp.

Her eyes widened. "Why?"

"Because I'm afraid you'll add," he gestured, "all of that."

She crossed her arms and stared at him with sharpened determination. "I would never actually say that to him. I had no plans on telling anyone until you came along."

"I think he should hear it."

"I don't think I could tell him."

"Maybe I will."

She didn't tell him not to, she just watched her envelope as he cradled it with the rest of his own. "You're not really sending my letter away, are you?"

"Of course I am," he replied with a smirk.

"But if you do then..." Her gaze lifted to look out the front window. "That means I'd have to go back outside."

George glanced over his shoulder and searched the world, missing where the predicament was. "What's wrong with that?"

"Wedding arrangements," she groaned. "My entire family is walking through town getting ideas for Victoria's wedding. I enjoyed having an excuse to not join in."

He hummed. "If only there was someone who owed you a secret. Someone who, perhaps, knew there's a way to sneak you out of here so your family wouldn't know you had left."

Molly's face lit up in three different hues of excitement. "Really?"

George tipped his head and stepped away. "Follow me."

He led her to the counter, relieved to see that Henry had returned.

"I was wondering if you were coming in today," Henry said as George approached him, Molly not far behind. "Running a bit late, are we?"

George waved off the comment and handed him the pile of envelopes. "This is Miss Jones, she's..." The moment he couldn't think of an appropriate term stretched too long, he gave up and went for the only thing that he could. "She's a dear friend, you could say. This is Henry, he's Edwin and Cecilia's son."

Henry acknowledged Molly with a kind nod and sorted the envelopes away. "Pleasure to meet you."

"I'm wondering if you could do me an extra favour," George added.

"What is it this time?"

George smiled. "She's in need of a discreet exit."

"I see." Henry balanced his forearms across the railing in front of him and focused on Molly. "I hope you don't find it out of place, Miss, I am aware I don't know you personally. However, I feel compelled to warn you about the company you keep."

Henry knew all too well what it meant to be in George's company, oftentimes having been present when certain things had failed to work in George's plots. Henry had stepped in as a clumsy uncle type figure, teasing and defending him when he was a boy. He'd often fast-talked the way out of George's troubles on the streets with various merchants after various stunts.

Molly looked unfazed. "While I appreciate your concern," she replied giddily, "I assure you that if you did know me better, *I* wouldn't be the one you're warning."

Henry's eyes widened in surprise. "Well, if that's the case." He unlocked the gate and motioned them through to the back room.

Molly skipped past, thanking Henry with a curtsy and spun around as she reached the back door. George couldn't peel his eyes away, even when Henry grabbed his arm and held him back.

Henry's smile was wide and jesting. "I'm sensing you're in dangerous territory."

"An increasing amount of it, too," George admitted, unaware of exactly what he was doing. He patted his good hand against Henry's shoulder. "However, I have never been able to keep away from a little trouble."

"It's about time you use that power for something good." With that, Henry pushed George out the door.

Molly crouched along the sidewalk, arms folded over bent knees as she smiled towards the cobblestones. She reached out and grazed her fingertips against a stone with a hollowed paw print on it.

"A cat walked across these bricks as they were being made," she said distantly. "So many people pass by here every day, filling this alley with stories. Do you think anyone ever stops to think of them?"

"I know of at least one." George knelt down beside her. Brown dirt was packed between the grey bricks, covered in crisp moss. He pressed the pads of his fingers against the closest stone and looked down the alley, across the street to the shops and businesses. "I happen to know a few of the stories."

She brightened. "Such as?"

George straightened to stand. "One of an old businessman bringing his grandson to a cigar shoppe for free candies. A story of a girl who is only moderately aware of how to mail a letter. Some tales of her sister, who isn't entirely bad, nor entirely good, but is always entirely annoying." He grimaced. "And horrors of the sister's lover and the events that led to needing a signal during our courtship."

Molly's face filled with colour. "It's because she kissed you, isn't it?"

Why had he even hinted towards *that* story?

"Molly!" The call came from a gentleman running around the corner, waving his hands far above his head. An overwhelming smile did what it could as the man desperately tried to catch his breath. "I've been looking everywhere for you!" He grasped onto Molly's arm as he folded over to suck in air.

The man asked her questions, speaking a mile a minute with sentences that repeated the same words in a different order. His hat was nearly falling from his head of thick brunette locks. Despite the fact that everything was clean and trimmed, nothing was all that put together. His deep brown suit clashed with his coat and scarf.

The ease of the gentleman's smile and the way he clung to Molly without her flinching away showed a softness they had together. She released his hand from her arm with a familiarity that brought a throbbing pain through George's pulse.

"Who is this?" the man questioned territorially, stepping in front of Molly, his deep hazel eyes piercing into George's soul. "Who are you?"

"George Clarington," he said, extending a gentlemanly hand.

"George, George, George. I've heard that name before." The man squinted in concentration, shaking his hand a little too long. "Where have I heard that name before?"

"You can't be serious," Molly placed her hands on her hips.

"Ah!" The man's face lit up. "George! You're Victoria's George!"

George's eye flared wide. "Don't ever call me that again."

"Definitely Victoria's George." The man laughed. "I've heard all the stories. And before you ask, yes, that includes all the ones you probably wish I hadn't. Molly, why didn't you tell me this was George?"

"Because I knew you would react this way," she replied shortly.

"How absolutely rude of me." The man ignored her comment and spun back to George, taking his hand to shake it a second time. "The name's Felix. I'm Molly's favourite cousin."

"You're my only cousin."

"That makes me the best." Felix gave a disarming grin, one familiar to George, though he couldn't place why.

George forgot how to form a sentence. "So you're... cousins?"

"We're not *those* kinds of cousins." Felix raised his hands in surrender. "No, I'm happily married—Sylvia, she's everything that's good in my life. Her and my son, George. George!" Felix pointed back and forth to George and across the street. "George, George, I love it! My father's name is George as well."

George cracked a laugh. He turned to see what Molly was doing as Felix did the same, and found her hiding her face in her hands.

"Am I embarrassing you?" Felix asked.

"No." She ran her hands down her cheeks. "You're embarrassing yourself, and I'm experiencing it on your behalf."

"Splendid!" Felix returned to facing George. "You don't remember me do you? That's a shame. I remember you."

Molly scowled. "Felix..."

He waved her off. "Aunt Cat is by far my favourite aunt. Which is saying something because my mother has many sisters"—he waved himself off —"that's besides the point. What I'm trying to say is that Aunt Cat is my favourite, but Aunt Lizzy is my only honorary aunt, and I love her almost just as much."

George's world circled around the sound of Felix's voice. "Aunt Lizzy?"

Felix smiled gently. "She always brought over the most amazing biscuits. Your sister never wanted to share them with me, that's probably why I fell in love with her. Long before I met my wife. Long, long before that." He chuckled uncomfortably. "And you! You were my little shadow and probably my best friend, despite how much younger you were."

George paused to take a breath. "You knew my family? You and I used to know each other?"

"Well, I still know you. We've seen each other since then." Felix turned to glance at Molly, then quickly spun back. "But that's a story for another time." He winked.

"Why hold back now Felix?" Molly challenged.

"Your sister would have my head if I continued." Felix's laugh tapered off fast. "Speaking of which, it's imperative that you have a story to explain the tall handsome fellow you were conversing with. Victoria and mother are very curious."

"Who was I conversing with?" Molly's eyebrows gathered together.

"The tall handsome gentleman in the post office," Felix repeated, much misreading Molly's confusion.

"He means Christopher," George clarified.

"Oh!" Molly's face deepened its shade of red as she met his eyes. "Oh, Christopher. Right. I forgot about him."

Felix's eyes darted between George and Molly. "This is very endearing."

"Felix." Molly's voice was heavier, her eyes boring into him as he smirked back at her.

"To stay in good faith," Felix continued, "I'll give you two minutes before I collect you back for the family. After that, I need you to return. George is demanding to be held every thirty seconds"—he turned to George—"not this one. My George. And the only person offering to do so is Victoria. But George doesn't like Victoria"—he gestured to George—"Again, not this one."

"It actually fit that time," George couldn't help adding.

Felix grinned. "I knew I'd still like you."

George smiled back.

"Well, I'll see you in two minutes." Felix spun around to leave. "And don't forget about a good story concerning that Christopher fellow. You're practically already married to him in mother's mind."

George watched Felix leave. Sentences and words weaved through his mind, every detail and all the theories that could possibly knit together.

"George," Molly's voice drew him back. "I'm sorry if Felix was insensitive about your family. I'm sure he meant well."

"It was refreshing, actually."

Her brows peaked in curiosity.

"People never speak of my mother or siblings. If they do, it's only between condolences, as if they have only been names on tombstones above false graves. But Felix..." George stared off to where Felix had turned around the corner and disappeared. "He spoke of them like they were real people."

Her smile came back, beautifully filled with all the songs he couldn't write.

She cleared her throat. "And how's your hand faring?"

He looked down at it as if he'd forgotten it was there. "Everyday there's a little improvement."

"Any luck with the piano?"

Warmth spread across his torso like a tidal wave crashing against the surf. He thought of the familiar keys, how he'd spent the last weeks collecting all his favourite sounds, reciting the tones of the piano notes through his memory and folding them together into songs. He remembered the evenings at the Towsons' house, how he knew exactly what notes matched the melody of Molly's laugh.

"I don't have the mobility yet," he said, extending and stretching his fingers.

"Hopefully soon."

His eyes ticked up and matched hers. She held all sorts of hopes with her that glistened in her eyes and shone through her smile. It had him almost believing in something as helpless as hope again.

"Perhaps," he replied.

She flipped a necklace into her fingers, twirling it around with musical momentum. "I guess I should go," she said hesitantly. "Before my Aunt Vivianne has some choice words."

George was hesitant as well. "I'm sorry the escape didn't quite last."

"At least we kept our tradition," she said brightly, spinning around to leave, jacket and skirt circling her legs.

George watched, he couldn't stop himself. Though, he did decide to relax against the brick wall and scrutinize himself for jumping to assumptions about Molly's love life, an entirety of *three* times. None of which had any foundation—every one of them thoroughly contrived fiction.

Molly paused at the corner and held onto the bricks, looking up in the final moment and caught him watching her.

He tipped his hat and tried to pretend as though they had simply glanced up at the same time. She smiled and disappeared.

Oh, sweet murderous cruelty. Her smile was capable of utterly evil things.

George walked in the opposite direction, finding his way back to the office. He pulled out his pocket watch and squeezed it into his palm. It didn't matter that it was unwound and inaccurate. He already knew he was running very behind.

Back in the hallway with dripping stones, George stood alone outside a cell with no bars. Inside sat a piano with three legs and keys that were out of order. He crept towards the instrument, reaching out a hesitant hand to press on the notes.

It did not release music. The loud clang of a clock rung through the prison, ever growing, ever more horrid. It scratched against his skull in a sharp pain.

"Well done, George."

He spun around to the voice.

A man emerged from the shadows, tall, black leather boots ticking against the floorboards. He was draped in a lavish long coat that was stained and pitted with gore.

His father.

The room veered to the side. George slammed into the bricks. He held his head and stumbled forward, the room rolling in the opposite direction so that he was shoved into the opposite stones. Saltwater dripped through the cracks, coating his hands and his suit.

His father stared at him, large sinister grin curling over bloodied teeth, each coming to a point that sought to devour.

"What is this place?" George called.

"You're where you belong, George." He motioned to an emotionless maiden spinning through the room, dancing to the alarm of the clock.

George stumbled back from her, colliding into a wall of shattered mirrors. He dared a glance at his reflection.

It wasn't his own. His father's face sneered at him from the glass.

"That's right, my boy." His father laughed in the background. "There are no happy endings for us here."

George woke from the nightmare, but the savage laugh of his father still filled the silence.

He rolled over, pulled the blankets over his head, and screamed into his pillow.

Chapter 33

First came tea.

The delicate cup was etched in gold filigree and caught every spark of light from the nearby fire. It was Molly's third visit to the Northern Estate; this time it came with the promise of no boys, whatsoever.

She sat with Viola on the settee, both of them enjoying the afternoon sunlight. Everything in the room glittered as much as the snow outside. The high mural ceiling kindled the imagination, and the gold and white pillars in the corners gave the impression of more fairytales than Molly could count. However, Viola's stories were the most riveting.

"I was atop my favourite bridge when his horse was spooked. I toppled into the pond and was pulled under the water. Then came an explosion of bubbles because this radical gentleman dives in." Viola fanned herself, her face flushing to an adorable pink. "I only dream of this, you see, I was far to busy fighting for survival at this point. I shall always imagine

Johnathon looked quite handsome though. Tossing his jacket aside, leaping onto the stone fence to dive into the water."

Molly sipped her tea to hide her ever blossoming smile.

"I had no idea what was truly happening until it was over. I was laying on the riverbank with this man above me and he had the audacity to smile, as though it wasn't difficult to breathe as it was!"

Molly pictured it all. The blooming trees in late spring, the gowns, the parasols, a burly Johnathon and petite Viola back in their prime.

"Of course, I couldn't allow him to realize how handsome I thought he was." Viola placed her teacup onto its saucer and folded her hands onto her lap. "So I hit him. To which he merely laughed and reminded me that if I had swam on my own, he wouldn't have had to jump in. So I informed him that I had never been swimming, not once in my entire life. And he only smiled wider and claimed that once I married him, he'd teach me to swim. To which I swatted him again."

"You just met, and he was talking about marrying you?" Molly placed her empty cup next to Viola's.

Viola sighed. "Times were different back then, and Johnathon was a hopeless romantic." She patted Molly's knee and grinned. "But I knew he was special. Completely insufferable—*still* insufferable. But when I hit him, and he smiled in return, I knew. If he had asked me to marry him there, I would have said yes."

"Sounds like a fairytale."

"Every once in a while, life presents a fairytale." She squeezed Molly's hand and then stood. "Speaking of which, are we ready for riding? I'll ask for the horses to be prepared."

"Absolutely." Molly rose to her feet and followed Viola out of the room.

In her mind she saw the park and the pond. She imagined a family of swans swimming amongst the waves, the little ones nipping at the flower petals that fell down from the trees. Open carriages and horses strolling along park paths of different sizes, the fashions of all the pedestrians, all the stories looming around every corner, and the magic of fifty years into the past.

A door closed in the distance, making Viola pause and face the foyer.

"I wasn't expecting any more company." Viola listened to the footsteps that padded across the floor. "I most certainly wasn't expecting him." She abandoned her original route to the back of the estate and headed for the grand staircase in the centre of the home.

Molly had no choice but to cluelessly follow.

"George?" Viola called out.

He appeared in the doorway. "Oh." He took sight of Molly and turned away. "I wasn't supposed to be here today."

"No, you were not," Viola agreed. "So why are you here?"

"I forgot what day it was."

Viola's brows crinkled together. "You forgot what day it was, or you forgot it was today?"

"I don't see the difference." George raked back his hair and raced towards the grand stairs. They spiralled up to the many floors above, with hidden shelves every few steps and lanterns that dangled above fresh blooming roses. The estate felt increasingly more like a castle.

George had just gripped the stair railing when his grandmother caught up.

"George, I demand answers."

"It's nothing that concerns you, Gran," he said respectfully. "It's business related."

"Your grandfather did something." Viola held her forehead. "What was it this time?"

George's eyes flickered to Molly. "I'd rather not say. Especially since I'm not actually here."

She sighed. "Give it over."

"To what are you referring to?" he asked in a voice far too innocent to be truly his.

"Whatever it was that sent you racing over here forgetting what day it was." Viola's hand impatiently hovered in the air between them.

George retrieved a slip of paper from his pocket and dropped it into her palm.

She read the page thoroughly, scrutinizing every word. "He sent this to you, in a *letter*?"

George shrugged.

Viola stepped around him towards the stairs. "I'm going to sort this out."

George held her arm, stopping her. "That's what I'm here for. You have company to attend to."

Viola looked over to Molly and something in her expression fell. "I'm sorry, I need to handle this."

"I understand," Molly assured lightly, "family comes first."

Viola patted George on the shoulder. "I'll return soon." She fled up the stairs and disappeared around a corner.

"It's not going to be soon at all," George muttered as he walked across the floor.

Molly wasn't certain he was talking to her. There was a chance he didn't even know who he was talking to.

He fell against the wall and pulled out his pocket watch, swirling it through the air and catching it in his hand before spinning it in the opposite direction. It was a mesmerizing motion as the chain hooked around and the links clinked together. His hair was a mess and his cuffs were unbuttoned, allowing them to poke out beneath the thick charcoal sleeves of his wool coat, which had never been fastened. It looked as though he hadn't even completed his suit. His waistcoat was left open, no jacket was in sight. His wrinkled, pinstriped shirt was in great contrast to his weathered, blood-red tie.

She didn't have to ask him if he was doing all right, or if everything was okay. It most certainly wasn't.

Molly grasped her hands together and glanced towards the windows. The world sparkled, everything was glittering with ice and frost. Indeed, the snow was out to get her into trouble. She couldn't let George sulk against the wall. And only one thing came to mind.

Molly took a breath. "Tradition."

"Tradition?" George repeated, peering at her as he caught his watch before it had finished spinning.

"I was thinking of sneaking away somewhere." It was then that she realized her plan had only gotten as far as wanting to lighten the weight on his shoulders, and not to the point where she had a location in mind.

His smile shimmered. George slipped his watch back into his pocket. "Last week Gran mentioned she intended to guide you riding through the woods."

"We were headed there when you arrived."

"Seems a shame you'd miss out on riding here twice because of me." George pushed himself to a stand and walked towards the hall. "But there's a detour we should take. I'll meet you at the stables."

Molly wiggled her fingers inside her fuzzy mittens and pulled her hat down over her ears. The air was cold; snow coated every tree, and ice glistened on every surface. But the stables were cozy and warm.

She walked past the stalls, smiling at the horses who noticed her, and made it to the end where two beautiful animals were saddled and waiting.

The mare was lovely, blanketed and chocolate brown with caramel patches across her belly. Her eyes were kind and eager as Molly allowed her hands to be sniffed.

The stallion, however, was a different sort of creature altogether. Menacing dark eyes, a coat as black as midnight, and an attitude that conveyed trouble. He gave a huff of hot air, which Molly assumed was a demand for attention.

"I wouldn't do that if I were you," George said, entering her vision from the other side of the large black animal. "Excalibur doesn't take kindly to strangers."

Molly looked back at the horse. "He seems fine with me."

Excalibur brushed his nose against Molly's arm and let out an agreeing snort. She hummed and brushed Excalibur's mane with her mittens.

George stepped beside her. "Remember the story I told you about Desmond and horses?"

Molly's laugh burst out of her. "That was Excalibur?"

"His brother."

She turned back to the large creature. "It makes me like him even more."

"You *do* remember the horse story, don't you?"

"Surprisingly, yes." She coddled Excalibur a bit further. "Such a good horse."

"You're on the horse's side?" he asked disbelievingly.

"Completely."

She gave Excalibur one last pat and went closer to the mare. With George's help she mounted into the saddle and acquainted herself with her horse, Misty. They were already getting along quite well as George and Excalibur rode up on their right.

"Whenever you're ready." He motioned for her to lead the horses from the stables.

There was no possible way that the forest wasn't enchanted. Sparkling bark glistened on every tree, snow-dusted logs and boulders slept in the earth along the path. The wind blew glittering snow through the air, catching the sunlight in the most dazzling way. Pure magic.

Even Molly's riding habit sparkled. The sewn rhinestones caught the light and cast it out in twinkling bursts. Extravagant for riding attire? Yes. Completely wonderful? Absolutely.

"Here," George called out from the side. He brought Excalibur to a stop and began to dismount.

They had arrived at a small clearing of trees, where more light shone through the mystic tree canopy.

Molly dismounted Misty clumsily, but efficiently, and met George a few paces away.

He presented her with a leather satchel and dropped the strap into her waiting hands. "Look inside."

The buckle opened easily, jingling through the hushed winter world. Molly reached in, grasping onto straps and pulled out...

"I didn't think you should go another winter without learning how to skate."

Molly held the blades higher. They caught the light and shone like freshly shaved ice. "These look dangerous."

"They are if you wave them around." George lowered her hand and took the blades back. "It was a bad idea to give these over before you were sitting down."

He led them to the pond, where tree stumps became chairs. Molly wrapped her skirt around her legs and retrieved the skating blades from George. The buckles were easily fastened, though George instructed her to make them one notch tighter than felt necessary. Standing up, however, wasn't what she was expecting.

"This feels...strange," she said, flailing her hands.

"Because you're walking on ground. They're for gliding on ice." George pushed himself onto the pond, skates scraping against the frozen pond and casting off a cloud.

She hesitated at the edge. "I just step on?"

"You glide on." He gestured with his hands before tucking them into his pockets.

Glide on. Sure, Molly knew exactly what that meant. Annoying boys.

She stepped onto the pond, nimble and slow. Her feet kept moving, even when she wasn't the one moving them. "Now what?"

"You keep gliding."

Of course. Annoying, handsome boys.

George skated backwards, watching as she tried to figure out how to move.

"Don't pick up your feet," he called just as she was about to, in fact, lift her foot. "Feet stay on the ice moving forward, lift from the ice only to bring them back under you."

"*Right.*"

He chuckled. "I can't believe you've never been skating before."

"I almost went with a friend once." She tried to move her foot without lifting it, and found herself propelled—very slowly—forward. "But at the last minute she left me for a boy she barely knew. Which ended up being wonderful."

George skid beside her, completing a full circle around where she was still barely moving.

Molly pushed with her second foot. "That was the day I got back into reading. My life hasn't been the same since."

"What novel was it?"

"It was—" Maneuvering her next foot, she lost all balance, falling in a heap of shimmering fabric. She blew loosened curls of hair out of her eyes and adjusted her knitted hat.

George extended a hand to help her. He held her elbows, supporting her as she found her balance, then slid away. "I'm not doing this right."

"You?" Molly kept watch on her feet as she continued to move them without lifting. He was skating circles around her. "You seem to know exactly what you're doing."

"I meant, I'm not helping you properly." He came to a stop just beyond her, his skates casting off a glittering mist. "I'm used to planning things out, knowing the various outcomes before the moment is complete. Living life ten steps ahead. It seems I have lost that ability. This is the first spontaneous thing I've done in years."

Molly smiled, partly due to how far she had been able to skate on her own, yet mostly because of something unnamable. She looked up and caught him as he pattered his fingers along his thumb—a move that always reminded her of how he played the piano. With his dishevelled hair, his crumpled scarf and faraway voice, he was the same boyish version he had been that night at the piano in his closet of an office space.

She shook her head. She wasn't allowed to think of that.

Momentum came easier, each push of her foot became stronger and brought her farther. George skated in wider circles, noticing how much better she was getting. Her confidence had risen. So she pushed herself further, just a little too much.

She fell, making a terrible cracking sound.

Her shattered pride left her laying still on the ice. The cold crept through to her skin. Nothing was broken, except the height of her confidence.

"Are you hurt?"

She squinted her eyes open to the blinding, hazy light. "No, no I think I'm all right."

His warm hand scooped around her neck and shoulders, lifting her up from the ice and drawing her towards him. "You say that often. It's rarely true."

Molly let her eyes close.

"Did you hit your head?" His fingers found her hair and gently pressed along the back of her head.

Nothing hurt—it was the opposite of hurt. It was light and colours. It was worlds and dreams and secrets she wouldn't share.

Goodness. Maybe she had hit her head.

He sighed and pulled her in closer, sheltering her face in the crook of his neck as his lips whispered against her temple, "You're absolutely terrifying. Do you know that?"

George's hold was electrifying but easy to melt into. And for a brief, stolen moment, Molly allowed herself to enjoy the spectacular sensation of being in his arms. The way he felt solid but held her softly. The way he smelled; like rich spice and melted sugars spun together into something delicious. How strong the planes of his chest were. How wonderful it felt as his hands splayed out on her back with a comfort she didn't want to fade.

"We shouldn't sit on the ice for too long." But even as he said it, he took his time in moving, releasing her as hesitantly as she was moving away.

George pushed to his feet and dragged her up with him. "Shall we try skating again?"

"I've fallen more than skated." Molly wiped the ice shavings off her mittens. Her hands felt frozen as the melting slivers soaked through the knit. "I'm ready to sit by the fire, wrapped in a blanket with—"

"Steaming tea and a book? I know." He slowly skated around her. "The same way I know you'll go home feeling defeated if you don't try at least one more time. Skating feels a lot like flying once you get the hang of it."

Molly narrowed her eyes. "That's not fair."

"What isn't?"

"The fact that you know how to coerce me into skating again."

His smile mischievously met his eyes. "I'm not about to let you give up so easily."

Molly watched as he settled into a stance and shoved his hands into his pockets. She certainly wasn't enjoying how his eyes reflected the snow and ice in an incredible amount of silver, or how noticing they were looking back into her own made her feel very, wonderfully, warm.

She decided to turn the conversation around. "I don't like you very much."

He bit down on his bottom lip. "Oh," he drew out the word slowly, "I bet you wish that was true."

Her traitorous heartbeat thundered. "How would you know what I wish for?"

"The same way I know everything else."

"And that is..."

"A secret," he completed. "I digress; it is a story I've promised to share."

She placed her hands on her hips, wobbling on the blades that remained untrustworthy against the ice. "So, you'll tell me sometime within the next few decades?"

"I'll tell you in the next two minutes."

"What's the catch?"

"No catch." He removed his hands from his pockets and flared them in surrender. "Unless, of course, you consider the fact that I'm going to whisper the entire time, to be a catch."

"If you whisper, how would I—"

"Hear me?" He shrugged. "You wouldn't. Not from over there."

Her mouth gaped open. "You're teasing me with this story just to lure me into skating again?"

"Don't look so surprised." He grinned wickedly. "A desperate man resorts to desperate measures. I promised not to let you give up on this, and playing tricks is not beneath me."

Molly looked out to the forest around the frozen pond. The branches stretched to the sky, each one glistening where the sun reflected off the snow crystals. She turned back to George, who remained across the pond.

"It's time, Fairy Girl." He braced his hands on his knees. "I know you have it in you."

Molly looked down at her feet and hesitantly made one unsure swipe of her blades at a time, slowly making her way closer to him. She focused on nothing but the constant rhythm of her glides, the steady increase, the smooth graze of the ice beneath her feet. She was doing it, really doing it. One thing she didn't know how to do, was avoid divots.

The toe of her blade struck a hole and sent her stumbling as her balance faltered.

This time, she didn't fall. George caught her before she was anywhere near the ice.

She grasped onto his forearms. "I tried."

"You succeeded." He adjusted his hold on her. "I've been skating backwards the entire time. You would have caught me ages ago otherwise."

Molly swiped her hair away from her eyes and looked up to him.

"I knew you could do it," he added lightly.

"You believed in me?"

"Is that supposedly a hard thing to do?"

Seconds silently ticked away, but Molly wasn't aware of anything beyond him. Sparkles caught in his eyes, the rise and fall of their breaths bringing them closer together. Everything was a dangerous, rejuvenating magic.

"So," she said, breathless. "You owe me your secret."

He dipped his head sideways and released her arms. "Are you sure you want me to tell you right now?"

In all honesty, she wasn't sure at all.

"I don't think I could tell this story while standing still," he revealed as he skated away.

Molly watched as he swerved around the ice. "I'm not going to magically be able to keep up with you."

In twists of sunlight, the snow-dust swirled through the current of air behind him.

"There is a solution," he said, coming to a stop in front of her. "But I'm not sure you'll agree to it."

"What sort of solution?"

"I could...lead you around the ice, the same way I've led you around a dance floor."

She definitely could agree to that. "Only if you tell me the entire story. I want to know how you're able to read my mind all the time."

"As you wish." He slid behind her, lifting her hand into his own, while his opposite hand rested on the small of her back. "Ready?"

She nodded. Because that was all she was able to do. That, and shut her eyes as they moved forward.

"Everyone can notice a smile or a frown," he began. "The real talent of reading thoughts comes with understanding that not all smiles are happy and not all tears are sad." George strengthened his hold as their speed increased around a bend. "Things like that are only easy to determine if you've had a decent amount of conversations with a person. You, however, didn't even so much as look at me when I first started coming to your home, let alone talk to me."

"That's not true." Molly opened one eye, and deemed it safe to open the other.

"Ah, but it is."

"No, it's not. I remember looking at you."

"You sound very passionate about looking at me," he said, voice dark with trouble.

"You're infuriating," she grumbled, refusing to notice how his laugh was as decadent as his voice.

They had reached the other end of the pond, and George spun them around to continue moving. Skating may have been everything she dreamed it could be.

"You have to remember that I knew you, before I ever met you. Through stories and tales that Desmond shared. Only, you weren't quite what I anticipated."

Molly swallowed. "I wasn't exactly myself back then."

"And yet," he sighed, "you were more than I expected."

She glanced at him. "How is that possible?"

"Desmond's stories never did you justice, though I'm sure he tried his best. He's not exactly gifted in the art of story-telling. Secondly, I don't think you give yourself enough credit either." When his eyes met hers, she looked away.

Gliding against the ice with him was like waltzing through fantasies and realms. She almost didn't want to encourage the telling of his secrets, worried that once it was over, so would their journey through this delicate world be.

"What I knew about you filled me with just the right amount of curiosity to keep me drawn in. And I needed to know more." He adjusted his hold on her hand—it sent rivers of sparks beneath the knit of her mittens. "One morning, while I was getting ready to retrieve your sister and bring her to Jeremy, Gran hands me this book she'd like to get bound. Since I tended to have a surplus of time to myself once I united your sister with the Towsons, I agreed."

Molly settled into the sound of his voice as it wove a new landscape before her eyes, encasing the winter wonderland in a strengthened glamour.

"Of course, it was typical for your sister to keep me waiting. So, I sat in the tea room with you and your mother, each engrossed into your hobbies. Just so happens, the novel you started that day was the same one my grandmother handed me that morning. That's when the idea first came."

Molly held tighter to his hand. Was he possibly suggesting...

"You have these subtle expressions as you read," he continued. "Little smiles you try to hide, frowns you keep secret, worries or passions that colour your cheeks. I figured, if I knew what you were reading, I would know you a little better. Thankfully, you read at an...*absorbent* pace. It allowed me to finish books before you did." His tone dropped, reluctant of the feelings that came with sharing secrets. "I would spend evenings at your house deciphering which scenes you were reading, what actions brought forth which reactions. Through those stories, I pieced together yours."

Molly stepped around to face him, losing her balance and struggling to remain upright in his arms.

"You shouldn't do that while we're skating," he said, eyes wild.

Molly gripped onto the sleeves of his jacket. "You read my stories."

"Not all of them." George held her upright. "In some cases your taste in novels is quite questionable."

Crinkling pops sounded beneath her feet, growing louder and bursting into cracks as the ice split. One skate fell beneath the ice, water soaking through her boot. She yelped as her foot sunk deeper. George pulled her away and wrapped her around to his front before pushing her off to the shore.

It wasn't a big pond, so the edge quickly approached.

"George," she called, frantically trying to remain upright, "George, I don't know how to stop."

"What?"

"I don't know how to—" her toes dug into the crust of the dirt, hurtling her forward.

George caught the belt of her coat, crashing her against him as he spun himself to fall back first onto the ground, Molly landing in his arms.

His eyes remained closed as he lay still. "Did I hurt you?"

"No." She rolled into the snow, her head supported by his arm as it flopped open onto the bank beside her.

He started to laugh.

She pushed up on her elbows and stared at him. "Is there something you're finding hilarious? I almost fell under the ice."

He kept laughing. "That's highly unlikely."

"I've heard the stories; the horrors of drowning."

He rolled onto his side and propped his head up in his palm. "Miss Jones, this is a duck pond. At most, you would have ruined your skirt. The water, in its deepest parts, is no higher than your knee."

She gaped.

"I'm not sure what you want me to say here," he said, that laugh still rumbling. "You screamed, I reacted, and you kept reacting. By the time I remembered there was no immediate danger, it was too late to stop it."

He chuckled deeper, until it flew free in a vast array that she loathed.

She spun to the side and scooped a handful of snow into her hands, shaping it until it was perfect, and aimed it at his chest.

It ruptured against his buttons, spraying in all directions. His eyes brightened, and his lips flicked up in his usual sly manner. "*That* is very cold."

"So is my foot," she said with a high tilt of propriety. She brushed off her mittens and unbuckled the blades from her boots.

After rising to stand, she walked back to the horses, hiding her face as best she could in her loose hair.

Thoughts held her captive. Ones of his grin and the physical effects it had on her senses. How it felt to be in his arms. The way his voice filled with colours and stories she never wanted him to stop sharing. What it was like knowing he believed in her, or had read her books just to get to know her a little.

Her smile blossomed whether she fought it or not.

"You dropped this," George said from her side, holding out her hat.

His sudden appearance made her shriek. The horses stirred. Misty reined up and took off into the woods, leaving a cloud of billowing snow in her trail.

Molly covered her mouth with her hands, the initial shock wearing off as new emotions stained her cheeks.

His lips twitched, igniting his smirk.

"I'm sorry," Molly said through her fingers.

"No need. Misty loves running in the snow, it doesn't take much to persuade her. Good thing Excalibur feels differently, or we'd be without a horse entirely."

George shuffled his fingers to comb his hair to the top of his head, studying Molly and taking in her outfit from head to toe. When his eyes met hers again, she dropped her hands.

"What is it?"

"I don't suppose your fancy riding attire would allow you to sit safely in his saddle, would it?"

Molly looked at the layers of her skirt and fluffed it out. She doubted it. "I could try."

"It looks extravagant enough." His coat flared out to the sides as he headed towards Excalibur.

"It's not all that fancy." Molly kept stride with him as best she could.

"It *is* actually, whether you admit it or not."

They reached Excalibur, who watched the cloud Misty had cast off begin to settle.

Molly crossed her arms and watched as George attended his horse. "Well, I happen to adore this dress. There's no use in wearing things I don't love."

"You speak as though I don't understand the concept," he teased as he adjusted the saddle. "Are you sure you didn't put it on just for me?"

"Yep," she popped the 'p' proudly. "You weren't supposed to be here."

He hummed a note of approval and finished looping the buckles. Taking her hands in his, George steadied her balance and held the stirrups as she stepped to her seat on his horse. Once she was settled and he determined she was sturdy enough, he took a step back.

Looking at her through his fallen ink-like waves, George sliced into his smile. "I must say, I do think I've benefitted from you thinking I wouldn't be here."

Heat crept up her neck and to her cheeks. "Again with your casual flirtations?"

In a swift movement, he jumped his foot into the stirrup and swung his other leg over the horse until he was sitting directly behind her.

"Where do you think they'll take me this time?" His whisper froze her with the feel of his words fluttering in her hair.

"Apparently onto a horse," she gritted out. It was a battle to keep the distaste in her voice as memories flooded in. Perhaps the last time she accused him of casual flirtations, they never escaped their little world inside a row of bookshelves.

His laugh came deep and luscious, travelling all down her spine and across her shoulders as he wrapped his arms around her to tighten the reins. "I don't want you falling out of an improper saddle."

"Oh, is that it?"

He promptly shuffled backwards. "If it makes you uncomfortable—"

"I'm comfortable," she said far too quickly. She scrunched up her nose and squeezed her eyes shut, hoping he didn't see.

"As long as you're sure." He carefully adjusted his feet in the stirrups. "I'll take you home first. You can warm up while I search for Misty."

Molly remained silent, not trusting her tongue to say anything she wouldn't regretfully think over a thousand times.

Home. The word floated around in a forbidden little daydream.

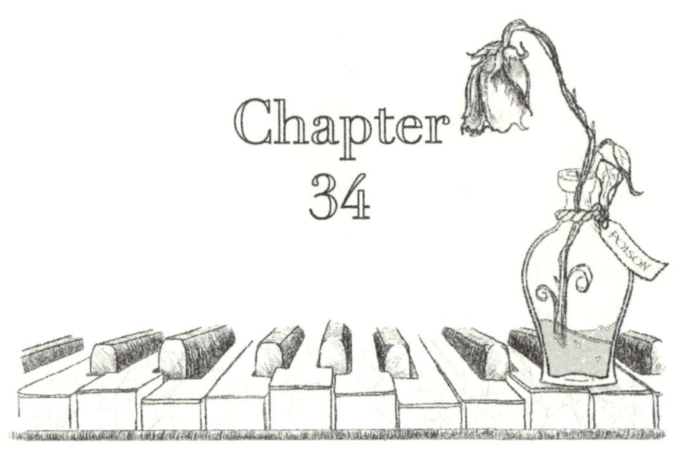

Chapter 34

George strode through the estate, following the song of flames as it crackled through the halls. His hands ached. Not from the cold. Not from yanking Misty through the snow. But from something he wouldn't dare to admit. He needed the fire just to remind himself of the truth that lingered in his haunting nightmares.

Hooking the fingers of his injured hand along the fringe of a wall tapestry, George stared up at the faces. His father smiled down at him.

He contemplated pulling on a thread and watching him disappear. But the portraits of his grandparents and aunt beside James wouldn't allow it.

George turned the corner, only to pause and consider the sight.

Gran sat on the sofa, flipping through an old worn book, wearing her old worn smile. "Welcome back," she called quietly, eyeing him from the corner of her vision.

George couldn't answer.

Sound asleep, Gran's arm around her, lay Molly, wrapped in a quilted blanket. Her hair spooled around her shoulders in soft ringlets, damp from the winter snow. Her lashes kissed her cheeks and fluttered gently, suggesting she was off and away in a dream. He caught himself imaging what her dreams might be when he noticed how her cheeks and nose seemed dusted with roses, with hints of pink among the freckles.

"You don't even realize it, do you?"

"Realize what?" he asked, blinking back to Gran.

"The way you look at her."

Maybe that was why his eyes always felt out of focus, even though everything was still clear. How the world blurred its lines, but nothing was completely in the clouds. Or how the colours were brighter and shrouded her at all times.

Dropping into the closest chair, George decided he would deny it all anyways. "I have no idea what you're talking about."

She closed the book and set it aside. "You can lie to yourself all you want, but you have never been able to lie to me."

He let out what he hoped was a dramatic sigh and stared at the flames.

"Your grandfather wishes to speak with you." Gran delicately swiped a lock of Molly's hair back from her face. "You should go to him once you're done pretending to watch the fire."

George raised a hand to his lips, keeping his involuntary smile a secret.

George sat in his grandfather's office. The wall behind Gramps was filled with shelves displaying his life and achievements. Family portraits hung in gold frames, certificates and clipped newspaper articles were scattered throughout. But it was a picture of Gran with a young George on her knee that sat proudly in the corner of his desk, watching over every task and taking up space where papers could have been.

A clock ticked away the seconds. George kept time with his fingers, tapping them across the arm of his chair with a song itching its way out of him.

"A letter?" George said.

His grandfather grunted, not taking his eyes off whatever paper he was signing.

"You decided it was best to tell me through a letter?"

Gramps peered over the brim of his spectacles. "Professionally, yes. As the owner of the company you're in front of."

"A face to face conversation was warranted."

His grandfather turned his attention to spinning his glass of water.

George rolled his eyes. "I'm not going."

"You most certainly are."

"I'd be gone for months."

"You're taking the voyage, George." Gramps slipped his glasses from his nose and tossed them onto the documents.

"There are many men you could have asked to go instead."

"They all have wives, children, families. I wouldn't ask them to leave their homes for nearly a year."

George braced his elbows onto his knees, dropping his head into his hands. "Please tell me this isn't another ploy to get me to find a wife."

"You came here to argue." Gramps leaned forward. "Very well. Let's begin."

"I didn't come here to argue." George grasped back his hair and sat up. "Well, technically I came here to argue. I was going to put up a fight and in the end resign to go on the trip anyways. But I've changed my mind."

"What changed your mind?"

George furrowed his brows. "I decided I wasn't going to go. There is no arguing if my decision is final."

"Uh-huh." Gramps grinned. "When was that decision made?"

"I'm not talking about this—"

"Was it soon after you arrived? Or perhaps during whatever excursion you went off on while your grandmother yelled at me?" He pointed to the foggy window that overlooked the hillside of the estate grounds, where it dipped to the forest and the hidden pond. "Maybe it has something to do with how you left with two horses but returned with one?"

His grandfather's expression was all too knowing, but George was transported back to the moment on the ice. The moment he knew he wasn't leaving. The moment Molly fit into his arms a little too well. When he had been there to witness how she would not give up on herself.

He wasn't about to admit it though. "I can't be halfway across the world from you."

"I don't buy that for a second, George."

But it was part of the truth. "If something were to happen to you or Gran while I was away, I wouldn't hear about it for weeks! If I needed to rush home, there's a good chance I wouldn't make it back at a decent enough pace. I won't put myself in that position."

"That's *a* reason. It's not *the* reason. And until you reveal the truth, I won't be changing my mind about you leaving." Gramps swung his glasses back on and filtered through more paperwork.

"I don't know what you want me to say."

"Poppycock."

"To what lengths are you willing to go to make me say what you want?"

"To what lengths?" Gramps folded his hands over his desk and cocked his head to the side. "One might assume there's a possibility I know how to get a certain letter delivered at a very specific time. One could also conclude that given your temperament lately, I could figure out your instant reaction to said letter. It's also possible that your grandmother knew nothing because I needed her reaction to be genuine; otherwise, you would have never bought into it. Of course, it was perfect timing since Gran had promised young Miss Molly Jones that you wouldn't be here. You were all so unsuspecting. So the lengths I took to get this to work, don't feel so lengthy."

"You played me?"

"Doesn't feel good does it?" Gramps grabbed the glass of water from his desk and took a swallow. "Similar to how it feels when your grandson pretends to be in a relationship with a girl he can barely stand."

George bit his tongue. There was nothing he could say to that. "You knew that my relationship with Victoria was false?"

"Of course I knew! You children are too naive to understand that while adults aren't with the times, we're not blind to them."

"You're an insane old man."

"I've been called worse." Gramps said with a wink.

"All this time, you've been setting up your game pieces, and now you strike. If your intention was to intimidate me into a marriage—"

"If I had intended for you to marry Miss Jones, that would have happened a long time ago. Back in January, when I stopped looking for the enclave behind the bookshelves just as I found it."

George blinked. "Nothing happened—"

"I believe you." Gramps held up a hand to silence any of George's further attempts at convincing him. "However, the entourage I was with wouldn't have believed you at all. So, I rest my case, George. If my intention had been to get you to marry anyone, *that* would have been my moment. But I chose this one instead."

George steadied his breaths. "Then what *is* your intention?"

"I want you to hear yourself say the truth." Gramps' voice shifted into minor keys, floating through the air in a way that was almost comforting.

Pressing his fingers into the arm of his chair, George played the chords, heard the silent reverberations, the echo of hope, a melancholy world gradually brightening...

Gramps went on, "The day I met your grandmother, I knew I wanted her to be the one next to me for the rest of my life."

"You barely knew her."

"She had a poor excuse for a gentleman at her side. Pity his horse spooked the way it did. I guess he should have been more careful about the things he said to such a fine lady." Gramps lifted a shoulder. "I was jumping into the water after her before realizing she couldn't swim. I suffered through her yelling and hitting, even though I had just saved her life. Because I knew I was going to marry her."

"That story makes less sense every time I hear it," George lied in a grumble.

"I'm a business man. I have a trained eye and know a worthy partnership when I see one." Gramps broke into an antagonizing grin. "I saw how you refused to look at Miss Jones in the theatre, but couldn't stop watching her during the play. It's why I sent champagne after you, because I had a sneaking suspicion she'd make fun of you for it."

And that she had.

George shut his eyes; the defeat ricocheting off every corner of his mind.

The truth.

George flexed his fingers at the memory. "Do you remember the accident?"

"Of course, I do. We made you move back in with us," Gramps replied coldly.

Before then, George had not known pain like that; a blackness so dark even shadows didn't dare to follow. A place where his blood filled with toxins, where claws ripped his veins apart and tore his skin from his bones. Life had become a virus of seeping wounds, consuming him like flames that shed screams in place of light.

He'd wished for nightmares, just for a reprieve.

And then...

"She laughed." George could still hear the snow ticking against the windows in the library, Molly's footsteps across the tile floor, the distress in her sigh as she peered outside. He felt the colours stain the air with the sound of her voice, the lilt of her words, and her laugh... "She laughed, and I heard music."

George played the song on the top of his legs, remembering how all at once the world had filled with colour again, how he knew he'd do anything to hear her laugh, see her smile, make sure she believed in herself.

Gramps nodded. "That'll do, son."

George shook his hand through his hair, straightening himself out of the memory. It was time to finish the conversation he had walked into the office for in the first place. "What does any of this have to do with me being gone for the rest of the year?"

"I don't know what you're referring to." Gramps pushed himself to a stand and walked around the desk.

"The months of worldwide excursions you had me taking?" George stood as well, waiting as his grandfather opened the door.

"I don't recall there ever being plans for something like that." Then Gramps was gone.

George pressed the heels of his palms into his eyes and stood in the office alone.

His fingers trembled until he mindlessly tightened his fist, the crescents of his nails biting into his palm.

He flinched and his hand shot open. He fixated on the deep set line of the scar left behind. It was a reminder that Molly took up space, bold and fearless, beneath his skin. Because all the best ones did.

He dropped his hand over his waistcoat and fiddled with the chain of his watch before pulling it out and twirling it around. His fingers teased at the dial, ready to wind it to the proper minute of the day.

Not yet.

He closed his eyes and didn't fight away the spinning colours as they twirled into shapes and figures. He was back on the ice. The sunlight warmed each strand of Molly's hair against the contrast of her cool skin. Her warm brown eyes brightened even his darkest moments. But it was in her smile that he got lost. It had appeared as a promise. *One day.*

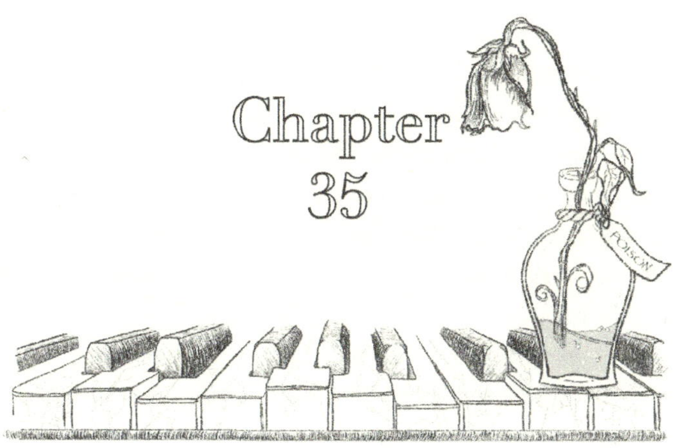

Chapter 35

Spring 1905

George stared up at Desmond's ceiling. A nearby clock ticked. Shadows constantly swirled. Alice's proof of George's darkest fears was deepening.

He was ruin and destruction, ashes and smoke.

He pressed his eyes shut, pleading for sleep, for relief. His pleas went unanswered.

George walked down the torchlit corridor, approaching the last open cell warily.

A man was curled on the ground. Each article of his clothing in shreds. Skin a pasty shell.

The room kept tipping. George gripped to the stone bricks for balance. "Are you all right?"

There was a groan as the man rolled over.

George stumbled back.

The man scratched against the floorboards, breaking his nails into gaping tears as he dragged himself forward.

His own face stared back at him.

The hall spun. George was thrown to the ceiling. His head cracked against the bricks, breaking them into pieces.

The entire space screamed as a gush of water poured in.

He knew that sound, the guttural hiss of torrential waters.

He was thrown back to the floor where he pulled himself up against the wall.

"We're on a ship?" He pushed off the stones, blistering saltwater covering his hands, thickening into blood in the centre. "With a hull made of stones?"

"You shouldn't have built so many walls, George." His feeble counterpart curled his neck to the side with a loud crack.

"You have to choose," his father said from behind. "Me." He motioned to the broken man in the cell. "Or that."

George crumbled to the floorboards, into the pieces he'd tried to glue together. He lugged his body to a distant rope ladder, forcing himself onto the upper deck.

He found his feet and made it to the stern. The ship's frame squealed in the fierce winds. A storm of navy clouds swarmed down from above, massive waves crashed against every side, splintering each mast. They towered high with the tearing sails. Nothing would last long.

Tick-tick-tick

George looked down at himself; at who he had come to be. A man torn into tatters, adorned in old rags and filth. An unsheathed sword was strapped to his side. He drew out the blade. It was as gruesome as the most spine-chilling phobias.

Weak, broken, unsure if he could survive the forthcoming onslaught, George turned back to the water.

Flames stretched up the port side, catching his skin on fire from the heat. The water was consumed with flames.

Shadows swam beneath the keel, revealing a creature of immeasurable wrath circling the vessel continuously.

Tick-tick-tick

"George." Her voice came in an enchanting song.

Out on the surface of the water, large waves crashing all around, stood Molly. Unaffected. Unsinkable. Devastatingly beautiful.

The beast roared from beneath the flaming currents. White fangs glistened, each ready to devour. Jaws rose from the ocean depths, raging with the force of a thousand infernos.

George jumped onto the railing, hanging tight to the rope that connected to the sails. With a weapon in hand and eyes on Molly, he had to choose.

Fight the abysmal monster... Or go down with his ship.

George woke with a start on Desmond's couch.

It had been a month since he'd skated with Molly, three weeks of wondering what might be, and seven days feeling within reach of hope.

Hope was such a useless thing.

Acorn stirred on the floor by the sofa, shaking her floppy ears and raising her head to peer a bit too deeply into George's soul. One paw reached up to his pillow, then her next one, until she wiggled her entire self to be right next to him and crush him into the sofa cushions.

Maybe George just needed a dog. He closed his eyes and stroked Acorn's fur, relaxing with each brush.

Early morning hours passed into afternoon ones. The large window on the adjacent wall had been left open, allowing sunlight to blare into the room. The heat barely touched him. George had removed his suit jacket and waistcoat early in the night, during Desmond's story. His tie was off somewhere with them. They were lost with who he had been before.

Memories flashed in painful strikes of lighting, things he had never been able to suppress.

The sound of Desmond's feet scrubbing against the floor had Acorn rolling against George's chest, paws in the air and fur in his face. When she licked him across the cheek, he wiped away the slobber and went back to scratching behind her ears.

Desmond stood above him, eyes heavy, his golden sunset curls a mess. After sleeping half the day, his hazelnut pyjamas were so thoroughly wrinkled they nearly looked pleated. He stretched his arms above his head and swiped a hand down his face.

"Coffee?" he asked gruffly, already heading to the kitchen.

"Absolutely not," George replied, earning a sniff as a laugh.

"Tea?"

"Please."

A few more clattering sounds had Acorn jumping off him and heading towards her food dish. George sat up and stared into his hands. They ached for a melody. And not one of the piano sort.

He lifted his navy suspenders individually over the shoulders of his no-longer-crisp white shirt. One by one he folded the sleeves down, unbuttoned and unruly. His cufflinks sat in his pocket. He took them out and stared at their reflections of stray flickers of light.

Cupboard doors closed, and a kettle came to a scream. George shuddered at the sound and rolled it away from his neck and shoulders.

"Here you are," Desmond said, holding out a cup.

George slipped the cufflinks back into his pocket and reached for his tea, the warmth penetrating his hands as if it were holding him in return.

Desmond dragged the table and a chair over. They scraped against the floor until they sat beside the couch. He collapsed into his seat and slurped his coffee. "How did you sleep?"

"I didn't." George lifted his tea, electing to just hold it for a while.

"I'm sorry I wasn't able to break the story to you easier, George."

"It wasn't your storytelling." He watched the steam rise from his cup, like smoke on a dark rainy night. "I can still smell it. I can still see the orange if my eyes close hard enough. I can hear the screams. Now the truth is clear."

George combed his bangs out of his eyes and demanded his voice not to waver. "I've always known I was the reason—"

"You were three years old." Desmond's eyes squinted in disagreement.

"And my mother came looking for me because I got out of bed. That's why she was upstairs when my father came home."

Desmond fell back into his chair. "George—"

"None of it would have happened if it wasn't—"

"Stop." Desmond roughly slid his coffee onto the table, waves of it crashing over the edge. "These are all just excuses. It's like we're boys again and you're taking the blame for the things that were never your fault."

"But—"

"I said *stop*, George!" Desmond leaned in. "I won't let you take the blame. It belongs in a multitude of places, and not a single one of them is you. It rests on your father's temper, on Alice for saving herself and not doing a thing to aid anyone else." He slammed a hand to his chest. "If you want to blame me, for existing, for being the reason behind the initial confrontation of that night to begin with, then do that! Because it's better than blaming yourself."

Acorn returned to the room, circling them before lying down on their feet. She peered up at George, tongue hanging loose from her gaping jaws, slobbering onto her paws.

"I would never blame you, Desmond," George said.

"Then don't blame yourself."

George stared into Acorn's eyes, somehow knowing there'd be consequences if he protested again. Still, it was easier to face her than it was to face someone who brutally rebuked him.

Desmond sighed and took a gulp of liquid courage. "Last night, we were joking about some girl you refuse to acknowledge. Is she real?"

Much, much easier to face the dog.

Tell him, the voice at the back of George's mind begged. *Tell him it's Molly.*

He looked up and met Desmond's gaze. The words lingered on the tip of his tongue, ready yet hesitant. Afraid.

"You're clearly not ready to tell me who she is. That's fine. I just hope she's there for you," Desmond said, his green eyes deepening in intensity. "You said she takes up space in your heart in the worst way. I think that's exactly what you need."

"That's a tad cruel," George muttered. "Albeit also true."

Desmond laughed under his breath. "Do you think she returns your feelings?"

"I feel very uncomfortable talking about this."

"You bugged me about Molly all of the time. What's the difference between this conversation and those ones?"

There were not many differences.

"Would you rather keep talking about your mother?"

"No."

Acorn scooted closer against George's legs. He stretched down and massaged between those cunning eyes.

Desmond lifted his mug and watched George over the brim. "How often do you see this girl?"

"Not that often," he resigned.

"You mean, not as often as you'd like."

George shrugged.

Desmond grinned, jesting at first, but ended in that grounding way he always seemed to have. "George, let her love you."

George stole a minute to savour his tea. The comfort seeped right through his fortified walls, warming him from within. It was exactly what he needed; sufficiently sweet to stave off the bitterness of reality, teeming with enough flavour to fill the void.

That was Desmond. There, always, despite it all. Despite running away. Despite not knowing how to be there in the first place. There after all their youthful tricks and troubles. There when George needed him but didn't know what for. Desmond, the ever loyal confidant.

Desmond, who didn't know George was falling for the same girl he had.

George cleared his throat. "No one said anything about love."

"You didn't have to." Desmond's expression softened further. "I can't pretend to understand anything about love. But I know you'll be good at it once you allow yourself to be."

He swallowed the final dregs of his coffee and took his empty cup to the kitchen for a refill. Upon his return, he flopped into place next to George on the sofa, bumping him playfully with his elbow. "There's nothing you haven't been able to do once you set your mind to it. Imagine what you could do with your heart involved."

To involve his heart meant unburdening locked away secrets. George would need to start at the beginning. And that wasn't with Desmond.

𝄞

"George?"

He stared up at her, not remembering being welcomed into the home.

Fresh flowers sat in vases that filled every table. The golden railing on the stairs caught every beam of light. The room was blinding compared to the shadows he had been staring at all day. Comfortably familiar though he hadn't seen them in months.

He'd played the words over in his mind so many times they'd muddled together in a mess. By the time he managed to speak, his voice wasn't his own. Each syllable was molten and scorched.

"My mother."

Cathryn's eyes went wide.

"I'm sorry," he tried again, keeping what he could delicate. "I don't know how to say this..."

She looked over her shoulder to their sitting room where multiple conversations flowed towards them.

"We'll start with tea," she said, resting a hand on his arm and ushering him in the opposite direction.

He blinked, and they were seated in the drawing room. A tea service appeared as if it were an apparition. A cup was in his hands. More time lost.

He fixated on the contents swirling in his drink. Crystals of sugar caught the lamplight, glistening as the heat curled the bronze liquid into currents. It burned his palm, the scars within, enlivening all the secrets.

"The fire," he began, seeing in her damp, somber eyes that he didn't need to specify what he meant. "It was all my fault. Alice confirmed it all happened when my mother came up to check on me. I'm so—I'm so sorry."

She took the tea from his trembling hand and placed it on the table. "Did Alice say you caused the fire?"

He gathered his hair back with a fist, begging to be afforded a final moment before having to go. One more minute... *tick-tick-tick-tick...*

"No." He released his hair and dragged his hands down his face. "I remember. And I thought you should know it was all my doing."

Cathryn pulled his hands into her own. "George, darling boy, I need you to listen to me."

His eyes refused to open. Unable to look at her. Unable to face a mother, a woman, whose life had been terribly altered due to him. The shadows swirled, devoured every colour and every light.

"You were here with me," she said, firm but tender.

He shook his head.

"You and your mother had spent the day here, and you left your little bear behind. You never could sleep without it." Cathryn combed his hair off his forehead. "Somehow you made your way back here that night, all on your own, through the most formidable storm I've ever seen. Just for your little bear, who you loved so much."

"A bear?" he choked out. "No. No I remember—"

"Memories are sinister if we allow them to take on a life of their own. They'll create stories that aren't even true." Cathryn cupped his chin with her fingers, drawing him to look at her. "I used to be certain the fire was my fault. My William had to re-assure me constantly."

"But I remember..." the words whimpered out, broken, in pieces.

"You have carried this burden for too long. It was never yours to begin with." She dabbed away his tears. "It is time to let it go."

He couldn't respond. He could only stare into the darkness beyond the window.

The years he had kept his guilt at the very core of all his secrets, stoked the fire of his anger, and fed the resolve to stay away from anything he could ruin; it was all gone. Fed to the flames.

He was gone. Nothing but ashes. Nothing but smoke. Nothing. Nothing.

Nothing.

"You are everything your mother ever dreamed of. She would be so proud of you," Cathryn whispered as she wrapped her arms around him. "I am proud of you, too."

An eternity passed before she pulled away. Time stilled as she looked into his eyes; at the boy he'd once been, the man he feared to become, the redemption he so desperately desired.

"I'll be back shortly," she promised. "I'm going to have a room prepared for you. This is your home for the night." Cathryn stood and stepped away, constantly checking over her shoulder until he was alone in the room.

His chest tore open as a silent cry ripped through him, unravelling all the versions of himself he had created. There would be no more personas. No more pretending.

No more.

Behind his many inner walls, in the most crypt-like of cages, waited his true self. He was a weak fragment of a man, blanched in fear of the haunting creature that crept up in the flames. After years of the piano keeping the monster at bay, those protective measures were now burnt to ash.

It was time.

Tick...

A battle of shadows with weapons forged in nightmares.

Tick...

George versus the beast.

Tock.

Chapter 36

Molly woke up on the cellar floor. She rubbed at her temple and tugged the pale lavender robe over her shoulders, wrapping it tightly around the sleeping gown beneath.

As the wedding quickly approached, Victoria had a vigorous beauty regime set out for them. By day, that involved copious amounts of pearl powders for their faces and a dusting of geranium petals for their lips. At meal time, it meant extra salad dressing and rich milk on the side. And for night, it meant silk only for the skin and hair. To help them look radiant.

Molly only ever felt cold. Not that the cellar stones did much to help.

It would have been worthwhile to bring a blanket with her during her escape to write her stories.

She retrieved her book from the cellar floor, holding it close to her heart to soak in the fairytales of her life. It was a diary by anyone else's definition, but so much more to Molly.

She closed the cellar door behind her and walked into her darkened home. Everyone had gone to bed, the world was asleep.

The faint grey glow of the moon flowed through the many windows. It cast the home into a hazy world of clouds and moonlight—eerily beautiful.

Molly grasped onto the stair banister and stilled. She heard something.

A groan through the dark.

It came again.

Her bare feet padded across the foyer, following the sound to the drawing room. Her hand fell onto the doorhandles and carefully clicked the door open.

Bookshelves against the back wall soaked in the moonlight. The settee faced the window and cast a long shadow behind it. A round table held a vase of flowers her mother had purchased at the market. The flowers filled the room with the scent of pollen and nectar, hinting at something richer.

The shrill noise came again.

"George?" Molly hurried to the settee.

His response was unintelligible, etched with sharp emotion that sent a deeper chill through her.

Curled under a knitted blanket on the cushions, was George, asleep, face pinched in pain, droplets of sweat collecting on his forehead.

His groan pierced into her chest, altering her pulse.

She tripped over the table and landed onto the settee with her knees, her book tumbling to the floor.

"George." She gripped his forearm. "George."

His hand caught her wrist, burning against the ice of her skin. He jolted up, clutching her waist and hauling her over his lap.

"Molly."

"It's me," she whispered, "I'm here."

He held tighter, seemingly untrusting of reality, unwilling to be torn apart. The fringe of his bangs draped along her nose as his rapid breaths whirled against her lips. His hand made its way to the nape of her neck, fingers tangling into her hair.

"This is real?"

She raised a hand in the narrow space between them and flattened her palm against his chest. His heart pounded beneath her touch. "This is real."

George dropped his forehead onto hers, and she couldn't move.

Worry folded between his closed eyes, desperation sketched above his brow. The pensive lines were like drawings on a map leading weary souls through worlds untravelled.

She lifted her hand and wrapped it at the base of his neck, anchoring him to her as his breaths softened.

"Are we sure this is real?" he whispered.

She let out a quick breath. "No."

His gaze shifted to take in the room as she slid off his lap. He scanned the knitted blanket between them. "I fell asleep. Someone let me sleep here?"

"My mother, most likely. She was saying how she wanted to give this to you." Molly lifted the nearest corner of the blanket, grazing her fingers across the loops. "This is a blanket your mother started. My mother completed it for her. You can see where the knit changes."

George swiped his hair with the back of his hand and lifted the blanket, expression shuddering as he held it closer.

Molly's hand rose to his arm, passing her thumb across the fabric of his wrinkled sleeves. His eyes were wide but sunken, as if he were staring at things unseen.

"What happened, George?" She bravely inched closer. "Can you tell me what's wrong?"

"Nothing important." Tendrils of inky hair dropped around George's features as his eyes fell closed. "And that's the problem, because I was sure it would be important. That the reason my family perished while I survived, would be significant."

Those puzzle pieces were more than enough. She wilted.

He blew out a heavy breath, skittering his bangs away. "I've put my whole life on pause because of an old toy. I neglected everything I ever wanted. For nothing."

Molly reached for him, slowly, carefully, until his hand lifted towards hers, and everything fit into place.

He stared down at their entwined fingers. "Do you remember our conversation at the post office, of what you wanted to add to your letter?"

She nodded.

His hand tightened around hers. "This is my chance. To build myself back up. I *will* build myself back up."

"I believe in you," she whispered.

His lips quirked up delicately.

And there it was again—their little world, holding them together. This time it was composed by his tender smile and her irrevocable wish to keep him that way.

George lowered his feet to the floor, accidentally kicking an object beneath the table. He bent over to retrieve it and held up her storybook. "Yours?"

She accepted it into her hands. "It's my book of fairytales."

"Stories you've written?"

"Stories I've lived." She indulged in watching him, picking up on how the quick shift in conversation lifted away another shadow. "Whenever something magical happens, I write it down. I've been doing it since I was a little girl."

Molly curled her legs up to her chest. Her robe drooped off her shoulders and caught in the crooks of her arms.

George's fingers lightly brushed her skin as he lifted the garment back to its place. His skin was flames against her own. He lifted the blanket and draped it over her shoulders.

She held the knitted throw close as the warmth billowed all throughout her.

His grin swept wider and met his eyes; another shadow dissipating. "What were you writing about?"

"Maybe it's a secret." She dropped her chin to her knees.

He twisted to face her, arm sprawled along the back of the settee, eyes filled with dancing sparks. She never could figure out why they did that.

But she loved it entirely. Things were always simpler to admit to in the dark; where secrets came out to play under the cover of night.

Her fingers grazed across the edges of her book, curling it open to the right page.

"You're going to let me read it?" He sounded surprised.

"Not if you don't want to."

His fingers thrummed a contemplating melody. "Would you let me pick the entry?"

"You don't know any of the entries."

"I'm curious about the first one." He slid closer. "The moment you believed in fairytales so much that you started looking for them everywhere. It's the moment you became you."

Molly's heart rippled in sparks. She couldn't properly breathe, let alone speak. She handed him the book.

He lifted the cover and examined the crayon drawing. And kept doing so for a very long while. "This is...something."

"That's me."

George brushed the surrounding doodles. "And these are?"

"Wings."

"Ah, yes." He tilted the pages towards the window for more light and gestured to the next item. "This must be a fairy?"

"A royal fairy, with a crown."

"How could I have missed the crown?" He looked at her with an overstretched smile.

She leaned over and pressed her fingers into the paper, unable to guess what the leftover shapes were. They could have been fairies or butterflies, or just bits of glitter.

She turned to face him only to find he hadn't looked away. His gaze was alight with tightly woven secrets; ones she craved to know, ones it felt like he wanted to share.

He closed the book and placed it back in her hands, never losing her eyes.

"It's very late," he said. "You should get to bed where you can do some proper dreaming."

"I want to stay with you." Her cheeks immediately heated. She swallowed. "I mean, I want to stay until you're done."

George looked out past the window and into the night, at the lurking shadows.

"I'm done," he said at last, voice thick with unspoken wishes.

He stood and helped her to her feet, making sure the blanket never fell to the floor.

They silently made their way to the stairs together and up to the second level of the home.

"Here." She removed the knitted throw from her shoulders and handed it to him. "You need this."

He wrapped his arms around it and held it close, looking both ways down the hall. "Do you by chance know which room your parents would have given me?"

His eyes met hers again, and their little world spun faster. She didn't look away as she pointed behind him. "Second to the right."

George's smile was as enticing as future fairytales. "I'll see you in the morning."

Chapter 37

Their little rowboat was gently tossed by pattering waves. Molly sat across from George, adorned in a ballgown woven of continuously blossoming flowers. It glittered more than the seawater; each new bloom catching each beam of light from the ever-changing glowing clouds. Her hair rolled in shambles around her shoulders, twisting with new flowers as they grew.

George turned to look over his shoulder. He watched the fire in the distance, the ship made of stone being pulled to the burning seabed in the jaws of that horrid creature.

They weren't too far away, but perhaps, they were just far enough.

"Did you think we'd make it?" Molly asked.

His eyes were on her again. "I didn't think so."

"You saved us."

"No, Miss Jones. You saved me."

Molly smiled and laid back on the little bench, staring up to the lavender sky, stars twinkling in her eyes.

The rhythmic lullaby of the crystal blue waters against the wooden slats lulled George into lying down as well. He took turns glancing between the dreamlike clouds and her. Each line blurred, the colours extra bright; everything soaked in an invisible magic. Whatever world they were in, it felt like home.

Molly rolled closer, resting her head into his shoulder and playing with the chain of his watch.

He stole every second he could to gaze upon each of her freckles, each curl in her hair, and her fluttering lashes. "I think I'm falling in love with you."

A rose budded on the sleeve of her gown, stem twisting around his palm as the petals unfurled. A thorn dug into his flesh, releasing a black liquid that puddled on his skin.

Molly laughed and plucked the flower away. She drew his hand to her lips and kissed the tender spot in the centre. When she pulled away, rose petals remained in his palm, wrapping around him like soft bandages.

Her eyes glistened with endless songs. She reached up and brushed her fingers against his neck. "Tick-tock, Mr Clarington."

A light rap at the room's entrance had George waking up before he was ready.

He pushed himself out of bed and fastened the buttons on his shirt for decency before opening the door.

"Good morning," Felix sang, bouncing a young child in one arm while holding a bundle of clothing in the other.

"Morning," George croaked, voice still thick with sleep.

Felix grinned at the little boy whose hair was in utter disarray but whose smile matched his father's. "Did you know this gentleman is a George as well?"

Young George chewed on the tip of his finger and examined this new George with his big hazel eyes.

"These are for you," Felix added, handing George the folded garments. "Aunt Cat discreetly mentioned that you might be in need. They're freshly laundered. Whatever fits is yours."

George scratched at the sleeves he'd been wearing for too many days and accepted the new outfit. "Thank you."

Felix nodded and threw his son over his shoulder. "We'll see you down at breakfast, George."

The child shrieked, and George went back into the room, laughing as he closed the door behind him.

He fell onto the edge of the bed, tossed the outfit to the side and thought back on his dream.

Dream.

It had been years since he'd last dreamed—with the exception of the waking moments he'd experienced as of late. Hiding behind the bookshelves. Skating on the ice. Last night poring over crayon drawings under a knitted blanket.

He got to his feet and went for the washing basin. He poured fresh water and drew it up with his hands, feeling the cool trickle wash away the last couple of days. He was in need of a good shave. Stubble scraped his palm as he brushed down his chin and neck. With the remaining droplets on his fingers, George combed back his hair, then headed to sort through the borrowed garments.

This was a suit unlike anything George had ever worn. Mostly because none of the parts of it really fit together. Each piece was extravagant on its own; less so after assembled. The checkered jacket and trousers were made of light pearl and beige fabrics. There had never been an outfit more outside of George's spectrum.

He finished dressing and brought his own cufflinks out with him to the hall, where he slipped them on during his descent down the stairs.

The dining room rang with commotion. No one tore themselves away from their conversations; too busy in family matters to be bothered. It was a refreshing neglect of formalities.

A chair was left empty between Felix and the girl with the amber eyes that aggressively shot their way through him.

"Good morning, Victoria," he greeted as he lowered to his seat.

Victoria's lips curled over her teeth as she turned back to him, coating her voice in poisonous syrup. "To what do we owe such an unexpected surprise?"

"That story would bore you." He served her a cup of tea, dropping in three sugars and a lemon slice before sliding it over. "Drink this and perhaps you'll hate me less."

Victoria pursed her lips and tilted her chin up, dismissing him but accepting the beverage. She'd come around in a minute or two. Not that there'd be much improvement.

Defying all reasonable sense, Molly's presence on Victoria's other side floated towards him; radiant, beyond his dreams. The cadence in her voice as she conversed with her family, her rhythmical way of playing with the pendant on her chain, the colour in her cheeks when her eyes locked on his. It was all so mesmerizing.

She dipped her chin, loose waves cascading around her shoulders, hiding what he knew was a smile that matched his own. The rose tinted lace on her blouse fluttered as she spun back to her cousin in-law, Sylvia.

"Will you be attending the Prescott Gala tomorrow night, Mr Clarington?" Though posed as a question, there was no hint of mystery in the words of Molly's aunt, Lady Vivianne Jones.

She was a woman about the age his mother should have been. Hair tightly pulled back, expression just as taut, eyes sharp and considering.

"We were discussing certain details of importance," Cathryn added with a kind smile. "William and I will be attending, Molly said she would join us. The rest of the family have dug in their heels in protest and will be staying home."

"They're throwing this party to attack my wedding!" Victoria retorted. Even Lady Vivianne seemed to nonverbally agree. "The only people who throw parties days before their neighbour's wedding are the ones simply trying to steal the spotlight." Victoria chewed her food angrily and continued, "They will come to regret it."

William Jones grumbled in agreement as he finished off the last bite of his breakfast. Even Felix and his father, George Jones, didn't hesitate to nod along.

George's own invitation to the Prescotts sat somewhere on his desk, forgotten about. He'd had no intentions of even considering accepting until that very moment.

"I will be attending, yes," he said to Lady Vivianne while dragging a slice of broiled ham to his plate.

"Very commendable, Mr Clarington," she replied. She made a high noise then looked across the table. "Cathryn, do you remember the last time we were in the company of a young Mr Clarington?"

Cathryn hummed. "I do."

Lady Vivianne's fork clinked off her plate, and she placed her utensils down and began to laugh; her propriety crumbled to pieces. "He didn't know what was coming for him."

"What was coming for him, mother?" Felix broke in with a delirious grin.

"You should know better than anyone else," she said. "No one crosses your mother and escapes unscathed.

"You scathed him?" Felix asked.

Vivianne and Cathryn locked eyes.

"Only for the night," Cathryn finished.

Lady Vivianne's gaze landed upon George a final time. "From what I have heard, you are nothing like your father. And I say that with the highest regards." She prepared a bite of breakfast. "It is a pleasure to know the Clarington name is back on track."

"Agreed," said William Jones.

"Hear, hear," added George Jones.

Felix clapped the back of George's shoulder.

"How thankful we all are," completed Cathryn. She watched George steadily, eyes searching for weaknesses or cracks in his facade. When she was satisfied, not finding any, she addressed the table, "The Towson family will be here soon. We'll be mapping out the grounds for the wedding ceremony and reception."

"We're very excited to meet the Towson family," Lady Vivianne followed the shift of the conversation easily.

George however, played with his food as he mused over the previous discussion. It wasn't uncommon for him to be confronted by his father's legacy. But while he scrambled for the connection, for any scrap of proof he was his father's son, he came up short. Disconnected. As if that legacy wasn't a part of his own.

He played with a medley of cubed fruits, tipping them over with his fork.

James Clarington no longer loomed over his shoulders or hid in his shadow. George was, for lack of a better term, free.

A wild scream soared through the room. Sylvia rose from her chair, steely eyes tracking her son as he ran in circles around the chairs.

George smiled at the sound and ate his food, finding peace in the scene of balanced chaos.

"George wants to be with Molly," Sylvia announced.

His shoulders went rigid.

Sylvia scooped her child off the floor with one hand and tucked loose strands of her raven hair back into its proper place with the other. She dropped the giggling child into Molly's lap before crashing into her own seat.

George released a breath. Too many Georges were in the vicinity.

"I saw that," Felix said, quiet enough for only the two of them to hear.

Lifting his cup to cover his mouth, George kept his words hidden and his voice low. "If you tell anyone," he paused, knowing he posed no real threat, "we could never be friends."

Felix's jaw went slack as he tented a hand above his heart. "All I ask is for recognition. The day you marry my cousin, I want it to be known that it was all due to my efforts."

George squinted and lowered his tea, flaring out a questioning hand.

Felix smirked. "You didn't deny it. Just think what that marriage would do for our friendship!" He waved himself off.

"We'll have time to talk about that later, I suppose. When there are less ears present."

George's shoulders dropped as he focused on his plate, entirely unsure of why he hadn't been able to deny a thing.

He pressed his thumbs into his temples and covered his eyes. What he needed to do was make it through the horrid gala the Prescotts were hosting. Maybe dance with Molly at least once to see how he'd fare in the aftermath.

Molly bounced her cousin's child on her leg, eliciting more laughter from the boy.

George caught himself smiling and looked back at his plate, ready to pierce his fork into a fresh piece of fruit.

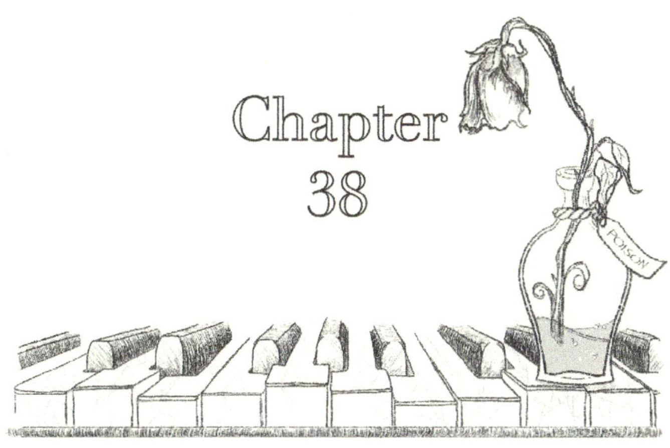

Chapter 38

It should have been assumed that the Prescotts would throw the ball of the century. Too bad it wasn't the century they were currently living in.

George was besieged by men twice his age. He stood near the doorway to the Prescott's ballroom, maintaining an attentive watch over the crowd as he pretended to listen to the tiresome conversations of old men.

Anyone who was anyone was in attendance. The most inspiring names in London, every influential family one could think of, and power hungry gentlemen of all stations. Gossipers huddled in their circles, glancing and giggling at the people around them.

Flames flickered in brass candelabras on the walls between hanging maroon fabrics, draping the mansion to look like a lair of the most vile creatures. How fitting.

The atmosphere clouded George's judgment. He tapped his fingers inside his pockets and kept a close eye on the guests. Something was amiss. He just couldn't figure out what it was.

He adjusted the lengths of his sleeves, the white cuffs peeking out from beneath the deepest midnight fabric. Sewn in nearly identically hued thread, were hidden roses. He brushed against them to find comfort in the fine suit. It was exhausting to pretend to be someone he wasn't, if even for a short while.

The clamour of the room dulled as George was drawn into a trance. That was the effect of Molly Jones. She was a siren song that lured him away from his better judgment. Her gown was layered in lilac frills that grew in size as they trailed to the floor. A loose braid sat along the curve of her shoulders, revealing the dangling florets of her crimson earrings. Even the most majestic gardens would envy her ability to bloom.

She caught sight of him, tucked away in the corner, and she smiled.

George didn't bother to dismiss himself from his current conversation, but made his way across the hall.

"You look...murderous tonight, Miss Jones," he presented with a shallow bow.

"Again with your casual flirtations." She curtsied.

"I thought you knew me better than that. I've never been one to dapple in anything casual."

She blushed. It was perfect.

A ripple of concentration crinkled her brow as she took in the room. "I feel like everyone is watching me."

George mimicked her scan, and several people turned away. That never meant anything good.

He tucked her hand over his and walked them over to a less crowded corner.

She peered over her shoulders and crowded closer to him. It wasn't long before she was plucking at the buttons on his sleeves. He drew her hand to his cufflinks, knowing they'd stand up better under the pressure. She didn't notice, and spun the stones around her thumb absentmindedly.

He tipped his head closer to her level. "Just say the words, and I'll whisk you away."

Her lips finally curled in the corners. "Am I that obvious?"

"Only to me."

Her eyes flicked to his.

Noises rushed together before George could think of a way to ease her into a laugh.

Harold and Alice Prescott entered the grand room as a unit. Harold's large barrel chest seemed further puffed in his pride; one misplaced pin could deflate him. Alice's dress was an interesting shape, curving around her midsection as her hand cradled her abdomen.

She locked her gaze on him, ticking her eyes onto Molly, then across the room to William and Cathryn Jones. She turned sideways, revealing her plump belly.

Alice's cruel grin was more than enough confirmation.

A child. A life.

One they would surely ruin if history had proven anything.

"They're bringing another child into this world?" Molly said towards where she was plucking at his cufflinks.

"I'm unsure," George muttered while holding Harold's glare. "Are creatures like Harold and Alice capable of bearing human-like offspring?"

Molly gave him a look, one fierce and wild as if holding in a laugh with great force.

George's mouth twisted into a sinister smile as he guided her around the corner into an abandoned hallway.

She released his arm and twisted the sash of her gown in her hands. "Who is this baby going to have? Desmond has you. Desmond had me. Who is going to be there to take care of them?" A ruby hue that matched her earrings spread across her nose and cheeks.

The giggles of gossips and busybodies came from the corner as curious guests scoped out the hallway. He eyed them carefully.

Molly blew out a breath. "I want to take that baby away, bring them home and love them. All children need someone to love them."

"We can come back to the subject of kidnapping in a few months, when it's more relevant," George suggested. "For now, why don't we leave this party behind?"

She nodded and showed him her trembling hands. "I need a glass of water first. The least Alice can do is hydrate me. Will you wait here?"

George fell back against the wall and crossed a foot over his ankle, using the dramatics to hide how hesitant he was about her leaving his sight. "I won't move a muscle, I swear."

Molly spun around and disappeared through the door to the grand room, music flaring out into the corridor from the ongoing dancing.

George thrummed his fingers. There would be no dancing with her now.

He lifted the watch from its hidden pocket and stared down to the dials. The mocking clock hands stood still, just as they had for years. All it would take was a synchronized flick of his wrist for time to move again.

William Jones bolted down the hallway, determinedly fuming. "Where's my daughter?"

George pushed away from the wall and slipped the watch away. "Retrieving a glass of water."

William's face reddened as he ground his teeth.

George wiped his palms against his pant legs. "I can find her and—"

"Get her out of here. Cathryn and I are handling the rest."

"Has something happened?"

The responding fire in William's eyes sent George's pulse raging with the potency of rallied nightmares.

Chapter 39

Molly's parched throat begged for more water. She reached across the table for a second glass, peering at the golden platters and fine china dishes filled with rich chocolate desserts. She trailed one of them across the table, fingers trembling against the plate.

"Brave of you to show your face," said an arrogant voice.

She spun around, clutching the plate and cup to her chest. Boris towered over her. "Can I help you with something?"

"You?" he taunted, eyes raking over her. "There's nothing I need from you."

After making a sound of disgust, she stepped past him, chocolate cake in one hand, glass of water in the other.

He followed her. "I heard you and Desmond had quite the experience."

Molly shook herself and kept walking.

The closest door had not led to the proper hallway. George was nowhere in sight, and she knew he would not have moved. She spun around and came face to face with Boris.

A few guests cast them some sneers, before evacuating the hall, leaving her alone with him.

"It's why Desmond left town in a hurry," he continued. "You're damaged goods now." His eyes travelled to places that raised bile in her throat.

The accusation was clear.

It was revolting.

She flung her cup at him. It soaked his suit and shattered to the floor.

Boris clawed into her wrist. "I'm glad to be here to enjoy your downfall."

"*Get away.*" She smashed the chocolate cake across his white vest and shirt, smearing the filth across the width of his chest.

He gripped her other arm and slammed her against the wall.

A darkness crowded her vision, leeching away the power she had left to struggle. The sharp pain travelled from her skull down her spine.

"You're done for," Boris seethed. "Now all will see you as a disgrace. You'll be unable to marry, to be loved."

Molly forced her eyes open, refusing to give up or show how close she was to defeat.

Boris snarled, a deep sound that was choked short. A hand gripped his shirt and a second struck him across the jaw, knocking him to the ground.

George winced. He stood over Boris and shook out his hand, the one in midst of healing. His eyes traced back to Molly through his mess of hair. He stepped away and reached out to her.

She ran and collapsed into his open arms as her legs tried to give out.

"I've got you," George promised, holding her closer.

"Georgie-boy," Boris patronized, adjusting the alignment of his jaw as he rose up from the floor. "How am I not surprised?"

A crowd had gathered by the hall entrance, greedy to decipher what they could of the exchange.

George's grip around Molly tightened. "Leave, Boris."

Boris sucked on his teeth before spitting out red. He wiped his mouth and glowered. "I have no intention of being caught in the company of a wretch like her."

George sheltered her beside him as Boris left.

Molly's stomach churned once he was gone. She curled over, feeling the sick fighting for escape.

"I'm sorry, but we need to go." George lifted her up and tucked her under his arm.

She couldn't protest.

George eyed every last gawker as they travelled through the foyer. His free hand flexed at his side, far more red than it ought to have been.

"Your hand," she whimpered.

He gave her a wink. Not obnoxious, nor arrogant, but with just enough irrefutable strength to help her carry on forward.

They raced outside, greeted by the night's breeze and a slew of silence.

George disregarded an attendant that tried to intervene and helped her to his car, aiding in her fall into the seat. The engine started, and he clambered in behind the wheel.

The truth crashed down on her.

"I'm ruined," she whispered thickly.

He had the vehicle in motion. "I'm not letting that happen."

"It already has." Molly hugged her arms around herself. "That's why everyone was staring at me."

George's eyes darkened. He wrung his sore hand around the steering wheel. "Do you want to go back there? I will fix this right now."

Tears streamed down her cheeks.

She craved somewhere far far away.

She imagined Quaintrelle Estate, lights filtering through nearly every window so it glowed against the dark. She thought of her family waiting there, laughing as they sorted out the details of Victoria's wedding. She could only hope her ruined reputation did nothing to spoil such an important day for her sister.

George reached across to her, soaking her tears away with his sleeve, passing his hand just beneath her lashes.

Her wrists ached as though thorns had pierced her flesh. Her breaths heaved, and pain rolled into every wave of her consciousness.

Molly sheltered her face into her hands and fell back against the seat.

His arm rested there, and so she'd fallen against him.

He maneuvered the car down the road. The hum of the motor carried over her broken sobs until she no longer had the strength to remain awake.

Chapter 40

A chorus of frogs and night birds woke Molly. She lolled her head to the side as her eyes slivered open.

George was sprawled in his seat, legs beneath the dash of his car, one arm curled under his head. He had fallen asleep, too. And for that brief second, in-between dreams and reality, nothing hurt.

Molly pushed herself higher and looked out over the hood. The lake glistened in the distance and trees cuddled around the rolling hills where a brick house sat.

In the silence, staring into the night, she felt herself sink deeper. She didn't want to go back there. Back into that pit beneath her waves where fearsome monsters awaited. Where wounds and misfortunes would befall everyone she cared for. Drowning. Bleeding. Anguish.

It was as though Boris' hands still clung to her arms. Alice's lies consumed every space in her mind. The sneers and the stares of onlookers. The worries about the upcoming wedding, her sister, her mother... And George.

Every thought tumbled over and under Molly, shattering her last nerves until they were indistinguishable from the pain.

She gasped for air.

"You're awake." George's voice was brisk with sleep.

She wished she was sleeping, still in that place where one could dream and forget.

Her fingers dug into her palm. Everything was destroyed.

And there was George, broken and healing himself. She could still see his cracks and fractures. No manner of fine suits could hide them.

"You should have brought me home," she said, desperate to sound stronger than she felt.

"Is that what you'd like me to do?" he asked steadily. Too steadily. He adjusted himself to sit straight.

"I'm *ruined*, George. Being with me is the last thing you need."

His gaze narrowed on her. "I disagree."

"You should take me home."

"I won't leave you."

She summoned all the courage she could, all the force to keep him away so her fate would not destroy his. "It's for the best."

A muscle feathered in his jaw. "I'm not doing this again."

He jumped to the ground, and marched around the vehicle until he was beside her. He offered his assistance to help her up.

She stared at his hand, fighting the reflex to take it. To stay. To be with George.

His lips thinned as he withdrew, heading for the worn pathway through the grasses that led to the water.

Molly scrambled out of her seat and ran down the path to him. "Why aren't you taking me home?"

He spun to her, jacket flaring out and hair tousling in the breeze. "You never specifically asked me to take you home. Simply stated I should. If the only reason you have for wanting to leave is how it would benefit *me*, then I get a say in the matter as well. And I feel like sorting through this at the lake."

He continued away, making it to the shore where an old dock floated atop the water. Each ripple caught a new burst of blinding moonlight and stars.

George grasped a pole and stepped onto the wooden planks.

She was right behind him. "No one has to know you were with me tonight."

He stopped short where the slats met the waves and spun around. She nearly plowed into him.

"Remember the last time we were here? How horrible I was?" she said, voice filled with angry tears. "I was not half as bad as this! Take me home so you don't have to endure that again. You'll be better. Everyone is always better once they leave."

"I'm staying with you."

"What of the effects on your name, the business—"

"Do you think any of that is more important to me?" He moved closer, leaving little space between them. "More important than you?"

Her heels caught on the lip of wood at the brim of the dock, the hem of her gown already trickling into the waves. She gripped at his jacket to avoid falling over.

George held her near, eyes boring into hers so she couldn't look away. "I am staying with you, no matter how deep you go."

Her fingers twisted into the floral fabric of his lapels.

Stay.

She wanted *him* to stay.

She shook her head, braid coming undone and loosened curls blowing in the wind. "Why?"

"I want to," he said, an oath. His fingers mapped out her elbows and slid up the back of her arms. "Despite what your scars would have you believe, I cannot leave you. My heart beats in tune with your hours—even those spent in the dark. So give me your worst, and if it is all I'll ever have, that will be enough."

The weight on her chest lifted, softened and metamorphosed. She pressed her mouth into a firm line to still her quivering.

George tipped her face up to his, heart-achingly gentle as he stroked beneath her lips until they relaxed. "In this world and those imagined, and every world in-between, I'll be here. Withstanding every storm. Doing what I can to reignite your dreams. For that is where I am, every time I am with you. Here dreaming even though I'm wide awake."

The stories in his voice wrapped around her in riveting symphonies. Melodies inaudible, yet so crisp, so tangible— daring her to believe.

Mellow colours rose from the horizon, illuminating the silver mist beaming off the waters. George lit up with every colour betwixt what was real and what was fantasy.

He combed his fingers across the nape of her neck and into her hair, lowering his forehead to hers.

"I'll take you there," he murmured.

Her eyes fell closed in surrender. "You already have."

George hesitated, holding in a disbelieving breath.

She swept her hands over his shoulders. "George?"

His arms roped around her waist and lifted her into the air, into their place between one dream and the next.

The world slipped away.

She allowed herself to forget. To go where fears no longer mattered. Where they banished their shadows as one day ended and a new one began, until the melody of the lake joined with the rhythm of their hearts.

George placed her back on her toes and tilted his head to meet her gaze. "Dance with me?"

Delicately sparkling in the bluest parts of his eyes was a little secret. She was sure a similar one shimmered in hers. There was no night dark enough, no storm strong enough, in times past or in times to come, where she would ever say no to dancing with him.

"Always."

His smile curled lazily in the corners. His hold swung open, and she fell into the free space. The hem of her skirt remained in the water, her head rested on his shoulder, and she fell deeper.

Glitter and sparks tingled across Molly's skin. "Is this real?"

George wrapped his fingers around hers, drawing his lips to the inside of her wrist. The kiss replaced every bit of reality that remained. "I'm entirely yours, Fairy Girl."

The sky burst into violets, with new colours blooming through the mist where the sun met the waves.

To Molly, there was only George. He was someone new. Someone she'd been waiting to meet her whole life. Yet, someone she had always known. He was worlds and dreams and magic. He was something to believe in.

Chapter 41

Victoria let out a string of expletives.

Molly groaned and fell back against one of the many pillows. Her bed was filled with all of the necessities for a pyjama night. Chocolates, cheeses and fruits, freshly baked goods, and sparkling drinks. Notepapers and ribbons, frilly blankets, and fluffy cushions.

"Perhaps Alice could have a little—" Sylvia paused to examine her finger nails. "A little accident, of sorts."

"No," Molly replied.

"You said she likes her trinkets. We could—"

"No!" Molly sat straight up and glared at the women in her room. The angry, loving, and fierce duo.

Victoria's face deepened its shade of scarlet, the colour reaching her ears. It was a bright contrast to her white lace sleeping gown, tailored to her to be perfectly fit for a bride.

Sylvia's face was a mask of serenity, dark eyes ever calculating. Her vixen red nightwear complementing the intensity of her schemes.

"We're not doing anything to Alice," Molly continued. "We're not sinking to her level, and we're not letting her steal any attention away from the wedding."

"Forget the wedding, Molly." Victoria's eyes hardened. "Alice will pay for what she has done."

"It's not my fight." Molly could hear George's reassurance as she thought back on his words on the drive home from the lake. It felt like an entire lifetime ago, when it had only been two days. One of which she had spent sleeping. "Alice did this to our parents, to her own son. She used me because she was too cowardly to face them. I don't want to fight her, she isn't worth it."

Victoria and Sylvia locked eyes in a silent conversation.

Molly curled up by the mass of blankets and sugary treats. She pulled down on the sleeves of her cornflower blue robe and cast her eyes away. "We're supposed to be having a fun last night."

"We don't mind talking about this," Victoria promised.

"Plotting revenge is one of my favourite things," Sylvia assured.

"I won't let Alice control my life by forcing me into decisions I'm not prepared to make." Molly stole a chocolate covered strawberry and devoured it in one bite. "If I do *nothing*, she loses."

"That's the most boring solution I've ever heard." Victoria lifted a cluster of grapes and popped one between her teeth.

Sylvia slathered a slice of bread with herbed butter. "I think the whole idea is that Alice deserves nothing but something boring from us." She lifted a nonchalant shoulder, silken hair coiling around her muscles as she lifted her plate for a bite.

Victoria added something through a mouthful of food. Molly was thankful she didn't understand.

"Sorry to interrupt," Felix said, knocking on the open door. "Our son is begging for one more goodnight kiss."

Sylvia's eyes lit up. She flicked them back to Molly as she crawled off the bed. "I'll be right back."

"I'm going to sneak downstairs and fill up on our refreshments." Victoria held up her glittering flask; one she planned to fill with their father's hidden liquors.

Molly watched them leave, wishing them well on their separate ventures.

Felix remained behind. "Having fun?"

"Hopefully soon," she sighed.

He took drawn out strides into her room, tucking his hands away into his pockets as though he had no care in the world. But the concern was written across his forehead in deepening creases.

She twisted her fingers together to distract from her persistent worries.

Felix formed an exaggerated pout. "I was in town earlier. Making my way to a certain office. While it ended up being the wrong office, I found the proper building eventually."

Molly let out a humourless laugh.

He reached forward to steal an apple. "Once I made it to the right place, Mr George Clarington informed me that gossip is swinging slightly in your favour. Apparently people are rather frightened of his grandmother, and she has made it very clear where her loyalties lie."

Her pulse quickened, in a splendid and frightening way. She did her best to hide it. "Why were you visiting George?"

"I was only inviting him out for a drink tonight. He asked about you."

"He did?"

"He did." Felix flipped open his suit jacket. He reached into the inner pocket and pulled out a cream coloured envelope.

She stared. "What is it?"

Felix's eyebrows flew up. "Do you want to theorize?"

Molly jumped off her bed and plucked it from his grasp. She ran her fingers across the scrolls of her name as she fell into the plush violet chair in the corner.

"Shall I leave you alone with the penmanship?" Felix coaxed with a smirk, tossing his apple into the air.

She gave him a look, which only stretched his smile.

Very carefully, she peeled open the envelope and drew out the folded paper inside.

Fairy Girl,

Tomorrow. That is the word I keep repeating. Tomorrow will be brighter, since tomorrow, I will see you.

As a man who has been lost at sea his entire life, you are my beacon in the dark, the one helping me navigate through the lingering shadows. I only wish I were there to return the favour in your time of need.

Remember your wings, Fairy Girl. May they guide and bring you back to the light.

Until tomorrow,

George

P.S. Will you save me a dance?

The paper crinkled in her hands as she held it close.

"I'm on my way to see him," Felix drawled into the silence, followed by crunching his first bite into the fruit. "If you hurry you could write out a reply."

Molly made haste to retrieve the needed stationary at her writing desk.

George,

Today is already brighter with the hope of tomorrow. While perhaps I'm not quite myself at the moment, I assure you I have improved much since yesterday. All with your help.

You have always been my wings, George. So you may have all of my dances.

Forever yours,

Molly

She folded the paper away and tucked it into a fresh envelope, sealing it with drips of wax.

"I was expecting that to take longer," Felix said around the apple. "With the way you were saying goodbye in the driveway yesterday—"

"You saw us?"

"Fret not, dear cousin. I was the only one peering out the windows. I won't be sharing your secrets. Especially the night before Victoria's wedding. She'd have my head."

She eyed him skeptically and dropped the letter into his all-too-eager hands.

Felix tucked the envelope safely into his pocket. "I'm surprised he didn't kiss you."

Molly tiptoed to her bed and fell back into her old spot, fiddling with her pendant to silence the memories.

"It's complicated," she offered lightly.

"Complicated? " Felix wiped his mouth with the arm of his sleeve and stared at her flabbergasted. "Remember how I managed to get my wife to fall in love with me? *That* was complicated. But this?" He shrugged. "Sure, he was in a false relationship with your sister for six months. And who cares if the last person you kissed was his best friend. Or was it his brother? Not to mention the rumours flying around about you and Desmond at the moment."

Molly gave him a sideways glance. "See? Complicated."

"Mere semantics."

She opened and closed her locket. If it were not for the prowling accusations against her that had overshadowed the night, kissing George would have been wonderful. A kiss that would have brimmed with fairytales and given her wings. A kiss she'd wish to remember always.

Felix examined his fruit, searching for the location of his next bite. "His affections must run deep if he could resist the urge to kiss you."

"You're not exactly an expert on restraint, Felix."

"My point exactly." He left for the door with a wink. "And I love my wife with everything I am. Imagine what that means for you."

As the door closed, Molly smiled. A secret little smile that no one would see. One stolen from dreams, since in reality she did not have much to openly smile about. She thought about George and wondered if he too was smiling. That would be reason enough to spread hers wider. She only hoped her message to him would be convincing.

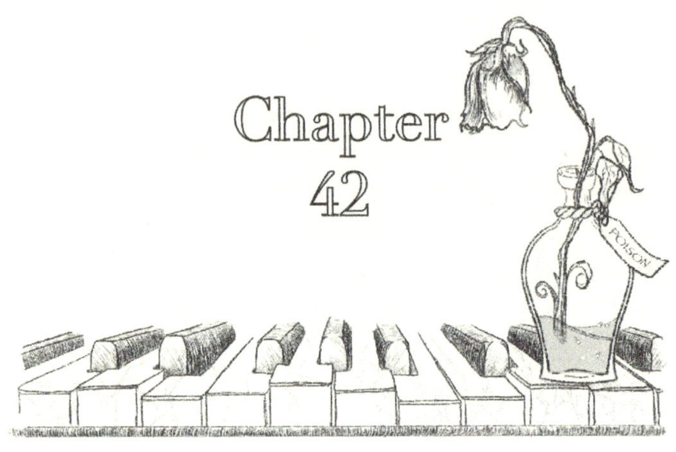

Chapter 42

George wasn't convinced.

He had read Molly's letter. Several times. While her words were soft and kind, something lurking inside George's shadows pushed him to better himself.

He'd had just enough waking hours to sew his tattered pieces into some guise of a gentleman. Mending tears and strengthening stitches, assembling shreds into an appropriate persona for the rest of the day. Locking away the wreck he was.

This would be accomplished with the help of his finest suit.

The black tuxedo fooled any untrained eye, for beneath the classic appearance was an indulgent red lining with several hidden pockets. His waistcoat was silver, but embroidered with ruby thread that glistened into blooming roses in the proper light. The matching pinstriped trousers were comfortable enough and sported the elegance needed for attending a wedding. It was a suit that meant George could be anyone he wanted to.

He walked to the foyer as he tucked his pocket watch into place, shoes clacking a song against the marble floors, the golden chain of his watch adding to the melody. His hat waited for him on its regular hook. He flicked it off and, mid-spiral through the air, tipped it onto his head with a synchronized flip of his wrist. It was a dance he had long perfected. He smiled.

Just as he turned towards the door, someone knocked at it.

Strange.

Jeremy knew to wait at their home until George drove up. Thomas was aware of that plan as well. No one else would come unannounced and so early in the morning.

The last two steps to the door was enough time for him to create a surplus of scenarios of who was on the other side.

It didn't matter.

Time never conformed to any clock known to man. Always racing or dragging, whichever was opposite to what was hoped for. A creature that moved at its own pace, revealing its imprints at the least opportune moment.

Which was exactly what happened when George opened the door.

He came face to face with several regrets all at once. Secrets he should have shared. Stories he should have told.

It was too late for him to choose his moment. Time had chosen it for him.

George swallowed and managed to compose a smile of sorts. "Good morning, Desmond."

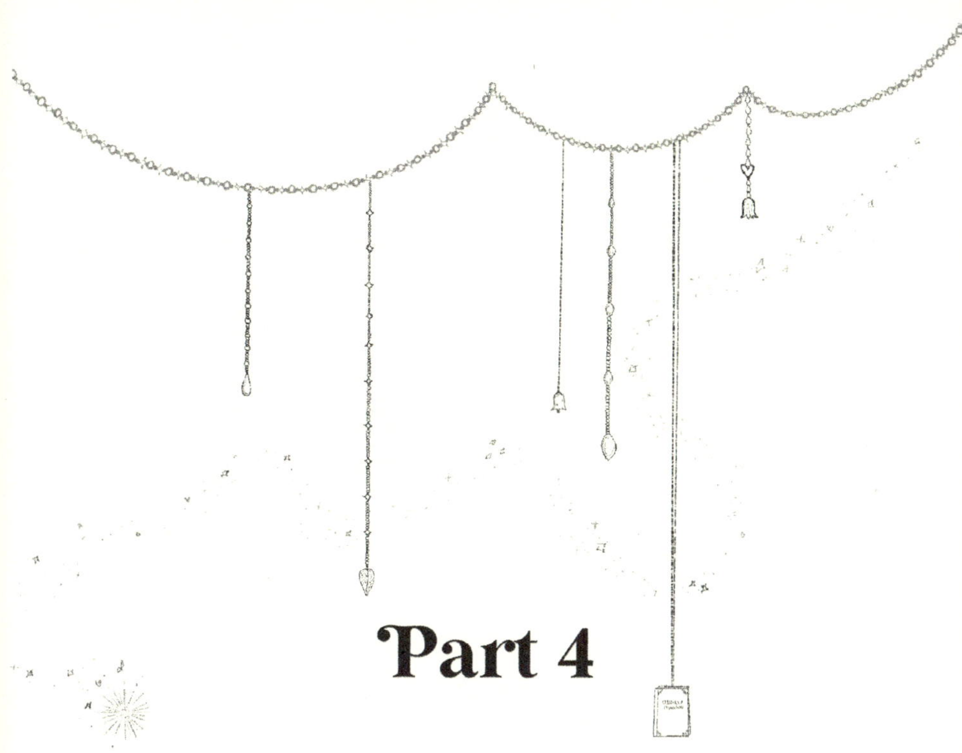

Part 4

Chapter 43

Desmond had finished his regular amount of morning coffee. Two mugs worth. Yet as George stared at him dumbfounded, an uncertainty set in.

Being in London the day of Victoria's wedding had been an unwise action. However, Desmond had found himself less inclined to wisdom than to adventure. Victoria didn't scare him. At least, she was not as threatening as one Miss Beatrix Thompson. And so, for what it was worth, he was ready to take on any obstacles in his way.

"Morning," he greeted.

"This is a surprise," George said, motioning him in.

The foyer looked different. Messy. A table along the wall was cluttered with envelopes, the walls were filled with bare frames, the clock ticked a few minutes too fast, and the house felt a little too cold.

George pulled off his hat and looked to the grandfather clock with compressed brows. "I'm sorry, Desmond, but I have to bring Jeremy to Quaintrelle Estate this morning, and I'm about to run late."

"Oh." He righted his jacket and put on a smile. "Yes, well, I was wondering if I could borrow a suit."

"A suit?"

"Apparently my wardrobe doesn't meet certain standards."

George's eyes narrowed, seeking out the hidden meanings between his spoken words. "Why do you need a suit?"

"For a wedding."

"Which wedding?"

"The Towson-Jones wedding."

George's mouth moulded to the beginnings of a variety of soundless sentences. He gripped back his hair. "I'm sorry, can you repeat that?"

"I'm here to attend Victoria and Jeremy's wedding," he confessed.

George dropped his hair and swatted his hat against his legs. "Fancy that."

The large ashen grandfather clock chimed from the corner, nowhere near following an accurate time. Desmond spotted the dusty reflection of the clock in a hanging mirror; the cracks in the glass distorted the time even more.

He followed the lines back to George. "I know you warned me not to come anywhere near town."

George closed his eyes and wet his lips. "How did you merit an invitation?"

That was most likely the worst question of all.

There was no way of truly knowing, but during some secret George had refused to share, he had crossed paths with Beatrix. Seemingly no-good-very-bad paths.

"I lost a game of cards," Desmond admitted carefully. "So I have to accompany Beatrix Thompson."

"Of course. Will you excuse me a moment?" George left to the adjoining sitting room with the fireplace and grand piano.

Desmond flinched at the obvious, open handed slamming of keys.

After a beat of silence, George sauntered back into the hall, brushing off his suit. "I'd like to apologize for that, and for what is sure to be a very interesting night for the both of us."

"How interesting?"

"That's infinitely unpredictable."

Desmond chuckled to make a joke of the matter. "More unpredictable than me showing up to attend a wedding where the bride has promised me physical harm?"

"That's a grave misdiagnosis for what's about to happen." George spread a hand across his forehead. "It keeps getting worse the more I think about it."

"Worse?"

George held out a finger, asking for a moment of quiet. It was a typical pose, one Desmond was used to when George formulated solutions to inexplicable problems. Clock gears clanged together, sounding abruptly through the room. It was George who flinched.

He opened his eyes and lightly squeezed Desmond's shoulder. "You need to find my grandmother as soon as you get to Quaintrelle Estate. Ask her about your mother."

"My mother?"

"It's of utmost importance." George stepped to the door and patted his hat back on. "Help yourself to any suit you'd like. Or anything for that matter. Take anything you need."

"That seems a bit exaggerated—"

But George was gone.

A slithering sensation crept up his spine. He shrugged and made his way to the stairs, not allowing the feeling to take root. One way or another, he'd reach to the bottom of George's antics.

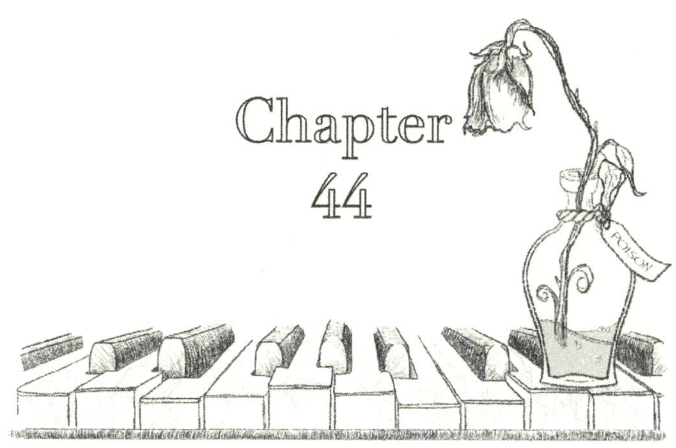

Chapter 44

George led the way to Quaintrelle Estate, his footfalls heavy against the earth. He kept his watch on the doors atop the stairs, the entry to a world he had been so close to being a part of, but that now felt hacked into fractured hopes.

Jeremy was restless at his side, in a way that was all sunshine and happy thoughts, bouncing as if he was about to take flight. His younger brothers followed closely behind, tripping each other repeatedly. Linus was all smiles, yet Thomas never laughed at it once.

After George knocked to alert their arrival, the tall glistening doors opened and chaos ensued.

Attendants criss-crossed paths in the foyer, little George ran around their legs while Felix tried and failed to keep up. Lady Vivianne hummed her way to the stairs where she ascended and faded into her room. Her husband, another George, wasn't too far behind, weaving around platters and fabrics being carried about.

"Do you know what we're having for dinner tonight?" Linus asked, removing his hat and shaking his hair out. "I'm starving."

"You're always starving," Thomas grumbled.

Jeremy stepped up to George's left. "You look more nervous than I do."

He rolled out his shoulders, where the tension of his shadows collected. "I can be better."

Jeremy's eyebrows pinched together. "That's not what I'm saying at all."

"Come, boys," Cathryn beckoned with a wide and tired smile. "Into the drawing room while I go get the girls."

The boys entered the room, but before George could disappear with them, Cathryn shut the doors.

"William wishes to speak with you," she said too kindly while leaving for the stairs. "He's in the tea room."

George's hands gripped onto the lining in his jacket pockets. His old walls, the bricks and mortar he used to lean on, were nothing but ash. They slipped through his fingers like granules of sand in an hourglass.

Each step to the tea room echoed through his bones, even the warmth of the sunlight pouring in did nothing to soothe his thoughts.

The tea room had been rearranged so that paisley printed chairs were huddled around a low table. Fresh flowers sat in vases on windowsills, and William Jones sat in his chair, reading the day's paper.

Without looking up, he motioned for George to sit. "I wanted an opportunity to thank you."

George lowered carefully onto the settee, the rhythm of his own breaths wavering his balance. "I'm not sure what I have done to earn your gratitude, sir."

"Call me William," he corrected, firm and fatherly, adding a new ache to George's muscles. "I was thanking you for everything you risked two nights past, for Molly. And that glorious bruise on Boris' jaw."

George's lips twitched as he stretched his hurting hand. The setback in healing had been entirely worth it.

"I used to pay you visits, you know." William folded his paper away and perched it onto the table.

"Visits?"

"Every month after the fire, your grandfather and I would discuss how you were doing."

He pushed back further into his seat, craving stability. All it took was the mention of those flames to bring them back into the corners of his mind.

William studied him for a moment, fingers cupping his chin. "Molly accompanied me once. You barely said hello before you took her hand and ran to the gardens." He looked out the windows, to where sunlight filtered over the lush garden and the rows of flowers strung with wedding decorations. "We didn't see the two of you again until it was time to leave. Molly ran to me all covered in dirt and flower petals, saying, *'Father, Father, we saw a fairy!'*"

George's heartbeat drummed through his chest, synchronized to the recollections of stories and the sighting of fairies.

"She was always in our gardens after that, speaking of fairies, never without that wild smile. You two have always had something special," William mused, his tone reminiscent. He sighed and gave George a smile. "Consider this my premature blessing for what I know to be your good intentions with my daughter."

Those so called *good intentions* had awoken the creature waiting in George's shadows. It clawed its way to the surface, slow and sure. Convincing him that it had never mattered how genuine his intentions may have been. It was already too late.

Following the tea service into the room was Molly. Her hair was a mess from sleep, her lashes batted slowly as though her sight wasn't fully crisp. He wasn't convinced she knew where her feet were landing.

"Morning," she said through a mellow yawn.

The sound of her voice settled into the cavity of his chest, bringing back his ability to pull a satisfying inhale.

"I'm going to check on Victoria," William announced, standing from his seat. Then to George directly, "It would be best if you were not here upon her arrival."

Her father had just left the room when Molly collapsed onto the cushions.

George opened his arm in time for her to fall into him, locking into place like all of his missing pieces.

"Good morning, Fairy Girl," he said into her curls.

Wildflowers.

She always smelled of wildflowers.

He drew her in tighter, fighting the desire to press a kiss to her forehead.

Perhaps that was his destination, the final mark on his map. To be a man who could come close to islands of paradise but who would never be afforded the chance to go ashore. Molly would only ever be a dream.

"I should go before your father returns," he said, and slid to the edge of the cushion.

Molly watched, confused and curious. "What's wrong?"

He looked into her eyes, savouring each speckle of cinnamon. She had always been able to see right through him.

Somehow, she already knew he couldn't answer her. He caught it in the spilt second between her rolling her lips in and looking to where her fingers plucked together.

"I want you to focus on family," he said for a soothing assurance. It was best to suffer with his secrets a while longer. He pushed out an angry breath and scooped away his bangs. "I should tell you one thing, though."

She looked up expectantly.

"Desmond is here."

Her mouth dropped open. "On Victoria's wedding day? How?"

"He came with someone."

She closed her eyes for two beats. "Does she have a big hat?"

"I'm not sure." He could only assume she would be wearing something ostentatious.

"If it's big enough, maybe Victoria won't see him."

There Molly was, making him smile when he'd forgotten how. "One can only hope."

Her eyes squinted towards the tea. "Desmond is really here with someone?"

He hadn't gotten as far as suspecting how she might react to that. "I'm not sure it's romantic."

"That's unfortunate. It would have made things easier for us." She turned to him with a warmth akin to a sunrise, clueless as to everything he wished to be forgiven for.

Victoria's voice sounded through the doorway; George's time was up.

He held Molly's hand as he stood, heart sinking as he had to let it go. "I'll find you after dinner."

She nodded, and he left the room before he was no longer able to peel himself away.

The ticking of a clock itched across his mind as he crossed the foyer to the drawing room.

Of all the ladies in all the countries, Victoria had to invite *Beatrix*. And of all the lads in all her history, Beatrix had to bring along *Desmond*.

That hardly seemed fair.

He distracted himself by helping Linus arrange his suit properly, assuring Thomas that spending the morning with his younger brother wasn't going to melt his brain, and reminding Jeremy that while Victoria was hardly a tolerable woman, he was still happy for them both.

At last it was time for him to join the audience. He slipped out unnoticed, leaving the front doors of the estate behind so that he could take the long route through the yard. The grass was a vibrant green, spring had brought forth the return of colours. A perfect day for an outdoor wedding.

George made it out to the chairs in the garden, keeping a portion of his focus on listening to whispers, prepared to escort a guest from the property less-than politely if anything was spoken in ill-intent against Molly.

Gran was easy to spot, and George let out an exhale when he realized she would have the largest hat in the audience. The brim alone would have him leaning sideways just to sit beside her. It matched her charcoal gown draped in ribbons of sheer violets.

"Gran," he greeted with a kiss to her cheek. "How is everything?"

She patted his shoulder. "It's just fine. I've finished my rounds. The rumour mill is as good as dead."

He nodded, fingers tapping at his sides. "And Desmond? You warned him about what certain people may be whispering about?"

"Only to emphasize how proud I am of him."

George flopped into his chair. He tore off his hat and pattered his fingers along the top.

Guests filed into the empty spaces with purposefully placed flowers to designate where each should sit.

Molly had been the one to design the floral arrangements. She had an entire canopy of blooms strung over the dance floor, bushels of ranunculus set along the pathways of the labyrinth and in lanterns by the aisles. They were accompanied by bouquets of baby's breath and white roses along the front steps of the pavilion.

A laugh, one too powerful, drew his attention.

Desmond had chosen a very ornate suit, a forest green jacket that George would have never worn, and a gold cravat that accented the fine golden leaves threaded into the brown vest.

"Who is Desmond standing next to?" Gran asked as she took her seat next to him and followed his gaze.

There were a lot of names George could have used. "Miss Beatrix Thompson."

"Oh."

"Mhmm."

"That's not good."

"I have a plan."

"That's really not good."

George donned what he knew was a convincing smile and stitched together the remnants of who he had to be. He adjusted Gran's hat and turned back to Desmond.

The boy's curls bounced out of place as he tapped his foot. He disregarded something Beatrix was saying and turned away from her to sit down. She crossed her arms and swung away from him, unfortunately bringing her eyes on George. Adorned in an orange gown, Beatrix caught the light the same way a match catches flames.

Her ensuing grin felt malicious.

George's blood went rancid.

A string quartet adjusted themselves right on time, signalling the beginning to the wedding procession. Vases, lanterns, and candles encircled the four musicians, and they were his heroes.

Music was, once more, a saviour.

Gran reached across and grabbed hold of his hand with her arthritic fingers.

The rescuing song of strings flared out with new fervour as the wedding began.

Jeremy stood with his brothers at the front of the aisle. Their matching tuxedos were dignified and classic, perfectly tailored to each of their builds. Jeremy smiled at his mother in the front row, who held a hand over her heart before blowing him a kiss.

Four matching flower girls marched down the aisle, tossing pink petals that matched their pink dresses along the way. Jeremy winked at his sisters before they took their seats.

Little George took his first steps down the pathway to the groom. His little hands carried the rings with all of the restraint a child his age possessed. Sylvia and Molly walked very carefully behind him. Every so often, Sylvia reached forward and tugged on the tails of her son's jacket to keep him from running away.

All of them wore different glowing shades of Victoria's favourite colours. Little George was in leafy greens, his tiny bowtie matching his mother's gown in golds and yellows, brightening Sylvia's otherwise cloudy disposition.

Then there was Molly. Silver thread glittered into vines around budding flowers that clustered at the waist of her forget-me-not blue gown. Pearls and crystals were woven through the translucent fabric that flowed in waves along her arms. Attached beneath her shoulder blades, delicate and sparkling ribbons trailed along the back of the gown like perfectly placed wings.

Felix knelt on the ground by the groom, motioning for his son to slow down. The audience laughed as the boy misread the signal and ran the rest of the way. He dropped the rings into Jeremy's waiting hands before collapsing against his father.

George laced his hands together and braced his elbows over his knees. Without the distraction of a child at her feet, more eyes were on Molly. Her breathing shallowed, her lashes fluttered too quick as her gaze lowered to the ground. The way he wished to reach out for her...

His scar ached as his grip tightened.

Sylvia looped her arm through Molly's, carrying enough strength for them both. She whispered something in Molly's ear that flushed colour across her cheeks and illuminated a smile.

The stress trickled out of his shoulders. Well, some of it.

Most would remain for a little while longer.

When Molly was beyond his sights, George glanced over his shoulder. Desmond and John Thompson were in deep conversation, ignoring the proceedings without being a distraction to those around.

A new song filtered through the garden as Victoria had her turn down the aisle.

Her wedding dress had a wide bell skirt and a long train that shimmered in her path. The white lace mixed with silken layers wrapped around her in her preferred way—mimicking her curves.

Halfway down the aisle, her steps had more spring, as if the overabundance of excitement needed a way out. Jeremy laughed and, unable to resist, met her partway. He exchanged an embrace with William Jones before guiding Victoria to the beginning of the rest of their lives.

Chapter 45

No force was strong enough to keep George in his seat once the ceremony ended. He sped across the lawn, making it to where the hedges met the cellar door. He snuck inside, breathing in the cool air of dusty stones and oak barrels, and crashed against the wall.

He watched the threads of sunlight cut through the space as afternoon sunbeams enriched into late evening rays. Soon the dinner would be over, and it would be time to share one last secret.

He brushed the dust off his jacket, realigned his tie, and snuck into the home. He rounded several corners and glided through new rooms, heart racing in his chest; a drum that drowned out the world around him. Somehow he found the parlour and sought comfort in the sight of the piano, hearing a song he had played more times than he could count.

Fairytales came in many different forms. Most happened on a fateful night where weather mimicked inside turmoil and someone inevitably did something they regretted. So his story wasn't special. The nightmares it had given him had informed him of that more often than not.

He closed his eyes and listened to the home.

Even in the distance, Molly's voice had the ability to play with his heartstrings.

He peeked his head through the windowed doors, catching a glimpse of Molly hugging Jeremy and stepping away so that the newly married couple could enjoy a few moments alone before dancing with the crowd outside.

She spun to leave and found George.

Her smile was instantaneous. His was not. The second of hesitation had suspicion written across her face.

She made her way to him and touched his arm. "You're whiter than the roses."

That made sense. He hadn't eaten all day, and all he could hear were ticking clocks and crackling flames and distant un-humorous laughter. *There are no happy endings here.*

George offered his hand, and she slipped hers into it and followed him through the parlour. He took her to the piano and fell onto its bench.

"I don't know where to start."

She sat down next to him and rubbed a hand over his shoulder. "All stories start at the beginning."

The beginning. A place he had neglected to go for far too long.

He stretched out his fingers and placed a palm onto the piano bench, desperate for the aid of music to tell this particular story.

"It was a society ball. I didn't want to be there, so as soon as Gran was distracted, I made it over to the windows."

He remembered the storm outside, the patter of raindrops on the glass. He had only gone to the windows for an escape, but he'd found *her* instead. She was watching the rain, feet dancing of their own will.

He swallowed the dryness in his throat and studied his palms. "I don't remember when she arrived or what convinced me to ask for a dance."

Molly's hand fell away from his. He couldn't read her expression, feared to even try.

"We danced every song, until I realized... I realized it was more than dancing. So I left. I left her there on the dance floor and ran outside."

Molly rose and distanced herself from the piano. Her fingers gripping into her gown. She stepped back, eyes darting from corner to corner as she relived her past.

"You left. Alone. She—" Molly shook her head. "George?"

He pushed to his feet. "Leaving isn't something I do. Please, believe me. I hadn't even been hit with a drop of rain before I headed right back in."

"Why are you telling me this now?"

"I had to." He pictured Beatrix, prowling around, hunting for him. "There is someone here who would have seen us together. She would have told you what I did."

She held a hand over her heart. "It's my sister's wedding day. I don't know if I can talk about this..."

"It is a part of my past that I am not proud of. But I needed to be the one to tell you. I had planned to. After the wedding. After emotions had settled. There is so much going on with—" *Everything.* Everything was happening all at once.

Molly clutched at the flowers on her gown, her eyes welling with tears as she dared to look at him.

He stepped towards her. She stepped further away.

"What happened next?" Her voice divulged every fear. "After you left, what did you do?"

Regret. Nightmares. Isolation in his shadows. He looked back up at Molly. Those details could go without discussing.

He skipped ahead to the words he had rehearsed. The part of his story that was easier to say.

"Over a year had passed when I was walking with my grandfather through town. We met your father and Victoria. I recognized their names and knew the connection your family had to mine. We left, and I thought nothing more of it until that afternoon. I was walking through town on my own and came face to face with Victoria and Jeremy. That's when she proposed the relationship scheme."

Molly swished her skirts around her feet, hands twisting into the layers of gleaming blue.

"I had every reason to say yes to her." George never pulled his eyes away from Molly, attuned to how her stress mounted into determination. Of what that determination was however, he had no inkling. "By saying yes, my grandfather would stop trying to force me to get married. By saying yes I would get to know my mother a little through the people she was closest to. Perhaps I would have been allowed to forget I had run away and deserted someone at a party. And last, but probably what enthralled me the most, was meeting this girl who Desmond always talked about."

He found the strength to approach her, leaving enough space for her frantic swaying. "I remember that night like it was yesterday. Walking into your home, meeting your family. Sitting on the sofa with your sister. I remember knowing you had walked into the room. I was drawn to you even then. I had to see you. The girl I assumed was made of glitter and gold. I wanted to know what all of the fuss was about."

She froze and inclined her head towards him. Her eyes slowly found his.

"You can imagine..." His heart pounded against his ribs, almost painfully. "You can imagine my surprise, when I realized I already knew. There you were. The girl I had left on that dance floor. The one made of glitter and gold. Who made me forget I was broken, even for a night. Who had me falling for her just by listening to her speak of raindrops and dancing."

"It was you."

"It was me."

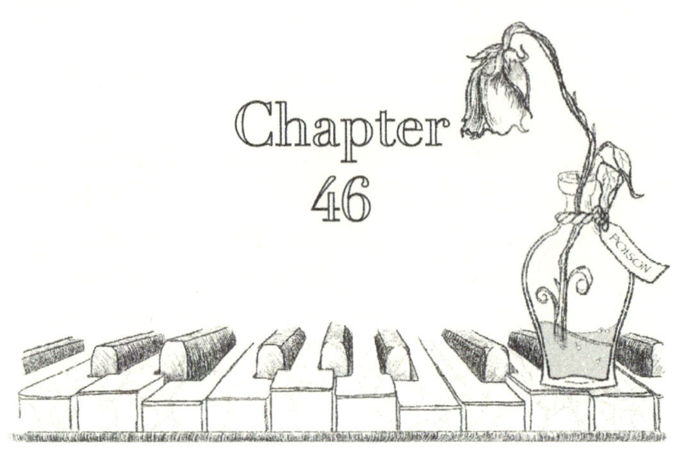

Chapter 46

George held his breath. Each persona, each wall he had used to hide behind, was gone. For Molly, they always would be.

Her eyes glistened with tears that wouldn't shed. "It was you," she repeated. "It was you."

He reached out for her as the door burst open.

"Molly!" Jeremy called. "Oh, thank goodness. Victoria has been looking everywhere for you. She desperately needs your assistance."

Molly wiped her eyes before turning away. "What is it?"

"She needs to... You know." Jeremy looked very uneasy.

Molly twirled the pearls on her gown, looking back to George as her determination was cleaved in two.

"Go," he suggested softly and against all inner protests. He tucked his restless hands into his pockets. "It's your sister on her wedding day. I can wait."

She narrowed her damp eyes at him and left both boys behind.

Jeremy gaped in her direction as the door swung closed. He turned his shocked expression to George.

"You didn't," he said.

"I may have," George collapsed onto the bench and dropped his face into his hands.

"You had to tell her tonight?"

"Your guest list didn't allow me to wait." Colours pressed into his vision as his palms covered his eyes; neither doing anything pleasant.

Jeremy sat next to George and patted his back, a condescending tone coming to his voice, "You did the right thing. Even if the timing was a bit off."

George gave him a sideways glance.

Jeremy grinned. "I'm sorry I can't be more sympathetic. I've married the love of my life, and right now I'm believing in happy endings for all. Even you."

Anything remotely close to happiness kept getting further from his reach. Telling Molly had been foremost. But equally terrifying was the fact that she wasn't the only person who needed to know the truth of his secrets.

Desmond sipped at a mug of hot coffee, grateful for some peace. He'd managed to escape Beatrix's attention since dinner. She'd seemed deeply interested in finding Molly, and so he'd refused to admit he even knew who Molly was, permitting himself to be a tad selfish. He started to make his way to a table, feet scuffing through the grass as he travelled across the lawn.

With light from the clear night sky shining over him, he looked down to his shoes. The old brown leather was a little worse for wear, but he knew a lot could be told about a person from their shoes. Like how George's were always polished, or how Molly preferred to be without them entirely. His were worn on all sides, but especially in the soles, for his feet always took him where he needed to go.

A hand clamped down on his shoulder.

Desmond spun around. "George?"

George was a mess. His blood-red tie was half undone, and there was a good chance he hadn't realized he had been playing with his pocket watch for so long that the chain was kinked.

"Maybe we should sit?" Desmond enunciated each syllable separately.

They fell into abandoned seats at a table near the back of the celebrations.

Desmond searched for a way to ease into the conversation. "So—"

"It was Molly," George blurted. "The girl I ran away from at the ball was Molly. She is also the girl who I haven't been able to get off my mind ever since."

There were many reactions Desmond could have had. Anger. Confusion. Shock. None of them were within reach. None of them felt like his.

"Molly. You're sure?"

George gave him a slow blink. "I happen to be very sure."

He frowned. "You left *Molly* on the dance floor?"

George pinched his bottom lip and silently kept staring.

"Right, it was Molly. It's just," how was he to say, "I think maybe I knew that."

"You think you knew?" George dropped his hand and poked the tablecloth. "How would you know, when Molly didn't?"

Desmond fell back in his chair, pulling his coffee with him, using the time it took to finish drinking to dig up what he could.

He reeled the memory in, details clearing. There had been a letter. One where Molly had written of attending a ball. It had been a big deal as it had been her first one. She had even spoken of dancing—a lot of dancing. And of her dance partner. Desmond looked back at George, whose face had a ghastly pallor. "She spoke of you in one of her letters."

"You never told me."

The accusation slivered beneath his skin. "Shouldn't I be the one upset about that?"

George stretched his hands out. "You're right. I should have told you. I just—"

"Yes, you should have."

Desmond felt the shift. They were on a precipice.

Lies and secrets collected like hungry hoards of creatures beyond the edge. Regrets and mistakes honing in on their weaknesses; waiting for them to plummet.

But he couldn't lose George. Not over this.

Desmond had always been hesitant, always naive. He'd always known that love, to him, would mostly be a weakness. A place he didn't feel quite safe. He never had been afforded a proper chance to even know what it was. No more than what George or Molly had been able to teach him.

"Look at me." Desmond motioned to the entirety of his suit, rather, George's suit that he was wearing. It strengthened his point. "I have never known anything about life or love beyond what you taught me. I never told you about Molly's letter because I was embarrassed. Hearing about someone's ability to make her happier in one night than what I had ever managed to do, lifted a weight from my shoulders. I was scared but...*relieved*."

He took a breath and calmed down. "I was starved of love, George. I was willing to force myself to get what I could, even when there was no way I was ever capable of fully loving anyone."

"That's not true."

"Do you remember when you found out my friend in the woods was a girl named Molly?" Desmond shook his curls back on top of his head, staring up at the stars. "You always asked about her or brought her up in every conversation until I started doing the same. You've always loved Molly. You loved her so much you were the one to convince me *I* was in love."

It was the truth. A solace in the guilt. Not a fix, but he knew the two people he cared about most would make each other incandescently happy, and that was worth something.

He followed the lines of the stars back to the earth. "You can give Molly everything she has ever wanted. And she can give you everything you need."

George tapped his fingers into the tablecloth, the wheels of his mind spinning. "She deserves better. I should have told both of you the truth long ago, back when Beatrix first— "

"Beatrix?"

"She has known Molly for years and was there that night, watching over her as we danced. And she was there during a dinner I had with Victoria. She recognized me when Molly couldn't, warned me to stay away from her or she'd tell her exactly who I was." George sighed and tipped back in his chair. "Which was really nice since Victoria overheard that conversation and has held it over my head ever since."

"That's why you hid in your car that day. You were afraid of Beatrix telling me your secret?"

"I couldn't lose you."

"There was never a chance of that happening."

George attempted a thankful smile, but the result was something broken and feeble. "Well, that's good since I may have lost Molly."

Desmond finished the final drops of his coffee. They were courage and strength, everything he needed if he was going to keep talking to George about Molly. "I'm sure it'll work out."

"You didn't see her face."

"I did once." He remembered it all too well. "She still forgave me."

"I acted as though I hadn't run from her for two years." George resigned with a heavy breath. "I wasn't ready. And now the only thing more terrifying than a forever with anyone, is the suggestion that it couldn't be with her."

He tapped his foot against the ground beneath the table. "Do you have a plan? To fix it?"

George rubbed at his eyes. "I don't know. I can't lose her again."

Desmond opened his mouth to say something—anything encouraging.

Two commotions interrupted him. One from the west end of the property and a second on the northern side of the dance floor.

George spun north, Desmond west.

The only person more unwelcome at Victoria's wedding than himself, would have been his mother. There, forcing her way towards the reception, was Alice Prescott.

Desmond's stomach turned to rock. He swung back to George for help, for a man to stand and fight for him.

George was gone.

He swallowed back a reserve and got to his feet. He stared at them, questioning everything. He wasn't sure he was ready for this. But his feet had never taken him in the wrong direction before.

One foot after the other, he approached the distant corner of the yard where his mother stood on the cobblestones of a patio.

He noted her unbalanced stance, how her arms crossed a bit higher over her swollen belly.

Anger burrowed and spread through all his limbs with each pound of his heart.

He faced her, stood his ground with fists on his hips, and summoned all resilience. "What are you doing here?"

Alice passed a hand over her unborn child. "I came to see you."

"How did you know I was here?"

"I was alerted by someone who is loyal to our family."

Family. The word slithered into his skull.

"You wasted no time making yourself a new one of those," he stated coldly.

Her eyes slitted. "This is your family, too."

"Don't." He squeezed his eyes shut, and he was back. Back in his old bedroom hiding in his closet. Back under the burden of Harold's thumb. A boy who had been forced to grow up too soon. A boy who had never been afforded to be a child. Scared. Full of loathing.

Until George. Until Molly. Until he had been reminded of what even a hint of love could do. The power in just a drop of belief.

The power in one small decision, every day.

His eyes shot open.

"Don't think that what I'm about to say has anything to do with you." He stepped forward, snapping a twig beneath his foot. "I'll come back."

Her shoulders relaxed. "You're coming home?"

Desmond shook his head. "I'll visit. Once a month, more if I can afford to do so. Not for you." His eyes lowered. "To remind my brother or sister that there is a better world out there. To listen when they're in need. To protect and take them away, if given even the slightest reason."

She gasped, as quiet as a breath.

He bent over to retrieve the broken branch and tossed it into the air, watching it flip before he caught it and tossed it again.

"While you're here," he drawled, relishing the smallest sensation of being in control. "You'll be telling everyone that you lied about Molly."

"You disrespectful—"

"If you don't repair Molly's reputation, I'll be telling everyone the truth about my heritage."

Alice stuck her nose in the air, a ferocity tugging at her shoulders. "You wouldn't dare!"

Desmond shrugged. "I'd leave out the Clarington name. But damage is damage, Alice." He turned away completely and headed back to the party. "Good to know your reputation is all you care about. You barely blinked when I talked of taking my sibling away. Dare I threaten your pride—"

"I am your mother."

He paused, only long enough to say one last thing. "Then do us a favour, and be a better one."

Desmond watched his feet, leaving her behind him and dreaming of where he'd be taken next.

"This wasn't the most glorifying part of wearing the world's largest wedding dress." Victoria sniggered as she and Molly left the water room.

"You do look beautiful, though," Molly answered.

Victoria jutted out her hip, white lace tears fluttering up with the motion. "Don't I though?"

The chapters of their sisterhood flashed through Molly's memories.

They'd been young girls window shopping for wedding dresses on the streets of London. With parasol swords and flower arrangements, giggles and sunbeams. Late nights whispering stories under the cover of fluffy blankets.

They'd been young ladies, mostly spending time apart but still able to enjoy tender moments. Victoria had cut out clippings of stories from daily papers and slipped them under Molly's door with sketches in the corners. They'd sometimes split the last sweet biscuit during their evening tea.

It was on to a new chapter now. One of long visits over the weekends, of parents becoming grandparents, and of gaining nieces and nephews to spoil.

Molly offered what she hoped was a smile. "I'm going to miss you."

"Don't cry," Victoria warned, her own eyes misting. "If you start, then I'm not going to be able to hold it back."

Molly had no power to hold the tears back. Not as Victoria glowed with happiness—pink cheeks and extra curly smile—one that had matched Jeremy's as she'd walked down the aisle. One Molly was sure would stand the tests of time.

"You got your dream."

Victoria's tears rolled down. "There you go, you've done it now."

Molly sniffed away a thick laugh and dabbed at Victoria's tears. She took her sister's arm and they left together for the stairs.

In the foyer, they each held back more tears brimming with happy memories. The clicking of Victoria's shoes rang sweetly along the marble floor as they arrived by Jeremy's side. His grin was overwhelming, and Molly turned away as the couple celebrated reuniting.

She didn't know where she was headed.

"Molly," Victoria called before she had gone too far. She rushed over to her side with a jiggle in her step. "Jeremy says that George finally told you?"

The mention of his name had her returning to that moment by the piano. When the truth about her fairytale evening had fallen upon her.

Victoria's arms were around her shoulders, holding her tight. "I know he was the one to run that night, but you were the one who found a place to hide." She released her hold and returned to her place beneath Jeremy's waiting arm. "You know better than anyone that chasing happily-ever-afters is always worth it."

They kept their arms around each other as they disappeared around the corner, leaving Molly all on her own.

She couldn't pay attention to where she was going and somehow had made it outside. Wedding celebrations went on in full force under the moon and stars. She passed the wine barrels and the flower canopy over the dance floor. The crowd seemed to love how it felt to be inside a floating garden.

An attendant called out in warning, but for Molly, it was already too late. The tray of water glasses spilled from his hands and over Molly's head.

She accepted his apologies and left, ignoring the whispers of those who had seen. She had gotten used to the stares, especially from those entrenched in believing false rumours.

A secluded place sat waiting for her by the white bricks that lined the outskirts of the glowing labyrinth. Molly removed her shoes and swished the frills on her skirt with her toes. Her hair pins came out easily, allowing the dripping rivers of her hair to trickle against the bare skin of her back.

"There is something I must tell you."

Her heart skipped into her throat. She spun to the sound of his voice.

George stood at the corner where flowers met the green hedges, moonlight glistening against his black suit and floral print vest. He turned his hat like a helm, compressing the brim in his hands.

An unknown balance kept her on her feet while walking closer. A tremble started in her chest and flowed to her fingers.

"Not here." She reached out and took his hand.

No second thoughts were needed. She pulled him through a doorway to the labyrinth.

Flickering lanterns lit the corridors. Alleys were decorated with strings of dried flowers that lead to the centre of the maze. Molly had memorized the way long ago.

A babbling fountain sat around the final bend, draped in jingling gems and beads. Floating candles wobbled in the pools, each one promising to grant a wish with just a shining coin. Garlands of roses twirled around the lantern hooks waiting in the corners.

She released George and stepped closer to the lanterns as he rounded the fountain. His fingers skimmed along the surface of the waves. He lifted his hand from the water and watched the droplets puddle into his palm.

"I wrote about our night in my book of fairytales."

His eyes ticked up to hers.

The memory laced her in with threads of moonlight and wisps of raindrops. How one dance had drifted into the next like infinite midnights and starry skies. How his eyes had been whispering the truth of his secret since that first night he had been in her home.

"You went back to find me, but I was hiding. I was scared because I wasn't who I wanted to be—who you help me to be. And I didn't want you to know."

George dropped his hat. It rolled into blackness as he abandoned the fountain, eliminating the distance between them. His fingers slinked into her tangles, hand coming to a rest by the nape of her neck.

"I have adored you in all of your seasons, Molly."

The sound of her name in his voice was an unspooling melody lighting its way through the night sky.

She stared into the sparkling stories in his eyes. "You make my name sound like a song."

"You are in every song." His thumb twirled and sent shimmers across her skin. "Even in silence."

Her hands fiddled with the collar of his jacket, down to where she tapped along the roses in his waistcoat. "I'm so sorry I hid from you, George."

"I'm sorry I left."

The fountain trickled in the background and flames sputtered in the lanterns. She saw the glow reflect in his gaze. The secrets were lifted; the shadows had gone.

She could have stared at him like that forever. "You said there was something you needed to tell me?"

A lock of hair fell before his eyes, looping over his brow in a mess he didn't brush aside. "I have fallen in love with you, Molly, and wish to do so endlessly."

She believed in magic. Not in spells, and wands, or potions in vials. But in the magic of teacups and sunlight, in snowflakes and blossoms. When certain songs came at the perfect time. How your favourite person always had your favourite laugh. Magic was believing in things that no one else cared to look for. It was in his smile. The glittering silver in his eyes when he battled not to divulge one of his secrets. How his voice danced.

She was in love with him. In every way. Even those that remained undisclosed.

George dropped his forehead to hers. "You must realize what happens when you look at me like that."

Molly watched each word, the movement around the vowels. "In what way am I looking at you?"

"Irresistibly."

She pulled him down so their lips met, sweetly curious and filled with lingering magic.

They lifted apart for a breathless moment and simply stared at each other.

He bent down and kissed her again; softly spreading sparks through her soul that unfurled like a thousand extra kisses.

His free arm hooked her waist, tugging her close enough that the buttons of his jacket entangled with the pearls on her gown, and her feet were nearly off the ground. Each caress brought them somewhere new.

He led her to the fountain with tender kisses and coaxing murmurs of her name. The hand that traced the length of her spine found its way to cupping her waist, pulling her in a solid movement onto his lap as he sat at the edge of the water.

The dangling gems chimed, tinkling as they brushed together. A simple song, never to be heard again.

His lips smiled against hers.

He stretched his fingers over his shoulder to the beads. "What are these?"

Her thoughts whirled together. His voice was dark and decadent, and she wanted to melt right into it.

"Fairy bells," she breathed.

He raised an eyebrow.

"To let them know we're friendly."

His second brow rose.

"I know fairies aren't—"

"A fan of being around three hundred people," he completed, catching his own breath. He looped one of her curls around his fingers and let it fall away. "It doesn't matter how friendly we are, they won't be coming."

Molly smiled. "You're every bit as charming as I always feared you would be."

"Is that so?" George's grin ignited a glow that tingled from her toes to between her shoulders.

"I love you, too, George."

He leaned in and trailed kisses along her shoulder. There he rested his head and reached back to flutter his fingers against the bells, playing the melody once more.

"I want to remember these." He looked up at her. His eyes had never shone so bright, their precise blue matching the hue of her dress. "To write a song later."

"Then I would like to hear that song. Later."

"Later," he murmured, close enough to kiss already.

Chapter 49

Desmond thanked his last dance partner and made his way out of the crowd. He stumbled over someone's discarded shoes and spun around children playing games and tricks. Different escape maneuvers were needed as he headed towards the back tables of treats near the estate.

Leaning against the brick walls, George held a plate with fruits and desserts. An auspicious smile tugged at his mouth as he ducked down to speak with someone on his opposite side.

"George!" Desmond called, gaining the attention of a wrong George as well as the correct one.

The older man grumbled and walked away.

Desmond gave him an awkward bow and rushed over to where the correct George lounged against the bricks. "I've been looking for you."

George swallowed his bite and pushed away from the wall. His arm stretched open, and Molly stepped out from his side, as though she had always been there.

"I was preoccupied," George admitted timidly.

Desmond couldn't say much. Nearby candle-lit lanterns flickered their glows into her hair. Tiny bursts of light caught on the crystals on her arms as she pinched the starlight fabric on her gown. George's hand reached out and gave hers a place to rest.

Molly barely met his eyes. "Hello Desmond," she said, voice coy and unsure.

"Molly. It's..." He sucked in a breath. Good? Strange? "Seeing you again."

She laughed and broke free into a smile. "Yes. Yes, it's seeing you again, too."

"Well," began George, setting his nearly empty plate onto a passing tray. "This is going just about as well as I thought it would."

Desmond flailed his arms out. "It's very weird for me."

George didn't seem to be listening, his gaze had travelled beyond Desmond's shoulders. "It's about to get worse," he confirmed ominously.

Desmond's first fear was that his mother had returned. He set his shoulders back and spun around.

"Molly!" Beatrix shrieked.

"Trix!" Molly beamed.

Desmond could only watch as his two worlds collided.

The girls ran to each other and embraced so strongly, they wavered back and forth, close to toppling over completely. They steadied as their voices hushed, and girlish giggles quickly turned into serious whispers.

"I may have underplayed their friendship a little bit," George murmured.

Desmond distanced himself from the girls. "By how much?"

"Oh, quite a bit. From what I've been able to derive, their fathers have known each other since boyhood. Molly and Beatrix have been friends their entire lives. Mostly at a distance, through letters."

Letters. Friendship was easy in letters. It was safer there.

Beatrix gasped and turned to glare at the boys.

"You," she shot to George. "You're very fortunate you found Molly before I did."

George rocked back on his heels and tucked his hands into his pockets. "I suppose I'll get used to being fortunate."

She gave him a sarcastic curl of her lips and faced Desmond next. "I don't even know where to begin with you, Desmond. The girl you ran from was Molly? You and your friend make the perfect pair."

Desmond grumbled and looked to George for support.

"She's not wrong," George admitted with a shrug.

A tall, broad gentleman in a tan suit approached Beatrix with two tall glasses of wine. "Here you are, sweet darling, love of my life."

She thanked him graciously and tucked herself close to his side.

The man extended a hand to Desmond. "I'm Christopher." He then greeted George, who dramatically retrieved his hand from his pocket to return the courtesy. "Good to see you again, George."

"As always," he replied with a grin.

"Molly," Christopher returned to acknowledge the girls. "Thank you for getting me an invitation."

She tipped her head. "You're most welcome. When Trix wrote to me, I knew I had to make it happen. It was perfect timing running into you at the post office."

"Serendipitous one might say." Beatrix curled herself around Christopher's arm and sipped at her wine. "If it weren't for Molly avoiding skating one afternoon, we never would have met or fallen in love before even exchanging names. Now, here we are, reunited once more; all thanks to you, Molly."

Desmond's nose scrunched up. "It makes no sense. How do you fall in love with someone before knowing who they are?"

Beatrix and Christopher laughed.

"Dance with me, Christopher," she purred into his ear, too loud to not be overheard.

He greedily accepted the offer and escorted her to the dance floor.

Desmond rolled his eyes at the lack of answers to his question.

George slung his arm over Molly's shoulders, and she sunk into his side. He slipped his hand over hers as she held her flowers. Molly gazed up at him as if she was reading pages of future stories, and George watched her like she was the infinite possibilities of songs.

Maybe that was love. When something lost had finally been found. Homes and families. Chaos and starry skies. Discoveries when you least expected them. How lovers danced with no music and travelled worlds without leaving home. In sunsets after thunderstorms and your favourite pillow after weeks of travel.

Desmond blew out a gust of breath that scurried his curls off his forehead. Just thinking about it was exhausting.

"Can we at least sit while the two of you stare at each other like that?"

George glanced over to him. "Shall we grab a table again?"

"I have somewhere else in mind," Desmond said, sharing a look with Molly.

She gave him a knowing nod.

"Where are we going exactly?" George looked between them both.

Desmond grinned. "Somewhere you've wanted to see for a while."

George's eyes widened. "Really? I get to come?"

"Yes. After years of begging, I'll let you come."

George's smile became everyone he had ever been. The little boy afraid of fires. The man who played with them. A person at odds within himself that had somehow found a way to love. George with his shadows where they belonged; behind and beneath him.

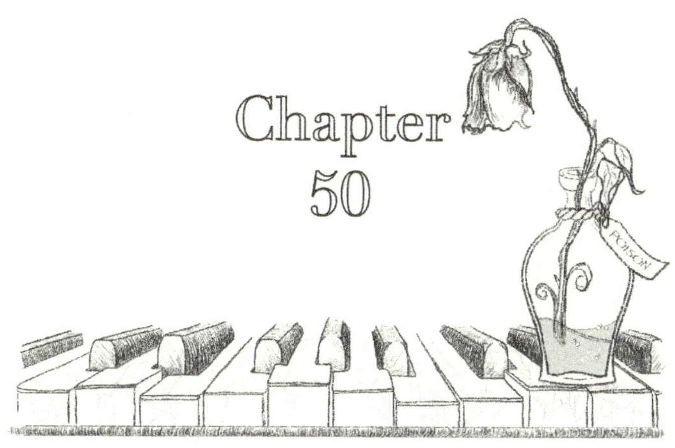

Chapter 50

George held the candlestick firmly, its light sending waves of golden shadows into the dark surrounding woods. Molly was under his arm, her hair still wet from her run in with the water tray. He didn't mind that it soaked into his sleeve while she stared into her bouquet. Desmond was to his left, picking up twigs and branches off the forest floor.

"I miss Acorn," Desmond said as he tossed a twig, the resounding crinkle of moss and leaves alerting him to its landing location so he'd pick it up again.

"Who is Acorn?" Molly asked.

"My dog."

"You have a dog?"

"She's more of an overbearing nanny," George added.

Desmond laughed. "That she is."

Songs of wildlife removed any silence from their trek to the creek. Cooing owls, chirping rodents, and the natural stringed instruments of insect wings came together with Desmond's stick slashing and Molly's humming.

Willow branches hung to the ground in a lush curtain that covered their path to the water.

George brushed aside the tendrils and allowed Desmond to walk inside first. Each leaf held a hundred different shades of green, and the tender swish of the wind sent them dancing.

"Hello, old friend," Molly whispered as she combed her fingers along the tree's bark. She smiled at the tree, secret wishes sparkling in the corners of her lips.

George leaned in close and lowered his voice. "Tell me your wish, and I'll make it come true."

"You don't have to be secretive just because I'm here," Desmond said, casting George a look as he crossed the space under the willow. "If you want to be all lovey and gross, be all lovey and gross."

"Careful what you wish for, Desmond."

"Just, maybe you could hold back on the kissing." Desmond grimaced.

"I wasn't even thinking of that." George paused. "Well, I am *now*."

Desmond groaned through a hidden smile, and made an opening in the next curtain of branches with his current twig.

It wasn't as though George had spent too much time imagining what the creek would be like. And perhaps it was more shallow than he'd imagined. It caught the moonlight in a way that somehow made it brighter, and the shadows of the tree canopy waltzed in the waves. Bubbles splashed against the rocks, welcoming them near with all sorts of glory.

George spread out his arms for balance, hovering the candle over the waves as he leapt from the shore to the largest rock. Molly gripped his hand and followed. He sat down in a comfortable lump with Molly lowering herself next to him, skirt puffing out around them both. She sat back against George's leg, resting her head against his shoulder as his arms wrapped around her.

Desmond jumped to the rock closest to the pebbled dirt and stood staring out to the trees of the Prescott property.

Molly drew out a single flower from her bouquet and spun it between her fingers. The blossom was a beautiful mess of petals. She lowered it into the water, and drew out a second one.

"We should have made this happen a long time ago," Desmond said, eyes on George.

George had not spent many nights at the Prescotts, but enough that he had been able to ask Desmond if he could join in his journey to the creek a fair amount of times. The answer had been the same every night. *No, I'll just tell Molly I can't see her tonight. She'll understand.* And so, George had never seen their secret place in the woods anywhere except his dreams. Until now.

"It's okay, Dez," Molly assured.

Desmond's attention latched onto the old familiar name.

George felt it, too. The ease of that detail erasing the leftover uncertainty.

"Uncle Dez," Desmond muttered, a loose grin spreading across his features. "I get to be Uncle Dez."

George's face contorted. "I missed something."

Desmond flung his stick into the creek. "I'm Uncle Dez because Molly's children need more than Aunt Victoria."

Molly nodded and lowered another flower into the water.

"I understood that part, Desmond. What I don't understand is what you're saying *theoretically*."

"I don't know what that means, George."

"It means..." His shoulders dropped as he took in the sight of Molly, watching as she smiled at each flower, skimming her fingers across every petal and finding enchantments in every detail.

"Theoretically," he started again, feeling the heat of a million fires on his cheeks.

"You're blushing," Desmond pointed out.

"Thanks, Desmond, I know."

Molly looked back at him then, all glimmering sparks in her eyes.

"Theoretically," the word sounded like three different sentences by the way he stretched it out. He shook the hesitation away and gripped tighter to Molly. "Theoretically speaking, my wife could call you Dez, my children could refer to you as Uncle Dez, but I would be calling you..?"

"Desmond," he replied with brash superiority. "That's correct."

George glared at Desmond's smile for as long as he could, fingers ticking across Molly's arm.

"I suppose that would be fine," George finally submitted.

Silence knitted around them in a comfortable blanket.

George retrieved new flowers; Molly set them free in the creek. Desmond played with sticks and stones. It was just them, and the old trees and new sprouts, the melody of the trickling creek meshing with the flickering candle, and the freedom of the waves carrying every last heavy weight away from them.

George believed in fairytales. In heroes and monsters, in damsels of immeasurable strength. And he believed that sometimes, even if you tried to battle against it, you could find your way to living authentically and happily, after all.

He pulled out his pocket watch, unsure of exactly what time it was, and set the dials into motion. Midnight seemed like a good place to start.

He slipped the watch away and traced his fingers along Molly's wrists, finding the final flower and drawing its petals up the back of her arm. "Last one."

She took it with a smile and twirled it under her nose. "We should all make a wish before we set it free."

Desmond nodded, ready for whatever was suggested.

George lowered his lips to the curve of Molly's shoulder. "Whatever you desire, Fairy Girl."

Epilogue

A midsummer eve, 1905

The crisp paper of Molly's novel sliced through her finger-tip as she turned the page. The sting wasn't unmatched to what the rest of her was feeling. The ache in her chest, the unnerving ringing in her ears, the smoke that clogged the air. It was only the constant patter of George's fingers across her arm that kept her in the moment, for as many fleeting seconds that were left.

His arm was draped behind her, and she had sunk into the space beneath it and against him, soaking in that feeling she had only ever been able to describe as *wonderful*. They sat together on the sofa, across from her parents where they sat by the fire, conversing with his grandparents.

She was in-tune with George, his breaths, and the syn-chronization of his tapping fingers that she had memorized. She could almost hear the music they were playing and patted them with her own when they seized their movement every time the fire let out sparks.

Their days together at the Lake House had filled her with reveries. With every new day, she woke up, prepared herself to leave her room, only to walk into the hall and see him there. That was a feeling she didn't want to fade. Two mornings of waking up and George being the first person she saw had spoiled all future mornings when he wouldn't be there.

And as the sun sank lower to the horizon, Molly knew their time hidden away in a place of dreams was nearly over. Tomorrow she would awaken in her own bed and travel out to an empty hall.

The emotions caught in her throat. She forced them down in a swallow and slipped her ribbon between the pages of her book before setting it onto the table.

George watched. His apprehension was palpable.

He leaned forward, voice a whisper across the curve of her ear. "Let's get out of here."

She nodded, uncaring about how desperate it might seem, and took his hands as he lifted her away from their couch.

Viola acknowledged they were leaving with a gentle flick of her fingers before she turned back to her conversation.

Through the doors to the wraparound porch, the warm glow of the sunset beckoned to them.

Molly drifted through the yard to the lake, fingers teasing through the long grass that tickled her palms as she kept moving forward. The lake reflected the yellows and golds of the sunset, waves deepening into sapphire blues. Just that afternoon they had been drifting across the waters in a rowboat; snipped right out of a fairytale. Laughing. Smiling...

Birds flew through the last beams of sunlight, singing their songs until they found their nests.

George grasped Molly's wrist from behind and spun her around to him under his arm. Her head lowered to his shoulder as they swayed in a secret dance.

"I don't want to leave," she mumbled into the folds of his shirt.

He pressed a kiss into her loose curls. "Then we'll stay."

"You have to go back to the offices tomorrow."

"I was supposed to be there today."

She looked up just in time to catch his guilty smile.

He raised an unabashed brow. "It's not like they can fire me. They most likely appreciate my absence."

"Then they're fools."

His smile sliced to the side. "I do love it when you defend my honour."

She poked a finger into his tie. "You are also a fool for not going back to work when you're in the middle of a big project."

His plans for the factory had started to take shape and grow wings. Soon it would be the safest and most productive factory in the district; morale was at its highest, with an outlook only for improvements.

"You really think I should have left?" he challenged, head lowering until his whisper brushed her cheek. "Even with the rain?"

Molly's blush heated her face as her eyes cut away. They had been caught together in the rain storm, dripping and soaked through. He'd kissed her beneath a tree, a kiss extra warm and soft, and more than magical enough to carry promises of a lifetime filled with more just like it.

"I enjoyed the rain," her voice was fickle, breathy.

His gaze dropped to her lips and tracked back to her eyes before snapping to something over her shoulder. "Hold that thought."

He took her hand and started to run. She kept pace as well as she could, following him to the hillside that was covered in a rainbow of wildflowers. Purples and pinks, reds, yellows, and blue, all darkened by the lessening sunset glow.

Their run slowed as the trek up became steeper, until they stood still on the incline. She stared up at him, the sky painted in hues of shadowed dusk all around.

She gripped tighter to his fingers, waiting as she felt his words tumbling around him in the breeze.

"Leaving this place is easier with hopes of next summer," he said at last.

She dragged her hands over his shoulders. "When you say it like that it sounds more like a promise of every summer."

"Every summer," he repeated, no hint of doubt.

It was a subject they'd tiptoed around; something spoken about at length without fully admitting what it was they were saying. Whispers of forever melting into them like sugared desserts; messy, yet delicious. Until they were insatiable, each more intimate than the last.

"Summer is the shortest season," he said through a sigh. "I find myself needing to know what you have planned for the rest of the year."

It was a game filled with dangerous admissions under the guise of something light. But the depth of it toyed around her heart, sputtering its rhythm faster.

"In spring, we can explore gardens as they bloom," she told him.

His eyes glimmered with something gentle and alluring. He nodded and raised his hand to cup the side of her face, fingers tangling into her hair, thumb brushing under the line of her jaw. "In autumn I'll write you songs; ones made up of memories we'll come to have."

She leaned into his hand, eyes just about to close as fluttering wings brushed past her nose.

The little bug landed on his cuff, legs testing out the terrain of it before the body beneath its wings started to glow.

"Fireflies," Molly gasped, laughing as it flew away.

George's eyes flickered to the valley behind her. "Take a look, Fairy Girl."

Molly spun around, feeling George's arm hook around her waist.

There had to be hundreds flitting through the wildflowers, out from petals and behind blades of grass. Lights dancing and flashing against the backdrop of twinkling stars.

George kissed the dip of her shoulder, sending out sparks that spread like fierce, undeniable wishes.

She had no idea summer could sparkle as much as the snow.

"What would we do in the winter?" she asked, eyes on a firefly skittering along her finger.

"I can only think of what we could do this winter. And it's a little terrifying." His hold fell away.

His touch skimmed her skirt and whisked her around.

He had dropped to a knee, looking whisper-soft and warm. In his hand he held a little velvet box, mauve and glittering. He lifted it higher.

She dropped in front of him. "What are you doing?"

"I was getting to that part," he said, a tender smile across his lips.

"Is that—"

The box flipped open. "There is a question I'd like to ask you."

Everything fell on her all at once. The gravity and sincerity in his voice. The caress of his fingers on the inside of her wrist. The dampness of tears threatening her eyes.

"Why?" It was a gentle whimper. Not sad or hurt, but frightened. Worried the question was coming for all of the wrong reasons. "Please, tell me it's not because of what happened last week."

Rumours were treacherous things, circling above only to dive down and drown you once you thought the coast was clear.

She had only been walking through the park, laughing beside a row of rosebushes, when she'd been spat upon by a passerby, ridiculed by strangers, and scorned by the crowd.

Her lungs filled with horrid, tumbling waves.

"I promise." George slipped the box into the grass and laced his fingers in hers. "That is not the reason. Though I won't pretend it didn't cross my mind. It crossed my mind enough times that it became the reason I did other things."

The words tickled her tongue, wondering what it was he had done. The twitch to his lips proved he had no remorse, no matter what it was.

"When I saw it happen, I saw you. Saw your heart sink, and the way you wilted." His hand cupped around the nape of her neck, tilting her eyes to meet his. "You cannot ask me to not be affected when you are hurt. It is not something I can give to you."

His kiss was feather light, landing right where a single tear had dropped. He broke away, eyes shimmering.

"But this, this is something I can give." The box was in his hands again, open and catching the first glint of moonlight. "It's merely a token of something that's already yours."

A collection of the very best dreams and fairytales would not have compared to the way her heart responded to the hush of forever in his voice.

"Every frayed, broken piece of me is yours. You bind me together in ways I'm not sure I could ever explain. So while I know we have only been us for a short time, I believe this is something we can always have."

Always.

The sparks in his eyes held so many promises; she desired to catch them all.

George's hand trailed down her shoulder until it was once again grasping her fingers. "All of the best stories leave you wishing for just a little bit more. I don't want to reach the end of mine, wishing I had spent more of it with you."

A million perfects danced through the air.

"Oh my," she murmured.

He grinned, sending shivers and flames teasing along her skin. "May I please have the honour of being in your story from this day on?"

Her heart skipped to a new rhythm.

How easy it was to imagine it all in their little world between fantasies and what was real.

Days would turn into years that would turn into chapters. Ones filled with his smile, even if she had to find it for him. Children with his eyes and her love for fairies. Enough memories to write songs about for decades, ones that would transcend the passageways of time.

She scooped a loop of his hair from his eyes. "Is this real? Really?"

"Yes," he said through a chuckle.

"Really?"

His smile flickered into something shy. "Unbelievably real."

A brave lone firefly flew between their noses, landing on him, sending a glow across his cheeks. Or perhaps it wasn't a firefly at all, but a creature far more magical.

Sometimes, when there was so much one would love to say, too many words filled the mind and bundled too tightly to be released. So, Molly nodded. Unrestrained and shameless. Hair tumbling in bouncing waves.

George lifted the ring from its cushion, slipped it on her finger, but never let go.

A solid pull, and she was falling into him, wrapping her arms around his shoulders.

It was him, only him. And his kiss.

His hands held her close and slinked into her hair.

Breathless and dazzling. A dance. Nipping kisses between adoring declarations. His lips found the delicate places along her neck, tickling as he toppled backwards into the flowers.

She fell with him, and her laugh had him smiling. He pressed it to the corner of her mouth as if they were sharing something secret.

"I love you," he whispered.

"And I love you."

George folded his arm so that his head rested back against it as he stared up to the stars and the flittering, glowing creatures. She nestled into the nook of his torso.

"We'll come back here every summer," he promised. "It is the most romantic place in the world."

Molly rolled into him further, enough to glance up into his eyes. "I imagine you can make anywhere feel that way."

His smile was playfully dreamy in every mischievous way. "How do you feel about getting married in the snow?"

She lowered her head and kissed his shoulder. "Sounds like the perfect way to welcome winter."

"Next year we will think of something new. And all of the years to follow."

"I have no doubts."

George wrapped his arms around her as he pressed a kiss to her forehead. And even though they were laying on the ground, they might as well have been floating through the clouds chasing stars; a place where dreams were closer in reach.

"George?"

"Fairy Girl."

She spun one of his jacket buttons around her fingertip. "Will you dance with me?"

His hand enclosed hers. "Always."

And they did.

Happily ever after.

Acknowledgements

I'm going to keep this short, sweet, and sassy.

First to my readers. This book would not exist without you. I hope it felt like a warm hug on cool nights, and steaming tea that soothes you straight to your bones. But seriously, thank you! From the bottom of my frost covered heart!

To the friends and family who have filled me with enough love to create the different pieces that make me whole. Don't worry, none of the bad guys are based off people I know.

Thank you to my editor over at Ryan Edits, this story really shines now. You're a dream to work with!

A special moment is needed to mention my dog. He highly inspired Acorn. Though I'm sure Acorn smells better...

My bestieeeeeeeeeee. GIRL! Those flame drawings make me laugh just thinking of them. And when George simply walks into a room and you wrote "hot move" every single time? Everyone needs a bestie like you! The number one hype girl. The best cover designer in all the universe. You ultimate superhuman and boss babe you. My next book is for you.

And my hubby. My hero. Hey hun, hope you loved that epilogue. I think you might find some of it rings a bell... Also, thanks for reading my books and cheering for these characters as if they were real. Oh, and thanks for retrieving the manuscript after I threw it into the recycling. I love you.

About the Author

There's no telling which world Shawna is currently residing in. Although, most likely it's somewhere with freshly brewed coffee and well organized bookshelves. She's an avid story consumer and lover of all things cozy. Her husband always indulges such endeavours, as do her spectacular offspring who might one day read and creates stories better than she could ever dream.